Praise for Andrew Pyper's bestselling debut novel, Lost Girls

'This is one scary book . . . you'll want to keep all the lights
on as you read this one'
Independent on Sunday

'This is an excellently written novel, brilliant in its evocation of atmosphere'
Evening Standard

'Extremely compelling'
Sunday Telegraph

'Think *The Shining* mixed with *The Sixth Sense*. A truly scary ghost story that
will have you turning the pages late into the night.'
Maxim

'*Lost Girls* is a hugely impressive and utterly compelling thriller'
Independent

'A remarkably fine debut novel . . . *Lost Girls* has a menace that is all its own'
Time Out

'*Lost Girls* is remarkable and compelling. But, more than that, it is a novel
that goes some way towards reinventing the literary ghost story.'
The Times

'*Lost Girls* is an excellent first novel; part thriller, part ghost story but always
original in style and compulsive reading'
Manchester Evening News

THE TRADE MISSION

In addition to *The Trade Mission*, Andrew Pyper is the author of *Kiss Me*, a collection of stories, and the international bestseller *Lost Girls*, a novel selected as a Notable Book of the Year by the *New York Times*. He lives in Toronto.

Andrew Pyper

THE
TRADE
MISSION

MACMILLAN

For Leonardo

First published 2002 by HarperCollins Publishers Ltd.,
Toronto, Ontario, Canada

This edition published 2002 by Macmillan
an imprint of Pan Macmillan Ltd
Pan Macmillan, 20 New Wharf Road, London N1 9RR
Basingstoke and Oxford
Associated companies throughout the world
www.panmacmillan.com

ISBN   1 4050 0559 9

1 3 5 7 9 8 6 4 2

A CIP catalogue record for this book is available from
the British Library.

Printed and bound in Great Britain by
Mackays of Chatham plc, Chatham, Kent

Meaning is served far better—and literature and language far worse—by the unrestrained license of bad translators.

—Walter Benjamin,
"The Task of the Translator,"
translated by Harry Zohn

BEFORE

THEY are only boys.

Tall enough to be men but something gives them away, even with parka hoods pulled tight over their heads. From a distance they might appear as two swaying drunks debating over which of the paths ahead will lead them home. But look at their faces: freckles standing out against bloodless cheeks, chapped lips held tight against the wind. Their fear is neither a child's nor a man's. Nothing is real enough to be entirely believed by boys like these, although they'd like to believe in something if it might make them look a year or two older. But for now they're too in-between, afloat in the not-quite-thereness of their boyhoods. Look at their faces: sometimes their eyes show a hurt they haven't even lived through yet. It's like a vision the two of them have shared, a premonition of the life ahead as an ongoing trade of damages. It's why boys sleep as much as they do. And in their dreams they are caped crusaders. Human but with impossible talents like x-ray vision or freezing breath or flight. Dreams that often end badly nevertheless, with an assassin's blade slicing their throats or tumbling out of the sky to gasp awake before they hit the ground.

"What's it say?"

"That way, I think."

"Which way?"

"Through there. North."

The slightly taller one returns the compass to the inside pocket of his parka and points a trembling finger into the trees that surround them. It's officially winter, but up until a couple hours ago the snow had been cagey, dusting and melting and looping around but refusing to settle in for good. Now it's coming down straight as marbles.

"It's getting dark," the shorter one says, and it is, the sky a purple sheet lowering over the cedar branches. It's also getting cold. A drop of several degrees within a minute of the sun's retreat.

They're lost, but neither has said so yet. It's their Outdoor Orientation exam—blindfolded then dropped off three miles in by sniggering prefects who kept calling them "lover boys"—and now it's clear that they've failed. Why did the parents of one and the guardians of the other send them to this school in the middle of the Canadian woods anyway? It's *obscene*, as the shorter one has taken to saying about all things that bore him. And to make matters worse, it's one of those schools without girls. Its unspoken specialty is keeping the young gentlemen of the wealthy out of trouble. But what kind of trouble could you get into up here even if you tried? Nothing to do but drink smuggled booze and look out classroom windows at the wall of trees and prickly creeks that lead to farther nowheres. It's as if the people that sent them here *want* them to get lost.

"You better get rid of that," the shorter boy says, eyes on the mickey of rum pulled out of the same pocket as the compass.

The taller one lifts the bottle in salute and throws back a gulp. Passes it to the shorter boy, who drains the spittled backwash. At first the alcohol had made being stuck in the woods kind of funny, then it had offered temporary blooms of warmth. Now it does little but root them to their places, as though all the stuffing above their waists had poured down their legs and into the frozen earth. The shorter one chucks the bottle away and it takes its time in midair. A half dozen tumbles before burrowing under the white blanket on the forest floor.

They go on. Put a few more miles behind them, or around them, for there's always a river or sudden cliff that pushes their path into spirals. And with the hours come new surprises of exhaustion. It takes all the talk out of them. There is little to be said anyway except the obvious, which, if stated aloud, would only make them more afraid.

Neither wears a watch, but the air is solid in the way the middle of the night is. Hardly moving at all now except for their arms, rubbering about them for balance. The cracked skin of their hands skimming in and out of view.

They come to a stop in a small clearing encircled by a solid web of brush. How'd they get through it in the first place? For a time each of them believes they are speaking, although it's impossible to tell. When they lift their heads to face each other the snow fills the air between them as falling bits of shadow.

"Which way now?" the shorter one asks, his lungs stinging from the air it costs him.

"It doesn't matter. We keep ending up in the same place."

"Or what looks like the same place."

"Same difference."

"But we have to keep going."

"Why?"

"To get out of here."

"We're *not* getting out of here."

"Yes, we are."

"And you're going to save us?"

"That's right. I'm going to save us."

"Here then."

The taller one pulls the compass out of his pocket and hands it over. But it's too dark to get a fix on the gyrating arrow, anxiously skipping between each of its four options.

"The compass is lost too," the shorter boy says.

"I'm really tired, man."

"We're both tired. But we have to move."

"I don't think so."

"C'mon. Another half a mile."

"Where?"

"Might as well be straight ahead."

"I don't—"

But the taller boy doesn't finish. Instead there is only the *whoof* his body makes as it collapses forward into a creamy drift.

"Get up!" the shorter boy thinks he shouts, but immediately begins to doubt it. Frightens himself with an oddly hollow laugh.

For a minute nothing moves. The night muffled as though brushing against a closed window. At his feet the snow already collecting over the body, sculpting its outline into another shape of the wind.

"You have to get up now." The shorter boy has fallen to his knees. Certain of his voice this time, at once fierce and cracked. "You have to." "No, I don't." "I'm asking nicely." "You go. I'll wait here."

The shorter boy considers this. Calculates the possibility of lucking out and finding a road or cabin. Getting help. Considers the particular darkness of the night, the particular hardness of the cold.

Even if he made it, the fallen boy wouldn't. The shorter boy tries to make the questions in his head as complicated as he can in order to buy a little time, but instead the answers come simply and terribly. He might leave and live, or stay and probably die.

He rolls the taller boy onto his back to show a startling mask of sealed eyes and lips. Drags him the few feet it takes to lean him up against a tree out of the worst of the wind.

"Hey, are you with me?" he asks, catching sips of breath.

The taller boy can only clench his jaw in reply. He's about to fall away into sleep, or someplace deeper, once and for all. The shorter boy knows this because he isn't far from falling away himself.

He lets himself lie down next to the taller boy and unzips their parkas. Slips his arms around the other's chest, brings him close in a wriggling hug. Stretches the layers of their parkas as tight as he can around their necks and knees.

"A sleeping bag," the shorter boy says.

"This is weird, man."

"Just pretend I'm a girl."

"But you're not."

"Pretend."

Their bodies find a hundred new ways around each other so that soon they are neatly joined as two lumps of clay. Under their coats their breath mixes in puffs of white steam.

Do they speak of things that matter? The odds they'll be alive to see the morning? Of their love for their mothers? For each other?

Serious words are not their talent. Instead the one who stayed behind whispers to the other practical jokes they have both planned and already performed. Lullabies the cruel nicknames of teachers into his ear. Then even he runs out of things to say along with the strength to say them. The snow drumming on their shoulders.

Soon they are blasting through the star-pocked sky with silver capes flapping behind them. Alert to the shouts for help below, ready to be heroes.

I

"LADIES and gentlemen, my name is Marcus Wallace, and I'd like to personally welcome you to your futures!"

This is in Brazil, but it could be anywhere.

A long conference room lit by dimmed halogen spots in the ceiling, a dozen rows of chairs, potted ferns circling the lectern. The front reserved for photographers, whose flashbulbs explode like distant artillery fire whenever one of the two people on stage makes a face or gesture of any kind. Behind them, slouching journalists scribble in notepads as they always have, or tickle laptops, as they do more and more. Then the rows of money: suits, silk shirts, Swiss watches of a price equivalent to an entry-level American sedan.

The person speaking to them is a boy. The other person on stage is a boy as well, although he hasn't spoken yet, and doesn't appear interested in starting any time soon. Instead, he sits at a small desk made out of a single sheet of clear, molded plastic (beneath it, his knees visibly jiggling within their cargo pants). He keeps his eyes squinted at a computer screen in front of him, and from time to time makes stabs at its keyboard, as though a cockroach were running back and forth across it. They are far enough apart that even from the back of the room you can't take them both in at once, so you move your eyes from one to the other. Decide that your first impression was wrong. They aren't boys at all. They are young men. But the word continues to cling to them, nevertheless. It seems right. You feel certain it will never leave them.

"Before we move on to this afternoon's presentation, I would like to introduce my partner—God, it sounds like he's my *wife* or something whenever I say that!—the real brains behind the success of Hypothesys, Jonathon Bates."

The young man at the clear plastic desk jiggles his knees more violently and raises his hand over his head in a kind of wave. A smile fractures across his mouth without him appearing to be in control of it.

"This is going to be one of the first public demonstrations of our product," the standing one says, "so we're pretty excited up here—or *down* here, I should say, seeing as this is South America."

A giggle escapes from his lips, which in turn initiates a round of chortles and cleared throats from the audience. He's cute. Everyone wants to like him. They already do.

"Why are we excited? Well, it's pretty simple. We feel that Hypothesys is something that is truly going to change the way we conduct our lives. And that's not just more of the same hype you guys have no doubt been served plenty of all week. Because this isn't *like* the stuff you've seen all week. It's not another Internet site where you can buy groceries or books or watch porn broadcast live from a rented room in Amsterdam or get twenty-four-hour webcam coverage of some Joe Nobody arguing with his girlfriend or brushing his teeth. Hypothesys isn't about any of that. In fact, it can literally be anything you want it to be. Something you *need*. Your confidant. Your best friend. Your nondenominational spiritual advisor. Night or day, it will be there to help. To offer guidance about life's most difficult questions, or even the easy ones you just feel you'd like a second opinion on. As the banner over our stall in the convention hall says, 'Hypothesys helps you make the best decisions of your life!' "

At this, the dimmed lights dim further, and at the rear of the stage a large screen glows blue. Gradually, the word HYPOTHESYS comes forward in white, a cloud taking shape in a clear sky. A jet streaks across with a roar, leaving "New Human Ethics Technologies" formed out of the dissolving exhaust behind it. Even from the back of the room you can see the encircled *c* asserting copyright over every one of these words.

Now the two young men are silhouettes against the perfect blue, except for pancake circles of light on their faces, spotlights following them wherever they go. They look like ghosts in a high-school play.

"Some have called our project a morality machine, but that isn't quite right," continues the young Wallace's disembodied voice. Only now, in the new darkness, do you notice how full it is, at once boyish and suggestive of experience. "Hypothesys doesn't deliver morality *per se*, nor is it a machine, strictly speaking. What it is, however, is a library of contemporary ethics. The process behind its development is known as collaborative filtering, but it's not as complicated as it sounds. It's just a survey, really. A *big* survey. One that has resulted in a collection of data that, once it has been thoroughly cross-referenced, can tell us something about the way we behave. So far, collaborative filtering is a process that has been employed for the most predictably commercial purposes. You know, the old 'If you liked *that* movie or CD, chances are you'll also like *this* movie or CD' based on the stuff other people have bought before you. Hypothesys is considerably more ambitious. It has nothing to sell but ourselves. It is who we *are*— all of us together—right now. It forms, in effect, a universal human mind."

Bates begins to work furiously at his laptop, and an animated brain appears on the screen, huge and pulsing with white bolts of electricity.

"Over the course of the past several months, we have conducted one of the most extensive studies of individual sensibilities ever undertaken," Wallace says, his spotlit head floating from one side of the stage to the other. "And we weren't asking about what color of sneakers people most like to wear, or what kind of car they drive, or whether they live in a house or a hole in the ground. In short, this was not the dead-tired market research you've all heard too much about already. We weren't interested in the *market* at all, as a matter of fact, but only in people's answers to hypothetical questions. Scruples. The way we decide to live our lives. Bates?"

As a buzzing swarm of static on the screen nibbles the brain away from stem to lobe, it is replaced by a shot of a crowded city street. People moving in undulating waves, half heading north, half south. It takes a couple of seconds to recognize the scene as computer-generated (it's only the slight over-vividness of digitized color that gives it away). Then you notice something else not-quite-right about it. The people are made up of men, women, old and young, skin of every graduated pigment between black and albino, a cross around one neck, a Star of David around another, a turbaned head and a veiled face. A street that had to be made by a computer because none could possibly be this perfectly representative anywhere in the real world.

"There is, needless to say, no single law that guides our actions. Our different religions, cultures and experiences shape our ethical orientations in a million discrete ways. But Hypothesys is indifferent to those distinctions. It's about what we have in *common*, not what sets us *apart*. And because the data we have collected does not take into account the identity of those who participated in its collection, it is a system that can be applied with equal effectiveness in any nation, and be relevant to any way of life. We have, in a sense, created an electronic Everyman. Or Everywoman."

Now the street scene blurs into a palette of brilliant colors that reassembles into a vision of the earth viewed from space. Different strains of shimmering, twinkly music seem to come from every corner of the room to converge between our ears. A chorus of synthetic human voices coming from the inside out. *Home*, they sing. *Home!*

Gradually, though, the planet's blues and browns and benign cloud masses become more detailed, hostile. Soon we are hurtling toward the surface.

"So how does it work?" Wallace's question cuts through the soundtrack, which has built up into a Wagnerian climax of swirling synthesizers. "Well, my friends, let's go *straight* into the mind of Hypothesys and find out!"

The earth entirely fills the screen in bulging 3-D and with a clap of thunder we crash somewhere in the middle of the Pacific, plummet down into the depths until the shafts of sunlight from the surface whither away and the entire conference room goes dark.

Somebody blows their nose. A goose honk in the silence.

Then a woman's face appears on the screen. As we watch, her features—hair color, skin tone, nose length, lip shape—subtly change so that she is never fixed. Never one woman, but an infinitely revolving carousel of women.

"Meet Camilla," Wallace says, softer now. "She has a problem. She knows something that her husband doesn't know, and she can't decide whether to tell him about it."

The woman's face fluidly morphs into that of a man. Of men.

"Camilla kissed Stephen last week. Stephen and Camilla's husband are friends, they play golf on the weekends, get together for family barbecues. But last week Stephen called Camilla and asked her to lunch. Now, this is important: Camilla felt something was strange about this. Camilla and Stephen had never had lunch alone together before. And the fact is, she's caught Stephen looking at her strangely lately. You know, giving her the old Latin lover eyes. But this is Brazil—you all know about *that!*"

There is appreciative laughter at this, along with a lusty whoop from somewhere among the journalists. *Hoo-ha!*

"But Camilla met up with Stephen anyway. They had some wine. They had a nice time. Then, over the tiramisù, Stephen drops the bomb. 'I love you,' he says. 'I won't get in the way of your life if you don't want me to. But I just had to let you know.' Camilla feels like a kid. She feels her cheeks get hot." (The women's faces reappear on the screen, all of them blushing.) "They pay and step out of the restaurant. And right there on the sidewalk, before she knows what she's doing— although she *does*, of course, she knows perfectly well—she kisses Stephen like he was about to head off to war. We're talking *passion* here, people."

The face of the men returns and the women and men kiss on the lips, a pink flash of tongue visible before they meet.

"Now Camilla doesn't know what to do. She'd ask her girlfriends for advice, but they'd blab it all over the place. And as for her priest? Her rabbi? She hasn't seen those guys since her wedding. Besides, it all feels so *complicated*. She might just love Stephen herself. But what about the kids? And her husband? Sure, she still loves him, but quite frankly, a good deal less than she used to. Is her last chance for adventure staring her right in the face? Or is this the tough spot she's heard about, when she goes to her husband and lets him know everything so they can try to work it out together? Is her duty to her own happiness or the happiness of others? As you can see, there's a *lot* of factors at work here, even in a situation as common as this. Too many for one brain to handle. And this is where Hypothesys comes in."

The word RELATIONSHIPS appears at the bottom of the screen, and then, rising up from it and branching out in different directions,

MARRIAGE and DISCLOSURE and CHILDREN and SEX. As the tree of words grows higher, the branches become more intricate, and eventually overlap into a single, wavering mass of dense leaves caught in a breeze.

"Camilla uses our system to sort out her problem one step at a time. She takes a good look at how she honestly *feels*, then enters the facts of her situation, detail by detail. She rates certain *perception factors* on a scale of one to ten, such as the pain she would endure if her husband left her, her physical and emotional desire for Stephen, the degree of discomfort she would experience in carrying on a long-term deception behind the back of the man she made solemn vows to years before, et cetera, et cetera. And these factors are then matched up with the responses of every other participant in the Hypothesys library. Within seconds, the system can give Camilla her answer."

On the screen, a spreadsheet appears with dozens of figures arranged in columns under the same headings that appeared at the base of the tree.

"And what do we tell her to do? Well, reading the responses is something of an art in itself—it's not exactly a simple yes or no sort of thing—but it's basically 'Go for it! Life's too short! But don't tell the husband unless you're *sure* Stephen's in it for the long haul.' Hey, it may not be the most honorable course of action, ladies and gentlemen. But it is the most true to who we really are."

The numbers on the screen skitter away, and in their place Camilla's faces reappear, nodding back in gratitude at Wallace's slender shadow before her.

"Thank you, Camilla," he says to the digital representation of womankind, then turns back to us, the broad swath of flesh and blood sitting at his feet. "And thank you *all* for coming. Of course, this demonstration has been only a most basic exercise of the system's capacities. Hypothesys is as complex as you are—and only you know what that *really* means. So I hope you get a chance to try Hypothesys out for yourselves at our exhibition area in the convention hall—and remember, confidentiality is guaranteed!"

Camilla disappears. The screen lulls into a fractal, one of those lines that create cities of fantastic architecture before wiping them out and starting over again. The halogen lights bathe the room in enough orange to identify us as separate heads. Wallace looks out over every one of them.

"I think we have time for a couple of questions," he says, glancing at his watch.

The journalists thrust pens, PalmPilots and index fingers into the air.

"Yes, Kevin?"

"Do you foresee any applications for your system outside that of a personal guide?"

"We're always working on things. There's been calls. The Pentagon has seen some potential for military deployments. Certain governments have shown interest in its use in policy development. NGOs, religious leadership, corporate management. Anywhere a decision has to be made, Hypothesys can be there."

"How are sales going?"

"This trip alone has been very fruitful," Wallace says, lowering his eyes in a half-second show of modesty. "Barry and Lydia, our associates on the money side of things, just yesterday sold world Portuguese rights for, well, what can I say? A *significant* amount."

"We hear four million."

"You hear pretty good."

"What about the movie?"

"What's with you guys and the movies? It's like you'd all rather be working for *Variety* or something."

"Hey, we're all in it for the glamour, right? So what's the deal?"

"The *deal* is that as of two weeks ago the film rights to our joint autobiography have been optioned by Paramount. I understand that a screenplay is already under development."

"Who are they thinking of to play you and Mr. Bates?"

"Naturally, I think the twenty-million-per-movie pretty boy of the moment would have to play me. I guess we'd need *two* of those, now that I think of it," he says, offering an apologetic pout over at Bates. "One concept the studio people have mentioned is an updated version of *Dr. Jekyll and Mr. Hyde*. I'm rolling with that. What do you guys think?"

"Would you be the beauty or the beast?"

"Very funny, Diane."

"Has the autobiography even been published yet?"

"Hey, we're still *living* our lives here. We haven't had a chance to *write* about them yet."

"This one is for Mr. Bates. Ever get tired of playing second fiddle to your exuberant partner here?"

The young man behind the computer looks out at us directly for the first time. His face elongated and blanched clean of expression, as though someone has accused him of something terrible. But this is more or less the way he always looks.

"There is no second fiddle with Hypothesys," he says evenly, though his knees are now thudding up against the underside of his desk. "In our partnership, we both play first violin."

"*Very* well put, Bates," Wallace cuts in and gives Bates an unnoticeable signal that turns his head back to his computer screen. "OK, everybody. Last question."

"What is your opinion with regard to the possibility of your team being the first to one day develop authentic artificial intelligence in computers?"

"I think that day is already here, Brad." Wallace blinks earnestly. "If our program can advise you as to how to live your life, and that advice is no worse than what most other people would likely advise, isn't that a demonstration of intelligence? Assume for a moment that wisdom is adhering to the law of averages—and who's to say it ultimately isn't? I mean, that's what rationality *is*—then what we have here is the old wise man sitting on top of the silicon mountain, my friends."

With this Wallace smacks a fist into his palm and Bates punches at his computer one last time. The synthesizer music returns, a single, thrumming bass note like a far-off freight train. As Wallace steps back from the lectern mouthing *Thank you* and pointing directly at recognized faces in the audience like a presidential candidate, the sound enlarges. The screen at the back of the stage becomes a slow strobe of colors that freezes the room in half seconds of blue and yellow and underwater green. And as the sound fully enters our chests (noticing only now that we have been painfully applauding since the first *thank you*) Bates rises from his clear plastic table and joins Wallace at the front of the stage.

They bring themselves toward each other with their smiles, arms rising to curl around the other's waist. These pictures of them stay in our minds longer than any of the catchphrases or special effects that preceded. It's somehow clear that this is the only part of the presentation that wasn't planned out. A gesture too fluid to be rehearsed, too familiar, without the stiff hesitations of thought. Two young men caught in the lingering wash of adult applause, standing so close they could be joined at some hidden point, tied to one another by a transparent wire that allows a range of individual movement but can also reel them back together at any time. They could be brothers. Or fashion models beaming their good luck out from a page of gloss. Or street hustlers starting their shifts.

I stand at the back of the room and hold them there for as long as I can. We all do. A last look at how things are, before they turn into whatever comes next.

2

LESS than two hours after Wallace and Bates's sales presentation, I'm shaking the prime minister's hand. (He's nice, clammy-palmed, shorter than on TV. As I pass him in the reception line I tell him he has my vote, but this is a lie. A harmless, favor-seeking sort of lie.) This is in São Paulo, at a reception in the ballroom of the Canadian consulate. There is "Canadian champagne" and Ontario Mennonite cheddar sweating on the buffet tables, the room lined with pale faces glistening like wet plaster. It's immediately clear that these people—government officials, international lawyers, CEOs, millionaire writers of Silicon Valley software code—are dangerously new to breathing unrefrigerated air. Almost all of them are men.

I am here with the other members of the Hypothesys team, have to be, as I'm the translator they've brought with them for the trip and they couldn't order a plate of rice without me. It's a good gig, as my fellow part-time interpreters like to say, imagining ourselves as seasoned journeymen well used to international travel, protocol, war zones. The truth is we almost never find work that takes us out of town. Surprisingly enough, holding an unmarketable Ph.D. in Economic History and having as my only other skill the ability to speak both English and passable Portuguese hasn't led to the most dazzling of lives. I live on my own. Galbraith, my mewling, tumor-ridden cat, recently had to be put down. A Friday-night watcher of rented Scorsese and anything with Gwyneth, in a basement one-bedroom, usually alone. I once counted nine and a half days between the ringings of my phone (and when the call came it was from my gym, asking if I was dissatisfied with their services, seeing as I hadn't dropped by for several months). So a free trip to Brazil, a per diem that would pay for an entire month of cable, a hotel room with a fully stocked mini-bar all to myself—it's a good gig, all right.

What makes it particularly sweet is that I am only responsible for the conference participants directly connected to the Hypothesys product, unlike some of my colleagues who, like overworked border collies, have to round up entire herds of departmental bureaucrats. In my case, there's only the four of them. Wallace and Bates (the two twenty-four-year-old "Boy Geniuses of Canada's Great White Web," as the cover of *Newsweek* called them); Barry, the managing partner they headhunted from an Atlanta pharmaceutical firm best known for developing prescription cures for male pattern baldness before their breakthrough discovery of the "female Viagra"; and Lydia, the English rose who is their European counsel, a few years older than me, forty and change, who "read *eek*onomics" at either Oxford or Cambridge, I can't say which for sure because she alternately mentions her "days up" at both.

I met them all at the boys' Toronto office the week before we came down here. A catered brunch in their "studio space" intended as a chance to "just hang out and chill," as Wallace's message on my answering machine put it. But the studio turned out to be the entire floor of a former button factory down in the docklands, now outfitted with a *Dukes of Hazzard* pinball machine, a sofa set covered with what appeared to be ostrich feathers, and a handful of desks draped with wires, distant as Pacific islands. Bates was the first to introduce himself. Shook my right hand and slid a flute of Pol Roger into my left, then pulled me to the center of the room to show how the remote-controlled blinds opened the windows up to the metallic field of Lake Ontario. Lydia picked a stray hair off my sleeve and kissed both my cheeks. Barry offered me Blue Jays box seat tickets he couldn't use the next day. Wallace challenged me to a pinball game and let me win.

"There's a lot of room," he said with his arm over my shoulder, peering through the forest of concrete pillars around him.

It was unclear to me whether he meant the office itself, or the potential opportunities within the company, or the global marketplace that everyone had begun talking about so much. I now know he was saying that there was room for me among them. If I chose to, I could be part of this odd family of English mother, cowboy father and two sons, all of them joined by the chemistry of commerce instead of blood.

"We're pretty close," Wallace explained after tickling Barry into weeping, "Cut it *out!*" submission on the ostrich sofa. And it was true. They had each made more money in the past four months than any of their parents had made over their entire lives. Their time together was a fluid mixture of laughter and shared secrets and initiation rites. They were *enjoying* themselves.

They called me only by my last name—with collegial affection—right from the beginning.

Now we're here. In sales. All of us are part of the official Canadian trade mission to Brazil, host nation of the Southern Hemispheric E-Business Conference, a "historic opportunity to introduce a new dawn of hope to the developing world" (as described in the prime minister's toast, glass of fizzing plonk raised high). The applause at this was loud and long. We'd heard sentiments like it before over the last few days, of course, in a number of different languages. But still, everyone seemed to be reassured by the endless mention of the sort of ideas crammed into the prime minister's sentence. They liked "making history" and "hope" and "the world." More than anything, though, they liked "new." All of them had fallen in love with the mere evocation of it. A single syllable acting as a universal polish, sprucing up almost anything you applied it to. Three letters to do the job of sweeping away the geriatric millennium that had passed and lifting the curtain on the next. It was enough to make even a room like this one giddy, to send blood rushing to cheeks and hands flying up to hide lopsided smiles.

And nobody has more new at this conference than us. What we offer is precisely what everyone wants. Or, more frequently, are *told* that they want, and that we're the only ones who have it. (I've been kept busy all week translating "buzz" into Portuguese—*expectativa!*—every few minutes.) As the banner over the conference hall stage declares, The Whole World Is Looking Forward to the Future! And we're here to sell it something so new it never knew it needed it before.

The particular slice of future that our boy geniuses have developed is a website that teaches you morality. This is not how they describe it, however. Instead, Wallace speaks only of the program offering "helpful advice," of "knowing what options are out there." He frequently reminds us of the expensive focus group market research the company had commissioned prior to the launch. Hundreds from a "cross-generational/racial/income strata" handed over their consumer profiles in return for fifty dollars an hour and all the donuts they could eat. Their principal finding is that explicit mention of terms such as morals, ethical good, guilt or even conscience has a distinctly softening effect on most respondents' "purchasing drive."

For these reasons, we prefer to say that Hypothesys answers questions for you. Not trivia game–type questions, though. Not "What's the capital of Idaho?" or "Who won the 1956 World Series?" Nothing with a determinable answer. Rather, existential questions, the tricky inquiries of principle, like "Should I lie to save my best friend from a life in prison for murder if I know he did it but I'm certain he would never kill again?" (one of Wallace's favorites) or "Is it wrong to take the bathrobe from my $350-a-night hotel room if I was assured I'd get away with it and the hotel is owned by a faceless, excessively profitable conglomerate?" (the one I entered on my laptop this morning after having already packed the bathrobe from my closet). What's ingenious about the thing—what Barry calls "the hook" while making quotation marks with his fingers—is that the answers come from ourselves.

For the purposes of my job, I've come to refer to it as a compendium of contemporary ethics. After months of conducting detailed questionnaires in chain e-mails and random door-to-door interviews around the world, followed by a cataloguing of the tens of thousands of responses, Bates's team of college dropout programmers (working for take-out Chinese and stock options) has put together a cross-referenced set of human behaviors. The trick is that when you mash them all together, the differences between the individual answers disappear, and you're left with a single stand-in for one of *them*. Your fellow man. The Joneses. The blue-shadowed households that constitute a Nielsen ratings point, purchasers of discount mail-order life insurance, the parents of the kids that soap your windows on Halloween. The *vast majority*. Just like you, but less determined somehow. Happily compromised, nameless, getting on with life. A backdrop.

This is how I have explained it to myself, at any rate.

Wallace is somewhat more poetic about it: *Hypothesys forms a collective mind.* Not just *them* but a them with you included. What's helpful from a sales perspective is that there's no right or wrong about it. As

Wallace frequently points out, the program promises not moral correctness but the law of relativism.

People seem to think it's something they've been waiting for. The current bid for world cable TV usage alone stands at $6.4 million, although Barry has turned it down in the expectation of "more heat" in the months to come. There is talk of industry awards, humanitarian recognition, secret military applications. The boys' personal website receives two dozen marriage proposals per day, on average. But as Wallace noted in a recent *New York Times* feature on the world's "bravest" web pioneers, "The real fun stuff will happen when we go public." *Forbes* magazine has estimated that Hypothesys' initial public offering could generate capital "on a scale equal to the GDP of smaller industrialized nations."

For the moment, however, we're just selling an idea. Everybody here is. Around us, the Caribou Ballroom of the Canadian consulate is overstuffed with buyers and sellers of ideas. With handshaking, decorative palms, platters of rolled Quebec ham melting in the air of cooked sewage blowing in through the open windows. I'm standing next to one with Wallace and Bates, ready to turn their English into something else if the need arises. It rarely does. Almost all the Brazilians in this room speak English (they claim it lacks emotion and is therefore better for doing business). Listen with eyes closed and all you can hear is the familiar dialect of American marketing.

Suits push through other suits to meet us. They know who Wallace and Bates are, they've been briefed and advised to show keen interest. Although they would likely come in any event. To *him*, anyway. People come to Wallace without knowing that's where they were heading all along, to step within range of his blithe masculinity. Too young to realize the brevity of his sort of physical gifts, but old enough to know what they could make others do.

Look: here they come. The Argentinean Director of Education, the Colombian Minister of Justice, a VP of personnel recruitment for Microsoft in a low-cut Donna Karan—they all drop by to say a word of support for the "dramatic change" young fellows like themselves are visiting upon the planet. Even the U.S. Secretary of Trade makes a special trip across the floor, bobbing at the center of half a dozen Secret

Service stiffs (three, I swear, wearing aviator sunglasses and wires trailing out of their ears).

"And how are you boys enjoying yourselves?" the Secretary asks them hungrily, lips bubbling out around his "boys" as though the word itself is an unseemly joke. I seem to recall that he was once governor of Mississippi.

"We're having a fabulous time. Aren't we, Crossman?" Wallace nudges me with an elbow. "Better than spending all winter in Canada, eh?"

"Y'all actually say that up there, don't you?"

"You mean the 'eh'? Not really. We just throw it in for the amusement of Americans."

"Oh?"

"It's like the igloos. And the Mounties. And all that damn hockey. It's for the tourists."

"And they say Americans are the ones who invented smart alecks," the Secretary of Trade says, giving Wallace a look of strained amusement. "*Way*-ul, *way*-ul. It should be no surprise that you're selling so much of your wares down here. They tell me you've got quite a little racket on your hands."

"Everyone's been extremely enthusiastic."

"I'm *sure* of it. Now, tell me, is it one of those games? What do they call them? A *virtual reality* game?"

"If you want it to be."

"How would I play?"

"You?" Wallace says, holding his chin in his hand and squinting down at his own reflection in the Secretary of Trade's Guccis. "You'd probably ask it the questions you couldn't ask your advisors, or your wife. You know, something like 'Based on my annual salary, projected pension and speaking engagement income, what is an appropriate amount of change to give to the heroin addict who lives outside my neighborhood ATM?' Or maybe, 'Is it wrong to decimate that defenseless rogue state that poses no real threat to national security—but happens to be run by a colorful demagogue—if it raises us five points in the polls?' That sort of thing. And then your questions mix with all the other subscribers' answers, and the program generates the correct course of action. Relatively speaking."

"Uh-*huh*," the Secretary says, wincing. "This could be of special assistance to those of us in the political arena. You know, we're *always* looking for the middle road."

"We're all looking for that, Mr. Secretary. It's natural to want to know what others would do in the same situation." Wallace gives him a confessional smile. "If the majority of others wouldn't run into the burning house to save the baby, then how wrong could it be if you decided to stay put yourself?"

The stubble darkens on the Secretary's sunburned jaw. Coughs his first inclination out of his head, then asks with all the restraint he can muster about principles being a different matter from following the herd, how perhaps sometimes doing the right thing is the opposite of what the majority would do. But Wallace has heard all this before.

"Hypothesys is a guide, not a bible." He shrugs. "It tells us what we are—you know, the current state of the *human condition*—whether we're ashamed of it or not. A database offers truth, not ideals. And in the case of Hypothesys, we offer assistance when you need it, to let you know what the most popular answers to life's questions might be. And while that answer might not be the most right in the eyes of God, well, we're not designed to be holy, are we? We're designed to get by. And doing what most others are doing has been shown to be the most efficient way to accomplish that. I mean, you're a Republican, right? Or is it the Democrats now? In either case, surely you can appreciate that."

At this moment the Canadian Minister of Foreign Affairs jumps out from behind a melting ice sculpture of a maple-gnawing beaver. Former head of Transportation, Defence before that, and a successful year mumbling his way through Indian Affairs straight off his first election. Cheeks so carefully shaved as to be waxed. The sort of career bureaucrat born with a gift for sensing V.I.P. discomfort from forty feet off. He works up a doubtful guffaw, squeezes the Secretary of Trade's shoulder with a meaty palm. They appear to be old friends. Everyone in the room appears to be old friends.

"Well, I'll be leaving you now, Mr. Wallace," the Secretary almost shouts our way as he steps back into the waiting circle of Secret Service linebackers. "I wish you luck with your video game, or your igloos. Whatever it is you're pushing."

"Thank you! Come up and visit us any time, eh!"

For a second, the two of them share a real smile.

When the Secretary has left, the Minister of Foreign Affairs is careful to avoid eye contact with Wallace, so deliberately turns to Bates.

"And how are you enjoying things here, young man?"

"Very well, sir. Brazil is such a beautiful country," Bates offers, although I know for a fact that all he's seen is the convention hall, the view from his executive suite at the Hilton, and this place.

"It *is* beautiful, isn't it? And you haven't even been to the rainforest yet, have you?"

"No, sir. But we're scheduled to fly out to Manaus tomorrow, then up the Rio Negro for a few days of sightseeing. We're really looking forward to it."

"So am I. Us government fogies will be traveling in a sister riverboat to your own, I understand. Don't forget to bring your bug spray! We don't want our country's business future being devoured by mosquitoes, or struck down by malaria or some such thing, do we?"

The minister shows us his bleached front teeth for a long second. Winks before clenching both of the boys' elbows and melting back into the crowd behind him.

"'No, *sir*. Looking forward to it, *sir*.' For Christ's sake, Bates," Wallace snaps, "have some pride."

"The dude is paying for this trip."

"No, he's not. The Canadian government is paying for it, and we don't owe them anything but a percentage of what we're going to make. Isn't that right, Crossman?"

"Death and taxes," I say through a mouthful of orange milk solids. "The only certainties."

"And the future," Bates adds so softly I believe I am the only one to hear him. "That's certain, too."

O futuro.

How many times have I translated "the future" into Portuguese on this trip? It appears in every other sentence, perking up conversations like a sprinkling of exclamation marks. Hypothesys is technically nothing more than an IP service provider you can link up to right now for a special introductory rate of twelve dollars a month. But it is also, according to Wallace and Barry's pitch, "the way all of us will be living tomorrow," and thus unavoidable. And these boys apparently come with it, grinning with dyed blond tips and wearing Rage Against the Machine T-shirts, inevitable as the clock ticking off the hours. This is their trade mission to the rest of the world. But what do they have to sell but themselves? Faces of a North American future, a reliance on gadgets-to-come, answers to questions we haven't yet asked coming down the line. They offer nothing but promises. Tomorrow on sale today, threatening and absent.

Just look at them. Uncomfortable in borrowed shirts and ties, scuffing prep-school loafers over the marble floor. Laughing between themselves. At what? I can never tell for sure, aside from knowing that the joke is always on us. Or on me anyway, only half a generation too late to get it. Less golden boys than the whitest kind of white, the masters of something repeatedly called a revolution. Could anyone afford not to buy whatever nothing they had to sell?

It should perhaps be noted that I wasn't the only one to meet the prime minister at the consulate reception. Later, Bates told me he was surprised how bad the old man's breath was, and Wallace admitted to having forgotten his name.

We see our first blood two days later.

This is in Manaus. The regional capital of Amazonas built by the European rubber barons in the middle of the nineteenth century and now the principal eco-tourist gateway to the rainforest. Before we see the blood, though, we see the river. As we descend through the clouds in our chartered jet, the pilot instructs us to look out the windows at the *encontro das águas*, the point just outside the city at which the dark waters of the Negro and the milky brown of the Amazon run side by side like a pair of ribbons for several miles before finally mixing together.

At first we can see nothing beyond this but jungle, which from ten thousand feet up appears as a field of broccoli that spreads out farther and farther until the earth gets tired of it and drops away. After a time you can see other things in it, too. The perfect rectangles of clearcut forest, for one thing. Shaved tracts stretching back from the river's edge where the barges take the timber away and down three thousand winding miles to the ocean. And along with these, irregular gray divots that I know to be open-pit gold-mining excavations. I know because some of the men I'd met at the consulate reception were Canadian investors in wildcat operations like the ones below us, and they told me I should keep an eye out for them on our approach into Manaus. "We get in and get out," one of them said, in a tone that indicated he meant doing so without the tedium of attending to environmental regulations. "Get the rocks we want and *bang!* We're *outta* there!"

Farther in, beyond the patches and holes, is a jagged line of smoke. This was caused by lightning. But the others, the ones unwaveringly straight as if drawn by a ruler, are manmade. Fire lines set off by corporate ranchers making way for new cattle farms. "Each one the size of a Texas county," the pilot says over the intercom, and we all laugh a little without knowing why. Sometimes one of the ranchers' fire lines and the bald patch of a clearcut meet, and we can see how the fire has carried on into it, ripping through the dried stumps and whatever else has been too small to load away, so that only a slice of charred earth remains. Even from up here we see how some of it is still smoking, the branded mark left by the jungle's new owner.

We bank around to line up with the runway that is presumably somewhere below us, although Wallace calmly points out that this looks more like a crash landing. There could not possibly be anything down there meant for us, let alone for planes. And as we lower the horizon is lost too, leaving only the particular square mile directly under us, one exactly the same as the other square miles between here and Belém at the Amazon's delta going one way, and going the other, the mountains where those Uruguay rugby players also crash landed and eventually ate each other.

Setting ourselves down here would be of little consequence to the jungle. One metal tube needling into the trees, finding a hole for itself. We would hardly leave a scar. Something about the ease of vanishing into this shag as seen from a pressurized cabin with your seat cranked back and a plastic cup of Chardonnay gripped in your palm makes the idea of it strangely inviting.

The plane completes its turn and the river appears once more. Both of the rivers, one black and one brown. Each noodling off into the broccoli garden, sending back glints of sun from miles down their course. And the *encontro das águas* just like the postcards: the two rivers shouldering close in the same bowl like a confection of chocolate and caramel ice cream.

Then, some way up the chocolate stream, a gray scab attached to the shore. Apartment blocks lined together like stucco dominoes, two or three office buildings with punched-out windows, orange shots from a petroleum smokestack, an accidental web of streets radiating out from the port. Manaus.

A forgotten Portuguese fort until 1850, when, in another part of the world, it was discovered what could be done when you combined rubber and latex compounds and factories. Within twenty years, three thousand tons of raw rubber were being exported annually. By the end of the century, the output had multiplied twenty times over. There was money. Money of the instant, preposterous, doomed kind. The barons sent their wardrobes back to the Continent to be properly laundered. Chinese work gangs, French prostitutes and Italian tenors were brought in on the same boats that took the rubber out. There were electric street lamps and a trolley system in Manaus before there was either in New York.

Soon, however, it was discovered that rubber trees could be transplanted to lands in southern Asia that the English, Portuguese, Spanish and French had already acquired for themselves. Why bring Chinese slave labor to the jungle when you could bring the jungle to the slaves? Within two years the barons had packed up, leaving the colonial souvenirs of a river port, children of mixed blood and the Teatro Amazonas, a world-class opera house, behind them. By 1920 the entire place was bankrupt. The only Europeans that remained were those who'd been too stupid to put aside enough gold to leave.

Years later, the Brazilian government designated the city a free-trade zone in an effort to provide the half-million hangers-on with a

chance to survive. Now Manaus boasted smuggling rings, drug traffi-
ckers and an open-air market that sold cheap electronics, American
porn and Taiwanese running shoes to all of Amazonas. It was also the
starting point for "sightseers from around the world" to head up the
river on package tours of "anywhere between six hours and six
weeks." I learned all this in the way tourists do, as facts pulled from a
pamphlet or shouted from a guide at the front of a bus.

We see the blood while on a bus tour ourselves. After landing we are
immediately hustled onto a private van. Our first stop is the opera
house. "Everything was brought from Europe for its construction—
the very best things. The stone from England, the flooring from Italy,
the crystal from France. You can imagine the difficulty of bringing
these materials all the way to this place," the tour guide says,
although only a moment's thought proves it quite impossible to imagine. "Many died building it," he adds with excited wonder, even pride.

We are led out onto the plaza in front of the building, each of us stag-
gering into the wall of afternoon humidity. The plaza is broad and
unshaded, the ground made of imported Portuguese tiles arranged in
a disorienting pattern of snaking white and black stripes. Enough
room to accommodate outdoor concerts on Christian holidays for the
peasants of a hundred years ago, or the several coachloads of squinting Americans, Germans and Japanese of today. The sun x-rayed
through their Bermuda shorts and cotton blouses to reveal the osteo-
porosis and suspicious freckles beneath. All of us looking up at the
facade of the opera house, its pink dome dotted with gold tiles winking
up at the sky. Around us, guides offer information in a goulash of
foreign languages. We half attempt to listen, fixed in attentive poses,
staring up at the Unique Piece of South American History. And what
we see is stunning, insoluble, ugly as sin. An absurd lump of European
culture heaved into the heart of the jungle.

"Those rubber guys must have really liked their opera," Bates says.

"That thing's not about music," Wallace answers him. "That's to
show who's boss."

It's about then that we hear Lydia's scream. Standing on the outside
of our small circle with her hands clasped to her cheeks in a Victorian
display of shock. A jurisprudence degree, important participation in

the merger of international media conglomerates and eight years busting balls at the London office of Goldman Sachs doesn't stop her from acting like a storybook English girl when faced with a pool of blood at her feet. And there it is. Red as salsa. Splashed over the marble tiles brought deep into the rainforest to decorate the plaza for the arrival of the great Caruso in 1901.

Everyone turns at once. The Germans, the Americans, the Japanese, Barry and Wallace. The entire world stops being educated about its colonial past to look at it: bright and thick in the perfect clarity of midday. Then we look to each other to see which of us has been knifed by the glue-addict pickpocket we'd been repeatedly warned about.

It's Barry I think of first—his white Brooks Brothers button-down seems just the thing to be seeped through with hot insides, his swollen fingers trembling over the wound. Maybe he knows this, too. Or maybe he just follows my eyes, for he looks down at his stomach with alarm before figuring out he is still intact, that what he thought might have been his own blood is only a broken bottle of *guarana*, one of those syrupy fruit drinks they keep offering him but, his ulcer being what it is, he would rather not try.

As each of us recognizes our mistake (it was the rather theatrical British scream that made us think the worst) and turns to husbands and wives and package tour strangers to register the fact that we are all still among the living, Wallace strides across the spilled juice and pulls Lydia to him. Tells her it's all right, we're fine, perhaps she should sit out of the sun for a while. And she yields to his comfort. His young arms.

"That's Wallace," Bates whispers to me. "Ever the gentleman."

And although Bates means this as men of his age mean most things, as a sarcastic joke, there's something truthful in it. The swiftness of Wallace's action—stepping directly into a pool of someone else's blood (as far as he knew) to offer aid to a woman in distress—was too automatic to not be built into his nature. It's true that one of us might have done the same thing a second later. I'm quite certain we would have. But still, he was first.

It makes me wonder whether Wallace might be a misplaced piece of history himself, as unlikely a leftover of Old World manners as the jungle opera house looming above us. A *gentleman?* Overnight millionaire, developer of a virtual morality machine, born and raised in the passively corrupted suburbs of North America more than a decade after what the century's-end coffee-table histories referred to as "the last gasps of idealism"? After the draft and its dodgers? After Woodstock?

I can only suppose that stranger things have happened.

Manaus is burning. The air as steamy as you'd expect of the equator (two linen-suited government officials traveling with us collapsed seconds after stepping onto the airport tarmac, as though the laptop cases they carried had taken on sudden new weight). It makes one aware of breathing, its deliberate ins and outs. The rainy season still a couple of weeks off and not a cloud in sight. But there's a wetness that still gets into everything, your socks, your wallet, behind the lenses of your glasses, your lungs. Within hours of arriving it's like carrying ball bearings around in your chest.

But the place appears to be literally *on fire* as well. A city where a city shouldn't be, boarded up and crumbling and what's left now set alight. Look from the windows of the airport hospitality van, our rooms at the Tropical Hotel atop a gated bluff on the edge of town, from anywhere, and there is always what looks to be black smoke in the distance, flapping like a villain's cape into the sky. But turn away from it and it moves—now spiraling up beyond a different rooftop. Is it from land being cleared to make way for cattle or of natural origins? Is it coming closer? Somehow these questions can't be asked out loud. None of us mention seeing it, at any rate, although I'm sure we all do. Nor do we speak of the black vultures circling high over the rusted church spires.

On the day before we are to embark on our riverboat trip up the Negro we take in what we haven't already seen of the city. An air-conditioned bus is chartered for the afternoon, along with another guide from the hotel. We spread out down the coach's length, each of us separated by several rows of empty seats that take up an entire block of the town outside. From where we sit, levitating six feet above the streets of brick and tar, Manaus looks uncomfortably full. Plaster walls push against men wearing jeans and soiled long-sleeve dress shirts in the visible blooms of heat. There are also girls young enough to have not yet lost their layer of chubby cushioning just beneath the skin, walking sleep-eyed in super-minis and V-neck T-shirts that say "Bad Ass" and "Sugar Baby" across their chests. We watch them all pass through the tinted windows. And they look back at us with what we imagine to be either lust or hostility.

We walk through the covered market by the river with its tables of futuristic fruits and fish that all seem to be grotesque variations on a catfish theme. Bates views them through his Palmcorder and the rest of us envy the protection the tiny machine offers him. No larger than an ice cream sandwich and yet, acting as a narrowed eye, able to block out the overly bright colors, the faces behind counters streaked with guts, even the smells. While Bates makes a movie, we are left to nod at the tour guide's comments (the market was built in 1902 by a homesick Francophile who modeled it after Les Halles in Paris) and feel our skin burning even here in the speckled shade.

Back on the bus, we park on the city's main floating dock and are told how long the river is (1,642 miles), how wide at its widest point (over 7,000 feet), why it is called the Negro (the water is black compared with the Amazon's brown, on account of its higher acidity levels) and where it would lead if you followed it to its source (some village in Venezuela). It is a river that reaches "many peoples, many nations." One of its main tributaries, the Rio Branco, breaks off into Guiana, and another, the Uaupés, stretches as far as southern Colombia. At the mention of Colombia, Wallace and Bates hold fingers against the sides of their noses and snort an imaginary line out of midair.

The final stop is to see what the guide calls "the poverty many Brazilians still suffer today." A shantytown built on the banks of a creek that feeds into the Negro and extends as far as you could see from where we are, fifty feet above on a concrete bridge. A collage of cardboard, bicycle rims, oil drums and jagged sheet metal making up the walls of each box in which, we are told, at least an entire family lives. Many of the boxes sit precariously on crooked fingers of timber, a black ooze falling out from holes in the floors.

Barry shakes his head. Lydia holds her nose. Bates studiously pans across the scene of filth and degradation with his Palmcorder, whispering notes into the built-in microphone.

"People live here. It smells very, very bad. The river is their toilet."

Wallace stares. For the first time since I met him his face is set without the hint of flexing tendons about to be employed for the purposes of amusement. Only his eyes move from box to box, lingering on the few shadowed sets of eyes that peer back at him. Hands gripped tight to the bridge's rail as though he would fall forward without the greatest effort. All of us notice his silence. Even the tour guide, who stands there watching him after he's run out of things to say.

Once we are back aboard the bus, I overhear Wallace whisper to Bates so low I'm sure I'm the only other person to hear it. An odd phrase that he repeats a few times before leaning back in his seat and closing his eyes. Odd too that Bates seems to understand him perfectly, though the words sound incomplete to me. Bates nods to his friend in what might be agreement, or acknowledgment of a point made many times before. Or perhaps Wallace's empty words put them both into a kind of trance that takes the entire ride back to the hotel for them to find their way out of.

"It's a world," he whispers. Amazed, as though he were the first to discover its roundness. "It's a world. A *world*."

The concierge is tall. He is also wide. From a distance, standing under a fake gaslight next to the Tropical Hotel's marquee, he could be two men held in a close embrace. Then he turns and you see it is only a single giant, looking out with empty eyes over the tennis courts and tiered parking lots and sculpted shrubs to the river below. When you come closer, you see that his eyes are more cruelly pleased than empty, that he is fat as well as tall and wide, and that his skin is bad.

Wallace takes to him immediately.

"Where's the action tonight, my good man?" he asks before he's even stepped off the tour bus.

"Action?" the giant says, his voice cruelly pleased along with his eyes.

"We've been *seeing things* from a refrigerated sardine can all day. But now it's time for some ex-treme adventure tourism. Right, Barry?"

"Does that include getting a drink?"

"Absolutely. It ab-so-*lute*-ly involves Barry getting a drink."

Wallace has put on one of his accents and is acting like a drunk conventioneer. Bates calls it "going American."

"Yes-*sir*, Bear-man," he says. "We is going to see what this May-naus *really* has to offer!"

As we wait for Lydia to collect her bags of piranha teeth souvenirs, the concierge drapes an arm behind Wallace's neck and folds himself lower to speak into his ear. I can't catch the words, but whatever the giant says prompts a lewd grin from his audience.

Wallace is a sexy kid. It's not the first time I've thought this. One is likely to think it a lot around him. Especially at moments like this, sliding his way into the middle of an indulgent plan, telling a dirty joke. Women like him for his secrecy, his good looks, the tall certainty of his frame. Men like him for all this too, although they can't speak of it. A little obnoxious, of course, but somehow always likable. The lean lips, forehead clean as a laundered sheet, freckles like buckshot across the tops of his cheeks—his face brings you into him, tells you that you could be in on things too, if you wanted. Or if he wanted. Yes, he is asking the concierge of the only four-star hotel in the jungle how he might spend his undeserved wealth and get into the kind of trouble he knows he can always get out of. So what? He's a trouble maker. He finds profit in trouble.

You can see all this and still be there next to him, want nothing but to be a part of things, an accomplice. You won't admit this to anyone. Perhaps you won't admit this to yourself—it makes it no less true. Have him all figured out and you are no further ahead than someone who looks at him and sees only a handsome boy. Even the most envious would agree he is not without his charms. All of America is in him. Every slasher flick, pool party blow job, microwavable snack product and skipped class. Unprincipled but proud, rich in trivia but poorly read, viciously easygoing. His total Americanness comes naturally to him. But only as a Canadian is Wallace in a position to perfect it.

After we have all hunched off the bus and stand blinking for a minute in the stunning light, Wallace turns away from the giant's chest to address us.

"My friend has made some helpful suggestions for tonight's entertainments," he says, and smiles. His smiles are large and promising and unwholesome. They tell the world that it is unavoidably part of his plans.

We spend the rest of the afternoon apart. Wallace wanders around the mini-zoo in the hotel gardens. ("What did you see?" Lydia later asks him with scientific interest. "Monkeys." "Oh! What kind?" "The kind in cages.") Barry makes some calls to the company's bankers in New York on his cell phone down near the river, where he believes the reception is better. Bates jogs along the groomed "tropical trail" on the hotel's grounds. Lydia falls asleep in her room while watching a CNN report on renewed violence in the Middle East and its effect on world oil prices.

This is what they claim to do with their time, anyway.

What is certain is that, later, Wallace and I are the first to arrive under the hotel's marquee where the concierge is trying to round up a pair of taxis to take us into Manaus for dinner. Wallace meets my wave with a theatrically gaping mouth. Steps out of the glass revolving doors and pretends to trip my way in shock.

"Where did you get your hands on *that?*" he says, raising an index finger at my chest.

"On what?"

"The push-up bra number, what else?"

"It's a bikini top."

"It's an engineering miracle, is what it is."

"I got it at the hotel boutique," I say, and feel the bloom of hot regret in my cheeks. What does it matter where I got it? Why am I explaining myself at all? What *right* does this boy have to treat me like a pig-tailed schoolgirl? "It was on sale," I add.

"Oh, really?"

Do you like it?

32

I'm about to ask this aloud, but something stops me. What answer would he give? It would be terrible, surely. Honest and mean and unforgettable. Something I would pretend to laugh at and never recover from.

Wallace continues to grin at me, waiting for further self-incrimination.

"Why are you looking at me like that?" I say. "It's not a big deal, for God's sake."

"Is that make-up, too?"

Without thinking, I curl my lips into my mouth, hiding their coat of Maybelline Dusty Rose. "I borrowed it from Lydia," I mumble.

He looks me over once more from bottom to top and I let him. Hold my chin up for an extra half inch of height.

"It's not *you*, Crossman," he says.

"Oh no? What is me?"

"Wool skirts and itchy turtlenecks. A scarf round the neck and your grandmother's brooch when you're feeling especially wild. But this— this is what *girls* wear."

"If you haven't noticed, I'm not a man, Wallace."

"Of course not. I just wish you'd told me sooner, that's all."

He must notice the collapse of my smile, because for a second he has his hands out in front of him, pleading.

"Look, Crossman, I didn't mean to—"

"It's only a *top*," I go on, though I meant to say nothing more. I cross my arms but it sandwiches my breasts into even greater visibility, and I immediately let them fall again. Nipples sighing audibly against the material as they go. "It's hotter than I thought it would be down here."

"You're not kidding," he says with a lurid wink.

The brief look of apology drains out of his face—it may never have been there at all—and is once again replaced by his patronizing nod.

"You're laughing at me," I say.

"Wouldn't dream of it. I'm wondering, that's all."

"Wondering why a pushing-forty old bag like me would show more of her flab than she needed to?"

"No, I'm wondering who she meant to show it to."

He means himself, of course. He thinks I'm wearing these ridiculous cups for him, to get the cute boy's attention on our one night out in Manaus, to see what interest I might stir up. You never know if you don't try, even with a candidate as unlikely as me. He assumes that, whether I'm aware of it or not, I want him as much as everyone else does. And he's right, though I do my best to compose my face in a way that says he couldn't be further from the truth.

The concierge's shadow falls over us. He touches my bare shoulder and bends close to tell me that our taxis are ready.

"These are our cabs," I tell Wallace, stepping away from the concierge's cold fingers and feeling for the door handle behind me. All I want now is to be out of the light. To hide my skin from his eyes.

"Thank you for that translation, Crossman," he says, bowing like a courtier as I scramble into the back seat and blink at my painted face in the driver's mirror.

Among the local diversions recommended by the concierge is a restaurant in the old district of Manaus, down in the brick streets where the rubber barons kept their offices, mistresses and men's clubs. Our taxi driver smiles at the mention of the restaurant's name. A *churrascaria* called Bufalo (a giant papier-mâché steer grimaces at all that enter the door). We order two bottles of wine as soon as we're seated, but the waiter rushes off without asking what we'd like to eat.

"So can we get any *food* around here, Crossman?" Barry asks me.

I tell him to hold his horses. And soon, platter after platter of meat arrives at the table—joints of lamb, roast pork, four different cuts of beef—all dripping off skewers to be sliced by grim-faced stewards and slapped onto plates the size of medieval shields. Aside from a couple bowls of grainy manioc and a sliced tomato, no vegetables are offered.

Within minutes the amount of food becomes ludicrous ("So *this* is what they're clearcutting the rainforest for!" Barry roars), and each of us becomes involved in its excess. Without prompting we start laughing through bloody mouthfuls, nodding for more from the waiters when they return to our table, as though powerless to shoo them away. An unstoppable orgy of meat pushing toward its climax with charcoal belches and slippery fingers.

Barry the most passionate of all of us. It's like he has something to prove, having already informed us that, coming from Georgia, he "*knows* bar-be-cue."

"Barry looks like he's going to start mooing or growing an udder or something," Bates announces, blushing under the buzzing fluorescent lights.

"Yes, Barry! You look positively *bo*vine!" Lydia shrieks.

And it's true: Barry *does* look more startled and hide-stretched than usual. He laughs along with us, though, his hand circling the air over his bald patch for another bottle. A man made of solid meat. Sausage fingers, ham hock thighs, fatty back ribs. A boundless deli case all sewn together into a new sort of animal, one with thinning blond hair who recites profane limericks. Nobody knows exactly how old he is (we all take guesses whenever he isn't around, but something in his winking, college-boy manner discourages direct inquiry). Would he be fifty? Sixty? You'd say he is in good shape for either. It has been said about him all through his life of barreling through office hallways, convention floors and airport terminals. An air of good shape in his designer colognes and forearms tanned and hardened from a million backhand returns.

We like him. He is the kind of American the rest of the world likes best: a laugher of unforced volume, a sunburned friendliness suggestive of mixed-doubles tournaments and long cocktail hours. He smells like an old hotel—bulk laundry detergent, cigar butts and shoe polish. A man to buy things from without speaking of the price out loud. Barry knows a lot of jokes that are actually funny.

"When I was starting out, you knew where the money was going," he's saying after more Chilean Cabernet arrives and he's filled our water goblets as well as our wine glasses to the brim. "You knew the deals inside out, you knew the players. Now? I'm just here to throw the cash around for these two—these two *kids*."

"Don't you mean *snot-nosed* kids, Bear?"

"It pisses me off," he continues, ignoring Bates. "We've *lost* something. From doing business. We used to *invest* our clients' money.

There used to be analysis. And prudence! But now grown men like me are chasing after these skatepunks, pumping millions into zero-revenue, zero-profit will-o'-the-wisps—into *websites*, for Christ's sake! I mean, what the hell *are* they, anyway? What do they *do?* Don't get me wrong. I'm grateful for the opportunity. I'm with the project. But on some fundamental level, I have to say that I don't get it. Honestly. I truly, truly, don't."

He slips in and out of a southern drawl whenever it suits him, which are the occasions he wishes to appear harmless or dim. But now he's suddenly grave, his bull's head shaking from side to side over the charred gore inches beneath his chin. It's somehow also clear that the moment is not meant to be entirely serious. This is his little *Death of a Salesman* scene. The touching confusion of the noble company man in the face of dubious progress. But he is a businessman first and an actor second (according to the Hypothesys business agreement, he stands to make fifteen percent of the gross profits, whether he eventually figures out what websites are or not). And sure enough, within seconds he is finishing the wine in his water goblet and telling the one about the priest, the rabbi and the Irishman walking into a topless bar in Las Vegas.

Each of us attempts jokes of our own after this, but none of them are as good. When it comes to Wallace's turn, his face shows that he isn't even going to make an attempt. He has been thinking of something else for a while now.

"I first got my hands on money when I turned nineteen," he says. "Have I told you this one before?"

"No," Barry and Lydia say at once.

"It was the final installment of my trust fund. Not a whole lot, but enough to do what everyone else of my age and means seemed obliged to do. We were taking a year off. We were *getting out there*. Some of us were even going to *make a difference*. So I did the only thing a fellow could do in such circumstances. I went to India."

"Oh, *India!*" Lydia exclaims, as though it's the name of someone she knows personally. "I've heard so much about it. Is it *wonderful?*"

"I suppose. Most of the people are what we would regard as dirt-eating poor. It's very hot. I'm no anthropologist. But what did strike me after I got back—and it struck me again today—is that India is still there."

"Of course it is."

"Yes. But *I'm* not."

"I'm sorry, Wallace. I'm not sure I—"

"I'm thinking of all the things I saw," he says, flattening the plastic tablecloth with his palms. "In Bombay, for instance. The billions of details that make up a single second—the streetcorner begging, the doorfront whoring, bedpans emptied out of *chawla* windows, schoolboys playing cricket on a pitch where the smog obscured every fieldsman from the batter—every unconnected incident in that paralyzing city, all of it going on while I am elsewhere. Bombay is still Bombay even after I left it. It didn't stop."

This observation crowds Wallace's mind. It makes him dizzy. And seeing the jungle from the plane brought it back to him. He feels the same about this place. That these grease-fingered waiters, the people who live in those boxes over the polluted stream, the line of fire marching through the rainforest—they will all be doing the same thing without him as their audience. For Wallace, this is almost impossible to accept.

"What you're talking about is nothing more than the most basic philosophical puzzle," Barry says, waving a glistening knife over the table. "It's the if-a-tree-falls-in-the-forest thing."

"No, it's *not*." Wallace circles his hands in front of him, his wrists loosened by wine. "Everyone *knows* a tree makes a sound when it falls, whether you're there to hear it or not. I couldn't care less about that tree. But instead think of *every* tree in the world that is falling at this very moment. Now, add to that every version of birdsong being sung. Every guy in a suit whistling for a cab on the island of Manhattan. Every mother telling her kid to *Stop that right now!* Throw in all the car alarms waking people up in East St. Louis, just for good measure. And you're not there for *any* of it. You're *here* instead. We're all trapped. Or blind. We can only see what our one consciousness allows us to see."

"You want to be everywhere at once?"

"Yes."

"And how are you going to do that, genius?"

"By expanding. And, in turn, by absorbing everything else around you, so that it *is* you."

"Wallace, with all due respect, what the hell are you talking about?"

"Losing yourself. To step away from the contingencies that bind you to a single identity, so that you can live more lives than one."

"I *see*."

"Bates understands it."

"Is that true, Bates? You get this shit?"

Bates says nothing, but keeps his eyes on Wallace to acknowledge his agreement.

"Jesus, the two of you." Barry shakes his head so low it nearly knocks a bottle of chili sauce off the table. "Really. It's like the world's smallest cult or something."

"It's too late for you anyway, Barry," Wallace says. "I already own you."

"What?"

"You've been absorbed."

"Well, not anymore. I quit."

"It's not about your *job*. Or money. Go ahead and quit. You're still mine. And the thing is, you know it."

They both laugh, though it requires some work. Until now I haven't seen the two of them talk like this, to tease so hard it hurt. For a time there is more eating. Barry asks if he can finish the wine that Lydia hasn't touched, knocks back one full glass followed by the other. We watch him with smiles. But there are no more words.

Steaming slices continue to be dropped on our plates, and we work away at them gloomily, as though a deserved punishment. All of us but Wallace, who chews and swallows at the same pace as when he began.

After perhaps five minutes of silence, it is Wallace who lowers his fork and wipes his blushing lips.

"Let's play a game," he says. "You and me, Crossman. We'll play it once between ourselves so the others can see how it's done."

"What's the game?"

"Simple. I'll give you twenty grand if you can guess who I'm thinking of right now."

I open my mouth and smack it closed again. *Twenty grand?* Wallace, money and a game involving the reading of his thoughts. There's a good chance of being made a fool of in this. And look at him now: sliding his eyes down the line of my goose-pimpled cleavage. Not a trace of lust in it, only humor, a reminder of the gap between who I am and who I might be trying to be. He had laughed at the way I had made myself look for him. Now he wants to laugh at the way I think.

"Not enough?" Wallace asks. "I don't blame you. Why risk losing unless the reward is worth it?"

He squeezes his chin between finger and thumb, and for a moment it seems that he's actually waiting for a response. But again, caution silences me.

"What do you say to fifty, then?"

"Fifty *what?*"

"Thousand dollars, Crossman. What else? Fifty thousand Brazilian *reals* wouldn't buy you a bottle of shampoo back home. Not that I'm suggesting anything about your personal—"

"You're offering that much money for me to play a stupid game?"

"No, gorgeous. For winning it."

I try looking down at Wallace's hands, then up to the blond ridge of his hairline, at anywhere but his eyes, but they follow mine wherever they go. Whether it is this or the understanding of precisely how much money he has just uttered—casually, plausibly—there is a tingling at the top of my head that trickles down over my skin like spiders.

"You carry that much around with you?" I manage.

"No, but Barry does. He's the one with the checkbooks. Aren't you, Bear?"

Barry grunts. He works for this boy. And he *is* the one with the checks.

"So what do I have to do?"

"Tell me who I'm thinking of."

"That's ridiculous. It could be anyone."

"It's not anyone. It's someone you know. And I'll give you three questions or guesses."

"How do I know you won't say someone else if I guess right?"

"Because you trust me not to."

"Look, I'm not saying I don't . . . I'm just trying to nail the rules down."

"Of course you are. Barry, hand me your napkin."

Barry takes the paper serviette tucked into his collar and crumples it into a ball, which he tries to throw at Wallace's head. But even with all the sauce smeared over it and the force of Barry's pitch, it arcs with accidental grace to bounce twice, soft as a cotton ball, at the end of the table opposite him.

"Does anyone have a pen?" Wallace asks, unfolding the napkin. "Lydia. You've always got lipstick in your purse, don't you?"

Lydia digs into her bag and pulls out the same lipstick I borrowed from her two hours ago. Hands it to Wallace, who slides the cap off and screws up its bright red head.

"Don't look," he says, and all of us blind ourselves by looking straight up into the fluorescent ceiling. "I'm writing a name on this napkin and turning it over. One name only. No tricks."

He claps his hands once to signal he's finished. When we bring our heads down to look at him again he is facing me alone.

"Take your time," he says. "Try to *occupy* the name. If you open yourself up to—"

"The prime minister."

"Courage! Who would have thought? Crossman ventures a bold guess, right out of the gate!"

"Am I right?"

"Afraid not."

"All right. A question this time."

"Think hard, Crossman. At the per diem we're paying you—let's see now—that works out to a whole *year* of translating you won't have to do if you get this right."

Barry snorts at this, but I cast him a look that prevents anything else from escaping him. When I return to Wallace I remind myself to take a breath. Who would he be thinking of? If Wallace is playing a game with me there must be an obvious way to win it. Otherwise, my losing wouldn't be any fun.

"Is it one of us at this table?"

"It *is!*" Wallace snaps his fingers and points at me, his thumb raised like the hammer on a pistol. "Last guess. But it's only one-in-five odds now. Not at all bad. Any sideshow gypsy could get this in a flash. Are you much of a mind reader, Crossman?"

"Depends on the mind."

"Not really. You just open it up and see what's there, one's as easy as the other. Like a book. I bet you read a lot of books, but not too many minds. Am I right?"

"You," I say.

"Beg pardon?"

"You're thinking of yourself."

"Is that your guess?"

"It's as good as any."

"Take a look and see."

Wallace makes no move to slide the napkin over so that I have to stand and bend halfway over the table to reach it, my hand over my chest to keep my breasts from slipping free. When I'm seated again I pull it up and read what's there. Read it again. Back and forth as though a carefully worded riddle. But it's only a name, scrawled out in garish capitals.

"Did you win?" Lydia asks.

"No," I say, the napkin held as a veil in front of my eyes. "I wasn't even close."

"How could you *not* be close? It was one in five!" Barry slaps his knee, snorting again.

"That's the funny part, right, Wallace?" I say. "No wonder you like to play this one. Make it so close they'll never get it."

"Who *is* it?" Lydia begs, her hands balled up into fists next to her ears as though to protect them from what they might hear next.

I turn the napkin over and lay it flat in the center of the table. Let all of them read my own name spelled out in crimson wax. *Elizabeth Crossman.*

"I was thinking of you, Lizzie," Wallace says. "I was looking at the answer the whole time and the answer didn't even know it."

I laugh a false laugh through my nose and feel something fly out.

"Well, that certainly was *interesting*, Wallace," Lydia says.

"Fun for the whole family."

"But it's not over yet, is it?" I say, wavelets of panic accelerating my words. "We know *who* you were thinking of, but not *what*. Why don't you tell us what deep ideas you had while you were staring at me."

Wallace raises his eyebrows.

"Tell me what you see," I demand, meeting Wallace's eyes but with my voice breaking in a bubble of sobs.

"That's a whole other game," he says.

For the second time none of us speak. This time, though, there isn't awkwardness so much as embarrassment. All of them silently feeling bad for me, not only for the money I could have made but for the way it was lost. The lips I can't stop from trembling. My failure to see that Wallace was never playing at anything, but making a point.

"When does it *stop?*" Lydia finally asks.

All of us glance up at the circle of waiters continuing to thrust spikes of charred livestock our way.

"Are we finished?" I ask the table.

"We're going to *die* if we don't stop now," Barry says, forcing something thick-sounding down his throat.

I flip over a red card on top of the napkin dispenser to show its blue side. The waiters disperse.

"They keep coming until you surrender," I tell them. "Non-stop meat."

"I love it!" Wallace smiles at Bates. "No need to ask for anything. No need for *need*. It all just comes whether you like it or not."

For a moment, I'm convinced he's going to ask for Lydia's lipstick again and make a note of this novel marketing plan. But instead he only nods his head with admiration while carefully finishing what's on his plate.

Outside the restaurant, three rumbling taxis wait to take the handful of other belly-slapping tourists and ourselves back to the Tropical. But Wallace has other plans.

"My tall friend from the hotel mentioned some places we could go after dinner," he says. "C'mon, Lydia. You and me mixing it up out there. Whaddya say?"

"I say I'm going to bed, Mr. Wallace," she says with a stagey yawn. "Tomorrow we go on our tour, and I expect I'll need all the energy I have for that."

"What about you, Crossman?"

"Sorry, but I think I'm going to have to call it a night, too."

"*Well*. I must say I'm a little surprised. I took you for a hellraiser. What with that sly little grimace on your face all the time. I assumed you were just biding your time."

"It's not a grimace."

"Fine. You're Chuckles the Clown."

"And Chuckles is too old for staying up all night."

"Barry's coming with us. And *he's* old."

"Watch your mouth, boy!"

"And furthermore," I say, bringing two fingers to my temple in a Boy Scout salute, "somebody's got to accompany Lydia home."

"Ah! So the ladies toddle off for their beauty sleep and the men are left to do the heavy lifting and tell you shrinking violets all about it in the morning as we steam our way up the—what's the name of the river we're going up?"

"The Rio Negro," Bates prompts him.

"That's right. The Black River. Mighty tributary of the mighty Amazon. Fine then. It will be our responsibility to collect some mighty stories for the trip," he says, pulling Barry and Bates against him so forcefully that they all lose their balance and look as though they might fall backwards together, but Wallace refuses to let go until they right themselves.

"Good night, Lydia," Bates says softly as we get into the first car, rolling his eyes at us as Wallace squeezes him even closer. "Don't let the bed bugs bite, Crossman."

The three of them wave as our taxi pulls away, arms cast high above their heads, their straightened teeth and white palms visible from two unlit blocks away. It's as though they are encircled by a spotlight, and these ridge-backed streets nothing more than a soundstage of poverty and abandonment for them to carry out their parts. Or this is what one could think from a safe distance such as mine.

What do they do next? There are different versions. Each of theirs in addition to my own. And even when pulled together there are still questions. I feel uniquely qualified in sewing these patches into a single story, however. I'm a translator, after all. And translation is nothing if not reading—and speaking—between the lines. A good deal of raw creativity is involved, if I may say so myself.

The real work is in making things up to bridge the inevitable gaps that language leaves between us. I often suspect it is not wholly unlike the task of writing fiction: more autobiography than is usually admitted to, perhaps, the collection of observed details, historical fact, all melted down into a credible beginning, middle and end. One must fall short of outright lying, of course. But if both sides can't understand each other, and whatever's lost in translation is lost forever, what's the harm in a fib or two to keep things going smoothly?

As Lydia and I drive off in the taxi back to the Tropical, the others ask themselves what they should do with the rest of their evening. It is clear that whatever it is, it should involve further drinking. A whiff of trouble might be nice. The kind of recreations you just can't get at home. Wallace mentions that the hotel concierge recommended the bars down near the docks. The recommendation was of the sort made with a wink, as these were not "places for ladies." And there is no lady with them now.

"The hotel guy winked?" Bates asks.

"Yes, he did. Why do you ask?"

"It's just hard to imagine him winking."

"Well, the guy winked, OK?"

Bates shoots Wallace a doubtful look but Barry is already striding ahead of them, so they start off to join him. They figure the river must be downhill from where they are, and begin zigzagging through the broken streets to find it. Women with children's faces poking out from between their knees stand in doorways lit by single bulbs. The smell of rice frying in vegetable oil and boiled bones. Rats scuttling through gutters so dark that only the last glimpses of their tails can be seen.

According to the afternoon's tour guide, the buildings the three of them pass now used to be the homes of the rubber barons. Slave owners, makers of opera houses. Now half of them stand derelict, long stripped of glass, doors and fixtures.

Without a word they stop before one that is two floors taller than the rest, as though they had heard their names called from inside. Barry and Bates are both surprised by their instant fear. An inexplicable chill that passes through them in the windless night heat.

"A haunted house," Bates says, but his voice is too conclusive to be taken as humor.

Wallace is the only one who is unafraid. In fact, the sight of the gutted grandeur thrills him. The vines looping down over stone balconies, gripping to the plaster cracks. It was beautiful once—even he can see that. And now it's a ruin. He finds drama in this. Not in the history it suggests but in the purity of its failure, the things-come-and-things-go lesson of economics. It's not the ghosts that lurk inside these buildings but their perfect emptiness that he finds exciting.

"There's some places down by the dock I've heard mention of," he reminds them finally, and gathers them up by the shoulders once more.

It is a street that only men seem to enter. On the far side of the small public square next to the British Customs House, where none of the light from the strings of colored bulbs over the vendors' tables can reach. Barry, Wallace and Bates stride around its corner as though it leads to their own homes, their clothes shining. But the hesitation in their legs is defeated only by an exercise of will. The street appears at once empty and full of faces. Popping out amongst the rubble of a burned-out storefront or floating over the edge of uncurtained windows. Each step is like moving into suckerpunches of stink: burnt machine oil, caramelized shit, gasoline. Without thinking, they form a line with Wallace at the lead.

"How's this place look?" he asks when they arrive at a new cone of electric yellow on the pavement. Barry and Bates look up and take in a high-ceilinged room with tables and a plywood partition down one side that acts as a bar.

"Good enough," Bates replies. "But where's the door?"

This is meant to be funny, for the room is entirely without a wall on the street side, so that walking into it is like stepping onto a proscenium stage from the orchestra pit.

They had all been in bars that felt dangerous before—roadhouses on the outskirts of college towns or a bus terminal lounge here and there—but this place actually *is* dangerous. Each of them believes these men around them to be storybook pirates, smugglers, switchblade thieves. Surely such men still exist somewhere in the world, probably in the lower hemisphere where it is hot and lawless and the people are desperate. Somewhere like here. So why not *these* men? Look at them: wrapped in a plastic sheet of sweat, fever-eyed, swearing in toothless Portuguese at a black-and-white soccer game on TV. Take the room in at once and it seems that they all wear expressions of addled hate.

"It ain't the Ritz, boys," Barry says in his southern voice, but there's a nervous whistle in it now. Nobody hears it though. Wallace is already seated at a wobbly plastic table, waving three fingers into the air and shouting, "Cerveza!"

"Cer-ve-*za* is Spanish," Bates tells him after he and Barry find their way to the table. "In Portuguese, it's pronounced ser-vay-*ja*."

"Ser-vay-*ja* then!" Wallace shouts, pulling an American twenty out of his breast pocket and slapping it down on the table. The pirates turn to look at the three of them—had been looking at them all along—but nothing changes in their faces.

Although none of the three really feels like it, they begin to drink with aggressive enthusiasm. Bottles of Antarctica beer arrive, two for each of them, and glasses of *cachaça*, the suspiciously clear liquor that comes whenever they make a pantomime of throwing a shot down their throats. Nobody suggests slowing down. Some powerful, unspoken challenge animates them. The entire room is part of it. Men keep coming in off the street to clog the aisles. Before long everything is slurred and stuck in tar. The air rank with something like boiled hot dogs and burned hair. It's so hot in the crowded fluorescence that vomiting or collapsing to the floor are constantly vacillating options.

"To Hypothesys!" Wallace toasts, raising his glass of clear fire. "And all who profit from it!"

"That would be us," Barry laughs.

"That's correct. But I think it's time we once and for all acknowledge the real talent in this operation, Barry. The reason our vaporware venture is going to succeed where others have failed before us. Our bard of software code: Master Bates!"

"Hypothesys isn't vaporware," Bates protests, but downs his drink along with them.

"Of course it isn't. It's the *real* thing, isn't it, Barry?"

"Ab-so-*lute*-ly. But remind me. What's vaporware again?"

"Software that doesn't actually do anything. At least not yet. A pure *idea*. Investors love it."

"Well, we'll just have to come up with some more pure ideas, won't we, young Bates?"

"Not me. Wallace is the ideas man."

"You flatter me, Bates. I'm not about ideas and you know it. I'm a *facilitator*. I bring things together and let them multiply on their own. Capitalism is human nature left to its own devices. That's my one and only idea."

"Put another way," Barry starts, and pauses to suppress a difficult-sounding belch. "You're a people person."

"Yes! A people person! I just *love* people!"

Something about the lighting shows their dandruff and the ash from others' cigarettes on their shirts so that a constellation appears across their shoulders, a starry map ringed around their collars. Barry takes a couple of ineffectual swipes at it, then excuses himself to lumber off in search of a toilet. Another round arrives without any of them having ordered it. A moment later Bates grabs Wallace's arm across the table.

"Hey, isn't that the guy from the hotel?" he whispers, head turned to the wide-open front of the bar.

"What guy?"

"The monster. The one you were talking to."

"The concierge? Where?"

"There."

Bates points at a Volkswagen Beetle parked across the street. Behind it, what may be the figure of the concierge, or a shadowed doorframe, or nothing at all.

"I don't see shit," Wallace says.

"He kind of unraveled himself out of that car and stared in here. At us."

"Maybe he wants to join us for a drink."

"Did he tell you to come here, Wallace?"

Wallace turns to him, his nostrils widened into perfect circles. "We *happened upon* this particular bar, remember?"

"It's just that you were talking to him for so—"

"What's your problem? So I talked to the hotel guy. Now you think he's the goddamn bogeyman, who's got nothing better to do than follow your ass around." Wallace throws back his shot without taking his eyes from Bates's, then abruptly pivots to face the street. "Look again," he says over his shoulder. "There's nobody there now."

And Bates does look. The Beetle is gone. But the black space that could have occupied a man remains.

"He must have left in the car."

"Must have."

Bates looks nervous. But his face has always been long and vaguely haunted, as though as a child he'd witnessed something he hadn't expected and his expression had kept traces of that initial horror with it ever since. A minor sort of horror, mind you. The common kind that most children toddle away from but others remember forever, as though it were their appointed duty to display shock for the benefit of those who hadn't seen anything quite that bad yet.

Barry returns from whatever corner he found to relieve himself in and they wave another round of warm *cachaça* and warmer Antarctica to their table. Nobody mentions the Volkswagen or Bates's vision of the monstrous concierge. Nobody wonders aloud what they're doing here, people who had been quoted in *The Economist* and favorably profiled in *Wired*, sitting in this bright hole, drinking with these damp-looking river thugs. A fluorescent tube spasms over their heads, freezes the curdled humor on their lips. Each of them wishes it would burn out once and for all and leave them in the more forgiving light of the Marlboro clock on the wall.

It's around then that they notice the girls. Half a dozen of them of various dimensions, ages and mascara colors suddenly materialized in a witches' circle at the far end of the bar. Denim shorts cut even higher than the Manaus average, passing the same lipstick between them.

"Well, well, well," Wallace and Barry say at the same time.

"Jinx," Bates says.

They come to understand that there are rooms somewhere in the back where a customer may go with these girls. From time to time one of the girls glances in the direction of the hallway behind the bar as though catching a flash of movement from out of its shadows. Mostly, though, they keep their eyes on the three drunk American tourists who, by the look of them, could be a father with his two sons.

And the Hypothesys men stare back at the girls. When they speak among themselves they find that now they share tight, business-like grins.

At first, the question of who they would each choose is only a vulgar hypothetical. The little smiley one with the huge tits? That would have to be Bates. Got Bates written all over her. And the older one with the dimpled ass and gold tooth? Definitely up your alley there, Barry! This sort of thing for a round or two.

But the drinks and the waves of cigarillo smoke and the way the girls keep looking over at them, now frankly amused, as if their table might be especially adorable—it turns their speculation into a grim selection of hardware.

"The one with the dark hair," Bates says. "She's the prettiest."

"They *all* have dark hair, at least under the dye jobs," Wallace points out. "And *none* of them are pretty."

But this isn't strictly true. The rules of prettiness are somehow altered for them here, such that the girls at the bar (no matter how "technically flawed," as Wallace puts it) have small but particular charms to offer. There is no embarrassment in plainness in this place. It's too humid and smells too much of rotten fish for the prim demands of beauty. The girls are brown and speak a different language and associate Wallace and Barry and Bates with characters in Hollywood movies. These things alone cast a certain spell. One that relieves the men from the ongoing subconscious North American search for the perfect wife, a woman of the right sort to sit beside them in imagined convertibles driving down imagined Malibu highways. There are definite advantages that these girls and boys can offer, and as they appraise each other across a room too bright and in a country too poor to hide one's most basic proclivities, they silently announce them.

"They all look sweet to me," Barry concludes, an added downhome twang to his *su-weet*.

"Sweet," Bates echoes, but it's lost in the hammering of Portuguese rap thrown down on them from the overhead speakers.

Wallace says nothing. He's listening to the voice singing in his head. *Strange and new. Strange and new.*

This is Wallace's sexual song. It comes on whenever a woman clearly wrong for him—too old, too fat—turns to cast him a second glance after passing him in the street. It isn't the satisfaction of vanity that arouses him, but the potential delight in making a bad choice. *Strange and new.* The melody wouldn't last—what pop song does?—but it delivers a pleasure all the same, cheap and mindless, like speeding in summer with the windows down.

When he first stands up, Barry and Bates assume that Wallace is going to order more drinks. He moves through the vivid light with his white boy hip-hop swagger, but with more lubrication in his joints than usual. A scuffling, buttock-pouting sort of walk, as though the referee had just ejected him from the game and he is making a leisurely show of removing himself from the field. Not the walk of an athlete but of someone who has watched enough pro sports on TV to simulate the attitude.

He bends to speak with the girls at the bar, saying something in what can only be English that nevertheless makes them laugh instantly. Barry and Bates watch him, admiring the ease with which he is putting what they didn't know they wanted within their reach.

As though to acknowledge this, Wallace turns to them, his arms now comfortably encircling two of the girls' waists. Raises his eyebrows.

And in this moment of men being men together, well away from the prissy constraints of law and good breeding, they know that whatever is about to happen cannot now be stopped. That Wallace must bring three girls back with him to their table, randomly assigning one for each Bates and Barry, and saving his surprise choice—the gold tooth—for himself. That they will make their nameless introductions, raised glasses indicating who they are and their capacity to carry out the exchange about to be made. That they will stand and possessively lift their chins to the pirates around them, then allow themselves to be led down the hallway behind the bar.

As they blink their way into the darkness they share the belief that now, finally, they are no longer tourists. Wallace is their new guide. And he has somehow found a way into the heart of what the pamphlets sticking out of their back pockets call "The *True* Brazilian Jungle Experience!"

They are taken farther into the back than they would have thought physically possible. Have they entered the neighboring building some-how? It's too dark to tell where they are or what corners they have turned, their feet too weighed down with booze to judge distances. Later, two of them will recall climbing a set of stairs, and one will deny it. No matter. Let us say there are stairs, and that they have some difficulty climbing them. So much difficulty, in fact, that the girls have to give them their hands to pull them up to the landing where the absence of light is now complete.

The girls open doors. One for each of them. Inside every room there is a single bed with a hollow trough down its center. A cross made of tied-together popsicle sticks pinned to the wall. The only illumination a string of red Christmas lights looped from the ceiling. Bates first, then Barry, and Wallace with the gold tooth at the end.

Now that he's here, at once unbelievably and undeniably *in this place*, Bates finds that he's more relaxed than he would have ever expected. His girl turns her face up to him. She's small and looks like no one he has ever known. The first thing he does is name her. This makes him even more relaxed.

"Lydia," he says.

"Tipfomaid?"

"Sorry?"

"Tip for maid?"

Her hand held out, cupped for offerings. He gets it now: an up-front commission for the management downstairs. After a swift calculation, he determines his standard fifteen percent restaurant gratuity and counts out three American dollars, watches them settle before being crumpled up into her fist. If her face shows any response on the spectrum between gratitude and disapproval, he can't see it. Through the dim light his vision has become selective: a snapshot of her lips without the nose or eyes above them, his fingernails laid out over his knees like bits of quartz. She is so small. Possibly the smallest girl he has ever seen in his life, but he still can't get a good look at all of her at once. There's a single flap of nausea as he wonders if he really wants to.

"You like love?" she asks, apparently satisfied with his tip.

"Love? I like it, I guess. Yeah."

She shakes her head once, sharply, as though from a squirt of lemon on her tongue. "No," she says. "What you *like?*"

He must tell her without speaking, because in a moment it all begins. It occurs to him that this is the last thing he was prepared to consider, let alone do—her skin, another's particular skin, a stranger's strange hands inside his shirt—but he can't stop it. This is the idea he has, anyway. A notion of unstoppability captures his mind in a way that, in turn, becomes unstoppable. On the other hand, he knows he could walk out right now. Pull her hands away, toss some greenbacks on the soiled mattress as the good man who changes his mind in the whorehouse has been seen to do in films. This is always an option, of course. But quite aside from the scientific matter of desire (does he possess it? does he not?), leaving is simply a less appealing idea than staying. There is the outstanding question of conclusions: where will this whole unlikely business lead him?

It goes on as it should. All the maddening, quick-edit peeks and allowances. He feels grateful. For the girl, yes. For his Lydia. For the surprise of his own competence. And for the fact that he seems to actually *like* it. He'd had doubts that he would. The publicity was massive (is there anything more hyped than fucking?) and he is as skeptical of bold promises as the next educated consumer—which explains, in part, his years of conscientiously missed opportunities. But as it turns out he likes it, all right. This at once foolish and straightforward thing he has never done before.

He is grateful for all of this. But more than anything, he gives thanks for the evidence it provides that he might not be gay after all.

The three men come at the same time. They hear each other clearly through the plaster walls that stop two feet short of the ceiling: a feminine moan, weary sigh, a gasp of childish surprise. Their noises mix together into a single echo down the dark hallway. And although each of them is only showing their pleasure, or at least relief, when taken together the sound they create is a collective expression of fear.

Barry can't believe how young his girl is and how young he feels inside her. After all the beer and the returning certainty that he was about to fall off the mattress in a dead faint and the troubling whiffs of his own armpits whenever he moves, he is stunned by the simple space she offers him. Nothing like his wife. (She crosses his mind, but only long enough for him to note how briefly she crosses his mind.) Nothing like sex at all, really. More a prolonged dream of childhood. An endless game of tag, a fit of giggles. Pushed higher and higher on a playground swing.

In the next room, Bates is occupied with the task of acting like a man. Holding his breath, his muscles. Imagining his individual parts clenching and thrusting in an athletic tribute to himself. But still, when the moment arrives, he hopes he won't hurt the girl, so small beneath him.

And what does Wallace feel at the end of the hall?

He feels that it cost too much.

• • •

Afterwards, they talk to the girls. There seems to be no rush to usher them out, so the men prop themselves up on stained pillows and answer the questions the girls put to them. They don't think it strange that they are asked questions in the first place. And not just the expected ones about where they are from and whether they are married and what their names are, but specific inquiries into who they work for and what business they have in Brazil.

The fact is the men don't think any of this is at all strange. They'd done a shameful thing far away from home that nobody would likely ever learn about. There is now a secret between them. They feel more interesting than bad. It seems like a very good time to talk.

Some of what they say are lies, and some of it the truth. Either way, a good deal of it is information that, in the wrong hands, could get them into trouble. This is a dangerous place. They've been warned about thieves who'd slice your throat for ten American dollars, Colombians who specialize in kidnapping tourists for a confused mixture of political and financial ends, smack-addled street gangs who do it for fun. It doesn't stop them from telling the girls about all the things they possess—money, insider trading tips, the most desirable passports in the world. And the girls listen, unsmiling. The men don't think it at all suspicious that their audience seems to care as much as they do. Or that the girls' eyes often close in concentration, as though etching the men's possessions into their memory.

When the men finally find each other in the dark hallway and make their way back out of the bar, a taxi is there waiting for them. They don't think this is strange, either. It's just the kind of good luck they've grown used to over the course of their lives.

Barry thinks of mentioning the black Beetle he notices parked at the opposite end of the street, one with a fellow cramped into it whose face looks a lot like the concierge's. But his stomach is upset by the jarring start of the taxi, and the fact is he doesn't feel much like talking anymore anyway.

Only Bates kisses his girl good-bye.

3

OUR boat, the *Ana Cassia*, is a good deal smaller than the *Presidente Figueiredo*, the one that the Canadian Minister of Foreign Affairs and his gaggle of "officials" are to travel on. There are only five cabins arranged around the length of our forty-five-foot deck, none of them much larger than the toilets at the back of buses. Somehow, though, there is a set of bunks and a shower jammed into every one, where "shower" is a hose that pumps water up from the river, over our heads, and drains through a hole in the floor that also admits such nocturnal ticklers as geckos, harlequin frogs and army ants into our beds. Barry and Lydia and I have cabins to ourselves, Wallace and Bates share one ("Hey, we've been roommates since puberty, or at least *my* puberty—we're still wondering about Bates's—so who cares?") and the entire crew have apparently been left with the remaining one directly above the engines.

There are four of them. The captain, who has a face slapped around by sun and liquor and a life of blunt razors; our bespectacled guide, whose name I don't catch and whose movements are as drugged as a tree sloth's; Americo, the first mate with a grin fixed to his lips as though tattooed there; and young Maria in the galley. Maria might be eighteen, and might be pretty (shyness keeps her face lowered in the sinks or turned toward walls, so it is hard to be certain) and Americo might be twenty-five and handsome, so within fifteen minutes of climbing aboard we, or at least Wallace and Bates, wonder aloud if the two of them are sleeping together.

"He'd like to," Bates ventures, "and he tries sometimes, but she won't let him."

"What makes you say that?" Wallace asks.

"You look at her. You see things."

"I see things too."

55

"And you think she's doing him?"

"Maybe not. But she'd like to be taken away by someone. Working on this boat, tourists coming and going, slipping dollars and pounds and euros into her apron. She wonders where they all go home to."

"You assume she's desperate."

"And you assume she's honorable?"

"Not necessarily. Just scared."

"Well, you'd know about that."

There is a walkway around the main deck so narrow that if someone comes the other way you have to flatten yourself against the wall or stretch dangerously over the rail to let them pass. At the very front is the bridge, just large enough for the captain to lean back with his Keds resting on the wheel. Immediately behind it, the ladder up to the galley. You can tell this is the boat's designated meeting place from the table, the art (a map of the Rio Negro next to a depth chart of the Anavilhanas archipelago, a clustering of several thousand islands dotted through the river like a spilled bag of marbles), and the entertainments (a deck of cards and three bottles of rum each with a murky ounce left at its bottom).

Another ladder leads up through a hatch in the galley ceiling and onto an observation deck, the front quarter of which is covered by a flapping square of canvas. That's where all of us are standing when the boat pulls away. Nobody says anything. Except for me, when Americo comes up to offer us beers to mark the occasion, and I have to translate for the group. They shake their heads without looking at each other, Bates and Wallace and Barry because of their near-death hangovers, and Lydia on account of it's ten-thirty in the morning. So I have one on my own.

The truth is, I'm a little excited. Yes, it's only a sightsee scheduled to return to this very place in five days, and we will never be far from a boatload of Canadian bureaucrats. But it's still the Amazon, isn't it? There are snakes here that can stop your heart with a single bite or swallow children whole. Vicious schools of piranha. And still malaria, yellow fever and other airborne concerns. Not to mention a million ways of getting lost. Anything can still happen in places like this, and we are going directly into it. The moment of adventure demands to be acknowledged. But when I invite Americo to join me he only continues to grin his permanent grin, which I take to mean that, although he'd like to, as first mate he can't possibly start drinking with the dock still plainly within sight.

We stand and watch Manaus recede into a jumble of plaster cubes, the opera house rising up from them like a painted nipple. It feels strange to see it shrink away, and the strangeness fortifies our silence. It is a city, after all. The only one for thousands of miles. We'd heard this over and over on the tour. But it is believable now. For already, only a few hundred feet out into the river, we can see the green beginnings of the jungle rising up at both edges of town. And after that, we can see nothing but more of it.

We tremble north through an afternoon of light so pure it brings a perceptible weight down on the tops of our heads. For the first hour or two we can spot the last traces of the Manaus outskirts—a rusted water tank lifted upon knock-kneed struts, a brick building the guide tells us was once a brewery—and now there are only trees. The river is wide and we travel in the middle of it, so that we are too far away to see anything in particular. Just the trees. A jagged line of green scissored into the sky.

"It's beautiful," Bates says.

"It's boring," Wallace says.

"It's beautifully boring, then," Bates says.

When the sun finally starts to grow and die, Americo brings the cooler of beer up once again. This time each of us takes a can. Conversationally, this helps somewhat.

"So, Mr. Americo. Where the hell are we headed?" Barry asks the big man. Naturally, Americo had been grinning when he arrived. He goes on grinning. I translate the question into Portuguese, then he startles us all by adding a nod to his repertoire of facial expressions. And when he speaks, his voice is surprisingly soft, even womanly.

"Nós viajaremos para o norte à noite e continuaremos de manhã."

"He says we keep going like this through the night and the morning," I tell the others. "This should get us up into the archipelago, where we'll stop around lunchtime. Then we'll do a little piranha fishing"—Americo pulling his grin wider and making a gnashing motion with his jaw—"and navigate through some of the islands. Stop for the night, and the next day go on a jungle hike."

"Lions and tigers and bears, oh my!" Lydia singsongs.

"After that, we'll head over to the *Presidente Figueiredo* to have a traditional Amazonian dinner with the government folks. But we must first catch some piranha, so that Maria can make soup out of the bones."

Barry offers one of his southern laughs at this, and it makes us all feel less far away. Soon Lydia is slipping full cans of beer into our shirt pockets and between our legs.

"Sounds like a plan," Barry announces, and gives Americo two slaps against his shoulder.

Later in the afternoon the captain comes up to greet us. Shakes our hands formally and then, once he's completed the circle, begins to laugh. A hee-haw braying at the enormity of Bates's high-tops, Lydia's bleached skin, Wallace's questions about the possibility of piranha finding their way into the toilet bowls. Despite his wrecked face, everything about the captain seems to encourage a spirit of blameless fun: the Boston Red Sox cap tilted back on his head at a boyish angle, the gray hairs blossoming out from both ears, the long arms freckled and pink as a dog's belly. Soon all of us are laughing for no better reasons than these.

"Hey," Barry eventually stops us. "If he's up here with us, who's *driving* this thing?"

The captain guesses the meaning to this, and in reply throws his arms around to deliver two thumbs up directly under Barry's chin. Laughs again. And again we join him in it.

The *Ana Cassia* is navigating itself. Straight and slow right up the middle—where else could it go, aside from shutting off its engines and sliding back to where it came from? Out here, where the river is as wide as a sea, there are only these two choices.

After the captain returns below, the dusk drapes itself over the river and the smell of Maria frying bananas blooms through the hole in the deck. Americo brings up a bowl of fried pork rinds and unfolds chairs so that we can sit looking out at our own pieces of darkening forest. Each of us seeing it as something else. An aspect of ourselves, multiplied and swollen. It is shame. It is grace. It is terror. Grafting these internal states onto the forest so that we start to envision it as a kind of horizontal totem pole. A neverending line of different versions of our own heads. Some true as mirrors, some leering gargoyles. All of them us.

Although we watch in our own ways, we all listen to Wallace. Bates is the only one who turns away from the jungle to look at him, though. Intent and unblinking, as if he has never heard any of this before.

"The first lie we're told, after the tooth fairy, Rudolph the Reindeer, Jesus-loves-you lies of childhood, is that you can find meaning in history," the voice is saying into the night, now blue as an old bruise. "But there's nothing real in the past. There are only events that have already taken place. Courses taken. Death. The only lesson you can learn from them is that they can't be changed. It is *done*. Meanwhile, the present is busy going about its business and—*whoops!* Look at that. Another moment gone. And you can't change that one now, either. You've already moved to the next second and it's only in *that* second that you have any power at all. All that precedes us is written in the third person. It's about everyone but you. But in the present, there is *only* you. That's where meaning is, in the now, the only place it can be because it's the only place that can be shaped according to an act of will. Now pinch yourself. Make sure this isn't a dream. You feel that? That's the realization that you are the only history that can be changed. Which is the same as saying that you are the only history worth knowing . . ."

Something like this. It's hard to know if his words make sense as you hear them, and they are impossible to remember exactly once they're said.

But he uses some of them, he must, in one order or another. What is certain is that while all of us listen, we are in complete agreement with this voice. When Wallace controls it in this way—or releases it to go where it chooses—it sounds older than mine when I hear myself interrupt him from time to time, or even Barry's when he offers a joke. Soon we stop speaking at all and let him consume all of the rainforest's air for the sake of keeping this voice afloat.

A lot of what he says I take to ultimately be about money, although he never mentions it outright. It's not that I believe him to be greedy. Greed requires covetousness, and Wallace seems to covet nothing but the desire to please. A good boy (from a distance, from a résumé), near the top of his class, the straight-As coming as much for the special thing he is as for the special things he can do. "Promising" and "boy wonder" and "gifted" are the words the magazine profiles use to describe him, and he loves all these words for their buoyancy, the sheer hope they offer. Not just to him but to the world. For surely everyone can take some comfort in knowing there are gifted, promising wonders at work among us. Who knows? The world might just be a better place thanks to the youthful innovation of the rare sort that he alone can deliver—clean, clear-eyed, stacked tight with fresh ideas. To resist a fellow like Wallace only shows something far worse than greed. It shows one's age.

"What could history possibly mean in this place, for example?" the voice is asking us. "What does this river know of its past? It knows only to run fast when it's dry and to swallow the land when it floods. It knows to be alive."

Now I'm watching him, too. Watching Bates watch him. They both seem far away, unreachable. Or this may only be how I feel. Wanting to come closer to them but knowing I cannot.

I am older than they are by a difficult gap: my thirty-eight to their twenty-four. Too young to be their parent. But still an obvious difference between us that is more telling than years. I suppose I'm among the very last of the Boomers, or a proto-Gen Xer, or lost in some such uncomfortably dissociated middle ground. As Wallace puts it, I am "demographically challenged." A product of mild, middle-class, midwestern disappointment, brought up in a small city in southern Ontario that wouldn't be noticed if plopped down in Minnesota or Pennsylvania or Ohio, any grid of streets named after trees you now have to drive out of town to see, somewhere past the stadium-sized hardware stores and automated pork farms. A place of vague promises meant to keep you there, and slammed doors if you decided to leave.

I left. And since then I've seen some things. Thought I had plenty of time. Held unlikely ambitions, and went on to observe the better part of them fail. I no longer expect greatness. Somehow all of this shows even in my brightest smile.

My parents were immigrants from Scotland who came to Canada because it was rumored to be friendlier to Scots than the States, and to the particular town I grew up in because my father found a job advertised in the *Edinburgh Evening News* as a lab technician at our county hospital. He liked to say that he had analyzed the blood of all our neighbors over his thirty-seven years of test tubes and rubber gloves. He was proud of these simple accidents, his wife, his only child, the careful avoidance of both misfortune and windfall. I loved him. I thought him a fool.

Perhaps surprisingly, it was the humility of the immigrant experience that filled me with the notion of entitlement. But despite the encouragement of nominal scholarships, polite letters of recommendation, near-miss appointments to the second-tier faculties of Lethbridge and Saskatoon, the ascendancy never went far up the ladder. And now I am left a blamer, given to conspiracy theories, outraged at those fortuitously born a few years before or after me.

Take our still peach-fuzzed Wallace and Bates, for example. What about *them?* They are nothing *but* expectation, rolled out flat and conclusive as a new highway. Will they *ever* fail? Who cares? They don't. This is the gift of their kind of certainty. Success has attached itself to them without the formality of waiting to see it borne out.

But this is too critical, perhaps. There is a sharpness to these observations that may have more to do with me than them. One must keep in mind the sort of misgivings someone like me has a right to, after all. A less-than-first-rate Ph.D. acquired at my own expense (I am already of an age of bubble-wrap cellulite and barren follicles, yet can barely pay the interest on my student loans). Now and forever cloaked in the woolly layers of impractical education, the fastidious crafting of unread essays, the growing certainty that none of it matters much. And these dubious honors followed by the professional purgatory of overqualification. Watch them go: the passing seasons of part-time tutoring and unpaid electric bills. Despite all the warning signs, still taken aback to find myself staring down an unavoidable Old Maidship, a spinsterhood no less musty for being visited on a supposedly free-willed woman of the twenty-first century. I have never been pretty, but in the years before these last few I had at least been *youngish*, which counts for something among those who are no longer youngish themselves. And now? Now the mirror plays the joke of turning a daughter into her mother, in this case a homely Scot, thin-lipped and a scoop of mashed potato in place of a nose.

But even with all this, there is surely still something of value I have over these two boys. Experience. Or something like that. The ragtag wisdom that comes with chronic underappreciation.

Yes, Wallace is clever (who isn't clever who has idled and bullshit-ted their way through the very best schools?) and he has talent of the most general sort, forever unrealized and all the more beautiful for it. And charm? Lots of it! Or at least what we've come to call charm but is really a good-looking version of self-absorption. All white teeth and cracks made at others' expense.

But what this boy has more than anything else is appetite. It doesn't matter what, or whether its flavors agree with him. Taste doesn't even come into it. Look at him and you're peering down a hole that needs to be filled but never will be.

Maybe this sounds as though I hate him. But approached from a different angle, it may be that I love him instead. Among my handi-caps is the inability to tell the difference.

Americo gives each of us a stick with a rusted hook tied to the end. I translate to the others that, when we get to the designated spot, we will pierce the hooks through cubes of rotten beef that Maria has sluiced into plastic bags and handed, blushing, to Wallace in the back of the canoe. When he takes them he grasps Maria's wrist with his other hand and tugs, ready to catch her if she falls against him. She squeals and jumps back from his grip. Wallace pouts at her and she giggles in reply, then draws her hand shyly across her mouth.

"Hey, Crossman," Wallace calls to me, still glaring playfully at the girl. "Tell Maria I'll catch so much piranha we'll never have to eat that . . . Bates, what do they call that sawdust they eat down here?"

"Manioc. It's a dried root that they combine with farina to—"

"—won't have to eat manioc ever again."

I translate all of this for them. Or at least provide a slightly personalized version, one with a few words added to suggest that Wallace thought Maria would make a perfect wife, with her spoiled meat and pretty face. It makes Maria's blush turn into a shudder of delighted horror and, briefly, removes the grin from poor Americo's lips.

Then the nameless tour guide starts up the canoe's motor and, with a single turn around a finger of land, the *Ana Cassia* is lost behind us. He points out animals and birds and tells us their names, although most often, by the time we turn to look, they have already disappeared. The one thing we all manage to see is what he calls a sunbittern. Watching us pass from a tree so close we could touch it with our fishing poles. A profile of a beak as long as chopsticks atop its withered neck, skeptical and cloudy eyed, like an old woman used to better treatment than what she's been getting of late.

We float through a series of turns around what might be either islands or outgrowths of shore. This close to the water, what we learn is that the Rio Negro is not black after all. It's a shadow. Deep and untouched by the sun except for a skin of purple scales on the surface. But look down from straight above and there is nothing but oily shade, licking and curling upon itself.

When we finally stop it's in an inlet where the branches come down low enough to scratch our cheeks.

"The piranha, they come for blood," the tour guide explains in his slow manner, which, combined with his troubled English, makes him sound a little like a surfer dude. But then he spanks his hand on the water, drops his hook in and, within the space of a single breath, pulls up a flapping fish with can-opener teeth.

"The splashing, it makes them come. The blood makes them bite."

And it's true. Soon all of us are jerking demon dentures into the hull, where they clack uselessly against each other. As it turns out, piranha aren't as frightening as all those matinee horror movies and *National Geographic* pictorials had led us to believe. They are nothing more than dime-store novelty items. Sardines dressed up as Halloween vampires.

Lydia screams each time she catches one, not out of actual fear but because she is an Englishwoman and therefore expected to. She looks to me to join her in this feminine ritual, but I won't let myself. I'm afraid my voice would shatter altogether if I used it now.

"Oh *God!* They're so *slimy!*"

"No worse than the investment bankers you have all those lunches with," Bates says, squinting down the throat of his most recent catch.

"Good point, Bates," Wallace cuts in. "Which is not to mention Barry here. Slimy as they come. Albeit toothless."

"Hardy-har. How many *you* caught, kid?"

"Looks like eight."

"Gotcha. I'm counting"—he pulls another up—"an even dozen."

"Bates, what time you have?"

"Quarter to one."

"Fine. Thousand bucks says that by one o'clock, I'll have more little nippers than old Barry."

"You're on, fancy boy."

"Gentlemen," Lydia says, "I'll have you know that you're recklessly wagering with company money." She shrieks once more at something moving around her toes. But for the moment Barry and Wallace aren't listening. They're staring into the water's shadows, waiting for the tug that tells them something has taken hold of their bait.

Lydia lays down her pole to peer into the surrounding jungle. "It's like spring here," she sighs.

I turn and follow her gaze into a deepening madness of green. *Spring?* It must be an idea made exclusively for the British. Only Lydia can look into the jungle and think of it as a wild companion to April in Kent. Striving palms an analogy for bold tulips, the web of vines seen as untended hedgerows just beyond the vicarage.

"Not in Canada, man," Bates says from behind the Palmcorder's lens as he records Wallace and Barry's competition. "There spring is all brown grass and dog shit."

"Or the South," Barry adds with a grunt, tossing up another piranha. "In Georgia it's *full-time* summer, sweetheart. Sweatin' lemonade three hundred and sixty-five days a year."

Lydia smiles at them, knowing that none of that matters. The rest of the world could keep its perspiring summers and salt-burned winters. England would always own spring.

I expect nothing less of her. She's an English girl, after all, and with an English girl's face to match: button mushroom nose (cap thumbed northward), freckle-seared skin (pale as liquid hand soap), all of it dolled up with make-up that somehow hints at the 1970s (the Twiggy Effect). Sweet, you might say, if she is sitting still. The vulnerable fleshiness, the hint of spongy jowls that suggests sympathetic attention. But *only* when she is still. There is something in her movements, heavier and more decisive than you'd guess possible, that makes her business capacities perfectly clear. Even her breasts are businesslike, thumping up and down inside her T-shirt like a pair of fists bringing a point home on the boardroom table.

Her face is white and her hair is dark in a way that somehow says more about her body than her face or hair. What does she look like beneath those Marks and Spencer pullovers that are too tight in the shoulders? What new version of paleness and black curls awaits the one to tug down those pleated, knee-length walking shorts? She must be British under there, surely. Dimpled and pliant as clotted cream, but with a rude whisker or mole thrown in. She has her appeal (all women must, as any attempt to count the categories of porn fetishes on the Internet proves). You just wouldn't want her in too much light, that's all.

Lydia finally turns away from the shore and, despite the overhanging branches, a shaft of light lands square across her face. She almost reels from the violence of the heat, and for the first time today I think of where we are. Of the hundred corners we rounded in the half hour after leaving the *Ana Cassia*, of the one quivering twenty-horsepower outboard engine and its single tank of gas no larger than Lydia's purse. The piranha could be silently laughing at our feet.

"Well, who's winning, Bates?" Lydia manages as she slides back into the shade.

"Looks dead even to me."

"How much time?" Wallace asks. His eyes unmoving from the water. You can see the man he will become in the corrugated edges of his eyes. It's the light here on the river: fierce and insistent and shadowless. It has a way of turning every face into an unfavorable prediction of how it will turn out.

"About a minute."

"I'm outpacing you, Barry. I've counted four to your two in the last minute alone."

"You know, there's more to life than winning stupid games, kid," Barry says and tries at a laugh. He's the only one of us exposed directly to the sun, and half of him has already liquefied through his shirt.

"Said like a born loser," Wallace says. "But you're right. There's more than winning. There's knowing you always can."

In the same moment, both of them bring another in, as though they are merely directing the fishes' own desire to join them in the canoe.

"What's the time, Bates?"

"Ten seconds," Bates says, one eye reading his watch and the other stuck to his Palmcorder. "You've got Barry by one."

"Hold it! Fucking *hold* it!"

Barry is standing now, his head wavering in front of the sun. Something stronger than any of the other fish pulls at his rod.

"—five, four, three—"

"Jesus Ch*rist!*"

The piranha on the end of Barry's line leaps out of the water and lands on a circle of sweat on his shirt as though it were a dart finding a bull's-eye.

"I got it! It's a tie!" Barry shouts, looking at all of us at once with goggled eyes.

"Don't look down," Wallace says.

The fish still clings to Barry's chest, its jaw snapping at the air, the fabric of his shirt. Then Barry does as he was told not to. He looks down. An odd sound that might be a whimper escapes his lips.

"Just stay still," Wallace tells him, working his way over our knees. "I'll get it."

"I'm bleeding," Barry says. "It's *eating* me, for Chrissakes."

A circle of red spreads out from over the place his heart would be. But it's not the fish's doing. It's the rusted hook, curled through the piranha's jaw, a layer of cotton and half an inch into Barry's skin.

At the sight of it Lydia falls limp against the side of the canoe as though struck from behind.

"No, no, *no*," Barry says as each new layer of bad news reaches him. "Get it *off* me, Wallace!"

"Don't worry. I'm coming. Keep your eyes up."

And then Wallace is there, grabbing the fish and ripping it off the hook and tossing it back into the river in one motion. He does it quickly, but not so quickly that Barry doesn't scream from the new pain it causes.

"Get it *out!*"

"I'm here, man. Stand still. Count to three."

We watch Barry's lips move like a brave little boy's.

One, two—

Wallace tries to twist the hook out at first, but this only brings another whimper out of Barry. Widens the circle soaked through his shirt, already drying into a glistening wax.

"*Count*, Barry," Wallace tells him. And the big man tries again.

One, two, three—

With a single pull the hook cuts its way free, and Wallace tosses it into the ripples.

But on the count of four, something else joins the hook and fish. A spout of blood that spits out from inside Barry and through the hole in his shirt, a purple arc thrown into the air. Smacks against the water's surface hard enough to send drops of it back our way.

All of us wait for the next spurt, for surely this much blood can only be followed by more. But there is only the one. The stain on his shirt not much bigger now than it was when the hook first caught it, Barry's hand sufficient to completely cover the wound.

"You're going to be fine, man," Wallace says in the voice that is older than he deserves. "But I'm afraid you'll have to concede defeat. You took in that last fish a full second past the buzzer. And Bates got it all on tape to prove it. Didn't you, Bates?"

. . .

The next morning our nameless tour guide repeatedly tells us to put on insect repellent for our jungle walk, but when I ask him if it will make any difference he only shrugs. The river so broad here that either shore appears as nothing more than the edge of a freshly cut lawn. Rolling over the chop in a motorized canoe, the wake bubbling up behind us like stirred Pepsi.

"Are there snakes?" Lydia shouts over the engine, her scarf parachuting out above her head.

"Yes," the guide answers with a shake of his head, as though awakened from a dream. "I should speak about these things."

'These things' turn out to be the hundreds of creatures that can do you unique harm in the forest. Among snakes, there are several that can knock you out for a week or two with fever or a violent seizure that ends in paralysis, one that turns your limbs to wood. But there are also those, like the *surucu*, that freeze the diaphragm muscle under your lungs within seconds of delivering their venom, so that you are otherwise perfectly conscious except that you have lost the ability to breathe and are left to observe what it is to slowly drown in your own saliva.

"I have seen this," the tour guide says in a tone that clearly suggests he wishes he hadn't.

"What else have you seen?" Wallace asks him.

"Not all things. Some I have only heard of."

He tells us of spiders that scuttle up nostrils to weave egg sacs deep in the sinuses. Jaguars that come in the night to grip men by the throat and pull them off into the bush from where, only seconds before, they had been sleeping next to a fire on an open beach. Then the many imaginative bugs, like the beetle whose specialty is burrowing into the back of your eyeball via the tear ducts, where it can take its time chewing through the optic nerve (a process that offers unmatched discomforts, we're told). And most exotically cruel of them all, the *candiru açu*, a microscopic catfish that, lured by any warm stream of urine, travels up the urethra and releases a series of hooks out from along its sides that fix it there for good.

"How do they get rid of it?" Bates asks.

The tour guide offers nothing but a blank look in response.

We are quiet for a while after that. Breakfast leaps in our stomachs. Neither shore is yet the closer one. The tour guide glances up at the sun, down at the water, at each of our faces, without a hint of interest in any of them. He might like us. He might wish us dead. Then, slowly, he starts to talk about parasites.

"They come inside you," he says clearly over the slap of water and the engine noise. "Where they will live. And eat. Eat you."

"But we drink the bottled water," Barry reminds him. "We can't get them."

The tour guide blinks. "They come inside you," he says again.

It's an imprecise science, apparently. Some eat you hollow, so that you are constantly ravenous, and are left bony and dried-out as a famine victim. Others coil up to grow unnoticeably over time until they push out a round, pregnant belly in even the fittest men. Nothing, the tour guide tells us, not even "your American medicines," can be assured of getting any of them out. Although the people who live in the forest have some methods of their own that have proven to be quite effective.

With this the tour guide pauses and looks to each of the distant shores, as though searching for something he might recognize along the unchanging line.

"What do they do?" Wallace finally asks.

The tour guide turns to him, cocks his head. "Do?"

"The jungle folks. To get out the parasites."

Now there's something in his face. A raised eyebrow, perhaps, a subtle show of teeth. Or maybe these are only the signs of effort that speech requires of him.

"First, you cannot eat. For long time. First, you starve," he says, his eyes set upon Wallace's, who meets this stare with one of his own. "No water, no food. Some die from this. And if you live, the snake inside—"

"The parasite—"

"—the snake begins to dance. Hungry. You are hungry, yes. But it is more than this. Days go on. The pain is lovely."

"Exquisite," I say. "I think the descriptive phrase is 'The pain is *exquisite.*'"

The tour guide doesn't acknowledge me, keeps his eyes in line with

Wallace's several rows ahead in the canoe. Holds them there even as the boat strikes through a new set of waves.

"It is eating *you* now," he goes on. "It cannot wait for something else. And so the snake that went inside, now it wants out."

"So you offer it an alternative," Wallace says. The tour guide nods, and may even attempt to shape his lips into a smile.

"Milk. Of pig, of goat, of woman," the tour guide says, the smile, or whatever it is, still hanging on his lips. "Or blood. Meat. Not cooked. These are the things the snake likes best. And so the man with the snake inside of him is held down, and his mouth is opened wide as a door, and his jaw is tied down to stay. And the milk or the blood or the meat is brought close to his tongue. Not to feed the man, but to be very close. The people around him—they wait. In time, the snake comes out. Often, it is not small."

Everyone turns away to fix their eyes to the horizon except for Wallace, who seems to have accepted the tour guide's strange smile as an invitation to return one of his own.

Within seconds the sun lifts itself higher above us and the river sends back a million blinding flashes. Even with sunglasses on I have to close my eyes against it. And keep them closed longer than I would guess, because when I open them again the canoe is no more than a few hundred yards from shore.

"Ooga-booga, everybody!" Wallace calls out. "Hear those drums? The natives are definitely restless!"

Something in the tour guide's tales of poison, parasites and violation has given Wallace a new energy. He could be spirited when required to be, of course. But there is no strain in his enthusiasms for this place as there had been in Manaus and São Paulo. He is looking at the real jungle for the first time. The thing we've all been hearing about since we arrived in Brazil, although each of us had brought our own ideas of it with us from illustrated travel guides, from adventure books and childhood TV series, from dreams. Now it is startlingly particular: those leaves, this black sand beach, that dead branch pointing at us like an accusatory finger. And Wallace pointing back at it, already standing at the front of the canoe. All of it exciting him in a way I'd never seen in him before. Bates, too. Except it isn't the wall of crowded plantlife that he is taking notice of. It isn't the cackling, chattering animals that can see us but remain invisible themselves. It is the sight of Wallace seeing and hearing these things that excites him.

Bates pulls his Palmcorder out of the bottomless pocket of his over-sized Stussy shorts to record Wallace being the first out of the canoe. His foot landing on sand that farts under the foreign weight.

"I claim this continent for Hypothesys!" he declares.

"Very good, Wallace," Barry says, the second one out, extending his hand to Lydia, but not to me. "But there's not much of a market for us here. Unless you plan on training the monkeys basic keyboard skills."

"There's more here than monkeys," Wallace says, peering into the trees as though he's already spotted something there.

For the first hour or two, it reminds all of us but Lydia of summer camp.

"Remember the hikes they used to make us go on at Kilcoo?" Bates asks Wallace, slapping at the leaves directly behind the tour guide, who slashes a narrow hole for us to pass through with a machete.

"Can't say I do, Bates. Nothing aside from the broken promises that they'd be *fun*. But I do remember the blue flame contests we'd have in the bunkhouses at night."

"Blue flames?" Lydia inquires.

"A science experiment involving a butane lighter, bare asses and canned beans for dinner."

"I see."

"Down where I grew up, along the big Oconee in Georgia, we'd have to go through woods a lot like these to get to the best fishing spots," Barry says, shaking his head. "It's a wonder we didn't get lost in there more than we did."

"Soo-*wee!*" Wallace howls. "A plump young Barry lost in the Georgia woods! Squeal like a pig!"

Our laughter is shallow. We're breathing too hard for anything else. It's a lot just to keep our eyes down and move. The forest stroking over us, leaving behind powdery seeds or streaks of jam or dollops of glassy

71

ointment. Soon we are camouflaged by the jungle's ooze. There is little point in trying to push it aside. It finds its way to us anyway, and we soon give up the polite habit of holding branches open for whoever walks behind us. There are too many of them to make a difference by snatching on to only one, and eventually even they must be released, whipping back into the next upturned face.

We seem to be weaving slowly up a slope of dense stuff (up close it is impossible to discern trees from ferns or whatever other things grow here), or it may be that the high steps required to move over the roots and grasping vines at our feet only make it feel like we're trudging uphill. Either way, it serves to make Wallace more cheerful. Telling us stories of the Kilcoo Polar Bear Club (being thrown into the frigid water every dawn), failed panty raids on the Catholic girls' camp at the other end of the lake (mustachioed Sister Julia, the nun who *never* slept), all the while petals of sweat blooming across the back of his T-shirt ahead of us.

Eventually, even Wallace loses the breath required for speech. When he stops, we notice for the first time since entering it that the forest is quiet.

"Where'd the birds and monkeys go?" Bates asks the guide.

"They are here. They are only watching us."

"They're afraid?"

"They do not fear us. They have never seen us before. Why have fear? They are only watching."

The tour guide stops us in a tight circle that is as close to a clearing as we have yet come across. Looks up into the branches as though to give whatever watches us from there a view of his face.

"Everything comes from the jungle," he says. "Before, most of the earth was like this. Now there is only this small part left. And these trees—they will never grow again. The soil is made of sand. It will wash away. All of it will be gone by the end of your children's life."

He says this without any change in his voice, although he delivers the last line specifically to Lydia, which causes her to reflexively rub a circle under her stomach.

The tour guide takes his machete and hacks a piece out of the tree nearest to him. Instantly, a white glue falls over the bark.

"This is *seringueira*. What they make rubber out of. And chewing gum. And this"—he hacks at a similar-looking trunk—"is where your digestion medicines, the Pepto-Bismol and the Milk of Magnesia, come from. All those things, these trees—it's what brought your grandfathers to Manaus."

He makes us press our fingers against the wood and taste the sap. Chops at other trees and vines within his reach, and we in turn drink fresh water from them, press healing balms against the cuts on our ankles, suck on quinine that keeps away fever and chew on fibers that the Indians use to cure impotence.

"Are there Indians here?" I ask. "Nearby, I mean?"

"Once, yes. Once there were many. Many languages, too—Arawak, Je, Carib, Pano, Tupi, Xiriana. You'd have much trouble translating them, I believe."

"Where are they now?"

"Now? Now most of them work for the lumber companies or in the mines, and live in camps next to the big rivers. Others live in the government villages, where they do nothing. And far from here, there are the last of the Indians who move from place to place. Hunters. Yanomami. The ones who have never seen you before. Like the birds in these trees."

"Have you seen them?"

The tour guide cocks his head and gives me a disapproving look, as though I am speaking of some foolish, not-quite-human creatures, of leprechauns or Bigfoot.

"Nobody does. They run from us, because they are dying."

"From disease?"

"From us. We are killing them by taking the jungle from them. By giving them things they don't need. By taking their blood to study and making them sick. Doctors and science men and andro . . ."

"Anthropologists."

"All these people. They have come and brought vaccines and cameras and helicopters. And it has killed them, in their ways. But you know this. You have already killed the Indians in your home the same way."

He says this without anything that can be interpreted as accusation.

It's the same tone he used to explain how a remedy for snakebite can be sucked out of a leaf.

"So now they're all gone," Bates says, looking around for some evidence of them having been here.

"Now they hide. Or they have given up. Moved down to the government villages, where they watch television and learn Portuguese in order to understand television, and write letters to the state representative in Manaus asking for more televisions. They die there, too. They forget themselves."

There is no air in these trees. It doesn't reach down this far. But Wallace hasn't noticed this yet. For in a moment it's his voice again, and his desirous eyes, holding the tour guide entirely within them.

"So they *could* be here, couldn't they?" he asks. "If nobody knows where they are, they might as well be here, right?"

"The Amazon has more than a thousand tributaries. Each of those has a thousand more of its own. We don't know what lies at the end of all of them."

"But you're our guide. You're supposed to know."

"I guide *you*. I don't look for *them*."

"You mean the Yanomami?"

"Or other things."

"Well, aren't you being tantalizingly vague."

"I'm sorry?"

"What *other things?*"

"There are stories."

"We're listening."

The tour guide keeps his eyes on Wallace alone. It's very hot now. A heat that comes from within as much as from the unmoving air.

"Places that nobody knows about," the tour guide says. "They have different names, and people have thought they exist in different places. The lost city of El Dorado. It is made entirely of gold, maybe five or six hundred miles inland from here. Maybe. Or the Mines of Muribeca. Many secret people live there. Not the *Yanomami*. Others without a name. They have built pyramids that have been seen from the sky." He points directly above his head.

74

"By satellite, you mean."

"The cameras have looked down, and they have seen things. Made by man. But they cannot be reached."

"You've tried?"

"Others have. For hundreds of years, one and then another. Even now, scientists from America, Germany. The great British Colonel Fawcett. You have heard of him, of course? All of them turned around. Or were lost. Many men have died in these expeditions."

"How do you know for sure?" Wallace persists.

"For sure?"

"That they died. Were there bodies found?"

"There are no bones in the jungle. The ground is too wet. Too hot. Bones don't stay."

"There are no fossils."

"That is right. No fos-sils. You cannot know if anyone was here, ever."

"So they could have found what they were looking for and just not come back to tell anyone else. We wouldn't know one way or another, because their bones would be gone by now anyway, right?"

"That is right," he admits, with a doubtful smirk. "They would all be gone." The tour guide then pulls his eyes away from Wallace's to glance at his watch. "These stories are not part of the jungle walk," he says, looking at all of us now. "They have made us late."

We turn about in a close circle, flattening the grass like a dog settling down for a nap. But instead, once we are in something like a line again, we strike out into the trees. Whatever path we made coming to this place is now apparently gone. And although we seemed to have come uphill to get here, we must go farther uphill to return to the river. The going is no easier, at any rate. All of us fall silent except for Wallace, who talks on ahead of us about Indians and secret cities made of gold.

Have I mentioned the heat? Not that it exists, that it is hot, *very* hot, for what else would you expect of a jungle in this sorry year of the ozone layer's history? It's the *character* of the heat that I mean. The way it changes. Minute to minute, even within the seconds, as though manipulated by a tireless artist constantly adding colors to create new shades on his palette. Sometimes the heat is wet. It *makes* one wet, but not from perspiration. Here it is permanent, a sticky second skin, as though from a glaze of tears. Sometimes the heat decides to be pitiless, inarguable as death. In other moments it has a hallucinatory invitation to it, bidding you to dream. Sometimes it is a gun at your temple, firing, firing. And once in a while even the heat is too tired, and is merely hot.

After a half hour or so I lag behind to relieve myself of Maria's toxic breakfast coffee. I'm grateful for Wallace's voice and the slap of branches against the backs of the others moving forward to cover the sound of my zip, squat and splash. It doesn't take long anyway.

But by the time I'm finished, they're already gone. No more than five seconds after I stopped to lean against the nearest tree and all of their noises have been sucked away. The green has swallowed them whole.

"Hey! Wallace! Bates! I'm back *here!*"

Nothing.

I'm not even certain which way they went. Or if I've just made a sound myself. Somehow the forest has instantly repaired itself of whatever trail they left behind.

There?

Or there?

What is *there?*

Every detail around me—the leaves, the sculpted ladders of fungi clinging to the trunks, the strings of ants marching over my boots—all of it has multiplied, so that what seemed particular a moment before (*those* ants, *this* jagged leaf) is now impossible to discern from whatever is next to it.

It is in this understanding of being lost, the plain fact that I will die here if nobody comes back to get me, that the jungle acquires an identity. And it is a villain. Or worse. A body of lush malevolence, motiveless, hateful for no other reason than it always has been. It took me from the others and now it gathers round to watch me become part of itself.

I hold on to whatever breath is already there. Push it out in a scream. No names this time. Just the shattering sound of a child's terror after

76

seeing the worst thing a child could see and, at the sight of it, the last of childhood falls away. A voice that is new to me, tumbling and fading into the identical trees.

And then the tour guide is here with me. Arrived from exactly the opposite direction I would have guessed he'd gone. His hand on my forearm, breath smelling like old cheese. A beautiful, human stink. I could kiss him. I almost ask him what his name is.

"Next time you go pissing in the jungle, bring a friend," he says.

The Canadian Minister of Foreign Affairs is already drunk by the time we climb aboard the *Presidente Figueiredo* for dinner. After twenty minutes of amusing us with his impersonation of a chattering spider monkey, his aides take him belowdecks to bed. That leaves us alone with a half dozen of his policy advisors, who manage to disappear into the few corners the boat offers before the main course is served. The *Presidente Figueiredo* has better food than the stuff Maria makes, though, and there is wine instead of Americo's lukewarm rum behind the bar. For the first time since our night out in Manaus, we have a good excuse to get drunk.

Wallace and Bates take up position at the back of the observation deck, their faces lit by the lamp beneath the Brazilian flag. After a while, Wallace waves me over.

"We need your help, Crossman. Your *insight*. It's a Hypothesys-type situation. And seeing as we didn't bring our laptops with us, we thought we'd let you decide the matter the old-fashioned way."

"Happy to be of service."

"When is a lie not a lie?"

"That sounds more like a riddle."

"The best questions usually do."

"I don't know. I suppose when it doesn't do anyone any harm. That makes it a white lie, doesn't it? Although if it's untrue, it's still techni-cally a lie."

"So the moral implications depend on the damage done. I see. But exactly how *much* damage is permissible for the lie to remain white? I think we still need more specific facts to determine where to draw that line, don't we, Bates?"

"Like what?" Bates asks.

"Like that shit you told those girls at the bar in Manaus, for instance."

Bates blanches. Blinks his surprise at the river that is somewhere out there below him.

"Go on," Wallace urges him, but in a near whisper. "What did you tell our dates?"

"I didn't tell *them* anything. There was only one. One *her*."

"Tell Crossman what you told *her*, then."

"What does it matter? Why are you bringing this up?"

"Because it's *funny*, Bates." Wallace grins, crossing his arms. "And Crossman would be interested, as it sounds like you did a fair job of translating, for an amateur. You managed to get across the fact that Hypothesys was not a website at all but rather a top-secret government project, possibly concerning a new generation of sophisticated weaponry. The perfect bomb. Yes! Isn't that what you told her? You had come up with the plans for the *perfect bomb?* I mean, none of that could have been easy, unless you've been taking Portuguese lessons on the sly."

"You *said* that, Bates?"

He turns to face both of us. There is nothing there to indicate shame. There is only the vulnerability that comes with the wish to be understood.

"I was bored with explaining what Hypothesys really is," he pleads, his palms open on his knees. "And it was just *talk*. You know, here we all are in this weird bar in the Brazilian jungle, acting like spies, and then this girl—it was a movie, and I was saying movie things. And you know something? I swear she understood me. Like she *expected* to hear the stuff I was telling her."

"You see, Crossman? Bates here is not as squeaky clean as he looks. He *lies* to *girls*. He's invented the *perfect bomb*. Behold: the new Oppenheimer! This boy has an imagination."

"What made it perfect?" I ask.

Bates succumbs to a trembling at one corner of his lips that could as easily be a reflex of pride as restrained tears.

"It does everything that A-bombs do, but without the nasty fallout," he begins modestly. "And it has far greater target specificity. So it could neatly flatten the downtown core of a major city and everyone in it, say, but do no harm to the suburbs around it. A useful tool in those tight trouble spots—think the Balkans, think Israel—where the town on the hillside is full of good guys but the town in the valley three miles away is full of bad guys, depending on your perspective. One drop and you've made your point either way. No tedious months of artillery tit-for-tat. Plus no radioactive clouds roaming the earth to worry the folks back home. It would be the first environmentally friendly weapon of mass destruction ever devised."

By the end of this, Bates has worked up some enthusiasm. His breath popping at the back of his throat. Opens and closes his eyes in Morse code. This may have been the longest continuous speech I have heard him make.

"So what powers the thing if it isn't nuclear?"

"That's the secret."

"The secret that doesn't exist."

"The secret that doesn't exist."

"And you told all this to your girl?"

"It didn't hurt anyone."

"Thus it's only a white lie, by Crossman's definition," Wallace says. "And nobody would ever think Bates capable of hurting a fly. He's *sensitive*. Are you sensitive too, Crossman?"

"When it matters." It's the look on Bates's face that makes me add, "More than you."

"I doubt that. You've read your Dickens. You've watched your *Oprah*. Who's more sensitive than an orphan?"

"You're an orphan?"

"De facto. A castoff of the New World Order. My parents were diplomats. I got sick on the water in the Cameroon when I was a kid, so they thought it best if I grew up a million miles away in a good old Canadian boarding school. Haven't I told you this? Bates was there, too. Except he was a *real* orphan. His parents weren't just selfish and neglectful, they were actually dead. So we did what we could. We brought each other up. Didn't we, Bates?"

"Best friends," Bates nods without meeting his eyes.

"And what's a best friend when you're alone? Well, I'll tell you. He's all you've got."

With this, Wallace pulls Bates against him and holds him in a long hug. Strokes his hand down Bates's back as though to warm him. It's partly another tease. But it lasts too long and appears too immediately comfortable to be wholly that.

When they part they both look up at me with canine grins.

"How's that for sensitive, Crossman?" Wallace says.

"You got me beat."

"Damn right I do. I'm all heart. Nothing but a walking, beating, bleeding heart."

This strikes us as a good time to finish our drinks, which we do.

"I'm curious," I start after we've clinked our empty bottles together on the deck. "What did you talk about with *your* date, Wallace?"

"Nothing at all, really. At least compared to Bates's disclosures. I just told her that I was an American millionaire. Which wasn't much of a lie, come to think of it. Of course, she didn't have a clue what I was talking about. Although the word *American* may have had some impact. It's the universal language, after all."

"American?"

"Money." He smiles at me with what appears to be real tenderness. "Something more to drink, my friends?"

A buffet table has been set up with platters of barbecued pork and magnums of wine, right next to the satellite dish that feeds the television sitting on a table of its own with words from home. Within only a few minutes I pick out "down twenty percent in the first quarter alone," "Tiger Woods missed his birdie putt on the 18th," at least two "dot-coms" and one "*You* are the weakest link. Good-bye!" The channels flipping on their own.

Wallace returns with a bottle of wine slung under one arm and a stack of plastic cups under the other. We stand with our elbows on the rail as though leaning against a proper bar, except one that smells of rain and dead fish. Stare into the jungle like there is something to see, but there is only something to hear. The coughing and burping and liquid complaint of whatever lives within it.

"It's laughing at us," Wallace says after a while.

"Are we that funny?"

"Stinking of insect repellent, sunburnt, blind as bats. I'd say we're worth a chuckle or two."

"It's not laughing, it's warning," Bates says. "Walk a hundred feet straight in there and you couldn't find your way back."

"As I found out myself this afternoon."

"Poor Crossman. Our Little Red Riding Hood who strayed from the path."

Now it is my turn to have my back stroked by Wallace's hand.

"That reminds me of a story," he continues. "Bates? Does any of this ring a bell?"

Bates holds his eyes down to the river but says nothing.

"What story?" I ask.

"Oh, it's nothing. Bates isn't in the mood. And I can never remember the punchline, anyway."

No one says anything for a time. I want to push them further, but Wallace anticipates my next question and speaks first.

"For a so-called party in the middle of the Amazon, this is unbelievably boring."

He grabs a can of Coke off the buffet table but doesn't open it. Without a word, Bates does the same, then me. The weight of grenades in our palms.

"What do we aim at?" Bates asks.

"The darkest part. That place between the trees where you can't see anything."

And to show exactly where he means, Wallace brings his arm back and his knee up to his chin, major league pitcher style, and launches the can into the jungle. We wait for the explosion, but it doesn't come. A flash of red and white caught in the light of the deck lantern and high quarter moon. Then nothing. No snap of leaves, no blast of fizz. Just the forest's uninterrupted hilarity.

Bates's throw next, tumbling high. Then mine, a spiraling bullet. Each of them disappearing into the same hole.

"They're catching them before they hit the ground!" Wallace says, and we all laugh in agreement, although it isn't clear what "they" he has in mind.

Wallace and Bates have a talent for removing themselves from others' company without being noticed. It's the most amazing thing. One minute they are tall and gleaming and saying things at a volume that is somewhat louder than the conversational average, and the next they have collapsed the space they formerly held and retreated to share secrets between themselves.

As they do soon after we run out of cans to throw into the rainforest. Our laughter has yet to exhaust itself, but when I turn they are gone. And in their place is Barry, swerving my way and thumping his heels upon the deck as though the *Presidente Figueiredo* is battling through a rough sea.

"They've disappeared on you, haven't they?" he says. He must have found a private stock: his breath is curdled with the horsepissy taint of rye whisky.

"How'd you know?"

"You've got that just-abandoned-by-the-boys look about you. It's unmistakable. But not to worry. They do it to me all the time. To all of us. You'd never guess by looking at them—and listening to Wallace and his yakking—but they're fucking Siamese twins, those two. Born sewn together."

"They're best friends."

"*I've* never had a friend like that. Have you?"

"Sometimes I wonder if I've ever had a friend at all."

"Well, that's rather more than I asked for, Crossman."

"I'm just saying. Whatever it is between them, I don't get it. I missed out."

"Compared to them, we've all missed out."

For the first time since I've met him, Barry looks his age. Whatever his age is. Maybe it's the piranha-hook incident that has gouged the lines around his eyes a year or two deeper. Or maybe it's the anger that he seems to have found in himself, in a bottle of rye.

"What am I doing down here, Crossman?" he asks abruptly, with more than a note of recrimination.

"Here? Right now you're a tourist. But mostly, you're here to sell things, Barry."

"No. They're here to sell. I'm *just* a tourist. A hanger-on. Which wouldn't be too bad, you know—I'm in marketing, I'm *paid* to hang on—except that it doesn't feel real to me. I mean, I understand what Hypothesys does, and I think it's an important product, or at least something that people will want to buy. But just being around it, being around *him*, gives me this unreal feeling. And look at us now! We're in the middle of a comic book adventure down here. The sort of stuff I used to read by flashlight under the sheets because my father would kick my ass if he ever caught me. It's like I've been thrown into my past, or somebody else's future, or some fucked-up business."

He shakes his head like a wet sheepdog. Pushes a hand through his hair. A second later, new lines of perspiration cut down his forehead.

"Are you all right, Barry? I mean, do you think you might—there's fever—"

"I'm fine. I'm just drinking."

Barry puts an arm over my shoulders as I have seen him do several times before with others. Except this time it feels like he actually needs me to keep him from falling over.

"None of it can be helped, Crossman," he croaks into the side of my neck. "The thinning hair, the mudslide of fat, mixing up the names of goddamned rock bands—sorry, it's *dj's* now—mixing them up with movie titles or the newest drugs that make them all dance for sixty-three hours straight . . . And yet *we* are blamed! For not knowing. For failing to keep up. But you want to know something? It's just time that we're blamed for."

"Nobody's blaming you."

"You might be right. Maybe it's me blaming them."

"That sounds closer to it."

"Fine. But don't tell me you don't do it too. You're not getting any younger yourself. And you resent them a little for it. Don't you? For the distance they've put between what we were and where we're all headed now, with them leading us by the noses. Admit it."

"I haven't given it much thought."

Barry scoffs.

"You're a good listener, Crossman," he tells me with a close-up of his businessman's teeth. "But you're a terrible liar."

At the end of the night it's Lydia who tells me things. She may not mean to at first, but she does. I've become used to it in my line of work. People tend to think translators make good confidants. There must be some line of reasoning that leads them to this, something to do with words and my being trained to understand them. It's thought that if I have a facility for comprehending the things people say, I will comprehend *them* in the process. It doesn't work that way, of course. But I never correct people once they get rolling. As Lydia is now.

And what does she have to report between the beginning and end of her one and only glass of British Columbia pinot noir? That for her, the narrative of life after thirty has been little more than a conquering of bad habits. Or an ongoing effort to conquer them. For years it had been smoking (learned in girls' school stairwells and perfected in London wine bars while negotiating the terms of selling off pieces of England to the rest of Europe). Then it was food, her butter addiction first, then the unspeakable chocolate sins, followed by shopaholism (bloody *shoes!*), and, most recently, falling in love with men she knew full well would never love her in return. She knows it's all nonsense, needless to say. *Utter rot.* But this doesn't stop her from hoping that if she did away with just one more self-destructive tendency, or shed one last pint of toxins—well, she wouldn't have to think about such crap so much and could get on with the real business of her life.

And what is that?

It's delivering the baby inside of her into the world.

"No, there is no man," she says in answer to the question I don't actually ask. "Well, there *was* a man. But not one that will stay. I'm thankful for what he has given me, nevertheless. I need to have a child. To save a life."

"Your life?"

"Maybe mine. Although I have someone else in mind." She pauses, as though tallying a sum in her head. "Do you have any children, Elizabeth?"

The sound of my first name silences me for a moment. But Lydia's smile is conspiratorial, indulgent.

"I haven't even thought about them much, to be honest."

"It was the same with me. Women like us, out and about in the world—we need our *space*, don't we? But then something happened. Something awful happened. And suddenly I saw the space I was living in as being nothing at all."

Lydia turns to look at me so directly it takes some discipline to meet her eyes. Whatever is there makes it clear that she is not talking about any mere pre-midlife stock taking, menopausal inklings or the tolling of some biological clock. There is not a hint of tears, but there it is anyway. Terrible facts being recollected, and she looks at me so that I can see them too. Yet it only takes a single sniff to put all of it back wherever it is usually kept, and she lifts her face up to the night sky.

"The stars are different here, Elizabeth. Have you noticed?"

"Closer looking, you mean?"

"No, they're just as far. But you get a different view of them. There's no Big Dipper, for example. Instead there's that absurdly geometrical square smack in the middle of things. What do they call it? The Southern Cross. Imagine. People live their whole lives down here and never see the same sky that we do."

An orange comet, vivid as an expensive special effect, spits across the sky directly in front of us.

"Make a wish," I say.

"You too."

We close our eyes.

"What did you wish for?" she asks me when we open them again.

"It's a secret."

"You're just a magnet for secrets, aren't you?"

"What about you? What did you wish for, then?"

I expect her to mention the baby inside her, her hopes for it to be born and grow up without accident and to read at the same Cambridge or Oxford college that she read at. But she doesn't. What she says surprises me, her words sure and swift.

"I wished for *them*, of course," she says, and nods toward Wallace and Bates, standing at the rail and whistling signals out into the jungle. "Those two will eat up all of our wishes before they're done with us."

We laugh. Saying and hearing more than we perhaps should beneath an unfamiliar sky. Of course we laugh. But perhaps it is because we have frightened ourselves a little, too.

And something else from that night. Back on board the *Ana Cassia*, after each of us has stumbled around the main deck's narrow walkway in search of our cabins. All of us except Lydia too drunk for goodnights.

Only a few minutes into my first attempt at sleep I realize I need some water and that I'll have to go up to the galley where the cooler is kept. I open my cabin door and there they are. Maria and Wallace. Her eyelids closed and darkly shining. His lips at her neck, devouring her.

It would be nothing more than this—an unremarkable scene of advantage being taken—if I were alone in watching it. But as I'm about to draw my head back inside the cabin, I notice another set of eyes peering around the far corner at the front of the boat. So yellow and unblinking I at first mistake them for a pair of glowing insects. But they're too still for that. Too focused.

They are Americo's eyes, frozen by injury. This is what I think at first. That the absence of white where his grin should be could be explained by the thing he is forcing himself to witness. He loves Maria. Now this American boy (who is in fact a boy, but not in fact an American) is kissing the girl he hopes—perhaps foolishly, hopelessly—to marry.

He takes a half step forward to get a better view and it allows me to see him, faintly incandescent from sunburn, a dying ember. It's Bates.

Watching, without any trace of expression, his best friend and a Brazilian cook embrace each other. Or perhaps an expression growing just under the skin that is being held there by will, by practice. An emotion so powerful that its suppression clamps all of him shut. It could be anything. Rage, despair, longing. Anything at all.

We are somewhere on two thousand miles of river on the less explored half of the planet. It's the middle of the night. It's impossible to say.

It all starts with that dream where there's someone in the house. Someone who shouldn't be.

You went to sleep alone in one of the upstairs bedrooms, the one with the embarrassing stuffed panda and buck-toothed graduation portraits where you did the better part of your growing up and left years ago. But now you're back, swirling around in some other, more dreamlike dream. Then you're startled awake by a sound from downstairs. Inside.

You ponder the precise nature of the sound you think you've heard. Only half a second has passed and already your memory of it is shifting. What you were certain was a single knock upon wood is becoming a metallic scratch, shattered glass, an exhaled breath. Although there is no sound now, whatever it was leaves an echo in the too-silent silence, pours down the hallway and under the door of your room.

How many times have you had this dream? Even as you dream it, it feels tired from repetition, although it never fails to frighten and make you do the frightened child things of pulling the sheet over your head and sending out a mental distress call to your mother, who, you know full well, has been dead for some time.

And then you hear it again. It may have been a knock or broken glass the first time but it is definitely footsteps now. Heavy zombie slides across the living-room carpet. How many times have you considered what to do next, decided to stay where you are and then pulled the sheet back and gotten to your feet anyway?

Nudged through the dark of your room (the smell of preserved suburban childhood clinging to your skin as you go) and into the hall-way. The footsteps downstairs have progressed to the front hall, where they stop. Waiting.

Is that the thing below, breathing? Is it you?

Nothing can be determined aside from how it will end. So on you go. A marionette dragged through the seamless dark.

You know you are taking steps down the stairs only from having done it a million times before. The darkness a screen you begin to anticipate things appearing on. Whatever waits for you below. Any number of images half-sketched onto a chalkboard and then wiped off to make way for something worse.

The nothing around you turns cold. You could see your breath if you could see. Christ, you'd like to go back up to bed! Or at least *grow up*. But you never will. This happens to be the particular nightmare you will have throughout your life and tell no one about.

Then you're there. Face to face with the intruding stranger.

And what does the intruding stranger do? It makes you wait. Or maybe there isn't anything there at all. This question is the next-to-worst part, because you know the answer even as you ask it.

A single pop of light shows it to be closer than you expected.

A horrible face whose horror lies in the way it is many faces at once: the squinty uncle who touched you in a bad place, the Doberman that took out a hunk of your cheek when you were six, a laughing birthday party clown with smoke-stained teeth. Even your beloved mother, who has heard your prayers but has instead arrived in a ghoulish version of herself, her eyes plucked out and her mouth growing wide.

What makes it so bad is that you couldn't conjure these faces-within-a-face as quickly as they appear. It's not your dream anymore, no matter how many times you've had it. This part always gets you. You'd like it to stop—right *now*, thanks—but it holds you a second longer until it pulls a wavering call for help from your throat.

It's this face made of faces that wakes you up.

Except this time it's still there. Looking back, real as you are.

4

THEN it's gone.

As soon as I've confirmed I'm awake (a slippery pinch of thigh under the sheet does it) the face disappears from the doorway. The open doorway. Not open when I went to sleep. Although it is instantly clear that I will never forget what this face looks like, there's not a single word I could put to describe it, aside from it being *there*.

A man.

Not Americo, or the tour guide, or the captain. Someone on board who didn't start the trip with the rest of us. Someone with a gun.

Despite my wishing for the door to shut on its own it continues to stand open, admitting a swift series of sounds I can't be certain about. A knuckle rapping on the wall? A word of Spanish? A woman's scream stifled so quickly it hasn't the chance to begin?

A drumroll of vibrations moving through every joint of the *Ana Cassia*. It may *be* the *Ana Cassia*, the regular complaint of its arthritic boards. But that is only one of the things I tell myself without believing it.

I pull on a T-shirt and pair of shorts and step over to look both ways down my side of the main deck. Will I go out? To see what's what? To offer assistance? It is embarrassment that answers the questions for me: *I can't stand here forever.* If it's really nothing, someone will eventually come by and ask what I'm doing standing here ("You look like you've seen a ghost, Crossman!") and I will appear foolish. For as long as there's a chance things may still be safe, it is amazing how compelling the fear of appearing foolish can be.

Outside my door the boat feels more steady, the hum of the generator and the notion of an absorbent forest somewhere out there smothering whatever I thought I'd heard a moment before. I decide to head to the front of the boat, in the opposite direction to where the face has gone. When I get as far as the bridge I look in the window, but the captain's not there, though one of his cigarettes leans against the inside of an empty coffee cup next to the throttle, still burning.

Turn around the corner and peer down the opposite side but there's nothing there either, just the wider part of the river, passing slow beyond the rail. But there is the impression that there *had* been movement a second ago. A trace of light in the empty shadow next to the ladder up to the galley.

That's where I start to go. To avoid embarrassment. To come to the end of the dream.

Then, from what is probably the observation deck directly above my head, come three sounds in equally spaced succession.

The scrape of boots over wood.

The Spanish words *¿Quién eres tu?*

A shotgun blast.

The last of these a single boom but with echoes following from every direction, and the echoes making echoes of their own, so that the sound grows louder before it begins to fade.

I will never move again. I will never hear another thing.

If I'm to be turned to stone at least I have a view of sorts, looking across the couple hundred yards of dark river to where the *Presidente Figueiredo* is tied to the trees on the shore. A light, then another, are flicked on behind its drawn cabin curtains. And see now: there may be the outline of human figures leaning at the rail. Impossible to say if the *Presidente Figueiredo* has been boarded by others as well, or if whoever is awake on its decks belongs there. Either way, they aren't doing anything in a hurry.

But what is to be done? Send some bureaucrats over in a canoe to save us? If it really is some of the government people standing over there, a groggy Minister of Foreign Affairs and one of his bifocaled tariff lawyers, say, and not just a pair of wet towels hanging out to dry, what they're doing is watching. Watching and wondering what the hell that noise was. Watching and wondering even though they know perfectly well what the noise was, along with what it means. Already their thoughts have moved on to deliberating over the wisest approach to the situation (*is* it a situation? can we be *certain?*) while entertaining private calculations concerning blame and responsibility and the potential impact of conflicting international jurisdictions. They're being *political*. But mostly they're wishing that whatever is going to take place gets on with it so that they may be relieved from even the possibility of action.

Just as I do. It seems an unlikely position to take, but I would rather be shot dead where I stand than have to make some effort to prevent it. What would that entail? Without even knowing, I'm certain I'm not capable of it. So I'll just wait here. And when it comes it will be very bad, but very easy too—

—another airborne face, the captain's this time. Not two feet from my own. Upside down as he tumbles from the observation deck into the water.

My ears still crackling from the shot so I don't hear the splash. But it's what I see in the half second of his descent that does the job. All the sunburn and alcoholic color in his skin bleached out, teeth bared, eyes pulled so wide it's like his lids have been trimmed away. Followed by a hole in his chest made of a thousand pocks and divots, each burrowing toward some different point deeper inside. Pieces of him still gleaming and whole. Organs I'm sure I could name if I knew even a little about human insides. Most of them blue. And finally his own pistol, the one I'd noticed tied within a leather strap under the boat's wheel, now spinning after the heels of his tennis shoes like a footnote.

He had tried to fight. It had still been bad, and not easy at all.

The captain must have heard the man at my cabin door at the same time I woke to see him there. Dropped his just-lit cigarette into his cup (drained of rum a moment before) and lurched out from behind the wheel, his legs asleep, still prickling. But he knew his ship. Even dreamy and liquored he could tell that the steel-toed boots clomping up the ladder to the observation deck belonged to none of his crew or passengers, but to a man of considerable weight who'd come aboard without notice in the night, a hundred miles from any town or mission station.

He took his pistol with him, held flat against his side. Climbed up to the observation deck with deliberate grasps and lifts, but without any special effort to be quiet. They both knew where the other was. But whoever had demanded to know the captain's name in Spanish was already waiting for him in the dark, a shotgun trained on the center of his chest. The captain had not answered. On his *own boat?* He had no need to answer. He considered laughing at the question outright, but told himself to wait until he could see the visitor first. Shuffled forward and raised his pistol waist high in front of him to search the shadows.

Before he has a chance to find who he's looking for, something is lifting him off his feet. A thousand baby fingers, but with nails sharp as drill bits. Buckshot picking him up and tossing him over the rail a dozen feet behind him.

It's the flash of his falling body that allows me to move. If I'm going to die I want to try to hide first. Another few seconds alone in the dark now seems worth the effort.

The *Ana Cassia* feels occupied by instant movement, although there is nothing that makes itself visible and the gunshot echo is still the only thing to be heard. There is more than one of them. They must have looked in the cabins first, and they'll look again if someone is missing. The top deck, the galley, the bridge. All rather obvious. It is a small boat.

Boot heels clinking down the ladder behind my back. The same boots I'd heard shifting around to line up the end of a shotgun with the captain's chest.

I go the other way. Around the open door to the bridge again to inhale the smoke of the captain's still smoldering cigarette, then straight down the deck on the other side. If whoever is descending from the galley goes the opposite way I'll meet him in the next second. Even if he stands at the ladder's base I will round the back of the boat and bump into him before I can stop.

But when I turn the corner there's nobody there. I'm standing in the shadows now myself. Maybe *I* was the trace of light I saw here when I first looked. A premonition: *I will be there.*

Then the memory of the face from my dream returns to me.

He is here too.

I climb up to the galley, then fall to my hands and knees, scuttling behind the bar. A move borrowed from my childhood terrier, Foxy. If she knew she'd been bad she'd always seek out one of the only two or three hiding spots available to her—behind the piano, my mother's closet—even though it never did her any good.

Once I'm sidled up against the piled cases of Antarctica empties, the *Ana Cassia* becomes quiet. Has been quiet since the gunshot. There is nothing but it and my own hoarse breaths that could be given a name. But now an idea of stillness has joined the silence.

Where are the others?

An immediate answer: the gunman has already spilled them over the side.

It wouldn't have been too difficult if he isn't working alone. Yet I would have expected Wallace to have posed a bit more of a problem, at the very least. Nothing heroic necessarily, just noisy. And who knows what resistance Lydia could put up against an unsuspecting pirate?

Perhaps there are so many of them aboard now that it was all finished in the moments when I was standing frozen on the main deck. Everyone but me and the captain asleep in their cabins. And when he awoke, he had gone up to face them and I had peered out from my doorway. If it has gone this way, then maybe, by the very best of accidents, I have been overlooked. The gunmen have already left, and when the morning comes, the others from the *Presidente Figueiredo* will motor over and find me, and my good luck will be rewarded with an executive-class ticket home and a press conference at the airport, where they will ask me about the boys, those photogenic millennial emblems—what a great loss to the future of technology and upbeat business journalism! But the real question, unasked but loud as a shotgun blast, will be why not *you*, instead of *them*—

—the tour guide sliding up off the ladder on his hands and knees just as I had. One hand pulling him forward while clenching his machete, the other cupped against the dripping weight of blood held in a pouch around the waist of his track pants. I must be able to hear again. The tour guide is making a strange sound. His lips foaming, releasing the air of a high moan.

He has been shot. Or knifed. Something sharp or terrifically fast has made its way through him, and now his face is contorted into a bowtie of pain. He is limiting himself to only this. Nobody is following him yet and he's trying to keep the noise to a minimum. They've left him for dead, and now he's taking the opportunity to find a place to hide on this small boat.

But he already knows that there's nowhere to go. He looks directly at me as he finally must. Is there room enough for two back here? Quite likely, with a bit of shifting. But how long will he take to drag himself to where I am? And no matter how quick he is about it, he will inevitably leave a trail of blood behind him, just as he has over the ladder rungs and across the galley floor, where it pools in the place his progress has stalled.

I shake my head. *Not here.* I may even move my lips. *There's no room.*

Does he catch these words, or the thoughts behind them? Either way, he stays where he is, the blood a widening spotlight of color beneath him. Gripping the machete so tightly it taps against the floor—*tee-dee-dip, tee-dee-dip*—as the high-hat beat of bebop jazz.

I could give him another signal, one to tell him to cut it out and stay still. But I don't. The taps get louder as he grows weaker, as though now he *wants* to let all below know exactly where—

—a shadow falling across him. Crawls along his spine before throwing itself full against the opposite wall.

It's the face from my dream. Poking up from the ladder, rising like a balloon on a string. A face sprouting a torso, a rifle, two bluejeaned legs and boots below them.

The tour guide turns from me without losing my eyes. Keeps his head facing away from the gunman too, now standing behind him. The tour guide stabs the machete into the wooden floor to drag himself another few feet forward. Then, with a gagging intake of air, he flips himself over to lean against the wall. The sudden motion tears his hand away from where he held it. He allows only the briefest glance down to see the new curtain of blood falling over his lap.

"*¿En dónde está la última persona?*" the gunman asks, but the tour guide says nothing to him. Instead he says something to me. A wordless expression cast between the legs of the dining table that seizes the held breath in my lungs.

And what does he say? I haven't the word for it. Like he's just now learned an obvious truth that is no less a revelation for being so obvious. He is instantly resigned to it, but not diminished. In fact it swells within him, whitens his eyes, cranes his head an inch higher on his neck. The moaning cut off in his throat. It gives him something anesthetizing, emboldening, this decision he's made, or recognition of what had been there all along. Wipes him clean of fear and lifts him to where he can be availed of comfort, although I'm certain he means this comfort and fearlessness to be for me.

He had saved me in the forest, even though I was the only one who believed I was lost. And now he is doing it again, without our knowing each other's names.

Bring a friend, his expression tells me for the second time.

The gunman slides another step forward. Raises the rifle above his head, takes a bite of air, then brings the butt straight down on top of the tour guide's skull so that it sinks halfway between his shoulders.

It makes me think of Whack the Weasel, that carnival game where you hammer at the heads of furry puppets as they pop out of their holes. But the sound of what the gunman does to the tour guide's head reminds me of nothing I've ever heard. A voice as much as anything else. A savage signal calling out to itself. And a second later, the tour guide's crown opens neatly as a trapdoor, spilling its custardy blues and yellows down the slope of his back.

He falls apart.

In the time of a camera's flash the tour guide goes from a man to a pile of unwieldy garbage spilling out of a cheap plastic bag. He requires nothing now but to be cleaned away.

But the gunman is not fastidious. He doesn't even bother looking behind the bar. Just turns and retraces the tour guide's wet trail down the ladder.

Funny thing: it's only after he's gone that the terror returns. It brings me to my feet, claws my fingers against the clasp of the window above the dining table. When it swings open I push my head into the outside air. It's cooler by a degree or two, and carries only a saccharine trace of the tour guide's insides that is already filling the galley behind me.

It seems for a moment that I might have to stay this way, jammed here like Winnie the Pooh going for the honey. But it turns out the window is just large enough for me to fit into its frame, yet small enough that I have to twist my way through it. When I drop away from the boat my head is facing upwards, looking into the flat black-board sky.

Other dreams end this way, don't they? The terrible ones where the only escape is to step off the cliff or the building's ledge. But you have to remember to wake up before you hit the ground, otherwise you're dead. It's a rule. To this end I try a scream, but I've forgotten how they go. And there isn't time, anyway. I'm already there. The moist soil of the river sliding into my lungs.

The water colder than you'd guess for a jungle. Its unexpected weight, thick as bitumen. Getting to the air takes three head-to-hip pulls of my arms—how far down had I gone?—and staying there once I've broken through requires a frantic bicycling beneath the surface.

I'm not a good swimmer. Not at all good. I remember this now.

Nothing to see but the *Presidente Figueiredo* sitting fat and pricked with lightbulbs only a three-minute dog paddle away. What may be more figures moving about on its decks. But it's all a painted stage backdrop, two-dimensional. Even if I reach it, it won't let me inside.

I thrash my way against the current. Surprise myself by making it to the end of the *Ana Cassia*'s hull. Past this there is only more river. And the hungry things that live in it. On the boat, there are people who may be my friends. And men with shotguns.

The devil you know.

I look up at the deck and there is one of the gunmen observing my escape. He doesn't seem to be at all alarmed. Probably been following me flailing along the side from the second I fell. Apparently he has as much confidence in my capabilities as I do.

"Help me!" I'm calling up to him before I know I am. "Please! *Por favor!*"

And with these words I begin to drown.

I've been coughing out a good part of the Rio Negro since I first came up for air, but now there's nothing for it but to suck it all back in. The water lapping over my eyes, and through it the sight of the gunman lowering the hooked pole Americo uses to pull in the motorized canoe.

I throw my hands up for it. But without using them to swim I only fall another foot down and the pole is out of reach again. Tell myself to try one more time but there's nothing left.

Down.

A lump of rotten beef for the little fish with all those teeth.

Then there is the hook sinking into my back.

Lifted up into the air now chilled and slow as the water. Slapping at the pole to take some of the weight off where it has cut through the fin of my right shoulder blade. The screech of metal against bone.

It reminds me how to scream.

"*¡Cállate!*" the gunman tells me as he pulls me over the rail, and I'm able to hold the sound back at my lips. It's not his command that does it. It's the sight of his face. At once particular and unreal, like those novelty store masks of ex-presidents.

"*Soy uno de ellos,*" I tell him in Spanish, which I cannot really speak. Still, I have picked up enough along the way to know how to ask not to be shot. Although I don't use those exact words. I tell him who I am.

"*Soy uno de ellos,*" I say again. *I'm one of them.*

He ignores me, as I expected he would. Steps around to pull the hook out of my back. I know this is what he does (I can hear it, the muffled scrapes, like sharpening a knife under a blanket), but it feels like he's putting something in there instead. A fistful of angry hornets. Along with the end of his gun. Pushing me along the deck to the rear of the boat.

The gun takes me to the Hypothesys team. Sitting on the deck with their backs against the rail and empty rice sacks pulled down over their heads.

It's not funny—of course it's not funny—but there's something comic in this pose. The way their hair-pricked legs are roughly splayed out in front of them like uprooted tubers, and each of their heads stuck in a sack. They could be a row of four prize-winning potatoes.

I startle myself with a giggle. And not just a solitary hiccup, either, but one of those nearly painful spasms—*hee! hee! hee!*—pulled out like a string of pearls.

It's probably only shock. I tell myself this as it's happening. That this laughter is not what it sounds like, so that instead of a scream out comes this sunny playground sound. Makes one wonder if perhaps this *is* rather amusing. Look at them. At me. These ridiculous men with guns. *Bang, bang!* It's kind of hilarious, isn't it?

No, it's not. It's the way Lydia's legs start jerking at the sound of my voice that tells me. She knows it's me standing here, still unhooded, untied. She's signaling for help and I can do nothing but laugh this terrible laugh, the most solitary sound I've ever heard.

But what happens next takes the laughter from my throat for good.

The gun at my back jabs me away from the rice sacks toward the front of the boat. Where is the Southern Cross now? The night is both cloudless and starless, so that even the sky has been shaved clean of life.

The gunman grabs me by the shoulder in front of the open doorway to the tiny bridge. Pulls me close enough that there is nothing to breathe but his clothes, stinking of sour milk. Now we can both turn to look inside, but at first only the gunman does before he pulls at my jaw to make me do the same. And there's the captain's cigarette in its cup, sending up the last licks of smoke against the windshield.

"*¡Mira!*" he says and pulls my chin down.

This is what he wants me to see. Americo and Maria, lying together on the floor next to the captain's chair.

They are holding each other. Americo whispering to Maria, who is sobbing without making any sound. Even now her face is turned away, so that it is impossible to see exactly what she looks like. But I believe she is pretty. And Americo is strong. Although folded up in a corner I can see that he is a man of bulk and capacity, wrapped around Maria as though to absorb whatever is to happen next using his body alone.

The gunman lifts the barrel level with them.

You might expect a pause now. But he just fires.

It is the kind of gun that allows him to shoot without reloading or cocking or whatever else you have to do with other guns, so that he fires and fires. The force of the shots moves their joined bodies in a jerking dance, the thrust and wriggle of hurried lovemaking.

It goes on for what may be a long time. For the gunman's amusement, I guess, although his face, now as when it hovered outside the open door of my cabin, shows nothing. Perhaps it is to make certain the job is done. As always with bullets and angles and unpredictable good luck—you can't be too sure.

He fires on. But Americo and Maria never let each other go. The big man's hands now cradling her head, as though to muffle her ears from the noise.

When the gunman is finally done he releases a tired sigh. He might have just finished doing the dishes.

A sigh that is cut short when Americo sits up.

And comes at us somehow. Throwing his giant shoulders forward one at a time and pushing his legs under him to make an attempt at rising to his feet. He does this wordlessly, his eyes fixed on the gunman's. It takes some seconds. And for the duration of his struggle there is only the steady draw and push of his breath. A working horse frothing under a midday sun.

The grin I thought would be there forever now gone. No sign that it ever was there, the skin around it veined with blue creases as though a layer of stage make-up had been cracked apart. His mouth coming closer even as his body comes to a stop. When I look inside there is only a furious swallowing. A hunger that will take in the gunman, me, the boat. The whole river poured into his chest.

But before it can, his mouth finds the end of the rifle. Pushed so far inside it jolts against the back of his throat. On his knees now, the blood a streaming apron tied around his ribs. Closing his lips on the gun without ever taking his eyes from the gunman.

To say what? Nothing I can translate. There is nothing in his eyes but this hunger that reaches back to his beginning and forward to our ends, on and on.

5

TWELVE hours or more up the river with the rice sacks still roped to our heads. Hands tied behind our backs so tight they balloon into boxing gloves. No water, no food. Regular jabs of a rifle barrel to keep us from sleep. Not that we could. Gnashing for air through our panic, the stinking canvas, the bile that crawls up our throats to be choked back the wrong way.

Someone bawling the whole time. Maybe each of us, taking turns. It makes the gunmen shout over top of it and bring their boot heels down on our kneecaps. Nothing they do can make it stop.

When the motorized canoe they have us in finally grinds onto a beach we are so weak they have to yank us up over the sides by the ropes at our necks. Leave us to bake on what feels like a field of stones. They take some time to smoke. Piss close enough to our heads that the spatter moistens through the sacks.

Then they argue over which of them will help carry us into the jungle. A competition decides the matter: whoever can make the old man cry out the loudest by kicking him in the ribs will only be required to carry his own pack.

After each of them has had a turn our arms, still tied, are looped over their shoulders. The bawling replaced by a layering of screams.

We are dragged uphill. Ascending in irregular jerks, each of which is punctuated by a weightlifter's moan as the gunmen heave another half step forward. Our cheeks bouncing against their slippery backs. Even through the canvas we can smell their sweat, cooked and sugary.

Our bodies are frequently thrown to the ground without warning so the gunmen can rest. Crumpled on the cutting ends of branches, on leaves that bite. Flies that find a way inside the hoods to feed on our molasses nosebleeds.

When the gunmen stop for good it's in a small camp from the smell and sound of it (the singed cherry of an extinguished fire, the flap and zipper of a nylon tent front). It has taken what must have been over an hour to get here but it may be little more than a few hundred strides up from the water. Two of them fight over which was worse: carrying the fat woman who wouldn't stop blubbering or the old man who'd shit himself. There are kicks to the sides of our heads every time we try to raise ourselves up. Building spirals of laughter.

When they finally tire of this they drop us in a hole.

A dug-out drum of soft decay, tickling roots, lines of bulbous fire ants trooping up to the surface and ripping out pieces of our necks and backs for the trip. The soil crumbling away at the touch of our fingers. Each of our movements releases a new bloom of gas from the earth. The rancid waves that escape from a long-unplugged fridge. The sour-ness of wet ash.

We arrange ourselves as best we can, telling each other where our limbs are so we might avoid snapping them under the accident of our own weight. A gate of planks slammed shut over our heads to keep us here. They leave us standing like pencils in a mug.

My eyes are open but I can't see. Not *I can't focus*, but a total blind-ness. They've kept the sacks on although they needn't have. I can feel the darkness with my fingertips, inhale it as a sickly musk. With some consideration, the different veins of odor may be sorted out from within it: the sharp ammonia of urine, fermenting rice caught in the sacks' material, the baby-diaper whiffs of our own clothes.

It's better to concentrate on the thirst burning in our throats, although it makes breathing even harder than it was before. And now the sun is up—we can feel its hot tentacles where it reaches down through the gate to touch us. Turns the air inside the hoods into a putrid soup.

There is always the changing character of pain to think about, too. The hole in my shoulder where it feels like the boat hook is still buried, separating muscle from bone. Along with a heat in my chest that sends up noxious burps of peppermint, like stale menthol cigarettes. What I imagine internal bleeding might taste like.

We speak as much as we can. Words that, as soon as they're spoken, scuttle away like the tiny sand crabs that gouge trails around our feet.

The first thing we ask is if all of us are here. Then we take an accounting of the ways each of us are hurt.

After that we tell each other how we are already shrinking. "Dematerialized" is how Bates describes it. An unexpected term, but no less accurate for that. Even in the darkness I can see the jigsawed pieces of my four friends surrendering by degrees the weight and color that make them real. Soon there will be nothing left of us, not even our bones. The tour guide was right. The soil here hates any history not its own.

We speak, but it is never clear who might be listening. Sleep comes over us like fainting spells, sudden and complete. I try to keep my mind on the pain to stay awake. To not be alone.

Their words remind me that we are still human.

Barry is first.

We hear the gate pulled open over our heads and the sun crashes down. Even inside the hoods the light is blinding—the *idea* of light, working its way between the threads.

Above, they tap each of our chests with the ends of their boots and laugh. Try to figure out which of us is which.

"*¿Es una panocha o un culo?*"

"*Cógela primero—pregunta después!*"

Is it a cunt or an asshole?

Fuck it first—ask questions later!

We're jammed in so close that we hear Barry screaming for a full second or two before we realize they're lifting him out.

"Wallace! What are they doing? *Wallace!*"

"Don't worry, Bear! Just hang on, man!"

"*No!* What are you—?"

Barry's voice is cut off by the gunmen tugging at the rope around his neck. Lifted high enough that his dangling feet kick at our heads. There's the grinding of his teeth as he works to push his jaw down for air. In the next second he's gone.

"Crossman! What's going on?" This is Wallace.

"I don't know. I—"

"You understand what they're saying, don't you?"

"They're speaking Spanish, not Portuguese. My background is—"

"You've got to know more than *we* do."

"I guess that—"

"What are they going to do to him?"

"They haven't—"

Now it's my scream that cuts everything off.

Pulling me up just as they did Barry, the rope a noose closed around my throat. A terrible quiet in my head. Every passage for blood and breath instantly squeezed off.

Then opened again as the hood is lifted away. So much unmediated light that at first it's a world of nothing—white on white. In a moment, though, the beginning of details emerge. The jungle circled around us. A body of waving limbs.

And Barry on his knees before it. They pull off his hood and the sunlight folds his eyes shut before he forces them open again. What he can see is a coil of rope on the ground reaching up into the tree above it, and three men with guns standing around him, smiling vaguely, as though what is to follow is little more than a frat house stunt.

Barry howls until he runs out of air. And when he takes another breath to go at it again one of the men raises his gun and slams its butt down into his crotch.

Barry rolls into the long grass poking up next to the fire pit, squeezes himself up into a tight comma. The gunman now bent down to unravel him. It requires two yanks of Barry's locked arms to get at his other parts. Then the gunman expertly clasps both of his wrists with one hand, and sends the rope that was on the ground up in showy circles above his head like a rodeo cowboy tying a calf. With a piece of twine he pulls from his front pocket, the gunman binds Barry's ankles together as well. When he's finished he stands back from his work to flick the sweat away from the sides of his nose.

"¡Ahora!" he says to the other men, who begin pulling on the end of rope that has been thrown over a tree limb. Lifting first Barry's hands, arms, his back, his wriggling legs up from the grass. The tree groans from the burden. Shreds of bark finding our eyes, our tongues. The limb bends low, but is so elastic there is no chance of it breaking.

With a dozen heaves Barry is completely suspended in the air, arms straight out behind him so that his wrists take all of his weight. Then the men tie the end of the rope around a neighboring trunk and sit down to smoke cigarettes in the reedy grass that Barry has already flattened.

There is nothing I can look at. Definitely not Barry, now bleating like a lamb above me. But there is the idea that if I close my eyes, it will only be worse.

I focus on the gunmen. Try to sketch the details of their faces into my memory so that I could immediately identify them in a lineup. But even as I look at them they blur into one another, exchanging broken noses for pockmarked cheeks for blackened teeth. It's as though my mind can only accept them as men, an interchangeable group of characteristics. Perhaps this is always visible in the faces of those capable of such things. The regular performance of cruelties has made them generic, fused a communal mask of violence to their faces.

They notice me watching them and jab their thumbs up at Barry. When I don't look right away one of them points a gun at my head.

What I notice first is that Barry's body shouldn't be shaped the way it is. His arms sticking up from their sockets like chicken wings and the rest of him, oversized, useless, hanging in a diagonal below them. It is the unnatural that makes it hard to watch him, to remember that it's Barry up there. Funny, handsome, ageless Barry. A southerner. A good man, from what I know of him.

But now the sound he was making has given way to something more frantic, an animal whimpering. He's only been up there for a couple of minutes and already speech eludes him. He's nothing but suffering. And it eats away at anything that might still be him. Especially his face. His cheeks full as though from carrying stones.

"*Tell* them, Crossman," he finally manages. His normally rich voice turned to a helium squeak from all the pressure poured down to his head, fattening his lips, his tongue. "For Christ's sake tell them I don't know anything!"

I tell them. I ask them to let him go, he's just an American businessman who'd let them in on anything if he knew. But it's hard to guess how much they understand. On my knees, eyes waxed with tears, I listen to my voice slip between Spanish and Portuguese, Portuguese and English. Soon there is only my shouting to cover the sound of Barry gagging for air.

If they get the message, they choose to ignore it. Flick their cigarettes away and stand up, bouncing their rifles in their hands. For a moment I'm certain they will now take turns beating him with their weapons, working to cut him open. But instead they take the snouts of their rifles and push Barry around on his rope so that it winds even tighter. The buckling line lifts him an additional foot off the ground. When the length of the rope is knotted into a single braid, his wrists snap.

He pauses before beginning his descent. His body hanging separated from his hands by four inches of skin that wasn't there a moment ago. Then he starts spinning in the other direction as a tangled yo-yo.

"Please, please, please," Barry screeches, over and over, so that I hear it every time his face turns to mine. Pleading to me as much as to the men. The one face he knows out of the twists of smoke and the jungle's swirling green.

In the hole, I try counting in my head to measure the time. But as it is with having sheep jump over a fence to bring on sleep, it doesn't work. It just goes on, producing only numbers upon numbers, and you lose track. Have to start again. But where are you starting from? What is now?

Gauging our hunger is the most unreliable timepiece of all. The gunmen feed us only once a day, or what feels like a day down here. Bring us up one by one to kneel before them, wondering if this time they will simply raise a pistol and put a bullet into the center of the hood. Instead they pull it off so that we can watch one of them dropping a single tablespoon of cooked rice into a coffee mug, then moistening it with a squeeze from one of their water bottles. They pull up plugs of it on the ends of their fingers and slip them between our lips. When we ask for more they fill the mug with rice and pass it under our noses before tossing it out onto the sandy earth where the flies cloud above it within seconds.

Hunger isn't emptiness. I'd always assumed that was the shape it would take, judging from the stomach growlings of a missed lunch or late dinner. But real hunger is being excruciatingly full. Not with food but with fumes that build up within. And when your guts are finally pushed out tight as they will go, the fumes are set on fire.

But the pain from the things the gunmen do to us is different. It has character. Each throb corresponding to a beat of the heart, which may go faster whenever the gate swings open and someone else is plucked out, and slower when exhaustion threatens to ease it down to nothing. Each ache or brittleness expressing itself in unison, yet still distinct. For the past while it has been my ribs. That one just below my lungs is a chalky scrape. And then there's the one that circles under my shoulders where the hook pulled me out of the river—that one's a gnawing.

In time each of the pains becomes familiar. I could give them names.

The pirates have devised something special for each of us. I'm the first to know because they bring me up every time. Ostensibly to translate. But they just want me to watch.

When Barry was returned to the hole after the first time we wondered if they wanted something from him alone. He was a man, the oldest—they may have assumed he was our leader and could give them what they were looking for sooner than any of us. But Barry had nothing to give them, and they hadn't asked for anything.

They would come for the rest of us in time. Although we never guessed that it would be so soon. And that they would choose Lydia next.

They pull her up as with Barry before, but she doesn't struggle as he did. Doesn't ask for help either. As she goes we can feel her body held stiff in an effort to not take up any space, to disappear. Then they pull me up too and crash the gate down behind us.

They take off Lydia's shoes and her hood. The gunmen aren't laughing this time. Standing around her rigid body, their faces fixed in concentration. The paleness of her skin stuns us. Beneath her shirt and her shorts we know she is whiter yet.

I'm powerless to stop them from doing what I expect them to, but I ready myself anyway. To ask them not to. To tell them not to rape her because she is pregnant. They will doubt this, naturally. She may be a bit fat, they will say, but that doesn't mean she's carrying a child. I will search for the right tone to assure them that she is. And surely even they could understand the special wrong that went with that?

For now, they only stare at the skin already available to them. I risk glimpses of their faces, and find only hardness. A stricken puzzlement. Not even words pass between the gunmen. Their lips pursed in consideration of her flesh, as though they will be tested on it later.

Finally the one standing closest to her orders Lydia's arms be held secure behind her back and for another to sit on her thighs to keep her legs in place. Then he walks to the edge of the trees fifty feet away and cuts a long branch from a sapling using a bowie knife. Hacks the smaller ones off its length. Demonstrates its elasticity by lashing it at an imaginary target.

Lydia rolls her eyes back to mine and I mouth the words *Don't watch*.

Now the gunman with the branch skips forward with a practiced grace, his arm suspended above him like a cricket pitcher. Slides to a stop before her while bringing the switch down. Slices the branch's tip across the bottom of Lydia's heel.

A line of blood appears instantly, clean as a razor cut. Three more lashes and there's a trickling star on the sole of her foot.

Lydia keeps her eyes closed the whole time. But even with the men holding her arms and sitting across her legs, she spasms so violently they leap off her body and into the air above her. The whip slashing the same pattern deep into the skin of her other foot.

When he's done the gunman holds his chin and examines his work. Examines the rest of her too. The possibilities of her skin.

"*¿Nadie se la quiere echar?*" he asks the others. *Does anyone want her?*

They think about this for a time. Twice I feel myself about to speak, and twice I stop short. Any break in the silence may be worse than letting it find its own end.

After more than a minute passes without an answer, the gunman holding the branch stuffs Lydia's head into the sack again and gestures for the others to drop her back into the hole.

Only when she's returned to the others does she allow herself to cry. She buries her feet up to her ankles in the earth to cool them. Asks for each of us by name and we tell her that it's all right, we're still here. We won't go anywhere without her.

Bates next.

For him, it's burning. Cigarettes held to his forearms. His cheeks. Then, dissatisfied by his refusal to scream, his shorts are pulled down. One of them cups his testicles, pink and shriveled as a newborn's. Kisses them with the end of his lit cigar.

Wallace is the only one they don't bring me up to watch. And when they drop him back in the hole, he's the only one who doesn't tell us what they did.

After the first round they start something new. Taking more than one up from the hole at a time. And now they sometimes take the others and leave me down here. I tell the gunmen that the others don't understand Spanish, there's no point in asking them questions without me there, or in hurting them when they don't answer. The gunmen understand this perfectly, judging from the single laugh they offer in reply. But they take them anyway.

"Who's here?" I ask the darkness when they shut the gate, swinging my arm through the new emptiness.

"I'm here." Bates's voice.

"Are you OK?"

"Dumb question."

"But you're with me?"

"I'm with you."

From above, Lydia screams.

"Who are they, Crossman?"

"I don't know. But they speak Spanish, they've got plenty of guns, they know a thing or two about stealing tourists. My guess is that they're Colombian guerrillas of some kind. Drug farmers. Jungle bandits. It's a good country for all that."

"But we're in Brazil."

"We were getting closer to the border all the time. I've read about Colombian paramilitaries crossing south to do this kind of thing. I don't fucking know."

"Tell me what they did."

"We're here, aren't we?"

"I mean on the boat. To Maria and the captain and the others. You were the only one who could have seen."

"I saw."

"So could they—?"

"No. They're dead."

"How?"

"They separated us from them. They knew who they wanted."

"They shot them."

"They shot them. And they made me watch."

"Just like they're doing now."

"Just like now."

An odd silence fills the pause in our talk. They have stopped making Lydia scream, and there is no movement above us. More than this, Bates seems to have stopped breathing. I can feel the building pressure of his held breath as though it is my own. Yet when he finally releases it his tone is neutral, becalmed.

"They're going to kill us too, aren't they, Crossman?"

"Not a chance."

"How do you know that?"

"They told me."

"Told you?"

"I asked them straight out, and they said they didn't need that kind of trouble. They're just going to mess with us until they get whatever they want. Then they'll let us go."

Bates pulls in another breath and holds all the shadows inside him before letting them out again.

"I don't believe you," he says. "But thanks for the effort."

I'd forgotten something I recognized at the very beginning. Bates is smart. With computers, yes, and numbers. But with people, too.

"How could you tell?"

"Down here, you start to hear a lot in someone's voice."

"Maybe you could tell the others anyway, Bates. When they get back. It might make them stay strong."

There is another silence, and I begin to think that Bates is calculating what other lies I might be capable of.

"Can I ask you something?" I say.

"Sure."

"What was it like to grow up without a family? After your parents died, I mean."

"My parents aren't dead."

"On the boat Wallace said that you were the real orphan."

"Wallace says things."

"You mean he lies."

"I mean he's naturally empathetic. Sometimes I think he lives my life better than I do."

"Trading places."

"Haven't you ever had a best friend, Crossman?"

"Sounds like you two are closer than that."

"Barry calls us the Siamese twins."

"To me you're not twins so much as an old married couple. The kind who knows each other's tricks but are still in love after all these years. You know?"

Bates says nothing, but I can tell that it isn't anger that stops him from correcting me. He's thinking of something else. In the hole, our trains of thought are allowed to do this, to randomly cut and paste.

He's telling me about his parents. Both still alive. A second-tier Canadian diplomat and his wife who had Bates back in the days when kids with degrees could get the government to fly them somewhere hot and poor where they could help the locals dig a well. Pretend they were changing the world. This is how Bates puts it, anyway. The problem was that they were so busy building good relations with complete strangers on the other side of the planet, they pretty near forgot about their own son. Although they sent a lot of photos of themselves to his boarding school. Pictures of Mom and Dad standing in front of raging sunsets or holding malnourished babies against their chests.

"I slowed them down," he says. "They figured they wouldn't get the groovy new appointment in Bali or Timbukfuckingtu if they had to carry some sickly kid around with them all the time."

"How do you know that?"

"I *know*. My mother comes right out with it after a couple of Manhattans every Christmas. She's remarried now. An orthopedic surgeon in Halifax."

"What about your dad?"

"I haven't spoken to him in three years," Bates says. "He prefers e-mail."

Sometime after the year of running the consulate in Reykjavik Bates's parents split up ("The sixties were over, and so were the seventies for that matter, and they looked at each other and could only see how much time had passed"). Today his father is a middle-aged hippie who was never a hippie when he should have been, so that the ponytail and soft drugs and scented candles are all fabulously new to him. He is more than merely "fucked," he is "*truly* fucked," which, in Bates's carefully hierarchical evaluations, denotes a terminal downgrade.

"He walked away from all of it," Bates continues, his voice lowering with anger. "Wife, foreign affairs, son. Shifted from Chivas to home-grown and headed west, snagged a live-in nutritionist named Memory. That's her real name—I asked to see her birth certificate when I first met her and there it was. Memory Pucinik."

Bates had visited only once. Never again. The condescending lectures on the immorality of unbridled capitalism were too much. The dipshit girlfriend was too much. The refusal to account for first leaving him, then his mother, was too much. The lush rows of pot at the back of the garden, the talk of having found a "muse" who happened to take the form of a twelve-year-old Sudanese girl, the exultant blathering of spiritual rebirth, the hectoring vegetarianism—it was all too fucking much.

"Do you think that's where the idea for Hypothesys came from?" I ask him. "Seeing your father make all those bad decisions?"

"I don't know if they were bad or not. But maybe he got me wondering how I could decide what was right for me. It was Wallace who brought all this up. We used to talk about the perfect set of rules you could make for living life, if your life was totally free to live. Without God or laws or habits. In the end, I came up with Hypothesys."

"And Wallace came up with something else?"

"He came up with himself."

I'm about to ask exactly what he means, but he starts on about the house in Ottawa where he lived for six months when his father was between appointments overseas. It was the only time his whole family lived in Canada at once. He was still a kid, nine or ten. The age when certain memories decide to burn themselves into the mind. For example: the house was across the street from an empty lot, which allowed him to take in the long row of red-and-yellow-brick Victorians on the opposite block. He thought of them as a line of faces, dollish and fixed as carnival game targets. The heads of the parents that came to visit the boys at his school in the woods, bricked in by lives of five o'clock cocktails, long silences and Sunday mornings that, no matter how bright, cast only dry, Presbyterian shadows. He'd sit on the sill of the bay window and watch their faces change with the feeling that they were judging him. The last sun on the upstairs windows. An orange rage in each of the eyes.

"The funny thing is, it's my only real family memory, and my family isn't even there," he says, and holds his breath again.

But is that *who he is?* A lonely kid seeing faces in brick and glass? That might as well be him. Everything else feels like details. Even the important things only feel like details.

For a long time I leave him there. Staring through a window at other windows. Waiting for dinner, for the rice sack to be pulled from his head, for someone he could love to walk in the front door and declare it home.

How do I know what they're thinking? I don't. They all say things but I listen more than the others. Soon it feels like they're speaking only to me. Whispers in the liquid space between us, murmurs over the laughter of the gunmen opening the gate to reach down to us. A narrative patchwork that, when sewn together, resembles something close to a whole mind. A translator's task, after all, is to take what can be understood and, when necessary, fill in whatever's missing. And what if there is nothing *but* missing parts? This, I suppose, is where one is obliged to tread into the foggier domain of fiction, a place I have been strictly trained not to enter. But surely such rules can't apply here. They say you come to know others most intimately through extreme situations. And I feel I know these people better after forty-eight hours in a dark hole than I know myself after half a lifetime above ground.

I confess there is power in this knowledge. Sweet and guilty, an eye held to the most forbidden keyholes. But why shouldn't I take a good long look? The others all have something else to think about. Lydia has her child within her, Barry his fishing lodge on the Oconee River. Wallace and Bates have nothing less than the new century beckoning their return. I, on the other hand, don't have any such distractions. So I'll stitch them into a new consciousness to replace my own.

These are skills that lie outside my formal education, I admit. But why *not* me? Perhaps this is my chance to expand, as Wallace puts it.

In a world without gods, am I not as qualified for omniscience as anyone else?

Counting the seconds on their own proves impossible, and soon the effort to count the heartbeats of pain collapses as well. Time is light. Even when the sun falls, the hours are measured in waiting for it to come back again.

But down here all that has been canceled. They've taken us to a place where time has no grasp, as in a fairy tale, or the grave.

Which has its consolations. Without time or light there is only the mind. And if one's own mind proves empty, there are always others'.

Right now, Wallace is savoring the last hints of stale coffee in his mouth. Imagines cigarette smoke in there, too, although he smokes only at corporate events to learn the secrets that the nicotine addicted tend to share exclusively among themselves. He lowers his chin and feels the islands of stubble catch on his first growths of chest hair. Sticks out his lower lip and directs his bad breath up into his nostrils. And with his lip out like that and his eyes slightly crossed he looks like a bulldog. If you could see him. A kid, making faces.

"Why us, Crossman?" he asks now, taking me by surprise. I'd nearly fallen asleep imagining I was watching him. "Why do you think they picked us?"

"They haven't told me yet."

"They could have robbed us right there on the boat. They didn't have to kill anybody to get us to sign over our traveler's checks."

"They haven't told me."

"You mentioned that."

I try to discipline my voice to meet the challenge Wallace is about to lay before me. It comes whenever he speaks. A degree of competition. Even here his voice carries a clear weight, quieter than before but somehow stronger for that. The rest of our words catch or break or boil up into sobs. But Wallace's seem to come from somewhere else altogether.

"I have some ideas," he says.

"Who else is here?"

"Just you and me."

"They only took up Barry and Bates last time. Lydia is still down here."

"They did a real number on her the last time. She can't hear us."

"I just wanted—"

"You say they're Colombian, right?"

"My guess."

"They had to be working on intelligence of some kind. To know where our boats were going to be."

"What's your idea?"

"They've got the wrong people. If it's some kind of political thing, they were probably after the Minister and the others on the *Presidente*. Wrong boat. Then again, maybe it *was* us that they wanted. Or they *think* they know who we are, but they're mistaken."

"I don't understand the last one."

"Somebody told a tale. In São Paulo. Or Manaus. Told a Colombian contact about our itinerary, gave up our secrets. Except the secrets were false."

"Like what?"

"Like Bates telling his girl at the bar that he'd developed a new kind of bomb."

"Are you saying that—"

"Notice how they separated us right away and killed the crew? And the way they've only talked to you. Our translator."

"I don't speak much Spanish."

"More than anyone else."

"If you're right, who told them? Why would one of us tell a story when we would be among the ones to get hurt? Take a look, Wallace. This situation isn't good for any of us."

"Not yet it isn't. Maybe it's always been part of the deal to hang out with the dead meat for a while longer. In order to find something out. Something they don't know yet but that they still need."

"You're not making—"

"Or maybe it's all gone wrong. They don't give a shit whose side we're on. They'll sell us all, or kill us all, and keep the traitor's fee for themselves."

"This is out of control."

"I'm thinking in the only direction we can think."

"So who is it? Bates? Because he lied to a whore?"

"I didn't say that."

"You brought him up."

"To illustrate a hypothetical."

"That's right. I forgot. *Everything* is hypothetical to you, isn't it? You just let yourself string things out long enough that anything becomes possible. But you never come to the end. Of course, if we had Hypothesys with us, we could just enter our names and it could tell which of us is a murdering liar."

"It couldn't do that."

"Then you probably can't, either."

"Bates says he saw the concierge the last time they pulled him up."

It's at this moment that I notice how truly *bad* it smells down here. I'd been concentrating on distinguishing the odors for so long that I'd never let them wash over me at once, the piss and shit and sick, familiar on their own but horrifically new when all mixed together.

"Bates is losing his mind," I say.

"He seemed certain."

"Are you asking me to consider this?"

"Said he saw the monster standing at the edge of the camp. The guy didn't say anything. Just stood there and watched the others burn his balls."

"And what was the concierge doing there? Bringing room service? Because I could really go for a club sandwich and a glass of Merlot about now."

"I'm just mapping things out. We need to know before we can act."

"Act? I can't even pick my nose. But you better tell me if you're going to try something, Wallace. Tell me *before* you do it."

"Why's that?"

"So I can set up a diversion."

"Or tell them my plan."

"What are you saying? Jesus Christ—"

"You're the translator. But how do we know you're telling *us* what they're telling *you*?"

"You're suspicious of everyone but yourself. Is that it?"

"I'll leave it to you to be suspicious of me, Crossman."

Lydia stirs awake. Her legs popping out from the cool earth like a pair of snakes pushing up to the air.

"Is anybody here?"

"I'm here," Wallace says. Although I can't see, I can tell he's holding her. "I'm here."

He doesn't tell her that I am here as well. But before I can announce myself, the gate above us is lifted open and I'm pulled up into the light to witness another round of pain.

. . .

Our only visitor is a rat. Slipping between the bars of the gate that squeezes its guts so tight they make a watery squelch as they press through. A prosperous, inquisitive thing no smaller than Galbraith, my deceased cat, and just as bloated and oily-haired. It comes only at night. Takes leisurely wanders along our limbs, its nails digging into the remaining soft zones of flesh as though to measure our loss of fat.

We never mention it to each other, although I can always feel some of our bodies stiffen at its arrival. Comes and goes as it pleases, sniffing through the canvas over our heads, wondering how long we can hold our breath. We follow each digression of the rat's journey so that the night is pulled out longer than it already is.

Wallace speaks to it once. In a whisper, my head huddled against his.

"Getting down here is no trick," he says. "But how do we get out?"

They have left us alone for what feels like the past few hours. Alone with the mosquitoes. The tour guide from the *Ana Cassia* had told us there were fewer of them along the Rio Negro on account of the water's high acidity. But what could the mosquitoes near *low* acidity rivers possibly be like? Because there's a lot down here. Definitely *many* mosquitoes navigating their way up my nose, enfolding my arms in a layer of extra hair, crushed in the blood-moistened crack of my ass. It's irritating at first. It was *irritating* for the first half hour, maddening for the second, before finally settling into a seamless, prehistoric, mutual hatred.

Although the heat is the same as it ever was, a shiver passes between all of us. An electric spasm that seems to excite the buzzing swarms. Moving from one entwined limb to another as though each of them belongs to the same head. It's enough to start Wallace's voice again. This time, he tells us of how he came to have a vision of God.

This was at the school in the woods. Where he met Bates and "convinced him to be my exclusive associate." They were both thirteen years old.

117

It started with a numbness in Wallace's lower back. The sort of thing you feel after sitting too long in a hard chair. Except it didn't go away. In fact it grew, spreading up through his shoulder blades, the back of his neck. Traded the numbness for burning. Bearable in the morning, the heat rising over the course of the day until it felt like a blowtorch held against his skin by the time he went to bed. On the sixth night he woke up shrieking. At the first sound of Wallace's cry Bates was running across the snow-covered playing field to the head-master's house in bare feet.

His kidneys. Spine. Probably already making its way into the marrow of his ribs. Inoperable.

"This goes without saying," one of the doctors told Wallace soon after he'd arrived at the Hospital for Sick Children in Toronto. There was chemotherapy, of course. But even this seemed to be undertaken without much gusto, the specialists feeling obliged to tick off this one attempt from their list of options. They called it a "hyper-accelerated form" of the disease. Quite rare. Extraordinary, really, in a boy of his age. Their tone suggested that Wallace should consider himself honored to have been visited by such an impressive accumulation of rogue cells.

Bates spent all his tuck shop allowance on the Greyhound down to the city. He didn't have anywhere to go at night, so the nurses let him sleep in the chair by Wallace's bed, hiding him in the staff lounge when security came around to shoo people out at the end of visiting hours. It might have been touching if the body in the bed belonged to an older man, and the vigil was being carried out by his wrinkled, loyal wife. But Wallace was still a child—an orphan, as he told anyone who came into his room asking where his mother and father were—and so the dedication of his slightly odd, narrow-faced friend fit no picture anyone had seen before, and was merely sad. The nurses kept Wallace juiced on "enough morphine to put Keith Richards to sleep" and smuggled Bates the Mountain Dews and chocolate milks he asked for in order to stay awake. The two of them had gone from reading the dorm's only *Penthouse* together under the sheets to a deathbed in less than two weeks.

At the end of his sixth day in the hospital the disease announced its final assault. The doctors never could have done anything to help, but now they said so out loud. Wallace remembers the night as unbelievably long. Taking a breath and holding it, afraid that if he exhaled he would forget how to take it in again. And when he finally did he slipped out of consciousness. Bates singing Clash lyrics in his ear.

"And in the morning I woke up like an alarm went off," Wallace says, and makes a bell-ringing sound with his tongue against the roof of his mouth. "Pulled the IV out of my arm. Asked Bates for a bite of his Snickers."

"What happened?" Lydia and I ask at the same time.

"That's what the doctors wanted to know. They ran tests. Then they ran more tests to see if the first tests were right. Shook their heads. And Bates? The little bastard couldn't stop laughing. The nurses didn't know whether to kiss me or him, so they kept kissing both of us."

"You must have been touched by an angel," I say, working for sarcasm, but it cracks apart in my throat. "Only you would be deserving of a miracle."

"It wasn't a miracle," Wallace says evenly. "It was a question of odds. Most of the time it killed you, but sometimes it didn't. We aren't special enough for miracles, Crossman. We're just these hairless, sentimental animals that come and go. Barely smart enough to think we have a right to magic. But we're wrong about that, too."

"For Christ's sake, Wallace. How can you say that?" Barry launches in, but is forced to pause so he can finish spitting something up. "You're telling us that you'd been completely written off, and then, out of the blue, you get better. It's like you rose from the goddamn grave."

"Not resurrected," he corrects. "But maybe reincarnated, in a way. I came back as something else. More alive than the old thing ever was because the new thing knew what it was to die. I don't think about it now. There's only a chunk of time and the choices you make in that time. Nothing more."

"You've picked a lousy time to be spouting this atheist bullshit, kid."

"Who said I'm an atheist?"

"Sounds like that's what you're getting at."

"I've seen him, Barry. How can I not believe in him?"

"You've seen God down *here?*"

"When I was sick."

"And what form did he take? The old bearded guy in the robes? A burning bush? George Burns?"

"It was different from how they say it is in the checkout-counter tabloids," Wallace explains patiently. "There were no tunnels of light, beckoning voices, the fluffy sense of peace. I saw him in what he *wasn't*, in all the space he'd left behind. Like when you fall asleep during a party but when you wake up, everybody's gone—more alone than if there'd never been anyone in the room in the first place. But there *had* been, and they've left invisible marks behind. Like ghosts or something. That's what I saw. That God is the original phantom. And you know something? It was more comforting than you'd ever think. I saw that his love was in giving us the freedom to do whatever we pleased. After he'd set things up, he just moved on to wind up some other toy universe and let it go. He doesn't even look in on us every now and then. Remember being a kid and having the house all to yourself when your parents went away for the weekend? Like that. Except in this case, the parents never come back."

Another shiver runs through our connected bodies in the still heat.

Soon, though, there's the scratch of rain on the gate over the hole. Some of the drops even find their way through to fall upon our hoods, seeping through to touch our skin. Although the existence of miracles has just been disproved, it's what they feel like all the same.

It's a common sort of fantasy, I suspect, but I believe I understand it better than anybody. You know the one: your entire life has been an elaborate experiment carried out by a mysterious, superior race. Martians, say, or angels. There to watch you react to artificial situations, with everyone around you actors, delivering their prescribed lines and you the only one improvising.

Over time, however, I have wondered if whoever is in charge of the experiment might not be so superior or mysterious. Maybe they're just people. Everyone you've ever known or glanced at across a subway car or shared a bed with. Observers. And you're the only one not among them (the *isolated element*, according to the language of scientific method), alone in not seeing the contrivance behind every accomplishment and agony of your life. What proof could possibly follow from such an experiment? Perhaps none at all. None but the confirmation that human beings tend to keep going even after they suspect they are the subject of a humiliating experiment. And that shows something, doesn't it?

I'm starting to wonder if this place is part of the same study. Thirty-eight years of floating around, note taking, chronic insomnia and avoiding eye contact with others, and the Martian angels are beginning to lose patience with me. It's time to see how someone who has so far lived entirely in her head handles a real challenge. They want to bring me out. For me to occupy my flesh and be aware of it at the same time. And once I'm there, to then cut off all escape to the hiding places. Science. The imagination.

They want to kill me. But first they need me to see what killing is.

I'm not going to make it easy for them. I'm a translator, after all. An academic, a career third party, an unrequited lover—expert at in-betweens. I can stay in my head as long as anyone.

They make me watch what they do to Wallace last. I had counted two occasions that he had been taken up before this without me, and because he didn't speak of what happened, I can only guess they did the same thing each time. Our captors don't go in much for variety. Once you've been married to the method of their choosing, it is for life.

At first it seems like they've lost interest altogether. One of them removes my hood and the other two circle around Wallace but keep their distance. He is taller than they are even though he stands slightly bent. One of the gunmen stands apart and crosses his arms. Perhaps they have grown tired of this. They've run out of whatever it is that makes inflicting injuries on others fun. Perhaps their hesitation shows they are still the kind of men who might change their minds.

But it isn't hesitation at all, only another part of the performance. By making Wallace stand in the heat with the sack still on they want the terror to grow within him. He knows what will happen; it is only a question of when. Although it involves no direct violence, this waiting strikes me as worse than whipping or burning or being strung up by the wrists.

Then the gunman with his arms crossed steps forward and pulls the sack from Wallace's head. I'm not sure what I'm expecting to see in his face but whatever it is isn't there. Even the gunmen are a little surprised. He looks good. If anything, younger and more alive than the last time I saw him, when he was kissing Maria on the deck of the *Ana Cassia*.

A second later I notice that this impression isn't quite right. His cheeks are hollowed out. Lips spiked gray with dead skin. It's only his eyes that I don't expect.

The sun doesn't seem to bother him at all. In fact he looks directly up at it as he moves his head around and takes everything in, as though burning this hacked-out clearing and these men and the sky's white bulb onto a photographic negative. And when his eyes reach me I see that they are only lenses. Their clarity forces my own eyes away.

I tell myself that it is the look of a boy. That there is nothing special in it but an immature will, or perhaps the first touch of madness. But when I force myself to look again it reflects an image of myself back at me. And it is the picture of a shuddering coward, hands clasped between her thighs, squinting against shame as much as the light.

The gunman who had his arms crossed steps behind Wallace to slam a boot against the backs of his thighs. There is a wince at the sensation of the boot but only that.

When I look again the gunman has pulled a revolver from his holster. It's one of those old kinds, with a spinning chamber in the middle of its body and a long barrel. He walks in a lazy circle to step in front of Wallace, holds the revolver loosely before the boy's face so that it dangles off the end of his fingers. There's something vulgar in the way he does this, as if he might ease the barrel past Wallace's lips. Wallace looks at the gun, but in the same way he looks at everything else.

Soon the gun's snout rises like a blood-stiffened erection. When it is lifted even, the gunman presses it between Wallace's brows. Pushes so hard that he is bent backward, but not so far that he falls. The gunman keeps him there in an awkward balance for what may be a full minute. Then he pulls the trigger.

The click of the hammer is quieter than I could have guessed it would be. But what's startling is that as soon as it happens, it happens again.

A look of surprise passes between the other men. A look that confirms that he didn't do it twice like that the last time.

Then the one with the revolver does something that surprises the other gunmen even more. Steps behind Wallace, unties him and puts the gun into the boy's right hand.

"¡Dispara!" the gunman tells him, and sticks a finger against his own temple to show what he means.

And without pause—so swiftly that he is halfway to doing it before he could possibly understand what he's been asked to do—Wallace lifts the revolver to his skull and pulls the trigger.

Another click.

Wallace hands the gun back to the gunman.

The others laugh. Clapping their hands and smacking my face until I make a show of joining them. But none of it can entirely hide their impressed shock. The boy they thought would be even less than a boy, an *American* boy, did it again. Just like the last two times. Didn't even stop to close his eyes.

The one with the revolver pulls the hood back over Wallace's head, ties it around his neck tighter than before. Then he motions to the other gunmen, opening the round chamber and repeatedly poking his finger into it. Telling them that the next time they bring this one up from the hole, he will add the other five bullets to the one already there.

"Elizabeth, are you here?"

"I'm here."

"Who else?"

"Just me."

"And Bates? I can feel him too."

"He's asleep. They took Wallace and Barry up a while ago."

Breathing. A calculation of words and the air they will require.

"Can you wake me up the next time they take Wallace out?"

"Sure."

"Do you promise?"

"I promise. But why?"

"I just need to know. Every time they take him and he comes back it makes me think we might still get out of here. And I have to get out of here."

"Your baby."

"How did you—I *told* you, didn't I?"

"You'll get out."

"I have to."

"Don't worry. You're going—"

"I have to have this baby, Elizabeth. I need to help someone."

It is very still in the hole now. The air heavy as the lead apron they put over you before taking your x-ray. It must be mid-afternoon up there. And through the stillness Lydia whispers to me. It is another of the stories each of us tells if only to know they have been told.

Had I read that story in the newspapers a year and a half ago? About the young mother charged with killing her two children? Remember? The ones in the bathtub? The mother's defense was that she had slipped on the wet bathroom floor and knocked herself out against the side of the toilet bowl, and in the time it took her to regain consciousness her two-year-old and six-month-old children both drowned, in no more than four inches of water, so close to their mother that when she woke her outstretched hands were still dripping from the spray of their struggle.

No, I wouldn't have read about it in Canada. This happened in a rowhouse suburb of Manchester. One of those real-people-tragedies-of-the-week they love so much in the British papers. Front page for five days straight and then it disappears, as though they'd made a mistake, it never happened in the first place, so may we now direct your attention to the rock star auto-erotic suicide or the schoolgirls abducted outside the Marks and Spencer in Leeds? In this case, however, there was no mistake. The woman was Lydia's only sister.

Lydia had never actually seen the bodies in the tub, of course. But she lived with the image of them as though she had, as though it was she and not her sister who had been the one to raise her head from the floor and find her two babies floating there, faces up. And more. Jessica's curls glued across her brow, eyes pallid and round as quail eggs. David, the little one, with fingers dug in his ears to block out the sound of his sister's skin screeching against the bottom of the tub. A vision of familial sympathy taken to gothic extremes. And something else. A picture Lydia needs to experience as a memory from her own life. She wants this baby for her sister. But there is something just for Lydia, too. She wants the baby to bring her back into the world.

For a time the heat pushes Lydia's words aside. I try to separate the pieces of her story into organized piles, but the work it involves brings a threatening tingle to the backs of my eyes and I give up before it claims me.

"I heard you and Wallace," Lydia eventually continues with a gasp.

"Maybe we should rest now. Talking only dehydrates you."

"I'm dried up already."

"Still, you should think about—"

"I *heard* the two of you. That Wallace thinks somebody brought these men to our boat."

"He told me you were asleep."

"It got through anyway. In a dream. Have you noticed that down here it's hard to tell the difference?"

"I suppose I have."

"Was it you, Elizabeth?"

"Me what?"

"Did you make this happen? Did you do this to us?"

Even in this dark I can see black spots play against my closed eyelids. The blood draining down and leaving me half here.

"No, it wasn't me," I say. "If it was anyone at all."

"Well, I guess it doesn't matter much one way or another. When we get out of here, I think I'll be able to forgive anything."

"You sound confident."

"Wallace said he's going to do something."

"There's saying and then there's doing."

"They're the same for him."

"You seem to think he's Superman or something. You think he's that good?"

"I think he's capable of anything. Does that make him good? I'm not sure. Have you ever really looked into his eyes?"

"Not since they put a sack over my head."

"You're trying to be funny."

"Tell me. What did I see when I peered so deeply into young Wallace's skull? Stock options? A computer chip?"

"You would have seen nothing at all."

"An empty shell."

"It's more that he's purged. There is nothing in him that would get in the way of his desire. And that's an extraordinary thing. You look into him and it's like a glimpse of freedom. Extraordinary."

Her voice falls away and I know that she is gone with it. It takes us more and more suddenly now, long fingers pushing through the earth to pull us back. No light, little food or water. The things the gunmen do. For how long? However long it takes them to separate our bodies from us. We might live a few days more, but it will only be this. Slipping in and out.

I try to find the pain again but it seems to have gone as well. Now there is nothing to mark being here but these thoughts as I have them, although the ones from only a moment ago have skittered off like pantry mice.

I had been talking. Been talked to. I had made a promise. I suppose it will have to be broken if I can't remember what it is.

Then the witch's fingers coming through the soil to pull me down.

We touch each other's hurt in the dark.

They've stopped tying our hands behind our backs and now we search for our bodies. Lydia's feet as swollen and moist as water wings. Barry's broken wrists corrugated with scars. The blotches of heat randomly spotted over Bates's skin like an unfinished game of connect-the-dots. Fingers looking for the point of contact to have it acknowledged. To heal. Except for Wallace, who, although neither of us has said a word about it, lets us know that he has been hurt in a different way.

"Nothing?" Wallace asks, as though into a pause in an ongoing conversation. He means the way there's no pain on me.

"So far," I say.

"And when they take you up alone?"

"More nothing."

"Why *not* you, Crossman?"

"I don't know. They need me to interpret for them, I guess."

"Interpret what? They haven't *asked* us anything."

"Take it easy, man," Bates tells him. "We're all in the same trouble."

"Apparently not. Crossman hasn't been whipped yet. Or been hung from a tree. As it turns out, we are *not* in the same trouble."

"I want out of here as much as you do," I say.

"And you're planning to do *what*, exactly, to that end?"

"I'll talk to them."

"I have doubts. With all due respect, Crossman, I have serious doubts that you'll do fuck all."

I can feel them looking at me in the double darkness, through the rice sacks, the closed air. Summoning my face to their minds just as clearly as if I were sitting before them under a noon sun. They aren't limited by surfaces anymore. In blindness, the skin doesn't prevent you from seeing within.

"I'm not going to die here," Wallace continues. "It's too dirty, and it smells bad. No offense. But I'm sure you all feel the same. So let's play focus group. The question is: How do we leave? Lydia, you first."

"Give them what they want."

"Thank you, but we've covered that already, remember? The problem is, we don't *know* what they want. I've handed over my Swatch and my Blockbuster card, and Barry has given them his Lambda Chi Alpha fraternity ring. They weren't interested. Bates?"

"We have to kill them."

"*Now* you're talking. *Kill them.* Say it again, but slower this time, in case anyone missed it."

"*We have to kill them.*"

"Excellent! Now, Barry. You're the American. How do we do that?"

"Do what?"

"Kill the bastards that strung you up, man."

"Do?" He pauses. "Nothing. There's nothing to *do*. And even if we had something to work with—"

"A weapon, you mean."

"—anything like that, once you put it in your hands and try to use it to . . . When a man stands between . . . Well, my bet is you couldn't."

"Couldn't *kill* these assholes? Is that what you mean? These apes who pulled us out of our nice eco-vacations and stuck us in this outhouse shit pit? Are you saying some *moral imperative* or something should prevent us from doing them harm?"

"It's hard to kill another man."

"Well listen to you," Wallace comes close to shouting, slaps the backs of his hands against the mud wall. "I'd like to know where all that inspirational Tony Robbins power thinking we hired you for has disappeared to. Perhaps you don't recognize our situation here. These people aren't going to let us go. I figure with the diet they've got us on we're dead in less than a week if we don't do something. But none of you are being terribly helpful with the brainstorming here. You're scared. You're tired. You think Crossman may be right. Fine. I'll come up with something of my own."

"Give it up, Wallace," I say. "Doing something stupid isn't going to help. We just have to hang tight for a bit longer."

"*A bit longer?* We've only been down here—what?—three days? Four at the outside? And we've pretty much packed it in. What good is *a bit longer* going to do?"

"They might let us go."

"Unlikely. By the looks of things, that is rather motherfucking unlikely."

Even this much discussion exhausts us. It's like we're all learning a difficult foreign language without a teacher.

"I have a question," Wallace tries again, his voice still strong, though quieter now. "A very simple yes or no type of question, to which I'd like an answer from each of you. Am I the only one here who wants to live?"

But nobody answers. Maybe they've passed out already, too weak for any thoughts but those of home. Wallace remains awake, though. I can feel the air from inside of him filling the hole. And I take it in with the idea that I have something to say. But before I can find the right language I too fall asleep.

Wallace was right to doubt that the gunmen didn't know what they were looking for. In fact, their inquiries were perfectly direct. They want to know about the perfect bomb.

Ransoms are messy, they said, and take too long, all those phone calls and the irritation of a police crackdown that comes after every "international incident." And for what? A couple hundred thousand dollars? They could get that anytime. A single briefcase of coke on the next flight to Miami or Heathrow would just about cover it. But we were special. We had a secret. The plans for a breakthrough explosive that could make them the richest guerrillas in Colombia.

I told them they were wrong. That it was only the stupid boasting of a boy in a whorehouse for the first time, coming up with the most dangerous thing he could think of. Jesus Christ, do we look like nuclear weapons experts?

Yes, they said. You do.

And perhaps they are right. What would the makers of the perfect bomb look like, anyway? They might as well be Wallace and Bates, clever boys with a talent for envisioning large-scale change and an indifference to the distinctions between building and breaking. Or maybe they think it's Barry, the kind of good-natured American who helped put men on the moon. You'd never think him capable of anything more strenuous than eighteen holes and a gin-and-tonic afterwards, but he's the sort who might also have some ideas about wiping out half a continent with the flick of a switch. And Lydia. Even these bandits know that women are getting better and better every day at appreciating the economy of violence.

It could be any one of us. They don't care who. They'll keep hurting us all until we let them know what they want, and if we don't, they'll kill us. I've known this from the second hour of our arrival. As soon as they figured out that I was the only one who could understand them— but also the only one who knew nothing of any importance—they decided they would play a game: torture the others until they talked to me. That's why they bring me up to the surface to watch. They want my observation of each of their suffering to become my own. Then they will put us all back down in the hole and leave the job of getting answers out of them up to me. To be the parasite finding a way inside.

Which I would do if they knew anything. I'd hand over the ingredients to the perfect bomb along with taxi fare to buy them if they would just let us go. I'd offer any lie if they might believe it. I attempted one early on, in fact, about how the plans were on a disk in the safe at our São Paulo hotel—this was as James Bond–sounding as anything I could think of—and if they released us we would courier them to their jungle headquarters as soon as we got back. This resulted in Bates having a lit cigarillo placed between the cheeks of his ass.

I was left with only the truth. Told them that the people in the hole are Internet entrepreneurs, not military physicists. Whatever the gunmen had been told by their contacts in Manaus was incorrect. If it is political types they're after, they wanted the other boat, not ours. And besides, even then it's only Canadian political types, which hardly makes it worth anyone's while. Let's face it. They'd been misinformed. It happens.

They'd stopped responding to any of these lines of argument some time ago. Now when I speak to them I offer only questions of my own.

Who told you about the bomb, anyway?

We just know, they said.

What would you do if you had one?

Sell it. Use it. Both.

Who's in charge?

The *commander*, stupid.

Is the commander that tall man I've seen at the edge of the clearing once or twice, the one who looks something like the concierge from the Tropical Hotel?

We have no concierge. What is a concierge?

So they will kill us. Sooner or later, according to the rules of the game that we were bound to lose from the beginning. I haven't told the others this yet in the name of preserving some measure of hope, but I'm not sure it's making any difference. Perhaps some of us are wishing for them to end it anyway. Bring us up for a last breath of real air and they can get on with whatever they have in mind.

And yet, even now, Wallace isn't the only one who wants to live.

It is a rather obvious desire, but still surprising when you truly face it for the first time. *I want to live.* Not to go home necessarily, or to right the wrongs of the past, or any such broad transformation. But to translate. To have at least one story to tell of my life, even if it's not my own.

In the hole we pass dreams between each other. At the moment it's the one from Wallace's childhood. The one where he's a ghost.

He knows even in his dream that wanting to be a ghost is a perverse ambition, something that would upset his mother if he told her. But she's dead now. His father, too. Besides, there are a good many things in death he can see as an advantage. To be a spirit and nothing else, rid of all the clammy, pimpled things that could fail or turn ugly. The eternal torment that supposedly comes along with a restless afterlife strikes him as overstated, a fearful adult myth told to children, like growing potatoes behind your ears if you don't wash there. It can't be so painful—where could pain come from if you were nothing?—it's only that it goes on and on. He can still *see*, can't he? Pass, Casper-like, through bedroom walls. Hide keys. Blow cold breath across the faces of those too occupied with living to see him.

But at the end of this dream it turns on him. He knows something bad is going to happen when he finds himself flying over a winter forest flooded white with snow. It is like any other northern forest but he still recognizes it, even at night, a thousand feet over the spiked tops of spruces.

He lowers in tightening circles as a hawk does until he lands beside a shape in the drifting snow. A boy. This is what it appears to be, although its face is concealed by the hood of its parka. The boy is asleep, but Wallace knows that he is dying also. For the first time as a ghost he is afraid.

Wallace bends down to hold the boy in an effort to keep him warm, but he has nothing to offer. His blood cold as the wind.

He stays with him through the night. He will stay with him forever. But because he is not alive he can't make anything happen, or prevent it from happening.

With the first pale hints of morning, he looks directly at the boy's sleeping face. Sees that it is Bates. The only face he could recognize from the living world, except now prematurely aged, freeze-dried. The color dwindling out of his skin and leaving only the blue taint of frostbite.

The expanding weight inside of Wallace presses him into a human shape. He looks down at the dying boy and feels solidified. His heart shocked into labor, brought back to earth by the gravity of love.

6

A boy's face sprayed with blood. Halloween-style. Each tooth outlined in red, as though from eating too many cherry gob stoppers. Eyes that want a push back into their skull. A boy looking altogether too amused for his own good, from speaking a dirty word, an act of vandalism, something cruel and thrilling. I blink against the light wavering behind his head. But when I open my eyes again the boy is still there. Closer now, panting. There is an awful lot of blood.

"We're getting out of here," the boy says in a strange whisper, almost choked with what could be either panic or delight. With his words the blood seems to thicken on his face.

And it's not a boy at all. It's Wallace.

"We're getting the fu-*uck* out of here," he says again.

"What's happened?"

"I did it."

"Did what?"

"I *fuck*ing did it, man."

I don't know what he's talking about but I believe him just the same. Look at his face, inches from mine in the cramped hole. What's left of what used to be his face. Oh, he *did* it, all right.

His features loom closer and for a second I'm sure he's going to kiss me. Instead he leans his jaw into my neck so that he can stretch his arms out full behind him. There's the rattle of his breath in my ear, a sound that might be a high giggle.

"You're going to have to move," he whispers against my cheek, so that it seems the words come from inside my own mouth. "You have to help me. And be as fast as you can."

When he pulls back from me the liquid spots on the side of his face have been smeared, and I know he has left some of it on my shirt, my skin.

"What's going on, Wallace? What have you done?"

"*Jesus*, Crossman. Would you wake up? He's getting us out."

Bates's voice. I turn to find it and there he is, hands held out before his eyes as though he can't believe they're still connected to the rest of him.

Of course Wallace had taken Bates's hood off first. Why did I think he might have decided to confide in me before anyone else? To gain my confidence before feeling able to carry out whatever plan he has already started on? Why, among all the thoughts I have a right to be thinking at this moment, is the one that registers hurt the very first?

"Crossman. Are you *with* us?"

It's the bloody boy again. I can't be certain, but I believe he may have preceded this question by slapping my face.

"Yes. I'm sorry," I tell him, hiccuping. "What shall we do?"

"You *shall* wake up Barry, and Bates will wake Lydia. Meanwhile, I'm going to think for a second. Catch my breath."

He needs to. Whatever he did up there that left stains like the ones he has must have required considerable exertion. Yet Wallace is more crazed with exhilaration than shock. There's a terrible electricity coursing the length of him, showing itself in random twitches and grunts. He leans against the earth wall, and for a time I watch the darting movement of his eyeballs behind his lids. I'm not sure I can move just yet. And now, feeling the gray light falling on my cheeks like warm powder, I'm more tired than ever before. We are free. Apparently. But I will definitely have to get some sleep before doing a thing to extend that freedom beyond—

"*Cross*man!"

Bates has grabbed me by the chin and pulled my gaze away from Wallace. Knocks the flat of his hands into my shoulders. Then does it again with more weight behind it. Within seconds a jittery energy is returned to me. The knowledge of where we are, what the gunmen will do if they see the gate lifted open, find us blinking against the dawn like puppies.

"Don't look at him," Bates whispers. "Don't do anything but take off Barry's hood, OK? Crossman?"

"No, I won't look," I repeat, and surprise myself by rising to my knees. Turn to the baggy figure that might be a man slumped next to me. "Barry," I say. "Wake up."

Once I finally coax my fingers into teasing out the knot around his neck, I pull the sack from Barry's head. He greets me with the smile of a blistered drunk.

"What did he do?" he says.

"Who?"

"*Wallace.* What did he do?"

"I don't know. But we're not clear yet. And we'll probably have to carry Lydia because her feet are so—"

"Wallace! Hey, man," Barry cuts me off. "I can't believe you did it."

Wallace may nod at him, or it may be the jerk of his heart pumping through his body.

"When we get back, I owe you something very, *very* good," Barry goes on. "How about all my Hypothesys start-up shares. Or my John Deere rider mower. I *love* that thing. Or my daughter! Regional Miss Georgia finalist, 1997. You can marry my only child, you clever bastard."

I'm expecting Wallace to shut him up at some point, but instead he allows Barry to finish before returning a smile of his own. The one that affirms his full participation in the fun, his born status as insider.

"I'll take your daughter," he says. "But you'd better throw your wife in, too."

"We can discuss that."

"We need to *leave* now."

"You're entirely right about that, Crossman." Wallace turns to me. "But we need to know how first."

"I suppose you're going to tell us?"

"You suppose right."

Lydia is with us now too. Her skin more pale than ever, her cheeks a fireworks of burst capillaries. And she has lost one of her front teeth. Now when she opens her mouth there is a space where her tongue bulges out, damming the trickle of blood that falls from her gums. But her eyes are here. Moving between us, reading our lips.

"I don't know how many of them there are." Wallace speaks directly to her, returning to his place against the wall.

"Are they up yet?" Bates asks.

"Not as of about three minutes ago."

"How did you get out of here in the first place?"

"I didn't have to. One of them opened the gate before the sun was out and took me up. Except this time he was alone. Started on his usual routine with me, but got a little overzealous. I, on the other hand, got his machete."

"Are you OK?" Bates asks him. "I mean, was it—"

"It was easy." Wallace exhales completely. "Once you get started on doing that to—well, it just *goes*."

He coughs now, and it's alarming to hear because it's not a cough at all but a laugh that he choked on before it made its way out.

"Now what?" I ask.

"We need to know what's out there." Wallace glances straight up, as though he means the last of the night's stars. "So we're going to go up to find their boats and see what we'll have to dance around to reach them. Then we'll come back, bring up the rest of you, and get the fuck out."

"We?"

"Me and Bates."

"I'm not so sure about that."

"What's your problem, Crossman? Lydia's obviously out—she can't walk. And Barry's not in commando shape at the moment, either."

"And what's my handicap?"

"You're just you."

"What the hell does that mean?"

"Nothing. Just that I don't know you as well. And three's a crowd."

"No way. I'm coming too."

"Is this a question of *trust* for you?"

"No, I'm only—"

"Jesus, Bates, would you listen to this? We'll have to add this one to the Hypothesys Sample Predicament Page, won't we? Even though there is grave danger involved, Crossman is wondering if that risk is worse than staying put while we tiptoe down to the river, hop on the first raft we find and never come back."

"I didn't say that. I just said I'm coming with you."

Wallace and Bates share one of their quick looks.

"Fine," Bates says almost immediately. "But we lead the way, and you stay quiet."

"Absolutely. A question first, though. Do we have anything to protect ourselves with?"

"My friend offered some assistance there," Wallace says and nods down. For the first time I notice a machete almost blackened with corrosion leaning against his thigh. One of the big ones, long as a baseball bat. And next to it, its snout nuzzled into the earth, an old field rifle, with a manual pump curled underneath the trigger.

"I would have thought you'd have a pistol, too," I say. "If the guy you took care of is the same one I'm thinking of."

"Very good, Crossman," he says, and gives me another of his smiles, although this one carries a less welcoming message than the one he offered to Barry. "Unfortunately for him, he had different plans for me today. A mistake. Any other questions?"

There are none. None that any of us have the courage to ask. Even when Wallace hands the rifle to Bates and pulls the machete out of the bare earth for himself—leaving me unarmed—I say nothing. They're leading the way and I was the one to demand the right to follow them. If there is to be any killing, the task falls to them. And at least one of them has some recent experience of that.

Wallace stands, hooks his fingers up over the side of the hole, and with a little jump, hauls himself to the surface. After all the time we've spent down here it's a surprise to see how easy it is to get out. In my mind the distance up to the light had lengthened, so that we were all sitting at the bottom of an empty well. But it's only what a couple of strong men with spades could dig out in an afternoon.

Still, I end up requiring some assistance. I knew I wouldn't be in top-notch shape after several days of white rice and twisted sleep. But I believed I was still thinking well, and so assumed my body would have more or less kept pace. Throwing my hands up to Wallace and Bates and having them lift me up, my feet scrabbling against the wall like a baby fighting against being put into its stroller, I realize I was wrong. I'm poured rubber, undisciplined and pliant. I'm Stretch Armstrong.

When I finally assemble myself on the ground I'm too breathless to whisper an apology. Which wouldn't have made a difference anyway. Wallace and Bates are already bent at their middles, hovering smooth and fast over to the trees at the edge of the circle of ash left from the gunmen's bonfire.

How do they know to do that? A way of moving that is at once absurd and familiar. Where have I seen men do that very thing before? Movies. Teenaged Americans blasting their way through rice paddies and Communism. Then they're waving me over to their position in the deepening shade and I'm doing the same. Folded at the waist, head down, dashing across the clearing with an imaginary M-16 slung low in my arms.

And nearly trip over a man's half-naked body.

Rolled face down into the earth, as though dropped from a great height. His shirt twisted into a headless snake beyond his grasping fingers. Shorts around his knees. No shoes. A gold-studded ear lying six inches from where it should be. Everything else cross-hatched with cuts.

He had different plans for me today.

The body more carved than torn. Liquid stripes of him now percolating up, each fissure blurred with flies. A white bracelet laid down the length of his back that is his spine, humped up to show its string of disks to the light.

A mistake.

Each of his buttocks methodically split open. A thick, almost clear mucus spilled over the flesh like two pierced egg yolks.

I wouldn't be able to move if it weren't for Wallace and Bates waving me over from where they stand at the edge of the trees. I step over the dead man and imagine myself passing through the floating spirit or aura or whatever it is that might be now exiting his body. But I don't feel a thing.

When I join them Wallace gestures, poking two fingers at his eyeballs. I shake my head. But I wasn't really looking for anyone, either.

Then Wallace is trotting out into the clearing again. Bates four strides behind him, his head turning to look into the thatch of low branches, then snapping back to check the tents. I hang back, part of me thinking that if something bad is to happen, I could still skip back to the hole, close the gate over my head and hope not to be noticed.

Even though I had been up here several times since the gunmen took us, their camp seems ragged and harmless now that we're viewing it on our own. The jagged charcoal of the fire pit, the red and yellow nylon of the tents, all muted in the smoky dawn. No larger than a football endzone.

We have to get within ten feet of the tents to start on the trail down to the river. Three of them clustered in a rough circle, each of a size that could sleep four. The front flaps zipped down to the bottom and tied in tight, delicate bows. The mosquitoes bother even pitiless guerrillas, apparently. But in the passing of another thought we'll be beyond them, into the cover of leaves and the first morning screeches coming down from the trees—

Wallace stops where the trail begins. When Bates and I freeze behind him we notice how much sound we've been making since emerging from the hole.

Someone rolls over inside one of the tents. Sighs.

Why won't Wallace move? Close enough to shake the poles of the nearest tent by just reaching out his hand. And maybe he will do just that.

We stand here for close to a minute. Maybe longer. Ahead of me, Bates's knees start to shake.

From within another tent, the trombone slide of a fart.

At this, Wallace finally moves. Turns his head back to us. *Smiling.* But before it can get too far the smile is gone, replaced by an index finger across his lips. It's hardly necessary. We're being as quiet as we can already. I'm not sure I've taken a breath since I climbed out of the hole.

Wallace walks on. Down the trail no wider than a broad set of shoulders such as his. Leaves slapping against them, whispered protests against his movement. Surely enough manmade sound to wake them. And I will be the first to find out if it does. Last in line and still close enough to the tents that I can smell the bodies of those inside them.

The light pushed stronger in irregular increments, as though by jabs at a dimmer switch. Soon the heat will force the gunmen from the tents. And the trail is longer than I remember it being when we arrived. A wandering course down toward a still invisible river.

"Wallace," Bates says.

Just his name to voice his concern. But Wallace keeps pushing on, taking us down in this ways and thats.

And comes to a fork. One arm of the trail carrying on in the direction we had been heading, the other off sharply to the right. Without pausing, Wallace makes the turn.

After about fifty yards I'm about to call ahead to ask if he knows where the hell we're going, or maybe just to speak his name as Bates had done, when Wallace holds still again. Raises his hand above his head for silence.

I can see nothing from where I am except for Bates's sweat-blotted back. But there's something definitely new about wherever we are. The sound of water. Not the big river but a smaller one off it. Tiny waves making polite applause against a sand shore.

Wallace lowers into his movie-soldier crouch again and enters another clearing. More narrow than the camp's, though this one is naturally made, the trees standing arm-in-arm along a line of beach. Beyond it, a sluggish creek no more than forty feet across, concealed from the big river by an almost ninety-degree bend off to the left. And there before us three longboats nudged up onto the sand. A perfect place for them. The riverboats that must pass on the Negro every once in a blue moon wouldn't have a clue that there is anyone here.

The idea of jumping in the closest one and steering it out right now is distracting enough that at first I don't notice him.

A man bent down at the back of the third canoe hammering a wrench at its outboard engine. He doesn't hear us step out of the trees and form a semicircle around the prow. The air vibrating with the metallic clang of the wrench. His breathing slightly labored, punctuated by frustrated grunts—he's been at this for a while.

For a time we do nothing but watch him. We cannot think of acting ourselves until he is finished.

The boatman eventually wipes his hands on a rag tucked into his jeans and rights himself. Grabs the engine's ignition cord and rips it back. It starts with a bubble of blue smoke. Loud as a chain saw and with a rattling that can't be good. But going. The boatman places his hands on his hips in satisfaction.

Wallace points at the boatman. As plain as it is, I'd forgotten that if we came across anyone, we would have to try to kill them.

Bates slides the end of the gun up under his chin and aims at the center of the boatman's back. Keeps it there as he turns his head around to Wallace. Asks permission with his eyes, his trembling chin. Not to know if the timing or his aim is right, but to be told whether, under the circumstances, firing a bullet between a man's shoulders without the man's being aware of it is an acceptable course of action.

Wallace nods. Once.

Without turning back to look where the shot is going to end up, Bates pulls the trigger.

It jams.

Or doesn't fire, no matter the reason. But it does manage to make a high-pitched *flink* that turns the boatman away from his work to take a look at us.

What could he possibly be thinking? Unlike Bates's face, his doesn't betray a thing. The only gesture he offers is to let his hands float up to wipe the machine oil from his palms onto his T-shirt. Black smears over the decal ironed to the front. An "In Concert!" photograph of Britney Spears.

The boatman looks at the rifle and appears to be wholly familiar with its mechanical shortcomings, for instead of seeing it as his most immediate concern he steps onto the beach and looks at Wallace. To the machete he holds at his side.

"*¿Cómo obtuviste eso?*" he asks. *How did you get that?*

By way of response, Wallace is already taking a step forward. Deliberate, his back held straight. The posture of a young soldier summoned to have a medal pinned to his chest.

Wallace raises the machete high with both hands.

The boatman looks past him, at us, searching for confirmation. He wonders if this is about to happen as it appears it is. *This* boy? The American who is in fact not an American whose distinguishing characteristics lie in being the only one of us not to cry and to have shown some notable luck with the pistol game? *He* is going to use that thing on me? How did he even get down here in the first place?

The boatman has many other questions in addition to these. But Wallace leaps off the end of his toes to bring his weight down where the blade meets the boatman's collarbone and all of his questions are knocked out of him.

It doesn't bring him all the way to the ground, though. The boatman slumps to one knee. Hands stuck out in front of him, his fingers linked together in a pose of marriage proposal.

Wallace stays at him. A straightforward lunge to the chest knocks the boatman back, legs kicking at the air. Followed by a red halo widening out from Britney's cleavage.

"Oh, fuck," Bates says, almost brightly.

Wallace stands directly over the fallen body now, one foot on each side of the man's hips. For a moment I'm certain he is about to drop his weapon as well as his zipper and piss on the boatman's face.

But this is only my impatience. Wallace is doing his utmost. The boatman simply won't die as swiftly as the cinematic precedent.

Look: Now there are clouts direct to the forehead. A dozen in a row until it cracks open. A glimpse of white noodles within.

Now it's jackhammering the sharp end into his stomach. This is softer. And produces more fluid than you would ever guess could be contained there, within the neatly organized pouches and bags. More a stirring than cutting through sinew.

The option of turning my head away never presents itself.

"Oh, fuck," Bates says again when Wallace finally turns to him, his tongue hanging over his lips as though trying to escape his mouth altogether.

"I'm done," Wallace says.

"He's still moving a little," Bates tells him.

"That's just what they do."

"Did the other one do that too?"

"Don't watch if you can't—"

"I can handle it."

"Fine then. Count to ten and he'll be gone."

Bates actually counts out loud.

One, two, three . . .

I'm not even here. They are doing it together, sharing whatever is to be taken away from this. Each second given its own name over the sputtering growl of the outboard.

. . . five, six . . .

Bates watches the boatman die. Wallace watches Bates. And I'm not here.

On the count of eight the boatman lies still.

"You were right," Bates says. "Not even ten."

"I'm two-for-two."

They share a single laugh.

"*Stop it!*"

"What?"

"What?"

"What the fuck do you think you're doing?"

"What?"

"What?"

I sidestep the boatman's head to turn off the outboard. It finishes with a cough, or laugh, in an echo of Wallace and Bates's.

"I said, what are you doing?"

"We're doing *something*, Crossman." With one stride Wallace is standing closer than I thought he could have. "As opposed to your preferred course of doing sweet fuck all. So *don't* play the lacy lady all of a sudden and tell us that this is too monstrous and yucky and you can't believe it's really happening. OK? You haven't earned that yet."

Without realizing it, Wallace has raised the machete even with his waist. I look down at my stomach, the skin exposed from my T-shirt being tied in a knot under my breasts. I'm pinker than I would have thought. Soft.

"C'mon. Let's keep it together here," Bates says. "We have to go back. Get the others."

"Shouldn't someone stay here?"

"With him?" Wallace looks down at the boatman. Touches the end of the machete against the tip of one of his Nikes. "What's the point? We'll all go. It might not be too easy hauling Lydia and Barry down here, anyway."

Wallace starts back up the trail before I can say anything more. And what would I say if he had waited? Not a thing, I suppose. It's what I might do that never has the chance to happen. If things were only slightly different I would let Wallace and Bates wander off, start up this engine again and try my luck on my own. But I know them too well to do that now. Or want to know them. And the idea of being alone with the boatman's corpse even for a moment, staring up with its lips pursed as though waiting for the answer to a question he'd asked long ago—

So I'm following them again. This time, going uphill, I feel the problem of my own exhaustion. Palms pushing off my knees for leverage. Mouth so wide open for air my jaw aches.

When we come into the clearing again it looks the same except for an added layer of colors. It's morning now. The indecision of only minutes before replaced by compressed daylight. Yet the gunmen still sleep.

Wallace and Bates share another of their looks and this time I join them in understanding it. We have taken too long. The pirates should be up by now and it's only sheer luck that they aren't. Or perhaps they aren't asleep at all and sit waiting for us somewhere just out of sight.

We look across the clearing. The opened gate over the hole impossibly distant in the new light. And beside it the hunched form of a man, his head lowered almost into his lap. A Raggedy Andy that's had all the cotton ripped out of him.

When he catches sight of us, Barry shows us the muddy elbows he used to climb out. Manages a one-fingered wave.

And with this child's gesture, the naive certainty that we would return for him, the possibilities of what we might do next are immediately taken away. Barry's wave decides everything.

We're running forward, not even bothering to circle around the long way using the overhang of tree limbs for cover. A bad tingling down my legs. A roar in my ears like hearing the tide in a conch shell.

Keeping my eyes on Barry's to hold back the black dots that now crowd my vision—

—Lydia still down in the hole, weeping just to see us again. Barry explaining how he'd tried to bring her out himself so that they'd both be ready to go when we got back, but his broken wrists wouldn't let him hold on to her, and the effort left him feeling not so good.

"Bates, go stand on the other side," Wallace says.

The two of them bend down to take each of Lydia's forearms. Then they bring her up, pulling at her like a wishbone.

"I don't think I can walk," she says when they set her down next to Barry. We look at her feet. Two unidentifiable lumps of meat, the sort of thing you might see hanging in a Chinatown butcher's window.

"We'll help you," Wallace says. Strokes the back of his knuckles over her cheek.

"You're bleeding," she says.

"It's not my blood."

"Thank God."

"But we have to go right *now*, Lydia."

She nods. We all nod.

"We'll run straight across to those tents," he goes on. "Beside them, there's a path to the river. Before you get all the way down, it forks— go right. That's where the canoes are. I'm going ahead in case they wake up before we get that far. Crossman and Bates, you help Lydia. And Barry, all you have to do is follow them."

"What if they come—"

"Is there a meeting place that—"

But Wallace is already striding across the clearing.

We do as we've been told.

Bates and I rope Lydia's arms over the backs of our necks and manage to lift her high enough that her shins snag and scratch over the roots. The sun pops higher into the top branches. And with it the heat. If I was struggling against passing out before, now every step with half of Lydia strapped to my back is an act of defiance against the black dots.

It's obvious after only the first few seconds that we're not going to make it. I'm certain I can feel Bates's agreement in the way his arm stiffens over mine. The way we hesitate before taking our next step to see if one of us will be the first to stop altogether, and it will end without our having to think, *It was me.*

Yet we keep going. In a way that could hardly count as actual progress, little more than an extended falling forward. Our heads down to push out everything else. The way the tents come no closer even though we shuffle toward them with a persistence we have no right to.

But we sneak peaks every third or fourth step anyway. Not to check how far we've come but to make sure Wallace is still ahead of us. So long as he is, we seem able to make it to the next time we raise our heads.

When we are only halfway across both Bates and I take another look. And Wallace is there, on the far side of the fire circle. Except now he stands perfectly still.

"Hey!" Bates whispers. "What are you—"

It's then that we see the two gunmen standing outside the tents. Arms hanging limp at their sides. One of them is naked. His penis still asleep in its nest of pubic hair.

Bates is the first to recognize what is about to happen. Starts dragging Lydia toward the cover of the forest. But he does it before I can move with him, and her arm, still clung tight around my neck, topples me to the ground.

The whole time I'm keeping my eyes on the naked gunman. Watch him calmly stoop, poke his head inside the tent nearest him and emerge with a pistol. Looks down at it for a second with what may be fondness. Clicks something next to the handle. Aims at us.

If Wallace doesn't move first I'm certain I will stay where I am, watching. But he jerks in the opposite direction that Bates and Lydia have started for, his arms waving over his head like an enraged orangutan.

What happens now?

A lot happens now.

There is no order to it, but it doesn't collide together all at once, either. It simply arrives.

Gunshots.

From guns of various calibers, champagne corking and cannon booming and castanet rattling at the same time. Shattering the air as if it were glass. All a *bit much*, as Lydia might say. Yet the bullets act the way I'd imagined them to. Ripping the bark off tree trunks, plugging into the ground with puffs of dust, leaving vibrating trails of hard velocity behind them.

And other, more discernible motion all around me. There's my own scrambling to my feet (the angle of my view of the gunmen's tents is changing, so I must be doing something). Dark bodies pouring into and through the clearing.

I can see the opening in the brush I'm heading for although I don't turn my head to look. The same direction Bates and Lydia took. If you could go straight through it for a couple hundred yards you would come to the clearing where the boats are. More or less. I guess this is what Bates is trying to do as well.

All the while a chattering tickertape update on whether I've been shot yet.

No.

And now?

Don't think so.

How about *now?*

Well, there's definitely a part that *hurts* now. A number of parts. But whether it's a bullet or another flare-up from the hook in my back or something else entirely is anyone's—

—curious how someone could be conjuring these words in the midst of all this terrible activity. *Where is this coming from?* one part of me asks even as it's happening. And another part answers: *You'd be surprised.* The guns making a sound like deerflies around my ears. Feet burning through grass as serrated and stiff as steak knives. And meanwhile I'm making up *sentences* in my head. It comes automatically. Turning the thing that's happening around me into something *inside* me. All I'm certain of is that I don't scream once the entire time—

—thrown into the green with eyes closed. The forest holding me back but with a sickening amount of give, like running into a cobweb of elastic bands. Nothing but the idea of something close behind me that I have to stay in front of. It may be Barry. It may not.

147

Then I'm flying.

Launched up from my last push forward, rolling off the balls of my feet. Some part of me should have met the ground by now but the ground has been pulled away. When I open my eyes I'm expecting to look down at the jungle canopy from above, fingertip-to-wingtip with one of those pretty birds the tour guide had pointed out to us a lifetime ago.

But it's only me. Slamming my shoulder against the earth and rolling into the clearing where the canoes are.

"Where's Lydia? Crossman! Did you *see* her?"

Bates is leaning against the edge of the farthest canoe. His feet close enough to the dead boatman's head that he could kick it if he wanted to.

"You had her last," I say, spitting a wad of mud out of my mouth. It takes a dozen distinct motions to rise to my feet again.

"She was there and then she wasn't," Bates says. "I'd gotten her as far as the trees and then—I thought you might have picked her up as you came after me."

"Picked her up? She's not a handbag, Bates. And she was with you."

"You saw how fucked-up it got. They were shooting at us and there was a bump or something—I'm not sure. I think maybe she was hit."

"How do you know?"

Bates swipes at the air in front of his face. "She was there and then she wasn't."

"Or you dropped her. So you could move faster."

"No," he moans, but it's not a helpless sound. There's anger there, too. "I didn't *do* that. There's no *way* I'd do that."

"I'm just saying."

"You're saying shit. And where were *you* back there?"

"Lydia pulled me down."

"Please! *Pulled you down!*"

I'm expecting Wallace to join in this line of thought at any moment. But Wallace isn't here.

"He was here when I got here," Bates says, reading my mind. "I guess he worked his way around in a big circle. Then he ran back in to get Barry."

"Barry? What about me?"

"You're here now, aren't you?" Bates twitches in a way that may be a reconsidered shrug.

"Jesus, Bates. I was *in* there—"

The *tat-tat-tat* of machine-gun fire clamps my mouth shut. Not far off. Up the trail where it forks. Close enough that we can hear the rip of leaves as the bullets blast up through the canopy.

Both of us turn to the canoes. One heave off the sand and each of us could be drifting away on the current, around the bend and out of sight.

"They're coming," I say.

"We have to wait."

"If we hide downstream in one of the boats now, we could keep an eye out for them."

"No, Crossman."

"There won't be a chance for them to get out at all if we don't—"

The crunch of deadfall. There's something coming forward from the bush directly behind me. Even the boatman's eyes are fixed on it. Ivory globes, astonished.

There isn't time to do anything that might help. There is only time to look over my shoulder at whatever is already there.

"Crossman. Bates," Barry says. "I found Wallace for you."

And it does look like the big man might have attempted tackling Wallace, slung over the younger man's back as he is. But it is he who is being carried. Wallace breathing in puffs that flap his lips straight out.

"They got him," Wallace says.

At the same moment he tries to slide Barry off his back but, once he starts to go, the big man falls hard. Ends in a plump coil on the sand.

"They got him," Wallace says again.

And they have. Nothing too bad, at least relative to the boatman's injuries. But something has started showing itself just below his armpit. A circle of blood where a sweat stain should be.

"I'm OK," Barry says, following our eyes. Places his hand over the wound. "I think it went in and out. No kidding. It's nothing."

His tone is no longer filled out by the forced good humor of a moment ago. The salesman in him has finally evaporated, leaving him hollow. It's not because of his wound, either. It's because he's afraid. What he fears isn't the gunfire but the possibility that if he's injured too seriously, we'll leave him behind.

"So you found your way here too," Wallace says, turning to me.

"Somehow."

"And you didn't see Barry in there?"

"I didn't see *anything* in there."

"He was yelling his head off."

"I was just running. But if I'd seen or heard him I would have helped."

"Does that go for Lydia too?"

"Bates was the last one with her."

"I'm asking you."

"Shut up," Bates says to no one in particular.

"Don't you see that he's lost it, Bates?" I say, pointing at Wallace. "Look at him. Soaked in blood and skipping through the woods like a rabid animal—"

"*Shut up!*"

The instant quiet allows us to hear it.

At first it reaches us only as the statement of her terror, the recognition that they have her now and that she is alone. But then we can discern the words within it.

Lydia screaming out each of our names.

The trees play with the shape of the sound she makes. Push it back farther than it probably is, flatten out the space required for an echo. There is somehow still a movement to it though, as there is with a voice picked up in a shifting wind. Except there is no wind. Only this one sound. At once far away and somewhere just behind the curtain of green.

I say something. I'm not sure if I mean whatever I've said—I'm not sure *what* it means—but nobody seems to have heard me anyway.

I try it again. Louder. "We have to go back, Wallace."

"No." He says this without his head turning away from where he has set it.

"For God's sake. They're going to kill her."

"They're killing her now."

"We could stop them."

"More likely they'd kill us, too."

"Not if we go through the trees and stay off the trail. Pick them off with the rifle."

"The rifle doesn't *work*," Wallace says, finally opening his eyes to us, his voice sharpened. "And even if it did, what's our chances? *Pop*. One down. Then they're all over us. Besides, why do you think she's still screaming? Because they *want* us to go back. They're not sure what guns we may have down here, that's why they haven't followed us all the way yet. We gallop up there and we're the best dead cowboys in Brazil."

"If we do nothing we might be better off dead."

"Well that's *romantic*, Crossman. You're saying the things you're saying because you like Lydia and you know what they're doing to her and it's not nice. But we're sitting our asses in that canoe and getting out of here right now. If they don't get here first. So why are we pretending that we're making a decision when it's already made?"

It's words that stop us from going back up the trail to save Lydia. Wallace knows that with words, once you start, you have to hear the end of them. He brings us back to ourselves less through what he says than through the saying of it, deadening whatever it was that would have taken us raging into honor and returning us to the ground we're all used to. The distracting rhetoric of self-preservation. Reason. Judgment. Heroes are merely those who lack the benefit of words.

And without another one we put our hands under Barry's loose parts and dump them into the back of the nearest canoe. Push it out into the water and throw ourselves in after it.

Wallace clambers back to the engine to pull once, twice on the ignition cord. On the third try it shakes itself to life, rattles like a school bell. Wallace yanks the tiller against his chest and turns us around into a sharp curve, into the channel we guess leads to the big river. The branches slapping our faces. Fragrant stings on our skin.

From somewhere behind or ahead, Lydia's screams continue undiminished.

Bates covers his ears but this won't keep it out. I know because I've tried myself.

He will hear his name spoken by the jungle for as long as he remains in it. We know this even now. That this calling of our names marks the end of ourselves, and that whatever follows will be a second life. One spent trying to keep the first hours of this morning boarded up, forbidden, a haunted house that you cross the street to avoid walking in front of. Lydia shrieks our names but they aren't names anymore. They are an incantation. A spell that allows us to see what actually lies behind the skin of *who we are*, its brittle, untested protections. And what is revealed is little more than terror. The whole of our lives as the empty ritual of appearing normal in a world of normal things.

I look back at Wallace to see if he hears it too, but he only stares ahead. Perhaps to steer the canoe. Perhaps the rattle of the engine blocks out the sound for him alone.

Yet it is his name we hear more than any other. Starting from inside of Lydia but passed along by the leaves, telegraphed through the network of vines. Crossman, Barry, Bates—we will take our names with us. But Wallace's will stay here.

Another turn and for a moment it seems that we are headed inland again. But it is only the final bend of the creek's meanderings before the big river is laid out broad and fat before us.

There is no idea of north or south, or where, even if north or south were known, would be the better direction. So Wallace takes us straight into the chop in front of us.

Beyond the forest's reach there is a tremulous breeze over the water and we snap at it as if it is freshly baked bread. And then the idea of real food occurs to us. We look down the length of the canoe at what we might have brought along. A couple of five-gallon jugs of what is either water or gasoline. A plastic case no bigger than a toolbox that may contain something we might eat. Nothing more than this.

In the next instant our attention is returned to the shore. There is something growing along the braid of yellow sand next to the creek's hidden entrance. Emerging from the end of the main trail down from the camp.

By the time the first gunmen make it to the beach and pull the rifles off their shoulders we are too far away for them to make a good shot, though they try for a few rounds, the slight jolt of their upper bodies from the guns' concussion visible more than a second before we hear the crack of the air.

When they give up they have shrunk in the growing distance. Still distinct—a lick of dark hair, the orange flap of an untucked shirttail— but already less frightening, playful even, like hand puppets. Shouting at us now, hopping from one foot to the other in a show of childish rage. From here they could be performing a tribal dance, although awkwardly, like they'd only just recently learned to do it for the benefit of tourists.

And standing behind them, partway up the slope into the trees, a figure that is taller than the rest. Not shouting or hopping, just watching us go as someone who has seen such departures a thousand times before, and it is his job to simply take note of them. We are already too far to say for sure, to even say there is anyone there at all. But to me it can only be the concierge. Tall and wide as two men fused together. Surely he of all people would know a thing or two about comings and goings.

I turn to Wallace and Bates to see if they have shared this vision. Do they see the jumping men as dancers as I have, or hear their shouting as a savage song? Maybe they don't see the tall figure at all. Maybe he is meant only for me.

And it's true that when I return my eyes across our wake toward the river's edge there is nobody there any taller than the others, only toy soldiers now. Jostling G.I. Joes that could no more do harm to another human being than bring their tinfoil machetes down upon a woman to cut the screams out of her throat.

7

WHERE is all this blood coming from?

There certainly is enough of it to make you wonder, curling up in little whirlpools in the water that has seeped through somewhere along the twenty feet of the canoe's hull. None of us know exactly where that's coming from, either. Bates bails out what he can with an empty coffee tin, Wallace keeps a grip on the stuttering outboard, and Barry lies jackknifed across the prow, a sickly mermaid, eyes shut in a way unlike sleep. None of us have spoken for a good while. The last English we'd heard was a woman's screams.

Dawn long given way to morning, morning to the hard hours that brighten everything into pastels, like an old black-and-white movie that's been colorized. Each blink a snapshot of where we are: the hunched back of jungle, the chocolate river, two of those white parrot things that mate for life but spend the whole time screeching at each other.

When someone finally speaks, it's Wallace. And when he does it is the words of polite conversation between strangers, the banter of elevator and waiting room. The most globally civilized words one can think of.

"It's going to be a hot one today," he says.

The morning after we left Lydia for dead we all go swimming in the river.

This is after our first night in the canoe, each of us having fallen asleep within seconds of Wallace cutting the engine and letting us drift back in the direction we had come from. It doesn't much matter where we go, seeing as we don't know where we are. So long as we get up in time to steer us back against the current away from the gunmen's camp, it's all the same to us.

A dreamless sleep. Not sleep at all, really. Something more total than that. A system failure. Fixed upright against the boat's side in the same way I settled myself half a day ago. Half a day without a single attempt at changing my position or getting blood down to my legs, now wet logs attached to my hips. *Move*, I tell each part of myself. *Move, head*. And it does, with the crack of a dry branch. *Move, hand. Move, toes*. It takes the better part of the morning to check if everything works.

I awoke thinking I was home. The sun didn't look the same (too low, too like a glistening egg yolk) nor did the sky (the too-blue of airport souvenir paintings). Didn't feel like home either—folded into a bloodless lump, heat blistered, dying. I'd never been in a dying situation at home. Or lost, in the final way that we are lost. Yet for a moment I mistook this sun and this sky for the northern kind, high and aloof. Then at once it fell down to smother the breath in my throat.

I pull myself up using muscles I no longer have much to do with, and before the first of the usual warning signals, jerk my head over the side to vomit into the river. A bar shot of Technicolor gastric stuff, spreading out over our flat wake. Followed by another. But this one sends something new into the water. A crimson string.

"You OK there, Lizzie?"

Wallace picking through the box that looks like it might be a cooler or a toolbox, now almost buoyant in the water collected at the bottom of the canoe.

"Just the worst hangover of my life," I say, which is only partly true. "I've been worse," I then add, which is not true at all.

"Really? It may strike you as strange, but damn if I don't feel almost *refreshed* this morning."

"You're right. It does strike me as strange."

"Maybe it's lightheadedness. Or what's that song? 'Freedom's just another word for nothin' left to lose'? That's been looping around my head since I got up. Christ knows what AM oldies station hell it strolled out of."

"You call this freedom?"

"Well, things have become a little *unconstrained* of late, wouldn't you say?"

"It's Janis Joplin. 'Me and Bobby McGee.' But it was Kris Kristofferson who wrote it."

"The Janis I've heard of. On the screaming banshee side of things, wasn't she? One of the tragic-sixties-genius-overdoses? But as for your Bobby and Kris—it's a bit before my time."

"Is there anything in there?"

A wildness twitches across his features, his skin pulled tight. Something that's been within him all along now dangerously close to the surface. It's a relief when he looks back down into the box.

"You mean anything to eat?" he says.

"I guess I do."

"What if I told you yes and no."

"I'd say, 'What do you mean by that?' "

"Well, there's one jar of technically edible stuff. There's your yes. But the problem is that it's that manioc grit, which bears the nutritional value of toe jam. Not to mention its unique absence of flavor."

"What about water?"

"You mean this here?" Wallace slaps the plastic five-gallon container next to him. "This is gas. And not too much of it, either. As for water, on the other hand, there's no shortage at all. Just look around."

"But it's not clean. There's fever in it. Bugs."

"Think of it as a science experiment." Wallace scoops a hand into the river and pulls a slurp of it into his mouth. "So far, so good."

"I guess we shouldn't complain then."

"You're right. We're out of doors, getting some air. Not stuck in some hole in the ground. It could be worse. Hey, we could be Barry."

Both of us take a look: Barry torn and bloated like a hooked fish left out in the sun. Before, back in Manaus, I thought of him as made of solid meat. Now he looks butchered. Still alive, though. Still breathing. A syncopated backbeat of rattle, catch and gasp. Turned away from us the way he is, we can't see whether his wound has expanded overnight or dried up some, although it is more likely the former. The water under him appears thicker than elsewhere, murkier, as though he is a metal drum dripping rust.

"I've already checked on him," Wallace says.

"How's he doing?"

"I'm no expert."

"Is it that bad?"

"Well, consider how you're feeling at the moment. Now add twenty years, no real food for several days and an untreated gunshot wound."

"He's dying, isn't he?"

"I suppose we all are. At somewhat different rates."

"What are we going to do?"

I realize with these words that Wallace is the only one who might have an idea. And even if he doesn't, he's the only one we will listen to.

"We keep going," he says. "I haven't noticed an exit sign along here yet, so I don't know of any way out. It seems that we're in the middle of a collection of small islands—that's what they call an archipelago, right?—or it may be that this is another river off the big river. Or another river off one of those. And as for what direction we're going in? I don't have a clue. My idea is to putter upstream, keep close to shore and see if we can't bump into somebody."

"Wouldn't our chances be better downstream?"

"Possibly. But downstream is where those pirate motherfuckers are going to be."

Wallace unconsciously lets his hand stray behind him to touch the barrel of the same jammed rifle Bates had tried to use. Beside it, the rusted machete. Less rusted now than stained.

"You think they'll come after us?" I ask him, and his hand returns to its place on the side of the box.

"We had something to offer them before. That hasn't changed. Or has it?"

"Why are you asking me?"

"I'm asking myself."

"And your answer?"

"Even if they've given up on whatever they wanted, I see no reason why they wouldn't still like to kill us."

"So that we won't report them if we make it back."

"That, and because it's what they do."

A grin etched into the corners of his lips now added to what was there before.

"If I didn't know better, I'd say you're enjoying this," I tell him.

"It's an adventure, isn't it?"

"We don't belong in an adventure. We belong in a computer lab. Or a study carrel. Or a Starbucks lineup."

"But we're here now."

"And you think that's just great."

"I wouldn't go quite that far," he says. "But I'm not frightened, either. It's too real for that."

A tall, storklike bird I remember the tour guide calling a *juburu* lifts into the air at our words, its legs dangling behind it like cut ropes. The few clouds of morning pull back to throw laser beams down upon the canopy on each side of us. Only a moment ago the air was a mustard haze. Now it's instantly burned away. And we can see how close we are to the jungle, crowding in on us, standing atop fifty-foot stilts. So high and uninterrupted our voices bounce back and forth in millisecond delay within the ribcage of trees.

Something about this makes me feel sick again. Or maybe it's the reappearance of the sun. It has no patience. Screwing down into our heads, lifting away pages of our skin clean as a scalpel. It can't wait to get to the end of us.

"Wake Bates up," Wallace tells me as he pulls his shirt over his head. "Let's go for a swim before we get started."

But Bates is already up. Standing behind me, all of his clothes a spotted ring floating around his ankles. Shivering despite the heat.

"I've got to get clean," he says. "I can still smell—I've got to get it off."

Trembles both his hands down the length of his front, his naked thighs.

"Are you all right?" I ask him. Offering a hand out to his. "You seem feverish."

"I've got to get—"

"Of course he's all right," Wallace says, now stepping out of his own underwear. His legs twisted bands of muscle. "Nothing that a nice tropical dip won't cure. Last one in is piranha bait!"

Then he's stepping off, one hand plugging his nostrils, the other tucking his legs up into the cannonball position. His spine a zipper down the smooth stretch of his back. The splash coats all of us with cold tea.

Bates next, falling rigid as a mannequin, and then me, keeping shorts and T-shirt on with the idea that they might be cleaned in the process. Or maybe I'm still shy around these boys. One likely struck with fever, one likely mad. And me the only woman among them.

Only now, underwater, is the jungle emptied from my head. The constant leaf-rustle of movement, the comic squawks and death cries all snuffed out. But when I break through again the jungle is still there, clamoring even more loudly, as though jealous of our having left it for these few seconds.

Wallace is at least partly right. The water seems to do us some measure of good. It may be teeming with the nastiest bacteria on the planet, but it certainly *feels* fresh. None of us have the strength to swim much farther than a stroke away. Instead, we cling to the side of the canoe and bob along with it, sharing looks that confirm we are here, together, sort of alive. Surely that counts for something. We even cup our hands to throw water over Barry, who seems to appreciate it, if we can take his chattering teeth as an expression of comfort.

It takes some effort getting back in when we're done, though, and for a moment it appears that this might be our end, drowning in the name of personal hygiene. But Wallace finally manages to slip over the side on his back, his chest shining white as rolled dough. Pulls Bates out, then me, before stepping across both of us to start the outboard. The engine loud enough to excuse the fact that none of us have yet spoken Lydia's name.

We're moving up the river, whichever one of the million rivers of Amazonia this one is. Slowly, slowly. Look up and there's the painful sun. Look down and it's blood-soiled water spilling over our feet.

Some or all of us will die here.

But where is here? I try to bring to mind the map tacked to the *Ana Cassia*'s galley wall, but it's nothing but white paper veined with restless blue lines. We are somewhere in South America. Brazil. Maybe southern Colombia or Venezuela or, less likely, Guiana. And where is *that*? All I recall is that the Rio Negro weaves drunkenly northwest from Manaus. To go back downstream to reach where we started from would take at least seven, maybe ten days, and given that the gas would run out well before we got there, we'd have to rely on the current alone, which would make it a good deal longer than that. And that route would also take us past the gunmen's camp. Not that they are likely to still be there. Nevertheless, it's a place we'd rather not see again.

That leaves us only with going forward, as Wallace said. I remember seeing little dots on the galley map representing villages farther up the Negro, but the distance between the stretched forefinger and thumb separating them might stand for several hundreds of miles. And this may not even be the Negro. We might not even be on the map at all.

There will ultimately be an explanation for this, if only you could gather all the facts and be certain about them at the same time. *How it all ends*. Every causal relation, both random and intended. The decisions you make. The manipulations of others. Secrets.

And as for the moral of the story? That's not the translator's job.

I'll leave it to a computer program to say how right or wrong all of us are.

You'd think that with all the unwanted excitement of the past few days a little uneventful time heading up a river would be welcome. But the jungle is too big, too constantly like itself to properly entertain what may be the last hours of a life. What had Bates called it? *Beautifully boring*. It's impossible even to appreciate the fact that we are moving. You need points of reference for that. A B running after an A. And us? We're just gliding over the black like a needle on vinyl, round and round.

We stare at the jungle but it doesn't bother to look back.

Other times we gaze into it without much thought of anything else but *look, there it is* and *there's more of it* and *more*, a parade of identical marching battalions. Everything around us reduced to the establishing shots of a Sunday-afternoon nature documentary, neatly framed within the borders of a screen. Then something reminds us of where we are. An extra pulse of sun, a mineral whiff of river, the cackling pair of macaws following us along the shore—and we are instantly returned to ourselves.

That's my hand, isn't it? A shock of bluish white, shaking below my chin.

That pop of bubbles is my breath.

Yet even with all the time that sits between them, things happen here. The gothic trunks of dead trees buried in the high water, their gray limbs clenched tight. A single lick of breeze, bracing as a leap through a garden sprinkler. The spectacle of an out-of-nowhere storm. Hard sheets cutting into the river's surface, into us, pushing the branches up and down as though taking a bow. It goes on for only a few minutes at most, but the volume is so great we are forced to start bailing out the canoe with our ballcaps, the coffee can, our shoes.

Then it's over. The jungle now calling out with renewed chatterings and squeals trying to locate misplaced mates, offspring, cursing the escape of lunch.

The wilderness holds its tongue only for one. The *uirapuru*. A natural soprano schooled in Schubert judging by its floating, aristocratic melody, whose song is so lovely it is said to silence all the other birds' efforts. Above us the thunderhead replaced by a textbook selection of cloud types. The flat, the explosive, the braided, the wispy. The trees shake themselves like wet dogs.

When the sun finally begins to wane, Wallace pours tiny cones of manioc into our hands and calls it dinner. We wash it back with water we know to be poison. Then Bates helps Barry drink and pushes a few of the yellow grains past his lips. This perks him up for a time. He looks at each of us with an almost fatherly pride, even whispers something to Wallace.

"What's that, Barry?" Wallace asks him. "We can't hear you."

Good boy, I'm sure he says. *You're a good boy.*

Later we take advantage of the evening's relative coolness by arranging our bodies as comfortably as we can for sleep. We drift back with the current so slow that now, in darkness, it seems we aren't moving at all. Nothing to watch that I haven't already seen miles of in daylight, yet I fix my eyes on it all the same.

It takes what may be hours to figure out that what keeps me awake isn't something I see. It's something I hear.

At first I think it's the trees themselves that are talking. Not like

Lydia's screams this time but several voices communicating with each other. Louder than a whisper but still intended to be secret.

I don't understand the words. Not because they are too far away but because it's the wrong language. Men speaking together in Spanish.

There is nothing to be seen behind or ahead of us that might suggest that these men are close by. No flashlight blink, no silhouette of a standing figure with binoculars held to his eyes. But I know they are there. Discussing their next move, putting together a plan. Looking for us.

I have the idea that so long as I stay awake listening to them they won't find us. Wallace and Bates slumped on either side of me, Barry snoring quietly in his place at the front. And me the only one to guard our silence.

The night settles over us. And every time that sleep comes there is something to push it back. Another spurt of Spanish words, their speakers about to step through the trees. Listen, and turn too late to see whatever caused the sudden splash from the shore's edge. The howl of discovery from the forest behind it.

Hunting.

Barry is dying. We can tell from the most obvious signs: he's barely moved from the position we settled him in a day and a half before, the slow but cumulative loss of blood, despite a strip of Wallace's T-shirt tied around his wound, the moments where his eyes flap open to show white stones inside. But more than this, we know because he's started to speak.

Right now he's talking to his wife. Even here it's a little embarrassing, like overhearing a personal phone conversation from the other side of an office cubicle. And for this I almost envy him. He's managed to do what none of the rest of us have. He's gotten out.

"I'm sorry, Leslie," he's saying, and phrases like it, in interchangeable variations. "I'm so sorry, baby . . . Leslie? . . . I love you, honey . . . Please . . . Where are you?"

It's so sad it even stops us from thinking of ourselves for a time. The quality of his voice now, stripped clean of southern ease, the leather and cologne of the affable salesman—the way it is so *plain*—makes us believe that he is a man capable of love. Love curled up in his belly like one of those discerning parasites that moves from host to host, checking to see which has the most nutrients to offer. It's been there too long to leave now. And it may have been the saddest thing any of us had ever heard.

"Leslie? Honey? Just wait for me, baby."

It's enough to make me wish I could shed a few tears of my own to take the place of the ones that Barry is too dehydrated to produce himself. At first, anyway. But after a while, it becomes just another sound we would rather do without. It would be a lie to say that there aren't moments each of us wishes he'd get on with it and die so that he'd shut up.

As though overhearing our thoughts, Barry is quiet again. Each of us begins to wonder if that is that. I decide to count to sixty in my head and if he's still silent after that I'll nominate myself to go over and check his pulse to see if—

—the voice returns, still plain, but now apparently addressed to us. Eyes darting from side to side, following the path of a fly.

"Remember what you said?" he asks. "Wallace? Do you remember?"

Wallace balances his way up the length of the canoe. Sits down on the edge in the crux of Barry's arm so that it appears like they are caught in an embrace.

"Remember what, Barry?"

"All that *stuff*," he spits. "About expanding? And absorbing everything. How you'd already absorbed me?"

"I remember."

"What about Lydia?" he says, his eyes rolling up to Wallace's. "Did you absorb her, too?"

"No. She was tougher than you," he answers without a pause. "There was more to her than just herself."

"More?"

"She was pregnant. It made her strong."

"How'd you know that?" I ask now, interrupting so quickly that even Barry lifts his head to squint over at me.

"Do you think you're the only one people speak to?"

"She told me she didn't talk to you about it."

"Horrors! A woman lied! And to *you*, the good Dr. Crossman."

"Somebody else must have told you," I go on, unable to hide the shrillness in my voice. "Not her."

"What difference does it make? The point is I knew, and that's what made Lydia the way she was. Strong," he says, placing a hand on the old man's shoulder. "Unlike Barry here, who gave up a long time ago."

"Jesus, Wallace," Bates whispers. "Leave him alone."

"He *is* alone," Wallace says.

There is another period of silence after this. Barry curls back into himself, as though one of those dolls that speaks only until the string winds away into its back. Ahead of us, the river suggests an opening into something wider that, if the last thousand such suggestions are any indication, will turn out to be false.

Soon Barry is mumbling again. Words dribbling out the corner of his mouth.

"What's our Chatty Cathy want now?" Wallace asks.

Bates steps to the front of the canoe to lower his ear to Barry's lips but does not touch him.

"A cigarette," he says, turning back to us.

Barry's voice continues. A new thread that joins the chortling of the outboard engine, turns the steady sound of the machine into a chanted prayer.

"Will somebody give him a fucking cigarette?" Wallace finally shouts, standing to return to the outboard.

Bates says, "You have one, Crossman?"

"No."

"Neither do I."

"For the love of Christ!" Wallace turns the engine down to an idling rumble. Pulls a tattered receipt out of his pocket—for his room at the Tropical, probably, or dinner at Bufalo—rolls it up and licks along the edge so that it's glued there. Then he bends to whisper something to Barry. Grips a hand on his shoulder.

Barry moves. He's been still for so long that just to see his knees bend and his arms lift into the air is almost frightening. All of him soft and heavy, as though the remaining blood within him had turned to warm milk. But still capable of this. Of dropping one arm over Wallace's back in appreciation and grabbing the fake cigarette. Bringing it to his puckered mouth and taking in a long, shuddering haul.

And what do I find myself thinking? Watching an imaginary cigarette smoked by a dying man lost in the jungle? I think: *That's not good for you.*

It makes me cringe, but it's typical of me. Sensible, proper, sidelined. I've always had a knack for restraint. Whenever I have imagined my own death, for example, there is a bed, drawn curtains, a bodiless spiraling into the netherworld. *Wasting away* was how my parents put it when they arrived at an age where they had to start visiting friends in long-term wards more and more, before they finally had to be placed in the same wards themselves. The possibility of anything unexpected or violent has never occurred to me—even pain is too melodramatic for my taste. As for dying of exposure? Hunted down by guerrilla kidnappers on the Amazon? It's just not for me.

This doesn't prevent such things from happening, I know now. Who ever *expects* to go down in the burning airliner? Or be strangled in the night by a penitentiary escapee? Or folded up in a front-page pileup? Yet this may still be the way.

I work at putting a name to what I would lose. Watch Barry smoking without smoke and summon to my mind that irrational collage that stands for a life, my own, *flashing before my eyes*: a childhood model of the USS *Eisenhower*, the sun falling behind schoolyard poplars, the Pacer hatchback bought with the savings from my first summer job, my mother's lips.

What strikes me with a bolt of dread isn't that it all may be disappearing but that there's nobody I need to say good-bye to when I go. There's the immortal Wallace and Bates, of course. And poor Barry. Lydia. But I'm not sure that they count. They're all part of here.

Wallace and Bates have a little more experience at this than I have. They both watched something die in their lives from before. A dog they discovered shuddering under their boarding school bleachers the first November morning the weather turned cold. They took it upon themselves to smuggle it food, even sneak it into their rooms some nights and let it sleep beneath their sheets.

Just before Christmas break, when they went out after chemistry class to drop off some paleolithic lumps of brownie as a treat, they discovered the dog was gone. They called for it from the farthest end of the playing field, shouted into the snow-drooped trees that surrounded the campus. Nothing. It was only then that they realized they'd forgotten to give the dog a name.

I'll check the road, Wallace said.

I'll come with you, Bates said, because there was nowhere else to check, and he didn't want to be left alone.

They ran down the school's snaking entranceway lined with barren elms. Their breath coming out in industrial plumes. They didn't worry how they might appear if anyone saw them. Everyone already knew Wallace and Bates to be weird.

Wallace was the one to find it. He thought of calling Bates over but didn't, not at first. Watched the dog scrambling around below him in the flattened margin between the road and the forest. At first he thinks it is only playing the old game of chasing its own tail. Except this time it had caught it. A frothing mouth clamped around a long stick of fur, spinning and swallowing. And then he sees that it's been hit by something passing on the road: a spiral of red dots following it in the snow like the curled arms of the Milky Way postered over their homeroom blackboard.

He'd thought about gathering it up in his arms and running back to school, but the idea of touching the dog with his own hands struck Wallace as improper, even dangerous, as if the animal's symptoms might be contagious. A rock to its head to put it out of its misery? Not a chance. He didn't have it in him and he knew it, although he could visualize how it might go: the dog's goggled eyes looking up and holding fast on the boy's, knowing, and then the weight of the rock coming down neat and sure. It would require more than a single blow. In his mind he saw no blood. But the sounds he anticipated it making made him close his eyes.

Then open them again in order to stand back and see. The dog still choking on its tail and turning in circles, repeating a trick it had been trained to do in the hopes of earning a treat. Wallace finally calls Bates over so that both of them can watch it. The animal performing for the boys even now, its side split open and the writhing snakes of its insides poking out blue heads and purple tails.

"You both seem to have remembered all the gory details," I tell them when they're finished.

"That's because it's the only thing like it we'd ever seen," Bates says. "Before this."

"And because we've never been to war," Wallace adds.

"What's that got to do with it?"

"I bet you had a grandfather who told you stories from the service, right Crossman?"

"One. On my mother's side. He fought at Dieppe."

"See? Me and Bates would have to go back to our *great*-granddaddies for material like that, and we couldn't even tell you their *names*. A dog spinning around in a ditch—that's about as real as conflict could possibly be for us."

So it wasn't apathy they suffered from, only privilege. They weren't wholly ignorant of world history, as the common accusation against fellows of their age goes. If anything, the many sacrifices made for democracy and freedom had been drilled into them, along with the national anthem in French and the chorus of their school cheer. Not to mention the Remembrance Day assemblies that featured hobbling veterans in bemedaled blazers and stories of the blood of friends spilling into trenches, none of them more than boys themselves at the time. For Wallace and Bates all of this was a considerably more engaging way to spend the afternoon than math or Social Studies. But it still lacked the tingle of reality. Wallace had been mugged once in Toronto by a man wearing nothing but Maple Leafs track pants. Bates suffered anxiety attacks where he was convinced he had been poisoned by inadequately washed vegetables. But no wars.

Yet we are now killers. Or one of us is. And the rest of us let a friend be killed, or worse, in all likelihood. That was something. Fear was something, too. And the exhilaration that came with irredeemable guilt—yes—that was new as well. True, it lacked honor or principle or the other supposedly good reasons that killing happened. But still.

Wallace remembers the dying dog and thinks he might be able to do it now. If he were there again, he'd take the stone and pound it down.

What had he learned in the intervening years that would stop him? It's only thinking that prevents you from doing such a thing, and God knows he's got that under control now. If the body is able, all that remains is for it to be given the command. Everything else is layers of fluff. He even imagines it this way. His skull spun full of cotton candy that need only be combed away to leave him capable of anything.

I look at him and believe that he has already managed this. Perhaps it is the strong light that exposes him. Shows how little of him is left.

It was obvious from the beginning that Wallace possesses certain talents. A man of his time, as they say. And I will concede there may be other, marginally special things about the kid, too: appetite and charm and a dulled appreciation of death—gifts given to him by birth and the accident of experience.

But down here he'd acquired something new and powerful on his own, a rare magic. He could bring an end to life. He'd done it twice already. If anything he found it easier the second time. And now there is this old man oozing himself into an already leaky boat, slowing us down. Why should the flimsy restraints of friendship or pity or the law stand in the way of his third?

He doesn't actually say this last part out loud, of course. That's me thinking for him. But there's no reason this should make it any less true.

I am becoming increasingly certain that something is growing inside me. There's movement down there from time to time, no doubt about it, and it's getting stronger every time it returns. A muscular flip, a coiling, a splash. It may only be the unfamiliar fanfare of Third World–class hunger, the intestinal shit-kicks known to famine and desert and slum. But the thing is I don't really feel hungry anymore. I just *hurt*.

None of this explains all the new activity, the *otherness* in my gut. The near-human murmurings. The sleeping weight.

Perhaps this is what it feels like to be pregnant.

Needless to say, this is an impossibility. But there it is anyway, persistent and absurd. When I start to have thoughts like this—when

I'm on the edge of being *convinced* of what I know can't be—I do my best to turn my mind to other things.

But there isn't much to turn to. There's the mostly futile search for wildlife in the foliage (which looks more and more like wallpaper to me, the velvet William Morris rip-offs that smothered the sitting-room walls of my youth). Once an otter followed the canoe for a time, gliding along on his back and watching us, unimpressed. And a *boto*, a freshwater dolphin that came up as a hump of pink muscle and blowing spray from a hole in its head before slipping back under. But overall you'd find more activity in a petting zoo. Only the most vain birds allow themselves to be seen for any length of time, along with the occasional tree sloth, its arms hugged to the branch like a drunk's around a lamppost. There's the continual speculation over what time it might be. If those books I ordered on-line would now be sitting in a puddle of melted snow in the front hallway of my apartment building. The condition of my spider fern. Whether anyone had noticed I hadn't come home yet.

Home.

More real here than it is there. The chewed pens and Post-It reminders scattered over my desk, along with the unfinished mug of coffee I had been observing as a kind of ongoing science experiment, tectonic plates of mold sliding into each other to form new continents on the brackish surface. The guy behind the counter at the corner store with the nosehairs that reached halfway down to his lips, fine and searching as butterfly antennae. The way the telephone wires make a tic-tac-toe grid in the air above my bedroom window. I can see them all perfectly now. Better than if they were right in front of me.

"Wallace?"

I turn to him sitting behind me. His hand on the outboard as usual, directing us upstream with his chin craned to the sun as though to get a tan over his adam's apple.

"Yo."

"Why did you tell me Bates was an orphan?"

"Did I?"

"You switched places with him. Switched lives."

Wallace frowns earnestly at this.

"I hear a story, I make it my own," he says.

"Part of your expansion plans."

"You may be on to something."

"So how *did* you lose your parents?"

"*Lose?* Now that's funny," he says, although he shows no sign of amusement. "As it turns out, that's just the right word. I *did* lose them. I mean, they died—you need that part to be an orphan—but it was more like they disappeared."

"That's provocative."

"I thought you'd like that."

"You beg the question. How did they disappear?"

"You want the *gory details*, eh?"

"I want only what Hypothesys would require to make a decision."

"A rebuttal worthy of your debating club days."

"You really don't have to tell me, you know."

"No, Crossman. It seems that I do," he says, having heard the brittle strain in my voice, an effort to sound normal I thought I had managed to keep to myself.

Bates stops bailing and shifts around to face us. He's probably heard all that Wallace might say before, but it seems that he needs words too.

"I am a *product of divorce*, as the saying goes," Wallace continues, turning the engine down to a wet cough that still manages to inch us up against the current. "But mine is a somewhat more tragic version than the standard irreconcilable differences. I see myself as nothing short of *symbolic* in this regard. Don't I, Bates? And now you're asking why. Lizzie wants to know more, as is Lizzie's nature."

Wallace looks down at his feet, flicks his toes up through the water still tinged with corroded Barry bits. His long, starlet eyelashes catching the sun and throwing it around with every blink.

He is aware that we are waiting for him. Watching each of these gestures and falling into them, into him. He's used to this. He knows how beautiful he is.

"It is the middle of the eighties," he starts. "The Baby Boomers' long dark night of the soul. A time when anti-sadness pills, spiritual journeys and seducing the teenaged babysitter still had a whiff of the original about them. I was only nine at the time, so I don't know what the exact story was with my own parents. But they were having problems.

North American professional sort of problems. Owen Sound, Ontario, population twenty-one thousand, Lions Club, de facto wife-swapping sort of problems. And all of my parents' cocktail party regulars—the doctors, the lawyers, the shady real estate flippers and complicit town councilors and the last of the main-street retailers with storefronts bearing granddad's name—were having the exact same problems. And their solution? Fresh air! For a while there all of them were busy dog sledding and mountain climbing and divorcing for the first time. In the case of my parents, the marital balm was decided to be sea kayaking. In the *arctic*. Eighteen months of marriage counseling and a two-week course in outdoor survival and they're flying onto Great Bear Lake in a bush plane with nothing but freeze-dried spaghetti carbonara and the idea that all this would bring the two of them closer together."

Wallace pauses now. To let his hand fall into the river, pale and rubbery as a surgical glove. To remind us that we will wait as long as he wants for him to go on.

"What were they thinking?" he finally asks with his hand still in the water, only a shadow now, a few inches lower where the sun cannot reach. The thought crosses my mind that the piranha might mistake it for a dead fish, but I say nothing. "I wonder about that. What the fuck were they *thinking?* Paddling out into a body of water the size of Iowa, thunderheads rolling in of a kind they'd only seen in nightmares and *The Poseidon Adventure*, all in the name of fixing themselves. Did they have a clue they were going to die? It should have at least occurred to them, but I bet it didn't. Not until the very end. This was only supposed to be an *experience*. Something to suffer through and return from with amusing photos to pass around at dinner parties. And then the rain starts to come down. An instant ice that turns their windbreakers and thermal pants into medieval armor. The waves rising above them like linebackers before tackling down on their heads. It rolls their kayaks over so that they're stuck there, hanging upside down. They try to bring themselves back to the air with *one fluid motion,* just as they'd been instructed at the boat-rental place. It doesn't work. Every time they almost get there a wave knocks them back the other way. They're exhausted after less than a minute. Which brings on the panic. Jerking one way and then the other, wasting whatever momentum they might have built up. The thing refuses to move at all now. Nothing but solid darkness all around, even with their eyes open. They've been set in stone. In the middle of nowhere, yet no more than ten feet apart."

Wallace's voice has entirely returned to itself. Or at least to one of his voices. The hypnotist's one, at once soothing and suggestive of deeper allusions. His words almost separated from whatever they are meant to refer to so that they exist only as sound, like humming a lullabye you remember from childhood. It's strange. And it makes you feel strange. It also brings you close to fear. A glimpse of some unspeakable subtext that can only be discovered by allowing yourself to enter the voice whole.

"Even as it's happening it seems ridiculous to them," he says. "Drowning in a lake cut in half by the Arctic Circle? Puh-*leeze*. But no. They die there all the same. Two sons back at home staying with the increasingly impatient neighbors. Scared and knowing that this is only the beginning of being scared. *When's Mommy coming home? Can I call my dad?* It's stupid. And sad and romantic and a little funny, you know, as with most terrifying things that happen to others."

He shrugs, and a collarbone juts above the collar of his T-shirt. A four-winged bug lands square within the parted hair of his crown where it rests for a moment before motoring off, wobbly as a biplane.

"It happened," Wallace says.

"How do you know?"

He gives me a hard glance. "How *else* could it have happened?"

"You had a brother?" I go on, not wanting to lose him yet.

"Name of Ian. He sort of disappeared too. Went traveling after graduation like everyone else, except he never came back. The last I heard he was bartending at one of those backpacker discos on Eos in the Greek islands. Lives in a cave. He prefers men to women, but I think he's alone more than not. Spends all his spare time working on this thousand-page essay on the moral vacuity of Western culture, or how paper currencies are the instruments of an international banking conspiracy, or the role of Hollywood in supporting the industrial arms complex. Or something. We don't talk all that much anymore. Our politics pose a problem, insofar as he has them and I don't. But that's mostly just the easy answer we tell others. The fact is that after Mom and Dad died we had to come up with some brand-new identities. Something *sharp*. Sharing the same continent would run the risk of reminding us that we're only make-believe. And we've worked too hard at ourselves for that."

"Are you angry at him?"

"Why would I be angry?" Wallace lifts his chin level with mine, his face pinched with real puzzlement.

"Because he's your brother," I say. "And he left you behind."

"He did what he had to." He shrugs again, which lifts his hand out of the water. "Just as I did. And as you already know, I found another brother."

Wallace smiles at Bates now. Full and wide, even with his chapped lips pulling it back the other way. But there's a vacancy just behind what it shows to the outside, a lack of the animation that comes with true expressions. It turns this smile into a threat as much as a display of warmth. Not toward Bates, but toward me, Barry. Anyone other than themselves.

With this look whatever it is growing inside of me returns with a thrashing leap. But this time its presence is almost welcome. Watching Wallace and Bates connect with their eyes, as brothers, has left me alone again. Excluding all others seems to be as much the point of it as anything else. It reduces me to a child. The gawky girl at the back of the class, four-eyed. Not hated, just ignored. An isolation earned by wanting to make friends too badly.

And the memory of this child's world brings the most childish of responses. A humiliating rim of tears, hidden from view only by the stomach cramp that sends my head down between my knees. It makes me think that whatever is inside me—river parasite or some other alien—it is still connected to its host, is still partly *me*, after all.

I must learn to be grateful for the company. In this place it is the only family I have.

We're about as far from anything as is possible in the Americas. I know this for a fact. Before I flew out from Toronto I studied the globe I still have from my undergrad days, one of those illuminated kinds with raised and gouged surfaces to mark the mountains and sea canyons. I turned it on and found South America glowing pink. Ran my fingers over where we are now. Smooth. The bulb within warming the great forest as I moved my hand westward from Belem to the Andes. No names beneath my fingertips aside from those few that snaked alongside the rivers.

And yet I'm still surprised that, aside from the Spanish voices following us and an empty container of motor oil that bobbed by on the second morning after our escape, we haven't come across any evidence of the manmade. It's not that I'm expecting much. Yet surely even the smallest tributaries accommodate occasional traffic. Maybe we just haven't been out here long enough to see any of it. We might stop here and wait three months before another boat chugged by. We might wait six. And only our bones to watch it pass.

And then we see the hut.

I see it, anyway. A constructed outline amidst the mangle of the lower canopy. Lines meeting lines.

A shelter, I think. *Somebody must have* made *that.*

Do I want to see it so badly that I have finally made the forest yield, however slightly, to my wishes? It may only be this. An illusion of purpose caught in the chaos of fallen branches.

But there is definitely a doorway, albeit a doorway without a door. And a peaked roof of dried palms. The entire structure—no more than five feet up or across—sitting atop slices of jacaranda trunk. An Amazon garden shed. And with a little imagination it becomes even more recognizable. There is something in the provisional look of it, the error and tilt that comes with a one-man job undertaken with haste, that reminds me of the home-fashioned bus shelters that stand at the end of Canadian farm lanes.

And for a second instead of river I'm driving over gravel. Seat-belted behind a windshield pricked with ice, passing a scene at once familiar and not my own. I expect a kid in a neon ski jacket to step out of the shelter as much as I expect a gaunt prospector, a jaguar, the unfolding height of the concierge.

I'm about to point it out to Wallace but he's already steering us toward the bank. Cuts the engine with a couple of boat lengths to go so that we drift onto the sand.

The hut stands like a primitive altar fifty feet up an overgrown trail directly in front of us. We all see it now but say nothing. Even Barry holds the noise of his breathing within him and peers into the shadowed doorway. Nothing moves. How could we tell if it did? The interior is so dark compared with the furious daylight around us that we can't see any hint of the rear wall. A man could be standing inches inside and we would never know he was there.

Bates points just to the right of the trail. There, stretched over a fork of dead branches, is a startling band of white. The middle of it sagging to form a cup. A diagonal slit that cuts it in half.

"Jockey shorts," Bates whispers.

"And just my size," Barry says. "*Christ* could I go for a clean pair of underwear."

It's more than a little alarming to hear Barry's voice again, but nobody responds. For in the second after we recognize what it is, we recognize what it means.

"Bates," Wallace says, balancing his way forward along the edge of the canoe. "Hand me the machete."

After passing up the blade, Bates finds the rifle as well and brings the butt to his shoulder. Wallace steps into the ass-high grass and gestures for me to follow him. Caught between them again. Unarmed.

It doesn't start well. Placing my foot down on the still earth starts an uncontrollable trembling down the length of my legs. The canoe's lazy rolling and my own weakness have left me struggling just to stand. But Wallace waves me on and I keep up with him as best I can. Because he has ordered me to. And because of the hope that perhaps this dark box contains something that might, one way or another, deliver us out of here.

Wallace holds the machete a couple of inches away from him, so that he could bring it up in an unobstructed arc if he needs to. He is now visibly comfortable with the weapon in a way that makes it only more troubling to be near him. Like he knows he can use it and wants to. And if the occasion doesn't arise on its own, he'll come up with an excuse.

When he reaches the doorway he stands directly in front of it, looking in. Although I can't hear anything it's as though he is in conversation, head down, meeting the eyes of whatever lies on the floor.

I step up behind him, and at the sound of my approach Wallace moves aside. Ushers me in with the machete, now poking into the shadows. But even as I bend low and enter it is too dark to see as far as its stained tip.

I'm expecting death. A dying figure in the corner, or something long dead. And maybe I'm half expecting to see myself. For Wallace's blade to find its way into me and leave me here, in this place that is not an altar or bus shelter but my very own crypt.

The available light finds its way to my eyes. No footprints, fire circle or animal remains. Only the most foreign thing you could ever find in the jungle. A totem left by some visiting extraterrestrial, almost glowing in the ribbon of light on the dirt floor.

A book.

"What is it?" Wallace asks, as I already have it in my hands.

It's the 1987 Amazon edition of the Get Moving! travel book series, "Complete with Regional Maps and 48-pages of GORGEOUS color photos!" The gorgeous photos are still here, but the maps have been torn out. The rest of it puffy with repeated soakings and dryings. So stiff that turning the page is an act of reverence.

There's no use in it, of course. Not unless we've gone a lot farther than we thought possible and Iquitos or Santarém or Manaus itself turn out to be around the next curve. Only then would we need to know the rates at the Best Western or where to get the "juiciest cheeseburgers this side of the Tropic of Capricorn." I hold on to it anyway, feel the calming weight of money and convenience within its covers. Step back into the canoe pressing it piously to my chest like a pilgrim and his King James.

"Looks like Crossman's finally found a friend," Barry says before returning to sleep.

Bates lowers the rifle, ignoring both me and the guide book. Speaks only to Wallace.

"What's in there?"

"Nothing to help us."

"But there *was* somebody there?"

176

"Whoever it was is gone."

"Was it the pirates?"

"I'd say not. Judging from Crossman's discovery, it was more likely a lost and absentminded tourist. Left his travel guide and his undershorts behind."

"That means he had a boat."

"He probably lost that, too. Or was dropped off here by others. Maybe he stuck his nose where it didn't belong. Poachers, miners. Indians. He figured he was better off walking into the jungle than waiting for the next bus to come by."

"Did you think of that too, Wallace? Like one of those shacks to keep schoolkids warm while they wait for the schoolbus?"

"What are you talking about, Crossman?"

"I just thought—you said *bus*—"

"There's no bus here. But you're welcome to stay to see if I'm wrong about that."

"Should we go and look for him?" Bates says.

Wallace lowers his chin at Bates. "Whoever it was made a stupid mistake," he says. "It doesn't mean we have to."

"If it was a tourist," I venture, eyes down at the guide book open to a full-spread shot of a tropical screech owl with a sloth in its talons, "he'd come a hell of a long way."

"Some do."

"Only if they have a reason. They come to *see* something. But what's out here?"

"Parrots, anacondas, nature. The usual. I bet if we searched a hundred-foot radius into the bush we'd find him. Crawled off like an old dog to decide on his own grave."

"No," I say, closing the book decisively as though it had just provided me with an answer. "I don't think he left this place to find a way out. I think he went into the jungle to find what he came for."

"Well, I hope he had a nice trip," Wallace says, pushing us off the bank and back into the river. The hut already shrinking into the scramble of life it came from. "Who knows, Crossman. Maybe we'll meet up with the poor bastard yet."

• • •

Dinner is a palmful of manioc and half a coffee can of river. It manages to be filling, as anything would be thrown into our stomachs about now, shriveled up into clenched fists. I fall asleep with eyes open. The last of the day's sun glinting off the water in the same rhythm as the slowed beats of my heart.

But before I'm completely gone Wallace wakes me with two jabs between my shoulder blades. He's pointing at the nearest shore. Somewhere in the dark below the overhang of knuckled roots exposed by the dry season.

I follow his line of sight but there's nothing there.

"I can't—" I start in little more than a whisper.

But my words cause something to move from the very place Wallace is pointing. A pair of eyes. Yellow rimmed with black centers, sitting atop a pimply log.

Wallace reaches down for the rifle.

The eyes stay with us, so bulging and still they take in the length of the river before them. But they say nothing. They could be expressing anything from doubt to hate.

The rifle now held against Wallace's collarbone. It occurs to me that if the thing turns out not to be jammed and actually fires, it will break him. He looks so small compared to the gun. Most of his upper half wrapped around it, pulling the stock into him as though it is an animal he wants to keep warm. One with a straight black tail pointing at a fallen log on the shore.

Everything waits. Wallace to find his aim and then to hold it. The rifle to find the power within itself to fire.

But before they do Barry brings a honking snore of breath into his chest. The pimply log thrashes forward into the water. The eyes atop its head the last of it to submerge.

Wallace pulls the trigger anyway, but the rifle remains jammed. Or broken.

"That could have been a real dinner," he says with something like awe.

"What the hell was it?"

"A caiman. I've been spotting them all along here, but none were as big as that beast."

"I could only see a dark line under the branches."

"And they're in there. Looking out."

"You must be getting jungle vision."

"It's true. I'm seeing things I never could before. Incredible things," he says, only now lowering the rifle. "Aren't you?"

"Listen, Tarzan. I think you're talking about hallucinations here."

"Who's to say? It all seems real enough."

"Virtual reality."

"You couldn't program this place. It's too hot and I'm too hungry."

"And we're too scared."

"I've told you before, Crossman. I'm past that."

Bates splashes back through the canoe to join us.

"Wallace nearly shot a giant alligator," I tell him.

"A caiman," Wallace corrects.

"Sounds dramatic."

"It was."

We all stare at the spot where the caiman entered the water as though it might pop up again to stick its tongue out at us.

"I know this shouldn't be at the front of our minds," I say, "but have you thought that if we ever get out of here, we'll make great cocktail party guests?"

"Maybe you'd like to look forward to that," Wallace says. "But in my experience, there's nothing worse than a travel bore."

"You call this travel?"

"Of an extreme sort. Heli-skiing, deep-sea diving, bungee sex. Kidnapping, torture, murder. It's all shit you can't get at home, Crossman."

"So would you say you two are well traveled?" I ask, sensing another opportunity for distraction. "Before this, I mean?"

"Not particularly. But we're supposed to be," Wallace answers for them both. "Travel is our generation's call to arms. Everyone Bates and I know is right now asking the exact same question. To recognize that you are civilized and lucky but not know what to do with yourself: Is this hell? All you're certain of is an interest in *being there*. Taking off for years in Southeast Asia, Chile, Prague, the Yukon. Me? I manage a couple weeks in India before the shits get the better of me. But at least I got sick. I *kept it real*."

"So what do *we* end up doing for the summer after first year?" Bates asks himself. "*We* go tree planting."

"Tree planting! Yes! Have you ever gone tree planting in the farthest reaches of northern Ontario, Crossman?"

"Can't say that I have. Back in my day, we spent our summers waiting on tables and smoking pot."

"Oh no, that won't do," Wallace says, shaking his head. "What you *have* to do is get on a bus with thirty other twenty-one-year-old existentialists and drive up to the middle of nowhere—almost as nowhere as here except still cold in June and a good deal uglier—and stick these pathetic Charlie Brown Christmas tree saplings into the frozen earth. And you get to sleep in *tents!* And try to fuck one of the fourteen *girls* within two hundred miles! And once in a while, they drive you into the nearest town to drink *beer!* Now that I think of it, it was on such an occasion that I saved Bates's life for the second time."

"When was the first?"

"That's another story."

"Tell me about the second time, then."

Wallace rests the rifle between his legs and leans back against the side of the canoe. "Bates, I think we may want to save this for posterity," he says.

Bates pulls the tiny Palmcorder out from the depths of his pocket and trains it on Wallace.

"You still *have* that thing?"

"They burned my nuts, Crossman. But the fuckers never checked my pockets."

Now he zooms in and out to frame Wallace properly. Only once the camera has found him does Wallace begin.

"It happened in one of those towns up there made entirely of aluminum siding," he says, looking directly into the lens, into Bates at the other end. "We settled in the local tavern—these places only have one, so the police know where to go to collect husbands and the limbs of barfight losers—and started to drink. We drank so much that we did what we had been told never to do: we started talking to the ladies of the town, instead of keeping to our own. You can tell where I'm headed with this, can't you? It's the oldest story in the book. Am I right, Barry?"

Barry says nothing to this. But his eyes appear to be open, and they're more or less directed at Wallace.

"Well there we are, chatting up a couple of backwoods lovelies who, according to the standard in towns of this kind, could be anywhere between eighteen and fifty. We're not doing too badly. They find our city-slicker ineptitude exotic, and we find their missing teeth and tales of snowmobile accidents a little thrilling, too. They invite us back to their place. On the way, however, they alert us to the existence of boyfriends. When I ask where these boyfriends might be at the moment the one says *Drinkin'*, as though it was a place on a map. When I point out that we were also drinkin', and in the only bar in town no less, the other discloses that yes, the boyfriends *was drinkin' there, too*. And I say, 'You wouldn't be doing all this in order to make your boyfriends jealous, would you, ladies?' And before they can provide an answer Bates is tugging on my sleeve and our dates are pointing over my shoulder with some excitement. At first I assume it's because of their spontaneous creation of a new word."

He waits, and so I have to ask. "What word?"

"*HolyJesustherestheycome!*"

Without lowering the camera from his eye, Bates picks up the narrative as though it's been rehearsed this way. He doesn't move the lens from Wallace's grinning face the whole time, though.

"They were no bigger than us. But they wore lumber jackets and their faces had the same confused expression carved into them, which gave them an instant advantage. We were drunk. But these guys were *pre-human*. Like in *Altered States*, after William Hurt spent too much time in that sensory deprivation tank jacked up on peyote. Kind of anthropologically interesting from a certain distance. And then just plain unsightly as they got closer. And then they were all over us. All over me, at any rate. I'd never been hit before. It was like waking up from a long dream. Just *there*, no arguing with it. Which is exactly the point, I suppose."

Bates has an Elvis mouth. How could I have missed it before? It's only as he speaks that it can be seen. All the vulnerability, but without the sensuousness. Pursed and full and dumb, but unaware of its being any of those things. You want to smack his lips right off his head, or pinch them together so he has to suck air through his nose. Kiss them hard with your teeth.

He pauses, the Palmcorder still trained on Wallace. Then his Elvis lips start to move again.

Tells of how one of the boyfriends knocked him to the ground and pulled his arms behind his back, so that he was sitting up, legs straight out in front of him like a cotton doll propped against a headboard. Bates offered them his wallet, his Walkman. He was cooperative in the way he'd once seen an urban survival specialist advise on *Oprah*. But these guys weren't in it for money. Or jealous rage, for that matter. This was *fun*. And with a good-natured whoop, they began kicking him in the face. It seemed to go on for some time. Having never been beaten up before outside of hockey body checks or touch football pile-ons, he was at first concerned about the pain. But there was surprisingly little of it, as the flash of shock was too startling to get a handle on whatever lay behind it.

More than the spreading heat of internal hemorrhaging or the worry of how much more he could take, Bates was aware of occupying the moment. Swinging their boots into his eyes, knocking the retainer out of his mouth and skittering it over the pavement, one of the lumber jackets repeatedly calling him the worst thing he could think of, *cocksucker*, the suspension of time when he would try to put his hands in front of his face or plead *Give me a second!*—in all of this he experienced nothing more than an overriding sense of event, of possessing his own skin. He thought: *Well, this is something now, isn't it?*

"Kind of like being here," Wallace says.

"Kind of, yeah," Bates admits, lowering the Palmcorder. "Now that you mention it."

But I don't want to mention it. I don't want any more about here.

"So what happened?" I ask him. "How did you get out of it?"

"Well, that's kind of funny," he continues, except now with a stutter of suppressed giggles. "I'm sitting there getting the shit literally kicked out of me, and I start to wonder where *Wallace* is. I swear to God, the guy's name only has to cross my mind and *shazam!*—he's right there! Waving the lid of a trash can over his head and screaming like a ninja on crack. You know, the whole kung-fu *yee-owww!* thing and spinning around and giving all these Sporty Spice kicks to the air. It was the worst fake-out I'd ever seen. But these mutated boyfriends, they totally bought it. They took off and left everything I owned in the world behind on the ground—my Walkman, my nose ring, my fucking retainer."

Wallace can no longer hold back his laughter, and Bates joins him in it, lifts the Palmcorder once more to get his friend's amusement on tape.

Without thinking I was capable of it, I feel my own laugh muscling its way up. I'm surprised by how much I want to be with them in this, seeing the ridiculous and showing that I see it too. There's an idea that if I can let myself do this now it might shrink all the trouble we're in.

But something stops it before it makes its way out. A new sound reaching us over the rattle of the outboard. Not an animal, either. Nothing the jungle might offer on its own. I recognize it without being able to give it a name.

Hollow claps of thunder. It makes us look to the sky, but the clouds there remain charcoal outlines. Even though it may be coming from as much as a couple of miles away we duck down in the canoe so that only the tops of our heads would be visible from a distance.

"What is that?" Bates whispers.

"A gun," I say. "A number of guns."

"Do you think it's them?"

All of them, even Barry, look my way.

"I didn't tell either of you before, but I heard voices the other night. Far off and close at the same time. I couldn't hear exactly what they were saying, but I'm pretty sure it was Spanish."

"You weren't dreaming," Wallace says.

"You heard it too?"

"Me and Bates. We both did."

"Why didn't you tell me?"

"Same reasons you didn't tell us."

"We should have messed up the engines on their canoes when we had the chance."

"We never had that chance. We needed to *talk* for a while instead, remember?"

"Still, it may not have been them."

"Maybe not. Although I wonder how many Spanish-speaking men who like to fire off guns into the trees might be *accidentally* following us."

"It's a river. It's not like we're leaving a trail or anything."

"They've figured we're going north, so they're doing the same. If we try to turn back, we'll smack into them first. And unless we get out of these islands and into more open water, they'd be right."

"So what do we do?"

"Keep going."

"How much gas is left?"

"I just pour in a cup now and then. We've got a day or two. Maybe less."

"And then what?"

"And then we start going back downstream. Or we row our way up to Bogotá."

"Or we sink," Bates adds. "Have you noticed? We're getting closer to the waterline all the time."

All of us reflexively look at Barry, but in the next second return our eyes to where they were.

"We'll just have to do some more bailing," Wallace says.

"We can't keep up," I say, "even if there was something aside from a coffee can that we could use. Sooner or later it's going to start pouring in over the side."

"If it looks like that's going to happen, we'll have to beach it and go for a stroll."

"It doesn't sound promising."

"It's *not* promising, Crossman. It hasn't been *promising* for some time now."

The guns continue firing into the evening. At times they are so close I can almost hear the hiss the bullets leave behind in the air. Other times they're so far off that the mating calls of the tree frogs are louder. We don't attempt conversation again even when the guns are at their most distant. Or when they stop altogether.

We stay close to shore. I offer to take the engine but Wallace waves me off, as though I should know by now that he has moved beyond the trivial requirements of sleep. I, on the other hand, would welcome it. But it only comes in waves, and these are filled with dreams that make it worse than being awake.

And in these dreams the gunmen's canoes are close enough that I can hear them talking again. Along with something else. Their sentences cut with words in our own language.

Our names.

In the morning, the boat is so full of water we have to push it over the sides with our hands. Keep at it until dizziness claims us. First Bates, then me, and finally Wallace, who works directly in front of Barry so that he gets rid of most of the blood.

We can't leave the leak alone for an entire night anymore. It is decided that the coffee can will be passed between us in shifts, so that whatever water is coming in will be met by one of us scooping and pouring. This seems at first a satisfactory solution, and not too taxing. But the sound that results, a repeated glug and splash, makes us think of the giant caiman of the day before, swallowing, swallowing.

So we try to listen for other things. The guns. The rumble of a motor coming around the curve behind us. Spanish voices. But the daylight has taken all of them away and left only the constant riot of the jungle.

If taken all at once it is pandemonium, the shouts and sniggers and weepings of a terminal-case psych ward. We train ourselves to separate certain voices from the others. Lend them order. With a little discipline, you can hear whatever you want in the birdsong here. Over the long hours, the ears pick out their own lyrics. I tend to find repeated chastisements, as in "What a wreck! What a wreck!" or, from an orange-winged macaw that looks down directly at me, "You're *lost!* You're *lost!*" Bates detects a single name. His girl from the Manaus brothel, three syllables sung in a variety of tunes. And as for Wallace, he can hear only multinational corporations. "AT&T! AT&T!" and "Mi-cro-soft! Mi-cro-soft!" along with one so distinct that I start hearing it myself. "G.E. Monsanto-*oo!* G.E. Monsanto-*oo!*" A proposed merger squawked out from the trees.

"I haven't even *seen* anything yet," Bates says after too much listening, his eyes searching through the forest's sharp edges.

"Like what?" Wallace asks.

"Something. A monkey, say."

"A monkey."

"Yeah."

"So if you saw a monkey taking a dump off one of those trees you think it would make you feel better?"

"I think it might."

"Then *look*, Bates! I'm a monkey! *Oooo! Oooo!*"

In a single motion you would think possible only after weeks of rehearsal, Wallace drops his shorts and shits a trickle of river water over the side of the canoe.

"There goes the neighborhood," Bates says to me in a wifely tone.

"What neighborhood?" Wallace stands above him now. His shorts stretched around his knees. "This is the jungle. Jungles are *built* on shit. That's why you can't drink the water, although we are because we don't have anything else to drink. And you know what's happening? Things are *growing* inside of us, Bates. You're the science guy. Figure it out. Meanwhile, *you're* concerned about how disappointed Lizzie here might be about my manners now that I've taken a crap off the side of a canoe?"

Bates looks at him the same as before.

"I just wanted to see a monkey," he says.

Illness comes and goes like some unwelcome waiter, laying down steaming plates of nastiness, then clearing them away just as quickly. It's not what I expected jungle fever, or malaria, or typhoid, or whatever this is, to be like. I thought that no matter what version, once it had you that was it. But at least in its initial stages, the sickness prefers to play a teasing game of tag, staying away just long enough to make you think it was never there in the first place, and then returning with a slap: *You're it!*

As the day goes on, Bates seems to be bearing the worst of it. He can feel himself cooking from the inside out. More poached, or micro-waved, than broiled by the sun. For the moment he believes he would still be rare (a shining pink if you sliced him open) but moving quickly toward a gray well-done.

"It's the third stage of dehydration," I tell him. "Even when we drink the water. It goes right through us."

Wallace scoffs. "Third stage? Where'd you get that?"

"The guide book. There's an appendix on health risks in the tropics."

"Sounds like page-turning stuff, Crossman."

"At only five percent fluid loss, there's impatience, nausea, lack of appetite."

"Ah, yes. The good old days."

"At ten percent, indistinct speech, dizziness, headache. It seems like we're coming up on the twenty percent level now, though. Delirium, dim vision, swollen tongue, numbness."

"What happens at stage four?"

"Over twenty percent is usually fatal."

Both of us look to Bates. It's his turn to bail but he spends most of the time with his head held over the side. Watches the waves twisting and knotting into bands of DNA. It makes him think of the intricate code of his own genes, the data carried within each wriggling sperm. The invisible things that make everything tick, microscopic explanations to every how and why. It provides no comfort here. He'd always taken science at its word before. He loved it for its completeness, its honesty. But here it is a joke. Cells, atoms, formulae. Now it makes him laugh out loud.

"What's so funny?" Wallace says.

"The waves."

Wallace looks down at them kicking against the side of the canoe.

"You're right, Bates. They *are* hilarious."

. . .

A remarkable thing stuck into the middle of the afternoon. A line of jet exhaust split through the sky above us. Coming from a definite somewhere, going to a definite somewhere else.

Bates is the first to see it. His finger follows the white stain it leaves behind like handwriting on a page.

I see Lydia that night.

We are drifting with the current to give the gas supply a rest, moving no faster than one of the palm weevils we see when the river narrows and we can watch the beetle scuttling along a tree limb with a single leaf held in its jaws. It's the hour when even the jungle shuts up. Everything that was meant to be eaten has been eaten. Everything that hunts is asleep.

She is standing on the shore no more than twenty feet from the boat, a faint glow about her that is the half-moon reflecting off her English skin. The thought that it might actually *be* her lasts for only the first second or two. Not because I am able to reason that there is no way she could have followed us, or that it is impossible that we have navigated ourselves in a circle that has brought us back to the gunmen's camp, where Lydia has been waiting for our return. It's because it's obvious that she is dead.

Only Wallace and I are awake, and even he sits slumped forward, staring at something of his own on the opposite shore. There's no point in asking him if he sees her too. She's mine. I am sunstroked, witness to things in the last week—in the last *day*—unmatched by anything else in the preceding thirty-eight years. Of course I'm starting to see things that aren't there.

And yet she looks real enough. Her eyes searching through the dreadlocked vines in the same way the caiman's had. Clear of intent, spellbound. Feet sunk into sand up to the ankles so that I wonder if maybe now they've finally cooled.

If I can't make her go away (and I can't—that was the first thing I tried) I consider some of the things I could make her do, if only to show that she is part of my imagination, and as such subject to my manipulations. I could give her scars. Have her hold limp in her arms the baby she would have one day delivered. Perhaps I will have her do nothing but whisper my name. Something the others would think is only the hungry whistle of a *potoo* bird gliding through the upper branches in search of moths.

Although she is of my own making, Lydia ends up doing something I don't expect at all.

She crouches down and slides out from the the hairy vines, then lifts herself up again when she begins to step into the river. Now that she's closer there's more expression in her eyes than I saw at first. Something vicious that the Lydia of before wouldn't have been capable of. They make a couple of things more clear than any words she might use. She hates us. She's coming for us.

But she sinks as the river bottom slips out from under her. Like the caiman's, her dead eyes are the last to go. They linger on the waterline as though detached from everything else. Two floating black pearls.

With another step toward the canoe the top of her head disappears below the surface without a sound. Nothing but the moon there now. Stretched and twisted in the ripples we leave behind.

It is not yet morning, not yet dawn. The promise of light a lipstick stain on the river's horizon.

I must have gotten some sleep. This scene—the jungle caught halfway between black and green, another twist of river, the last of the sky's unfamiliar stars—appears almost new to me. And then I recognize that there *is* something new about it. Something not here that was here before.

"Where's Barry?"

"He's gone," Bates says.

Bates is sitting one plank back from where Barry had lain across the narrowed front of the canoe. Staring at the same place I am. The brown smears the big man left behind on the white-painted sides.

"Where?"

"Well, I don't think he's gone for a swim."

"Don't you think we should go back? To look for him?"

"He's *gone*, Crossman," Bates almost shouts. "You can ask as many questions as you want, but that's the answer to all of them."

Wallace hasn't started the outboard yet so I assume he is still asleep. But now his hand is on my shoulder as he balances his way past to sit between me and Bates.

"Have you been awake all night?" I ask him.

"Not *all* night," he says. His voice calm and easy, almost amused. "I seem to recall a dream or two."

"Did you see Barry go?"

"Did you?"

"I just woke up."

"Do the math then. None of us saw him."

"Why didn't you tell me?"

"You looked so pretty there, all curled up. Besides, what would you have done?"

"That's not the point."

"Tell me what the point is."

"Barry has *disappeared*, Wallace. He couldn't have tread water for more than ten seconds in his shape. It means that he's dead now."

"I *know* what it means. And I know that we all cared about him. If we could have gotten him out of here, we would have. But he didn't have much left in him and you know it."

"We *lost* him!"

"And I'm just wondering *what* we've lost, exactly."

"He was your friend."

"A friend who probably slipped over the side in the night."

"*Probably?* We've had to lift him up just so he could take a piss for the past two days. He couldn't have rolled over the side on his own."

Wallace takes a step back toward Bates, crosses his arms. Cocks his head slightly like a dog waiting for some command it actually understands.

"One of us had to have pushed him," I say.

Wallace straightens his head. "So I pushed him," he says. "Or Bates did. Or me and Bates. Or maybe it was you. Maybe all this shock and horror of yours is a show. Quite a puzzler, isn't it? But I *can* tell you a couple things that are certain. This canoe is a lot lighter now that Barry's not in it. That means we can move faster, and won't have to bail as much. There's a bit more food for all of us. And if the time ever comes that we have to make it through the bush on foot, we won't have to drag along another body that was never going to make it anyway."

"You've given this some thought, haven't you?"

"Shouldn't one of us be thinking?"

"And that would be you. Who needs a Hypothesys subscription with you around? A man dies and within seconds you're tapping away at the calculator in your head. And guess what the final answer is? Who *cares!* It's all for the best!"

"Well it is, isn't it?"

I know he's wrong but I've forgotten the reasons to explain how. Isn't it enough to know that Barry is dead? Barry, the good American, capable of maintaining the finest of American balances—Democrat millionaire, Ivy League southerner, honorable salesman. He is dead and it cannot be for the best. It cannot.

"If we stop caring," I say after what may be a long while, "then we have nothing."

"There's caring and there's living. We have to worry about the latter right now."

"I'm not sure you're capable of anything but that."

"You're wrong there. But I'm not going to debate with you right now, Crossman."

There is no discernible impatience in his voice, but it's there in the tightness of his crossed arms, a coiled strength. It proves that Lydia was right. He is capable of anything. But it is a capacity that doesn't know its own power yet.

"When we first got here, Bates told me you were a gentleman," I go on, sliding back against the side away from where he stands. "I didn't think it was possible. I thought they were extinct. And now I *know* you're not a gentleman, Wallace. But Barry might have been."

"Maybe you're right. But he's gone and now there's just us. Not a gentleman among us. We can sit here and mourn all that or we can tend to what's coming next. I honestly think that's what Barry would advise."

"You didn't know the first thing about him."

"And you did?"

"He talked to me."

"Did he tell you he was going to die soon?"

"There's no—"

"He told me. Back in Manaus."

"Dying?"

"Cancer. Eating him up from the inside."

"Bullshit."

"Prostate. Not a thing they could do."

"Bull*shit!*"

Wallace closes his eyes.

"You're lying," I say.

The eyes open halfway. "You sound certain."

"He never told me he was dying."

"And I suppose he would have *had* to, given that everybody tells you everything."

"He talked about his wife. He wanted to go home."

"We all want to go home."

"I'm not so sure about that."

Wallace smiles at this, a flash of white from out of the shadow he sits in.

"What I'm saying," I start again, "is that he wouldn't have thrown himself over."

"It seems like you've got all of us figured out. Barry didn't have cancer because he didn't tell you about it. And he wouldn't have killed himself because he loved his wife. Simple! Then what about me, doctor?"

I smack my wrist. A reflex shot at one of the helmeted insects that land on our arms every couple of minutes to rip a patch out before floating off. But the truth is this one hadn't bitten me yet. I wouldn't even have known it was there if my head hadn't been hanging down, looking anywhere but directly at Wallace. And when I raise my eyes again he's still waiting for an answer, and Bates's back is still turned to me.

"Are you listening to this, Bates?" I ask.

He nods, but doesn't move around to face us.

"Don't you think we owe it to Barry to figure out what happened to him?"

"He's gone."

"But if we don't—"

"He's *gone!*"

Bates's shoulders contract all the way to his ears. My eyes search within their peripheral vision for the rifle, but it's nowhere to be seen. It could be behind me or lost over the side along with Barry. Or it could be gripped in Bates's hands where I can't see it.

"How's this?" Wallace offers finally, opening his palms and spreading them out before him in a fatherly gesture. "If we ever get out of here, you can tell everyone that I pushed Barry over because I was getting tired of him bleeding over my Air Jordans all day. You'll feel better because you've *done* something, and I'll enjoy the benefit of you shutting the hell up."

I should accept this. What do I hope to prove by staying at him? Out here, where no accusation or confession makes any difference?

"You're worse than the ones that killed Lydia," I tell him. "At least they don't do it to people on the same side as them."

"And whose side are *you* on, Crossman?"

"Not yours. Not anymore."

"I didn't *have* to get you out of that hole." Wallace raises his voice by a degree. Grips the machete's handle so that the bones in his hands push white against the skin. "I *saved* you. I tried to save all of you."

"That's right, you're the hero. Me? I'm just the translator. And I'm *definitely* not the maker of the perfect bomb."

"I only told Lydia about that," Bates starts in a protesting rush. "I never—"

"You told *Lydia?*" Wallace and I say over each other, both of us with our eyes on Bates's back now.

"No, not—the one in Manaus. *My* Lydia. The girl at the bar. I just got mixed up." Bates shakes his head in a show of correcting himself. "I didn't tell anyone but her. Just the girl."

"That's what you say," I jump in. "But even Wallace was wondering if maybe you told a few others."

"Don't, Crossman," Wallace says.

"Maybe you got tired of being the geek in the background, typing the code for some novelty game, and started imagining that you'd actually made something *real*—"

"*Cross*man—"

"—something that a *man* might come up with, a new idea for killing—"

I'm interrupted by what I think is Wallace trying to stick his fist down my throat. Less a punch than a rough sort of surgical procedure, one meant to pull something out from my insides that he'd caught sight of while I was talking and thought he'd better go after right away. He pulls his fist out of my mouth and drives it in again.

"*Not* him!" he's shouting through his teeth. "Accuse me of whatever you want. But *not* him!"

Bashing these words into my skull, everything loosening and pouring out my nose. His fist hammering through bone to grip my brain once and for all.

Bates has to throw his arms around Wallace's neck and lurch backwards in order to pull him off me. For a while we all just breathe. Caught in different unraveled poses, leaning on our thighs or slouched against the sides of the boat. And now there is a new source of blood. Falling off my chin to stain the water inching higher inside the canoe.

Maybe a full minute passes before I speak next, and even then I'm still panting. My lips swollen fat as wieners.

"She picked you, didn't she, Wallace?"

"Who?"

"Lydia."

"What are you saying?"

"Lydia," I say again, her name finding its way out through the spit held in my mouth. The blood lends it the flavor of liquid copper.

"You're bleeding," he says. "And you're not making any sense."

"Tell me."

"I believe we headhunted her straight out of her London office."

"Her *baby*, Wallace. She wanted you to be the father. And you were."

With a racking sigh Wallace stands up so that his head is haloed by the sun peeping over the farthest line of trees. All I can make out of him now is a tall outline of shadow. His face could be shriveled with fury, or he could be indulging a silent laugh.

"Where is all this coming from?" he asks, revealing nothing. "I'm curious."

"The way you knew she was pregnant even though she didn't want to talk about who the father was. How when she made a wish, she did it for your sake. Both of yours, now that I think of it."

Wallace moves his head a little to the right, blocking out the light more completely, like the moon moving across the sun in an eclipse.

"That's your evidence?" he asks.

"That, and as we've just seen, you're *loyal*." I spit a globe of blood over the side. "You might even be brave. Rare qualities in young men today, from what I read in the papers. And women tend to want that in the genes."

"Flattery, Crossman. Flattery."

"Am I wrong?"

Wallace launches back an unsteady step so that the sun, now rolling up heavy above the highest branches, cuts red lightning into my closed eyelids.

"No, you're not wrong," he says. "Although it may be the only thing you've got right."

I painfully focus Bates back to life. To see if there's anything he might be showing to indicate whether he knew about this before. But he remains just as he was, keeping his eyes on the stains Barry left behind.

"She asked nicely," Wallace explains without prompting. "We were business partners. She was *British*. It struck me as the right thing to do."

"And now that she's gone?"

"What are you asking?"

"If you cared at all or if you considered yourself merely the *facilitator*. Didn't you say that's what you're best at?"

"I'm still waiting for your question."

"I'm asking if you loved her."

"Of course I did. But that's hardly remarkable."

His hand slips off the machete's handle and the blade totters for a second before clanging against the side of the canoe.

"No doubt you'll find this difficult to believe," he says. "But I love everyone. Even you."

Wallace faints. Or nearly does, anyway. A hand rises to his forehead to cradle his skull atop his neck. In the next instant Bates is there behind him, buttressing the back of his legs, guiding Wallace's collapse down next to him. Takes the coffee tin and pours cool trickles of river into his hair, over his flaring cheeks.

We stay like this well into the morning.

Now I imagine that every new turn in the river will reveal something else entirely. A motorized canoe occupied by tourists, laundered and combed and taking snapshots. And as we get closer we see that it is ourselves. The clearly etched people we used to be coming back the other way.

They begin their versions at different points—one with the "chalky smell" of the winter air, the other a mickey of rum in his pocket "like a grenade"—but they both end in the same place. Two boys lost in the woods at night. One of them collapses and can go no farther. The other could leave him there in order to find help, or he might only tell himself this so that he could try to find his own way out before he too froze to death.

Because I have already heard the second, this, I assume, is the story of the first time Wallace saved Bates's life. But it may be the other way around. Their identities have become so flexible since the time it happened. And now it seems to matter less who did or said what than the simple fact that they were there, then, together.

They start without my having to ask. Sometimes they say the same thing at the same time, or utterly different things in a jumble of opposing meanings. Other times they take long pauses. To remember what comes next. To wait for the fever to boil higher and kick them back into speech. The result is a story that follows a shared thread while at the same time wrapping additional threads around it, thickening it like spun yarn. Was Bates the one who held the compass at first and

Wallace the bottle of Captain Morgan, or the other way around? Who led the way through the trees? Who was saved? Who is the hero?

They were only boys. Castaways at a private school three hours north of Toronto. The one where Prince Andrew once spent a term, a boast that still littered the promotional brochures and inflated the tuition fees years later. It specialized in athletics, the physical sciences, "nature studies." There were no girls and it was far away. It was *obscene*.

The grounds were set up as a kind of summer camp, with clapboard bunkhouses scattered through the trees, a dining hall with a vaulted ceiling of margarine-spattered cedar, and a boathouse on the lake that was frozen over except for the first and last months of the academic year. Beyond this were several hundred square miles of forest. A dozen creeks weaved indecisively through it, feeling their way out to the lake. Because the soil in this part of the Canadian Shield was shallow and studded with rock, the only trees that grew in it were a few ghostly birches and stubby pines, trees with needles instead of leaves and branches too low to walk under standing straight.

This is where the prefects in charge of their Outdoor Orientation exam dropped them off, blindfolded. It was a Tuesday, they think, in the middle of January. At the kind of school that believed that having children find their way out of the woods at subzero temperatures built character.

And this Wallace and Bates could certainly use a little toughening up. Always together, their heads lowered to share secrets. Worse, they didn't like sports. The shorter one argued that teams denied individualistic expression. The taller one had "bad knees." During free time, instead of touch football (broken fingers) or pick-up hockey games (shattered teeth) they preferred to curl up next to each other in the library's beanbag chairs, reading *books*. It was too much. The headmaster's letters home noted that Bates's and Wallace's futures were thought to be in some jeopardy without a good deal more "physical challenge." The older kids had their own way of putting this. They called them "lover boys."

They had to count to sixty before they were allowed to remove their blindfolds, a long minute spent listening to the prefects' retreating shouts of *faggots!* scrambled through the thicket. When they were finally able to look around them the sun was on its way down, blinding to the left of them and failing to make it through on the right, so that they stood on the line between night and day.

They use both the compass and the bottle of rum as best they can. Try to follow the prefects' footprints at first but a new round of falling snow soon fills them in. Every step shows the forest to be slightly altered, but without offering a clue as to which way might yield to something else. By the time of lights-out back at the dorms, they are lost.

One of them falls. The other stays.

"I didn't get the last part," I say, trying at a smile to show the confusion is mine alone.

"He stayed with me," Bates says.

"He stayed," Wallace echoes a half second later.

They go on to tell how they were discovered by a search team the next morning, still huddled together like "a couple of steaks you find at the back of the freezer." One of their heads tucked under the other's chin, as though seeking protection from a horror movie played out on the screen of the encircled forest. Look at their faces: their skin the fibrous gray of homemade paper. It was assumed that they were dead. How could people so still be alive?

But they were. They knew they were too, on account of the dream they were sharing. A flight high above the forest they had fallen asleep in. Looking out for victims to save using their superhuman powers. Searching for each other.

Their voices separate more frequently now as they struggle for the sequence of things. An epilogue relating how they had to be pulled out of the forest on a toboggan like two felled Christmas trees, then rushed into town to be placed into lukewarm bathtubs, hooked up to sugar drips, a circle of doctors with nothing more to do but wonder whether their frostbitten hearts would stop or continue to beat.

After days of identical turns the river before us widens, so that the shore is pulled away from either side. The details we've been using to judge our speed—every dead branch or spindly treetop that stretches forty feet higher than the others around it—retreat into the water-color gallery we haven't seen since the Rio Negro. Perhaps we have been returned to the big river again. Or this may be a new route altogether, one that will only take us farther into the interior and away from any chance of a village or passing riverboat.

Wallace and Bates have stopped speaking. Disconnected once more, one looking to the left shore and the other to the right. The same face looking away from a mirror.

"Why do you think you lived?" I ask them. "Did the heat the two of you shared make the difference?"

Bates looks at me. His expression a combination of pity and scorn, as though he'd only now remembered that I suffered from a softness in the head.

"It was love, Crossman," he says, taking time with his words so that I might understand them. "What do you think it was?"

"I don't know. God? Courage? Good luck?"

Bates shrugs and turns away. "Same thing," he says.

It starts to rain. Just as you would expect in a rainforest. Round about the same point in the afternoon that, were we home again, we would be visited by our first thoughts of dinner.

We hold our faces up to it. Warm, but still a few degrees cooler than the air. Coming down so hard it bruises.

When we bring our eyes level again and look ahead the river is gone. It has been replaced by a sheet of aluminum riddled with bullets. Holes blasted through and sending up molten shrapnel, licking onto our arms where I expect it to burn into the skin but it only slides down to my fingers and off the ends. There is no idea of surface to the water anymore. There are only tighter and tighter folds, and this fiery perforation. All of it blowing what looks like steam up to the tallest treetops.

Bates faces me and says something that I can't hear. Tries again. A child calling for its dog across a field. But Bates is no more than four feet away.

The water drenches us through within the first twenty seconds. In the minute that follows, it turns our shorts and T-shirts into translucent bags. I am naked before them for the first time, but there is no shame. There's not enough of us left for that. Our skeletal knobs and twigs animated without having a right to be. Bates throwing out arms to grip at the sides, Wallace attempting to stand but twice being thrown back against the prow. Me on hands and knees to get to him but the water in the canoe is too high and I choke on what finds its way up my nose. Even the flesh of Bates's Elvis lips has been suctioned away, leaving them spastic, doubtful.

Wind. That's new too. Normally there's nowhere for it to go through the endless body of forest. But this storm isn't bothered by that. That's because it's coming straight down on us. Pillars of air striking our heads, dunking the canoe below the waterline. The waves it makes are heavy, high and instant.

At first there is something ridiculous about all this fuss, the showiness of it, as though manmade effects on a theme park ride that will subside as soon as the tracks under our canoe lead us another few feet along to the next stage of simulated violence. The problem isn't that it fails to be threatening. It's the *venue* that doesn't seem right. A river? This is a North Atlantic gale, a cyclone in the Bermuda Triangle, an ill-timed rounding of Cape Horn. Here is all the fury of the ocean and we can still see the line of beach on either side of us, glowing yellow as though drawn with a highlighter pen.

"Jesus! *Je*-sus!"

Wallace's voice. But when I spin my head around there is nothing to see. Nothing but the grid of bones across his back—

—the guide book floating in my direction inside the canoe, nudging up against my shins. Begging to be saved. And it has come to me, its current master, for preservation. When the going got tough with its last owner he had ripped out its maps and taken off on his own. But surely I would prove a softer touch. A bookworm by nature, a born page turner, a *woman*. Surely *this* one would rather risk life than watch a disemboweled reference text go down.

I grab it by the spine and throw it high.

For a second it flaps its covers and falls behind the next swell. But before it disappears altogether it opens itself up. A Japanese fan displaying its seductive colors and painted characters. *Look at all this*, it says. *Just think what you'll be missing—*

—the canoe falling out from beneath us and we are cast in midair. Suspended like cartoon characters who have stepped off the end of a tree limb but not yet acknowledged their obligations to gravity.

The boat comes up on another crest to meet us. Hard. A wooden paddle to our asses.

There is so much water pouring in over the sides and spraying down from above it's unbelievable that the thing still floats. And it doesn't, really. Even if everything settled now it's days beyond bailing out with a coffee can. It is here only because the froth of the storm won't let it sink. But after this it will go no farther.

And then what?

We keep going. Wallace's answer to everything.

There he is now. Clawing his way to the outboard. Apparently the motor is still working because he twists the throttle and directs us into the oncoming waves in order to find the way to the closest shore. Although it isn't clear if this is making any difference, it's comforting just to see Wallace try.

And now he's doing something more. Shouting at us. *Hang on*, maybe, or *Stay down*. I'm already doing both.

The rest of me working to keep my eyes on him. Isn't that what they tell you to do at times like this? Focus on the one thing that is constant. The horizon. But I can't see the horizon from where I am sprawled out in the bottom of a canoe. Wallace is the only thing left.

And Lydia. Barry, too.

Perched on the end of the stern, leaning out from behind Wallace's shoulders to return indecent smiles. They don't look good. Not at all. No, they look *bad*. In their intent, in what they want to see happen to us. Mouthing Wallace's words with mock urgency.

Hang on tight, Crossman!

I look to see if Bates sees them too, but he's got his back to us, holding something against his chest.

"Bates!" I find myself screaming. "Bates! *Look!* Do you see them?"

He shifts around so that he's facing our way. Brings the thing clenched in his arms up to his eye. The Palmcorder.

"I see you!" he says.

"Not us. *Them.*"

"Don't worry, Crossman. I can *see* you!"

Water sheets over the lens. Even if he's getting Lydia and Barry on tape they would be no more than arguable blurs, two clouds poking out from Wallace's outline with streaks of light coming through. And they're *not* there. I know this even as I turn back to see them. Laughing outright now.

Swing around to Bates and attempt my own smile into the camera. If this is our time to go, we might as well appear presentable. Lift one hand out of the water and float it an inch next to my cheek. Shake it into a wave.

"Hi, Mom!" I say.

Wallace still shouting at us. With different words this time.

"What the fuck are you doing?"

Bates shifts the Palmcorder up slightly to get both me and Wallace into the shot.

"What the *fuck* are you doing?" Wallace asks again.

We're losing our minds. That's obvious, isn't it? Fever. Malarial, dengue or yellow. Take your pick. The specters that come with the giardiasis, typhoid, the cholera and tetanus. Look around. The sky and everything that it holds is falling.

We did quite well. As well as keyboard ticklers, screen gazers, channel changers like us could expect.

But now that's over. Now we are dead.

I consider saying some or all of this, but it takes more strength than I have just to stay in the canoe, and every time I open my mouth it's filled with rainwater. And now Wallace is saying something else.

"There they are!"

I'm pretty sure those are his words. Casting his head back to confirm it.

"They're coming!"

They?

The prefect bullies from Wallace and Bates's school in the woods. It could only be them. We're lost and they've been searching for us and now we've been found.

Why did they bother? To save us? To deliver a fresh round of harm? Judging from the folded-in look of Wallace's face, I take it to be the latter. They've certainly come a long way just for this. But a masochistic streak is always part of the bully's nature. Cruelty is only really fun if you have to work for it. Back home they would all be junior stock analysts and marketing consultants and VPs of daddy's business by now. And *this* is how they've chosen to spend their three weeks off this year.

Here they come.

Maybe a half mile back, bobbing around the last corner of the river before it opens up. Too far to see their faces but it's a canoe, all right, with maybe four or five heads poking up over the sides.

The *prefects*. The lucky ones who couldn't just get on with enjoying their luck but had to remind everybody that they had it, over and over. I'm not surprised to see them. They've been following me all along, even though I may not have actually caught sight of them before. The ones in charge of the emotional response experiment, the one I had originally guessed was run by Martians or angels. Showing up right at the end to announce that nothing that has come before has occurred without them being responsible for it, the bits of good as well as the steamrolled stretches of bad. And in the final analysis the experiment has proved nothing. Although it did provide some amusement to those who engineered it. Ha, ha.

Cup your hands into binoculars and take a good look. The past itself blasting over the waves to meet us.

"Down!" Wallace is wailing, his command directed at the river as much as to us. "Get *down!*"

Only now does Bates lower the Palmcorder from his eye. When we ride up on top of the water I can see that we've progressed—or the storm has pushed us—closer to shore since I last checked, now no more than a couple hundred yards off. There's something there in the middle of it, too. A dark line spliced into the trees. Another outlet into the river, not much wider than our canoe.

Wallace must have seen it when he first went back to the outboard. Had seen the prefects too, and knew he had to get to it as fast as he could. We know they are there. But they may not know we are here.

Perhaps our smaller boat has been obscured by the waves out in this wider part of the river.

Bates sees the outlet too. And the two of us set to bailing the canoe again. Pitiably, Bates with the coffee can and me with a cupped palm, although our efforts would likely be better spent opening our mouths to the sky and spitting the rain over the side. We're helping. Not that we think it will do any good but because Wallace thinks it might. And it's better to focus on that than on our pursuers. Or where we might go even if we do make it to shore. Or the motion of the water that calls up the last black strands of stomach lining to be spit between my legs.

"Get the oars!" Wallace tells us when we're close enough to the tributary's mouth to see the waves being swallowed into it. "Use them to push us along the bottom. Keep us from getting stuck on either side."

I'd forgotten about the oars. Those two logs at the bottom of the boat that screwed pencil-length slivers into my feet whenever I tried to stand up. I can see one of them lying there now. Looking heavy.

"Crossman! Let's *go!*"

Bates this time. Already swinging one of the oars above his head as though it's a helicopter blade he hopes might lift him out of here.

"Just pick it up," he says, too soft to be heard, but I can read his lips.

I plunge both hands in and grab at one of the sections of oar refracted by the water. And get stuck with another goddamn sliver. But I don't let go. Lift it up by pushing against the weight with my legs, so that I am standing too, dipping the paddle over the side for balance.

Wallace jolts the outboard back and forth against the waves. The engine cutting out and starting again and snarling blue smoke, but he manages to direct us into the break in the shore. This turns out to be a shallow, sharply twisting stream.

Almost immediately the hull is screeching over the rocks. Bates hammers against one bank with his oar and I nudge at the other, the two of us working together like a pair of gondoliers. Wallace holding the outboard down as it kicks up against the river bottom. Every contact between metal and stone sending a high-C up through the boat's frame to the roots of our teeth.

The storm shows no sign of easing but the wind is little more than a distant stir here in the cover of jungle. Because of the turns in the stream's course it's impossible to know how far we've gone in. The prefects may be right behind us. They may have set off on foot and have only to go fifty yards in before jumping out of the bush ahead.

None of this matters much.

We are simply putting the last of ourselves into going forward because this is all we have been doing. To make note of how long we last. To see where we end up.

Here, as it turns out.

Lodged in the crux of a fallen tree. In front of us nothing but the marshy circle of the stream's source. Lily pads the size of garbage can lids laid out over its surface. Behind us the stream somehow more narrow than the canoe itself. There's more water inside the boat than anywhere within sight.

Wallace shuts the outboard down. Without it there is only the drumroll of rain on the leaves.

"OK," he says, as though someone has been repeatedly asking for his permission. "*Fine*. OK."

The oar falls out of my hands but I remain standing. And with the surrender of its weight comes an almost soothing observation.

That's the end of me.

The prefects could follow us here, string us up, whip our feet and burn us. Do whatever bullies do. I wouldn't try to stop them.

Yet I'm still embarrassed by what happens next.

The way I hear my own voice say *My nose is cold*, possibly aloud. The way an unseen audience stands just outside what's left of the visible, blue lights popping off from within the crowd like flashbulbs at a prize fight. The way I don't feel a thing. Not the tickle of an idea, the current of misconceived outrage that I'd become used to, not even the prick of shame that still comes with every foul whiff of myself. Nothing but the last of my blood spiraling down the drain at the back of my neck.

But what I truly wish not to happen comes at the last second of what can be remembered. The way that, in the manner of the corseted heroine from a Victorian romance, I bat my eyes up at the dripping green before falling back into Wallace's arms.

8

A NIGHT of frogs.

Clinging to the trees, hunched next to our ears on the ground, asking us to leave. The rain has stopped but the air remains stiff with moisture. Look up and there is the moon stuck behind a sheet of plastic. Conditions that have only excited the amphibian population around this pond, their cacophony bouncing off the giant lily pads that float upon it. A congress of poorly behaved frogs, drunk and horny. Their calls reaching us in stereo. Belching, drumrolling, ripping fabric in their throats.

The three of us stretched out side by side on the bank. When we could go no farther Wallace and Bates dragged me out of the canoe before falling on either side of me, the rain scouring off the last layer of our skin. When it finally stops sometime in the night we try to sleep. And then the frogs arrive.

"The Indians here have a story behind where they came from," I say.

"The frogs?"

"The lily pads."

"Let's hear it," Wallace says, lying back and folding his arms.

"A beautiful young girl, Arari, wanted to look down on the world forever, to hold her face above it like the moon. So she climbed the tallest mountain she could find to take her place in the sky. But when she got to the top she slipped, tumbling all the way down into a lake. The moon knew what she was up to, though. And when she fell he looked down and took pity on her. Despite the insult of her vanity, he decided to grant her immortality after all by turning her into a lily pad. That's what these are," I say, sitting up to poke one underwater with the end of a stick. "The faces of an overly ambitious kid."

"No wonder they look so familiar," Wallace says.

Once again Bates pulls his Palmcorder from his pocket and trains it on the water just beyond his feet. Still works, too, despite the drenching it took in the storm. Bates touches one of its buttons and up pops a tiny spotlight that cuts an electric beam onto the nearest lily pad, its dimples and arteries. Then he slowly pulls it up, the light diffusing as it covers more of the pond's surface, exposing the more distant pads as a luminous sheet of polka dots.

"It's the Amazonian version of the Icarus myth," Bates says in his documentarian's voice, completing the lens's movement to the horizon. "The punishment you're meant to receive for flying too high."

"Except this kid got too close to the moon, not the sun," I say. "And Arari survived. Sort of."

"Very interesting," Wallace says, offering exaggerated nods of consideration. "Where'd you come up with all that, Crossman? I didn't know that you were an expert on Brazilian folklore."

"I just read it somewhere."

"Where? In all the rush I must have missed the commemorative plaque on the way in."

"It was in the guide book we found."

"Don't tell me you brought it with you."

"I threw it out in the storm."

"Did you *memorize* the whole thing?"

"I have a gift for storing useless information."

"Us too," Bates says. "We're in the useless information *business*."

Something plops up from the water's edge to land between my legs. Another frog. But a strange-looking one. A frog with see-through skin.

"Bates, shine the light down here."

"Where?"

"Right there."

The spotlight flicks up again and is cast on a tight circle of muck between my knees. At the center of it, a jellied orb with webbed legs and feet. Perfectly still except for what can be seen working away inside of it. Its pink fold of intestines. The clutching sphincter. Silver nerves.

"What is it?"

"It's called a glass frog," I say, pointing toward it with an open hand, as though by way of formal introduction. "Nocturnal, with transparent skin. The female likes to attach her eggs to the underside of leaves that overhang running water, which are protected by the male who stands by until the larvae hatch and drop into the stream below. This must be a little egg guardian right here."

"Let me guess," Wallace says. "You got that out of the guide book, too."

"It had a picture of one. Except this guy is even better looking than the one in the book."

"I can see its heart," Bates says, zooming in. "Pumping, pumping."

Wallace and Bates study the glass frog sitting before them bewildered in the alien light. And I study our own shapes in the glow of the moon. An underwater phosphorescence moving over our skin. Wavering layers of silk in the air still unsettled by the storm.

It lets me see what I have never seen before.

Our insides revealed as clearly as the primitive guts of the glass frog, although a more elaborate layout, our turbocharged six-cylinders to its lawn mower engine. Not so much x-rayed, as I had imagined the tourists standing on the opera house plaza in Manaus, but *laid bare*, stark and conclusive, the nakedness of where we have all come from and where it will end. It is our bodies and nothing else. Squeezing and flowing and congealing and otherwise getting on with whatever is required to keep going. And that's all. Not a word of poetry to be pulled from any of it. Not even the simplest metaphor is applicable to what is now exposed within us, the irreducible truth of our parts that, when hooked together and started up, can somehow generate the fictions that we come to know as ourselves.

Only now do we remember how hungry we are.

The glass frog leaps out of the light. Bates turns off the Palmcorder and slips it back into whatever secret pocket he keeps it in. We are left only with the noise of frogs again. The wet moon.

"How much manioc is left?" I ask Wallace.

"Remember that coating of yellow sand each of us licked off our fingers yesterday morning?"

"I do."

"Well, that was it."

"So we have no food?"

"You're quick."

"But we still have the rifle," Bates says, stroking its length in what may or may not be an attempt at comic intimacy. "We can hunt for . . . for . . . *You* memorized the guide book, Crossman. What kind of animals might make a good lunch out here?"

"You can eat pretty much anything that moves if you cook it long enough. Monkeys, tapirs, capybara."

"Sounds good."

"Two problems. One. We haven't seen any of these beasts, let alone lined them up for a shot. And we're not likely to. You've got to be born in a loincloth and with a bone through your nose to even think about walking in there and finding something to eat."

"You said two problems."

"Problem two is the rifle doesn't work."

"It may only be jammed."

"So it's jammed. It doesn't make much difference. Unless some furry thing leaps into our arms and slits its own throat with its claws, we're going hungry."

Then Wallace does a funny thing. Not unwelcome, just a surprise. He puts his hand on my knee. A snap of static electricity that sends both my legs scrambling away from his touch.

"Tell me, Crossman," he says, his hand hovering in the same place where my knee used to be, "when are you going to start having fun on this trip?"

"*Fun?*"

"I think your rather relentless concerns about survival are letting a great learning opportunity pass you by."

"I've learned plenty. And I'm sure Lydia and Barry were edified by this whole excursion too. That is, until we left her behind and threw him overboard."

"Now, now. That's not exactly the way—"

"Listen." I feel the words escaping before I'd even thought them. "Shut up and *listen* to me."

Wallace returns his hand to the rain-whipped mud at his side. "OK, Crossman. We're shut up and listening."

"Good. Because I want to make very clear how little *fun* I'm having right now. I have shit running down my legs I don't even remember letting go of, for starters. My temperature has been in the triple-digits for days. There's some creature in my stomach that's eating me from the inside out. In short, I don't *feel* well. And you two can't be in great shape, either, even though you're acting like this is nothing more than some reality-TV experiment and at any moment the producers are going to step out of the trees and hand you goat cheese sandwiches and non-disclosure agreements. You're losing your grip, in other words. You never *had* a grip."

I'm shouting now. Even the frogs have stopped to hear it.

"As for *learning?*" I go on, my voice breaking. "It's got me nothing so far. I've been trying to figure out who you two are from the start and I'm no further ahead now than when I was pitching Portuguese software in hotel lobbies on your behalf."

"Is this about you and the trust issue again, Lizzie?"

I'm looking into his eyes that are somehow sympathetic and teasing at the same time and I can't stop.

"I *don't* trust you. Either of you. You're all secrets. You just look at each other and there's another one. And I know what you're capable of. I *saw* the hatchet job you did on those assholes back at their camp."

I stop to catch my breath but it takes more than a few seconds to find its way up my throat. And they wait on each side of me. This is turning out to be a pretty good show.

"But I have to pretend that you're actually my friends, don't I, because there's not a thing I can do out here except hang on to your shirttails. Which would be fine if I wasn't constantly wondering when you're going to toss me over the side. Or lose me in the woods. I know what it is to be all alone in that stuff and I don't mind telling you I didn't like it. It's the most terrible thing to know . . . to know there is only *you*."

There are tears now. An involuntary convulsion that comes quick as choking. And yet I have no idea what they're *for*. Emotion that comes without any particular sentiment, the working of a forgotten reflex. One that proves it's still possible to pass through experience and come away with something even if you're not aware of it, like the burrs that cling to your pant legs after a walk in the country.

And along with the tears there are Wallace's fingers. Pinching each drop off my cheeks and rubbing it into the dirt grooves of his hands.

"We're all orphans now, Crossman," he whispers, and the jungle shrinks with his words. "There's nothing but us. Just our strange little family and the big bad green. And despite what you said just now, you *can* trust us. Besides, you're right. You can do nothing else but trust us. If you want to stop thinking and start feeling for a change, that's fine. I bet it's been a while for you, hasn't it? Go ahead and feel. I'll do the thinking for a while."

He's smiling at me. Making the kind of face meant to cheer up a colicky child. I want nothing more than to hate him for it, to see it as an intolerable insult coming from someone not much older than a child himself. But this time the hating doesn't stick.

"You sound like Mr. Hypothesys himself," I tell him, my voice now cracking in a single laugh.

"That's me."

"You've got all the answers."

"They're only provisional, of course."

"So, if you're the Answer Man, tell me. What *are* we going to do? Wait, wait! I know. We *keep going*."

"You want to stay here with the frogs? If I'm going to die down here, I'd like to do it in a quieter location."

"Where do we go?" Bates asks, sitting up straight, using the rifle as support. "We won't get far if we just start walking straight into the bush."

"The stream we came in on fed water out from this pond. So it follows that the water accumulated here must come from somewhere else. Like there," he says, pointing at a small opening in the grass fifty feet around the bank. "You can see it, trickling in. It might be a connection to something larger. The Rio Negro, maybe. Something that might have boats or people on it." He takes the empty manioc container and fills it with water from the stream. "Bates, you're in charge of the rifle," he calls to us with his back turned. "I'll go up front with the machete and the water we can keep in the coffee can. Cross-man, you just follow us."

"Wait a second," I stutter as Bates lifts himself on the rifle's barrel. "We're going *now?*"

"You saw them out there on the river, didn't you?"

"Them?"

"The pirates. They're even closer now."

"I thought it was someone else."

"Like who?"

A boatload of your private-school bullies.

"I was seeing things," I say. "Forget it."

"No matter who it was, they're almost on top of us. We have to move before they have a chance to introduce themselves."

"Couldn't we wait for morning? So we can see where we're going?"

"We don't *know* where we're going," Wallace points out. "So we might as well get started going nowhere right away."

Before I can ask them not to or beg for sleep, before I realize the implications of *crying* in front of them, they're lifting me to my feet.

From the river the jungle was an idea. Vivid in the way of a world viewed through 3-D glasses, almost touchable. Yet still *not there*. A painted shell protecting an interior that couldn't even be guessed at.

Now we're going into it and there are no more ideas. There is only the night, the tangle of branches closest to our faces. No more *I am here* or *It is there*. The jungle and our bodies and nothing more.

We don't get far before the sun shows up. Beneath every level of canopy, in what the guide book called the under-story, the light is so filtered and hesitant it seems to come from within the illuminated objects themselves. The leaves over our heads glowing the photosyn-thetic yellow that looks green from a distance.

But these gentle introductions of light only appear for a short time. Then it is morning, and the air takes on weight. It wants out of here as much as I do. Taking it in requires deliberate effort, as though it's wrapped inside layers of wet wool.

The heat is a different matter. The heat is nothing but itself. Neither this nor that, above or below, so that every step is like passing through solid fact. It stops us after less than an hour. No more than a mile in, and yet we have already lost the tiny stream we started out following.

I'm the first to fall to my knees. Followed by Bates, who rolls onto his back and immediately sticks both hands down the front of his pants.

"Jesus, Bates, you're scratching yourself like an ape," Wallace says, lowering himself next to him. "Is it from the burns?"

"The burns just keep on going. *This* is different."

"Different how?"

"Like it's coming from the inside."

"An infection."

"I think she gave me something, man."

"She?"

"Lydia. The girl in Manaus."

"What's it feel like?"

"Itching. Crazy, crazy itching."

"Sounds like the sort of thing a professional girlfriend would leave you with. But after a few days out here, who knows? It could be anything. You memorized the guide book, Crossman. Anything in there on jungle diseases of the skin?"

"A little."

"Maybe it's that catfish that follows your piss up your dick," Bates offers. "If it's that, they'll have to cut it off when we get back, won't they?"

"No need to wait until then," Wallace offers, sliding the machete up between Bates's legs. "Come on, now. Let's have a look."

"That's not funny, man."

"There's no way it's the catfish thing," I tell them, and Wallace reluctantly draws the machete back. "If it was the *candiru*, you'd know about it."

"Bates may be a little shy about his condition, but I've got a little problem myself I wouldn't mind showing both of you," Wallace says. "If you're interested, that is."

He bends down to unlace his shoes and in seconds his feet swell to take up the new space afforded them. Delicate pulls at his white athletic socks, now black with sweat-salt and blood. When his skin is finally revealed—what used to be his skin—we see that both heels and every one of his toes and toenails are riddled with pockmarks. A million points of entry.

In the next second a fungal sourness blooms up from them that sends me and Bates reeling back.

"A bit off, isn't it?" Wallace nods. "Haven't taken them out for a few days because of the smell. Makes me think of icing sugar, somehow. Icing sugar poured over something rotten."

"Jesus Christ, Wallace," I say, gagging but without anything inside of me to come out. "Do they hurt?"

"Yes, they do. They hurt a *lot*, actually." He looks down at his feet for a moment as though they aren't his at all. "Do you know what it is?"

"Chiggers," I say, recalling the little inset photo in the guide book that made me immediately turn the page whenever I came across it. "Little bugs that eat their way under the skin. Like maggots except they don't wait until you're dead."

Wallace looks at me with an expression I had never seen from him before. A glimpse of uncertainty in the downturned corners of his mouth.

"I don't suppose the book mentioned anything that might help," he says.

"Not specifically, no. But one of these trees must have a painkiller in it. The trees and vines here are like a pharmacy."

"But we don't know *which* vine or tree to cut, do we? Only certified Brazilian tour guides and Indians know about that."

The worried expression leaves him almost as soon as it arrived. He tosses his socks behind a fallen log and pulls his shoes back on with the vaguely disappointed sigh of someone returning the lid to a container of inedible leftovers discovered at the bottom of the fridge.

A terse breeze moves through the branches. But it is forty feet up, heard and not seen, and only solidifies the heat down here on the ground.

We drink some of the water from the manioc container, hoping for another miraculous round of energy to move us on. When it doesn't come we drink some more. Even though we don't know where we've come from or where we will lead ourselves if we continue, it is beyond question that we cannot die *here*. This tiny clearing of jungle is, by virtue of our sitting in it, worse than any other. Walking is difficult, and getting more so. Very soon it will be impossible. But it is always better than not moving at all.

This is when the terror comes. Finds us in our exhaustion, in the relative quiet of our settled breathing. Calling us to sleep and denying it at the same time.

"Listen," Bates says. A mass of mosquitoes racing around his head.

"Listen," he says again. And although there is nothing but the usual sounds of the daytime jungle around us, we hear it too.

There is something else here with us.

It's not a suspicion, either. Not the spooked-out sensation of a stranger standing at the end of your bed as you fall asleep, of not being alone in an empty house. This is certain. And without being seen or making a sound, it has let itself be known.

"Do you feel that?" Bates doesn't move, his hands still cupping himself inside his pants.

"It's been following us for a while," Wallace answers him.

"Since the lily pond?"

"From then, yes. And before. I felt it watching now and again even out on the river."

"The concierge," Bates says, triggering another round of scratches.

"You saw him?"

"I thought I saw him at the pirates' camp. Tall as a fucking under-taker. And now he's here."

"I'm not sure about that."

"It's him."

"Nobody else has seen him except you, Bates."

"And Crossman."

"Is that true?"

They look at me at the same time and the weight of it is greater than the two of them sitting on my chest.

"Bates told me that he thought he'd seen the guy from the hotel back when we were in the hole," I say, shrugging, but the shrug sticks and my shoulders remain rigid against my jaw. "And when we got away in the canoe I thought I saw somebody who looked like him standing on the shore."

"You think it was the concierge from the Tropical?"

"The power of suggestion, more likely."

"What did this suggestion look like?"

"I don't really remember. Like Bates said, I guess. An undertaker."

"The Grim Reaper."

"Something like that."

"He tries to hide, Wallace," Bates says. "But I can see him every time I close my eyes."

"Maybe you should keep them open."

"What do you think it is if it isn't him?"

"Something that hunts."

"Like the caiman."

"No, that was different. The caiman was all instinct. Whatever this is has a *mind*."

Directly over our heads a falling leaf comes to life. Grows wings that flap it back up several feet before becoming a leaf again, spinning down to the ground between us.

"Well, that's it, boys. It's official," I say, clapping my hands together once. The sound it makes startles the leaf to the air once more, or what is not a leaf at all but a butterfly dappled in camouflage. "We've finally lost it."

"Maybe it's the tourist from the shelter. The one with the maps," Bates says, ignoring me. "If it's him he could get us out."

"And in return we could lend him a pair of our underwear."

"If you think you're hiding how scared you are by joking, it's not working," Wallace says, slowly turning to me. "I thought you were going to do the feeling for a while, Crossman. So why not be honest and admit you know exactly what we're talking about."

"I can *feel* all sorts of things. The difference is I know it's not real. It can't be. We haven't eaten anything for a long time. We're ill. But as for something watching us—that's just a campfire story we're telling ourselves."

Wallace tightens the laces on his bulging shoes. "Sounds to me like you're thinking again," he says. "My advice? Don't try to fight what's scaring you. Use it. It's going to win eventually, anyway."

He brings himself to his feet by pulling against the machete stuck into the earth, followed by Bates.

"Get up, Crossman," Bates tells me. "I don't want to leave you here, but I'm not going to wait around to find out what whatever's out there looks like."

He means it. And by the way Wallace is already striking out in a new direction, he's not going to see if I'm ready to follow them or not either.

"See, Crossman?" Wallace says, squeezing the tendons at the back of my neck after I stumble forward to join them. "I knew that, under the right circumstances, even you would be capable of a little imagination."

We're walking and it gets brighter with every step for a dozen steps and then we're standing blind in a crush of light.

Too bright to open our eyes at first so we smell where we are before we see. Surrounded by fire. Or what was a fire, now extinguished. The air pricked with sulphur. When we're finally able to look around us it's the smoke that obscures our vision as much as the unveiled sun.

A field of war.

Blasted and cratered, the ground cooked by fire, still hissing. An arena of smoking tree stumps maybe a quarter mile across, the forest blotchy in the distance. Some of the trunks still standing though, whittled thin, their tops sharp as spears. And the ground an irregular thatch of blackened wood. Stripped bare but not yet turned to ash.

For a second the sight of it aligns with newsreel glimpses of mass graves. The entanglement of charred, disconnected limbs.

"I'm going to be sick," Bates says, as if we had shared the same image.

"Try not to," Wallace tells him. "We need to keep everything inside of us. We're into the fifth stage of dehydration by now, wouldn't you say, Crossman?"

"There is no fifth stage."

"Exactly."

I look back at where we've come from, but any path we may have made has already disappeared. In fact the wall of jungle is as solid here as it was along the shore of the river. By some trick of physics the fire has traveled in a perfect line along where we stand, neat as the cut of a tailor's scissors.

"How do you think this happened?" Wallace asks me as Bates leans against him, taking in deep breaths of drifting carbon.

"It seems fairly recent. Probably lightning from the storm."

"But what if it's not natural? If people caused this, they may still be around."

"I don't think so."

"Why not?"

"Because we're *nowhere*. Ranchers stay close to the rivers big enough to bring steamers through for supplies. As far as we've seen, there's nothing like that around here."

"It might not be ranchers."

"Then who?"

"Indians. The people the tour guide talked about. The ones who are running *away* from the ranchers."

"I see. Indians who have a thing for recreational arson."

"They start fires to clear patches to grow things. Maybe they started it so they could build a new camp or whatever they call the places they live. Those open circles ringed with a straw shelter."

"*Shabonos*," I answer for him. Bates is now pulling himself right by climbing up Wallace's arm. "Seems like you've been paying attention to the tourist books too."

"I like the pictures."

Somewhere far off the fire makes an almost inaudible rumble. A movement that travels through the ground like the approach of a train detected by putting your ear to the rails.

"Doesn't look like anyone's around right now, anyway," I say.

"You sound relieved."

"We've been running from things for a long time. It's hard to think that we may be going *toward* something."

"We need to find somebody if we're going to get out of here."

"I know that."

"Somebody aside from the pirates."

"Or the thing in the forest," Bates adds, spitting his mouth clean.

Wallace points directly ahead of him and across the burned field. "And if there *is* something following us, it might be better not to run right back into it."

"Looks hot," Bates says.

"We're no more than a couple miles from the equator," Wallace says, stepping over the first petrified trunk. "Everything's hot around here."

"Wait a second."

At first, by the way his mouth hangs partly open and his arms dangle so low they may have already fallen out of their sockets, I'm sure Bates is asking us to wait because he can go no farther. We knew this would come. The only surprise is I thought it would be me.

But instead Bates's hand pulls back against his body, finds the front pocket of his shorts. Slides out with the Palmcorder.

"I want to get this on tape," he says. "Wallace entering the Inferno."

Wallace turns. Even now he is agreeable to the camera's demands. This time going for the intense look, the great blue-eyed hope on last legs that keep going by sheer resolve. It comes naturally to him: the bored aristocrat gone discovering and conquering and grass-skirt chasing. Now it's different, though. The intensity and willfulness suggest not lust but something more refined. A gentlemanliness. Hands high on his hips, squinting against the sun, a shadow of beard I hadn't noticed before now. And behind him the landscape of experience. All around this triumphant young man is trial and punishment and death. But he isn't afraid of any of it. He's about to walk straight into what he can only assume to be the worst nightmare he's ever had, and he is able to do it not because he has lost the ability to care but because he has found it in extraordinary measure. You can see all this in the pose that Wallace strikes. The gift of leadership, buoyant and oblivious.

If we get out of here and deliver Bates's camera home again I'm certain this recorded moment will come to mean something in the larger scheme of things, to outlast us as a single image can sometimes do. It's a portrait of Wallace. But on another level, it's a portrait of what Wallace *is*. Look at him: at once self-conscious and candid, an actor who has been performing for so long he is only being himself when he acts. And in the role of the moment he is the noble soldier. One who has seen some action and taken to it. Animated by a curiosity too ravenous to know the trouble it will eventually cause.

You recognize all this even as the pose is struck. The lens opens its eye and there it is, proof that *this happened* and *he was there*.

It has the look of history about it.

Bates lifts his finger off the Record button and we're returned to the present. Wallace walking on ahead of us again, navigating a route around the piles of scorched stuff. Thin plumes of smoke rising from the farthest charcoal trunks like the most delicate of exclamation marks.

Every glance back at where we started from reveals our advance to be impossibly slow. And it only gets hotter as we near the center of the clearing, as though these aren't the remains of a forest fire at all but the lip of a smoldering volcano.

Everything we touch burns. The side of a leg brushing against a still-flickering stump, a hand grabbing a disintegrating branch for balance. It's like walking through a tunnel of barbed wire. A million razor points crowding in so that there is always at least one finding its way through the skin.

It keeps us going, though. We can't lie down here. We can't sit.

Halfway across, even the idea of going back is taken from us. There is only the tree line at the far side of the clearing growing more distinct at what may only be an imagined rate. And the scalding touches that won't let us stop.

"Almost there," Wallace says. How are these words coming to him? Where did he find the air? "Doing good. Almost there."

They work all the same.

Almost there.

What my father behind the wheel of the wood-paneled station

wagon turns around to shout at me, the travel-sick kid in the back seat. Hours shy of our destination but he says it anyway. He'll keep saying it all the way there. And not even the most trusting child believes it to be true.

We take a few more steps. Another twenty feet as the crow flies. Four times that distance given the snaking course we're forced to take.

Almost home now.

If we believe the lie long enough, who's to say it can't be made true?—

—the soles of Bates's shoes fling up into my vision. A near double kick upside my chin.

He's fallen for real this time. A sprawling face-slide into the gray as though tossed into an ashtray.

"Get up," Wallace slurs, standing over him. Nudges a foot against Bates's side. "You *have* to get up now."

Bates doesn't move. All of him coated with fine dust, his arms cast out in a breast stroke.

"I'm asking nicely," Wallace tries, but when he opens his mouth to speak again nothing comes out.

Bates hears him, nevertheless. His shoulders tremble in a half push-up, supported on his elbows alone, leaving his hands to grasp up at us, blindly clenching and opening. We can't see his face. His head is too heavy to move. It hangs off his neck so that it alone remains buried in ash.

Then falls into it again. This time, when Wallace tells him to get up, there is no stirring.

Wallace looks to me. To see what's there.

All at once we grab Bates by the elbows and start carrying him forward. His arms yoked over our shoulders and the toes of his sneakers leaving two furrows behind us. Wallace and I doing this together. Both of us soldiers now, dragging a fallen brother off the field of battle.

It's then that I stop even the remotest speculation over whether we will make it. This has been Wallace's advantage all along. While I've been threading a narrative together to preserve myself, he has been acting. What appeared at first to be fearlessness turns out to be only instinct. Something that was once commonly human but is now lost, atrophied from lack of exercise. He has always had it and now I've been given it as well.

We work to bring our friend to the forest on the other side. Relieved of maintaining who I am. The internal debates, the never-quite-right translations, the frittering worry.

Whatever Elizabeth Crossman was is gone. I'm only a part of this now. A part of them.

For the second time, I open my eyes and think that I'm home. Looking up at the crosshatching of wires paneled onto the sky, the same view up through the window of my basement apartment in Toronto. But these are too hairy to be wires. Lianas vines. Ones that like to lasso tree to tree. The guide book noted that they are so strong that even if one of the trees they have tied themselves to is dead it can remain standing for years, propped up like a piece of jungle taxidermy.

And look there. Strangling figs. There are no strangling figs in Toronto, as far as I can recall. *A most curious botanical parasite*, the travel guide called them. Its aerial roots flow out from a seed planted in the bark of a tree by some spiteful *chacalaca* or puffbird, which comes to form a mesh that will eventually suffocate its host. All that survives is the parasitic fig itself. A weed standing as a lookalike second trunk.

"Crossman."

Another thing unlike home. Back there, nobody says my name aloud when I wake up except for me.

"Crossman. Hey. You OK?"

Bates's face looming over me. Sunburned as it ever has been but his skin suggestive of a new paleness just beneath the surface. You can even see it where the dead layer has peeled away. Underneath he is white as a larva.

"You made it," I say.

"The two of you pulled me out of there."

"We *pulled* you?"

"You and Wallace. Total fucking marines."

"Is he OK?"

222

"I think he's got fever really bad now. He's saying things."

"That's not so unusual."

Bates doesn't hear the joke. Or doesn't find it funny if he does.

"Do you think you can walk?" he asks.

"Do you?"

"I think so. The sick feeling—it comes and it goes."

"I just need some sleep."

"We'll start again when Wallace wakes up."

"Couldn't we just lie here awhile?"

"I don't think we can," he says, shaking his head as it removes itself from my field of vision.

"Why not?"

"It's coming."

"The pirates." I hear my voice falter, trying to bring Bates back into view.

"It's the fire, Crossman. Along with whatever else is out there," I hear him say high up in the web of vines before I'm out again. "The fire is hunting us."

Cinders falling all around and making the snapping sound of extra footfalls in the grass. Maybe there are those now, too.

I realize that I'm running before I realize that I'm awake. How did I get started at all? A good question. An even better one would be how I'm running through the bush, still asleep, *and* leading the way? That's Wallace and Bates just behind me. Bates pushing against Wallace's shoulders, ready to catch him if he falls. Whatever strain of fever that afflicts us has become expert at jumping from one of us to the other, sometimes within the space of minutes. Apparently now it is Wallace's turn.

Sometimes the fire comes close enough that we can see what it looks like head on. A wall of curdled oranges and tentacles of smoke reaching out from under it. Coming around at one of our sides and rushing to link up with the other parts of itself. Moving in fluid springs and flights, graceful as the crosscurrents of a ballet corps.

Other times not like this at all. Punches of heat connecting with our heads. Entire trees thrown down before us, cutting us off.

Now the sulphur is so thick it closes our throats. A moment before we couldn't even smell it. With eyes shut you'd never know the world was burning down a few hundred yards away. And then whatever wind there is shifts direction and our nostrils are plugged with ash.

Fire that makes a sound. Wet and smacking, a thousand cats licking their whiskers. That's when it's far off. But when it comes closer, it turns into something else. A hiss that nearly becomes a word.

The one thing I don't expect is how fast it can move.

There it is up ahead and I angle us off to the right so that we'll pass it at a safe distance. Then it lunges directly in front us. Traveling along the vines, dropping down the next dead tree and bleeding out from its base.

Go the other way, turn back. The fire skittering in a circle to surround us. No way to escape its reach except straight into it. What may be raindrops or embers pricking against my face.

There is a shape here with us, too.

A shadow crashing through the heavy underbrush, the ground thudding as it pushes forward. Snapping whatever stands before it with its immense head.

At first I assume it's an animal. A jaguar flushed out by the fire. But it stays with us too long for that. Close, yet far enough off that it doesn't show itself whole.

I glance back at Wallace and Bates but they can't have seen it— their heads bent, blind. Somehow they keep up, falling through the branches I push open and let slap shut behind me. Bates so busy nudging Wallace back up when he's about to topple to one side that it's all he can do to follow my changes of direction. He doesn't even look out for the fire. I am their eyes now.

And their ears, because it seems I'm the only one to hear the voice.

Something that knows how to speak but has chosen not to. Wallace or Bates. Me. The shadow that follows us. Lydia calling out for us from the trees.

Something that starts to scream and doesn't stop.

• • •

We stop only when it hits us. All of us scorched now—Wallace's neck glowing an implausible red, his clothes soaked black—but it is the surprise of sound that fills our heads.

A voice.

Singing in English. Though "singing" may not be entirely right. An untrained whine, the noise the tone deaf make belting out the words to whatever's playing on their headphones. Instruments, too. Rhythm guitar, drums, harmonica.

It's the sound of home that stops us.

A song. Absurd and defiant and outrageously human. The last-call dance tune at all the C&W taverns that play host to lonely patrons of a certain age (i.e., every one of them). Something to drift out the open windows of pick-up trucks and be played by house bands not so good at the fast numbers. To make you inexplicably sad and think of prairie highways you have never traveled on and of good women whose only real shortcomings are smoking and failing to be beautiful.

The jungle acting as an organic amplifier, every branch and vine and hanging tapestry of moss hooked up to the same source. But instead of tribal drums it has tuned in to classic American rock-and-roll (American rock-and-roll that is in fact Canadian rock-and-roll). "Heart of Gold." The first song that every teenage boy of a generation asked to be taught on the guitar.

It would be a comfort, perhaps, or at least offer a last taste of the familiar, if it weren't for the thing that watches us being here also. The beast's movement can't be heard exactly, though it lends a bass vibration of its own beneath the recorded sound, the thud of a footstep under Neil Young's road-weary complaint.

It isn't odd to hear the jungle sing. It's what it has always been working toward. An artful surprise, something as soon beautiful as awful. An enveloping expression of itself.

Music.

9

THE *shabono* is much larger than the guide book photos would lead you to believe. An oval of straw-thatched roof set upon poles and in the center an open space about a hundred feet across. An empty bull-fighting ring of blinding sand, and above it nothing but treeless blue. I suppose a 35-mm lens can't be expected to capture the height of the sky.

But down here on the earth's surface, all the way around in the sheltered shade, there are so many new bits of color and human detail I can only take it in blinks.

Hammocks slung between the poles.

Wisps of smoke from cooking fires.

Bunches of plantains lying on the ground.

Tapir carcasses strung up by their claws.

I work to keep the panic down and fix my eyes open to watch these individual snapshots bleeding over one another. It's the tears that do it. Single-minded, unstoppable. The effect is something like a home movie, the pre-digital kind my parents made of me toddling around, the candy-coating of Super 8. Or perhaps it is simply that, aside from the sky and the fire that chased us, these are the only shades other than green we have seen since leaving the river.

A *village*.

This word arriving late along with the storybook images it brings with it, of Tudor cottages and a church spire nestled in a valley. Although this place has nothing to do with any of that. This is little more than a curtain to hide behind. A manmade wall that keeps us inside and removes the forest from view.

There is only one way out. An opening in the ring that is veiled by hanging vines, not much wider than a space two bodies could pass through walking side by side. Yet with an angled sigh of wind the vines are drawn away to offer a glimpse of where we've come from. For maybe three or four acres around the entrance there is what looks to be a garden. Rough, unbordered, carved into buckled furrows. Weeds so tall they sag over the fat lumps of plantain. Nothing but this and a foot-wide trough winding through it all and the scar of footprints connecting the *shabono* entrance to the surrounding forest. This is where we must have been dragged along, although I have no actual memory of how they brought us here. From *out* to *in*.

The dried vines pull back and there it is. The jungle still out there after all. The bony slouch of trees weaving like a crowd of zombies, waiting for a sign of life to feed upon. Beyond them a billow of gray low in the sky, a knot of darkness that could be mistaken for storm clouds if I didn't know it was from the fire. I try to determine by the bends of smoke whether it's coming our way or just waiting along with the undead trees, but before I can get an idea one way or the other the moment of wind dies away and the vines close shut. Only the ring of white sand again. The blurred spots of color.

And people.

Wallace and Bates in the hammocks on each side of me. Both still. But both alive, judging from the sounds coming from inside their chests. Every time I turn my head to check on one of them I nearly pass out. I risk unconsciousness every couple of minutes to confirm that I'm not entirely alone.

"Bates?" I whisper at the curled question mark his body makes lying on its side. Then turn to focus on the other twin straight on his back, mummified, his mouth pulled open into an unintended leer. "Wallace?"

Ba-tees?

Wal-less?

Giggles. Bursts of speech followed by mocking repetition coming from every direction. Coming, I know, from the ones that are hard to look at. The people I have refused to accept until now because they are surely not really here.

Just under a couple of dozen I would guess, though there may be more if you count the babies clinging to their mothers' necks or sleeping in scarf-sized hammocks of their own. Adult men standing in a circle closest to us, then the women shielding their eyes from the sun and looking across the open circle from their different sections of wall, each separated from their neighbors by a porous divide of straw. And every few seconds the fearless children pushing through the men's legs to lay their fingers against our skin, wipe the ash from our foreheads, tug at our shoelaces. It's the children who find our names so hilarious.

How did we get *here?*

We were running from the fire when we broke through the bush into a partial clearing. Things start and end there. And with the music. When I opened my eyes to this place I thought we were alone. Not even the daytime murmur of the jungle made its way over the wall. Nothing since Neil Young's voice and then a drowning into silence.

Once, I tried to find Wallace's and Bates's names but nothing came out.

Awoke some hours later and this time there was something. The scratch of my tongue over my lips. Followed by what felt like rain falling into my mouth.

The next time I'm capable of a definite whisper, though no one seems able to hear it except for me. Then there are different voices, the mispronounced echoes. It's only after this that I decide that I can see them, too.

People speaking a language unlike any I have heard before. Yet what they say is also dimly familiar, as though a child's poem once learned by heart and now forgotten.

They are Indians. The tallest standing no more than five and a half feet, their faces round and slightly flattened. An indeterminable combination of what we know as Chinese, Mongolian, even North African features, and yet not mistakable for any of these. Yanomami. The secret people the *Ana Cassia*'s tour guide spoke about. The ones the travel book had a mournful one-page essay on, along with a photo of naked men with feathers through their noses holding up spears three feet taller than they were.

The men's clothing is limited to cotton strings around their wrists, ankles and waists. Penises captured in a sleeve, the tip of which is laced up and connected to the string at their hips to hold the whole business in place. The women in similar gear, with only a flap of animal hide over their genitals and a decorative bone piercing through an earlobe or nostril. From any distance their gender is difficult to determine, at least right away. All of them wear their hair in uniform bowl cuts. The men's breasts can sometimes equal those of the women.

But then I notice the differences. It makes them hard to believe in all over again. You see it in the children first. The ones that pop out from behind their elders only partly wearing the traditional strings and sleeves. Most of them instead shifting around within soiled, oversized Bermuda shorts. And all the ones that can walk draped in extra-large T-shirts with pop-culture icons and slogans found in "vintage" stores back home. Tweety Bird. Bart Simpson (circa "Do the Bartman"). A sweating, Vegas-era Elvis. One bearing the fuzzy-font declaration I DO WHAT THE VOICES IN MY HEAD TELL ME TO DO.

All but the youngest infants chew tobacco.

One of the boys is now excitedly pinching my chin and pointing at a spot somewhere beyond the end of my feet. When I summon my eyes to follow I find a television elevated on an overturned stewing pot. Its screen blank, its cord coiled on the ground like a sleeping snake.

"Where did you get that?"

The boy doesn't answer, not in his or any language, but runs over to the TV and falls to his knees before it. Places both of his hands on the screen and makes two circles in the dust collected on its surface. Rubs it like a Buddha's belly.

"It won't work," I say, the bottom falling out of my voice.

His hands move inside the screen. Two drills spinning deeper into a block of black quartz.

"You need to plug it in. And you don't have—"

A cough sends something into my mouth from a long way down. I just manage to push it off my tongue before everything blurs once more.

When the world next comes together, one of their faces is held directly over mine. A man no taller but somewhat broader than the others, his shoulders rounded by smooth orbs of muscle. A glance to the side shows that everyone has taken a half step back to make way for him.

"You have found us," he says, amused, as though congratulating us on a particularly vigorous game of hide-and-seek. "Now you are here."

"Yes."

"Sick."

"Yes. We are very sick."

He nods, the smile broadening in the appreciation of some joke I'm unaware of telling. Shows gums molded like wax around the roots of his teeth.

"*Very* sick," he agrees. "But we will try."

"Yes. Try?"

"To make you well."

"Thank you," I hear myself saying in Portuguese. Only now do I realize that the headman is speaking it too. Not the strange language the others were using before but an oddly lilting yet coherent Portuguese. The kind they taught children in the old mission schools.

"Thank us, yes." He nods again, releasing his laugh at last. "Can I ask?"

"What?"

"Do you have anything to trade?"

I throw my head back to look at Bates in his hammock and everything swims for a few seconds. When I manage to focus he's too curled up for me to see if he still holds anything against his body as he sleeps.

"You want the rifle, don't you?" I say, my eyes shut against a rising wave of nausea.

"Your gun?"

"You can have it, if you haven't taken it already. It's jammed, though."

"We already have guns." He almost laughs again. "Many guns."

"I'm not sure what else—"

"Do you have any tapes?"

For a moment I'm not sure if I've heard him correctly. His face remains suspended above mine with the same expectant humor.

"Videotape," I say finally. "The very small kind. Inside the very small camera. Yes, I think we do."

"No, not *movies*. There is no VCR here."

"But you have a TV."

"That is only—how do you say the thing you keep to remember?—it is only a *souvenir*."

"There's no electricity for it to run on."

"But we have batteries. Many batteries."

"You have a radio?"

"A ghettoblaster, yes."

He says "ghettoblaster" in English. Every syllable carefully enunciated, as though a recently coined scientific term.

"That's what we heard before?" I ask the floating face.

"You found us."

"The music in the jungle. Neil Young."

"He is excellent, yes."

"That was your radio."

"No radio. *Cassettes*. This is what we trade with the *nabah* for."

"*Nabah?*"

"You," he says. "The ones from outside."

All of this is costing me too much. And here they come: the black fingers reaching through the holes in the hammock to pull me back again.

"Mostly?" the headman says in a whisper of giddy confession. "Mostly, we like the rock-and-roll."

He sleeps with his eyes open. If you can call it sleep. Gone wherever the fever has taken him. Down so deep there's no trace of him left, not as far as the light can reach into his pupils, wide as dimes. I think his name and will him back into its skin. But none of these prayers change anything in his stiffened body, arms crossed over his chest like ceremonial remains laid out upon their sarcophagus.

Yet there are still hints of movement if you watch closely enough. Each new gasp shocks him, as though breathing is a skill he thought he'd forgotten. And as his chest rises up to receive the air his eyes seize upon a fixed point in the sky. Once or twice I even let my own head fall back to see what he might be looking at. Each time I'm expecting a cluster of vultures circling a thousand feet up. But there is nothing there except the same old boundless blue.

I slip in and out of things myself. My stomach aches from hunger less than it did before, though I don't remember eating. They must be tending to us but I never catch them doing it. Everything hurts a degree less than it did: where the hook sank into my back, the singed flesh up my legs, the molars Wallace rattled loose of my jaw. Even the parasite has been quieted for a time.

But he still hasn't woken up.

"Crossman? You there?"

"Halfway."

"Any changes?"

"Still sleeping."

"Not with his eyes open like that."

"No, I think he's fine."

"He's not even throwing up anymore. That's got to be bad."

"It's only because there's nothing more to throw up."

"You talked to that one guy. Is that Portuguese he was talking?"

"Seems to be the only one who can."

"So what are they doing to him?"

"I don't know what they're doing. But I'm pretty sure they're trying to help."

Bates is in his hammock behind me. I could turn to face him but I might lose it again and I'm trying to hang on for as long as I can. Each time I'm awake I work for a bit more light and air and speech.

"Crossman?"

"Yes?"

"If he dies, we die too."

"He's not going to die."

"It's not that I'm frightened. I just wanted you to know."

"He's not going to die, Bates."

"Look at him."

It's all I've been doing. And Bates is right, of course. Wallace has the sucked-out appearance of one who has reached the end of an unnaturally long string of luck. And though he should have from the beginning, he never thought it could happen. Staring up into an absent heaven. Stricken, dismayed.

"If it comes to that, we'll just have to lean on each other," I say.

"There's nothing to hold us up."

"Enough to get us home."

"I wouldn't know what home is without him."

"I'll show you."

"You didn't know before you came here. What could you show me now?"

"My apartment. My books. My autographed Elton John poster. The place on the corner where I get coffee in the morning. That's all I know."

"And that adds up to more than here?"

"Here hates me."

"Maybe that's better than nothing. Better than being alone with your bookshelf and coffee shop."

"I don't have the heart for much more than that. Most people back home don't, either. Maybe they could all do with a nice jungle outing to perk them up. But I'm going back there all the same. And so are you. And so is Wallace."

"If he's not with us we'll never get back anyway."

"That's not necessarily true."

"It *is* necessarily true. Why are you always denying what you know?"

"Because it's ridiculous. He's only one man—a kid. He's not *magic*. He's not a *god* or anything, for Christ's sake."

"I never said—"

"Just because you love him—"

"Yes, Crossman?"

"I mean that your feelings may be getting in the way here."

He surprises me with a barking laugh. "'All human history is the digression of emotions.' He told me that once. Quite a thing for a teenager to say, don't you think?"

"I thought Wallace was against history."

"Only the way it pretends to be a single set of facts. He would say that there is no one truth, but as many as there are people to feel them."

"And what was the occasion for this insight?"

"It was when I first admitted to him that I loved him."

"What could you have known about that? You were still kids."

"The Awkward Age. I knew it might push him away but I said it anyway. That it was *painful* to love him as much as I did. And then he told me that the pain was the point."

Wallace shivers. Ripples sent down from his shoulders to his ankles like a breeze over water. It seems all he is capable of now, a tiny seizure issued from some place outside his control. I wait for another. Fight to stay awake so that my vigil might return some power to him. Bring his voice back.

"What about you, Crossman?"

Watch him lying there, pale as a plaster idol. One that comes alive for only the most faithful.

"Is it the idea of dying that makes you scared?" Bates tries again. "Or is it love?"

After a time Bates assumes I have fallen asleep and haven't heard him. I would have attempted to answer him, but it's all I can do to keep watch. Waiting for another fluttered eyelid, a snatch of breath. A signal meant only for me.

Another face floating over me when I wake. Not the headman this time. A gaunt mask whose features aren't quite right. The worst part is the mouth fixed into a show of teeth pulled partway out from their gums, long as piano keys.

"Good morning, Crossman," it says.

"Good morning, Wallace."

"I'm not even sure if it *is* morning. But from what I understand, it's been a long sleep for all of us, so we might as well start from the beginning."

"Or the end."

"Listen to you! Narrowly escaped the jaws of destruction once again and here is our Crossman, the irredeemable pessimist."

"There's not much to get excited about."

"Really? I'm *full* of excitement."

"We thought you were dying."

"It crossed my mind, too. But I decided against it."

"So you came back to us."

"Ta-da!"

"Trouble is, we still don't know where we are."

"Look around," Wallace tries to shout but his voice breaks, and instead he throws out his arms to take in everything within the *shabono*'s walls. "This is an undeveloped market if I've ever seen one!"

I can look into his skull. Perhaps it's from the lean wrapping of his skin. Both nostrils flared hollow, reaching back a foot or more inside of him but with nothing to see at the end. His mouth opens and there's the back of his throat, the abrupt drop, the clenching of the pink pipe that could accommodate anything you might push into it.

"Are they still here?"

He lifts his chin and looks around somewhere past the back of my head. "Of course."

"What are they doing?"

"Watching us, actually."

"Oh Christ."

"Not to worry. I've already engaged them in some economic discourse."

"You mean you gave them the rifle."

"No, I traded them my Nikes for some of their medicine." He sniffs, and everything inside of him rattles. "Fantastic stuff."

"It made you better?"

"*Better?* I'd say better, yes."

"Let me try some."

The mask returns to look at me. Two cut-out holes for the eyes, each with a single glistening spot of white within.

"I'm not sure you're ready yet, Crossman. It's rather heavy."

He runs a white stick of a finger under his nose. Flicks away a string of green ejaculate that has found its way onto his lip.

"You *snort* it?"

"My apologies. It has some rather unsightly side effects, I'm afraid."

"But it saved your life."

"Hallelujah!"

"You have a thing for resurrections."

"Our hosts are impressed with my recovery as well. They don't seem to have thought I'd make it."

"I prayed for you, you know."

"What was that?"

I'm frightened of him now. This is not the way he has always looked to me because I have managed to deny that he might actually be monstrous. I have feared him since I met him, but told myself it wasn't fear at all but only some kind of complicated resentment. A mixture of envy and moral disapproval and the most ungainly of generation gaps. But I can see now that he is a monster. And what had I done? I had prayed for him to return.

"What did you say, Crossman?"

"What are you going to do without your shoes?"

"*They* don't have any shoes. And besides, the soles fell right off them somewhere before the fire. That's what you get for cheap glue and Taiwanese slave labor."

"When in Rome, is that it?"

"That's right, Crossman," the mask nods. Recedes. "That's *exactly* right."

It may be the next day. Or the day after what would have been the next day the last time I was conscious. At any rate, there is a persistent chill clinging to my skin that feels like it came from the night before. And I'm much stronger than I was. Hunger like a boot to my guts and the worm inside of me has come back to furious life, but still better, I guess.

When Wallace's face next appears over me it is less like a mask than the last time, too. The features remain puckered and gray, but this only from the thinned blood of tropical fever. Nothing savage or inhuman.

I don't even think I fear him anymore, either. Look: I'm lifting myself up on my elbows, shifting in the hammock to get a better view. Getting closer. How could I have ever thought I could fear him?

"Did Bates make it?" I ask.

"He will."

"He's still sick?"

"It's that bug going around. Everyone seems to have it."

Wallace is wearing nothing but his shredded boxers, although he's cleaner than he was. His tan lines cut across thighs and arms. Even his feet seem to be healing from their chigger infestation, the holes now plugged with new skin, white as putty.

"I'd never seen so much enthusiasm over J. Crew shorts and a *very* stinky Phish World Tour T-shirt," Wallace says. "Imagine if they dropped a Wal-Mart down here. It would be madness."

"What did they give you in return? I assume you didn't hand over your clothes as a gift."

"Well, I'm not in much of a bargaining position, am I? A palm leaf filled with mashed plantain, some tree goo on my burns, a bit more of that crazy powder up the nose—that's fair enough for me. Besides, I'm kind of *into* the nakedness. It's a lot like skinny dipping, except without the water."

By hanging on to the rope around the hammock's edge I can pull my head even with the horizon and get a view of the whole *shabono*. A couple of the men have noticed my waking and stood up to peer this way. The headman and some of the children start walking over to us.

Wallace glances around to meet the headman's eyes, raises a hand above his head in a cordial wave of the kind offered to the next-door neighbor over the backyard fence.

"Here they come," he says. "The welcome committee."

A circle of them stop a body length from where we are. Except for the headman, who comes forward to stand next to Wallace.

"From what I can tell, Crossman, my friend here is very keen to speak to you," Wallace says. "He seems to be the one *in charge*."

"He speaks Portuguese."

"That's handy. So do you."

Wallace gives me a gentle slap on the shoulder that sends whatever parts I'd managed to lift up reeling back into the hammock. This starts another round of giggles from the Gap and Fruit of the Loom kids. Even the headman offers a droll nod at my feebleness.

"I knew we were right not to leave you back in that hole with the pirates," Wallace says, now facing the headman directly with a movie star smile. "A *translator*. Don't leave home without one."

The headman says, "*Você poole levantar e ir caminhar comigo agora.*"

"I can't get up yet. My legs won't hold me."

"What are you saying? What's he want?" Wallace asks.

"He's asking me to go for a walk."

"A *walk?* With who?"

"Just the two of us, I think."

"Like a date?"

"God, I hope not."

"You feel bad," the headman says in Portuguese. "But there are things you need to tell me. That I need to ask."

"Can't it wait? And if not, can't we talk here?"

"It cannot wait." He looks over his shoulder. "And it cannot be here."

Gently, but firm enough that there is no choice about it, the headman grips me by the arms and lifts me out of the hammock.

"You have slept enough. Now you must walk the sickness out," he says.

"It's too hot."

"That's good. The fever leaves with your sweat."

Without my being aware of any effort, we begin to shuffle out into the sunlit center of the *shabono*.

"Where are we going?"

"Outside."

"We *are* outside."

"You are not part of the *shabono* yet. We cannot properly speak within it."

My legs swing under me without touching the ground, my weight hanging from the arm slung around the headman's neck. He's taking me to the vine-covered entranceway. Out into the full sun that pulls up instant stings of sweat.

"Remember, Crossman. It's only your first date," Wallace calls after us. "Don't do anything I wouldn't do!"

Nobody else in the village comes near us, though they watch us go, and I try to read their faces. Is the headman going to kill me? If he is, what kind of expression might his people be showing about now? Excitement? Pity? There's no sign of either. What is there could instead be seen as hope. Who knows? If the negotiations go well between me and the headman there may be Adidas trainers and *Neil Young Unplugged* tapes all round.

We pass through the vines and out into the plantain field. The clearing here is just wide enough to permit the air to move about. Although little more than a hacked-out yard (slash and burn, just as the guide book said), there is a familiar purposefulness to it, a logic. For this ragged spot if nowhere else, the jungle has been denied.

It makes me think of home. Not mine, but what others would see in it, the heartening sign of human organization, of nature put into some semblance of control. Barry would have seen a version of Georgia. The leisurely, sentimentalized one of his childhood, "way back before they started calling the Old South new." He would have looked at this mess of palms and envisioned walking out from his family's fishing lodge with a rod and a jar of squirming bait, making his way to the creek that lies at the end of the trail, to the shady place his granddaddy showed him where the brook trout lingered on hot afternoons.

Lydia, no doubt, would have seen an only slightly neglected English garden.

As though I had been speaking these thoughts aloud, the headman asks if there had been more than the three of us traveling in our party when we started out.

"No, there is only us," I tell him, and the lie comes easily.

He lifts my arm off his shoulders and walks ahead of me. Without him I totter for a moment before throwing a step forward, at first for balance, and then one after another. When I catch up to him he has turned to witness my progress. It's impossible to say whether his face shows doubt, or whether the pause comes only with his effort to understand.

"No others?" he asks again.

"There's me. My name is Elizabeth. And Wallace, the one back in the village who you've already met. And the one who is still sick. His name is Bates."

239

"That's all?"

"That's all."

"Oh yes?"

"That's it."

"Why did you come?"

No pause at all this time. He doesn't believe for a second that there were only three of us at the beginning, but he can live with that. This question is different.

"We didn't mean to."

"But you are here."

"That's an accident."

"Accident?"

"We were tourists. *Eco*-tourists. Have you heard of them? There's package deals you can find on the web. Many of us want to save the rainforest. Or we at least want to see it before it disappears. To take in all of this, your natural—"

I stop. I'm about to say *habitat* but that's wrong. That's only for animals, isn't it? And why am I playing travel agent with an Indian jungle warrior anyway? If that's what he is. But the thought must be finished now that I've started it, because he's standing there, waiting.

"—your *home*. So we flew down to Manaus and went upriver on our own. We got lost. Then the storm forced us into the bush. We didn't mean to disturb you."

"Disturb?"

"I mean we weren't looking for you. But we're certainly glad we found you. Or you found us. It's no exaggeration to say—in fact I'd like to *express*—you and your people saved our lives."

"Yes."

"And we are very thankful for that."

"Thankful. The three of you. Yes."

There is no change in his voice, or in the way he looks at me, but there still seems to be some anticipation of more.

"Were you *expecting* others?"

"No," he says, finally moving his head into a shake of regret. "But I must tell you that there *are* others, nevertheless."

He turns now to keep walking toward the wall of forest. When I try to follow it seems I have already forgotten how to walk, and the head-man has to come back to take me by the elbow, guiding me along like a shrunken old lady. I might have dropped to my knees at any point up to now. But this news—*he knows about the others?*—has taken every-thing away.

"Do you know who they are?" I ask him.

"I have not seen them myself. It was only one of my hunters," he says very close to my ear, more than half my weight leaning on him now. "He saw a group of men, he couldn't say how many. They were gathered by the small river where you left your canoe."

"So they know we're here."

"Only if they know where here is."

For a second the absurdity of my situation strikes me—who I am and where we are and the naked brown man next to me who smells of smoked meat and tobacco. Then it's gone as soon as it arrives. No matter how foreign the setting, what surrounds me remains nothing but facts. I'm the only one who can speak to him. Given this, some part of me decides it will spend no more time pretending I'm not actually here.

"You know who they are," I say.

"They came for you. I would think you would know better than me."

"We're tourists."

"You have said what you are."

"Strangers in a strange land."

"But these others. You believe they are not also tourists? Strangers?"

"If I had to guess, I'd say no."

"And you are being *followed* by these *nabah?*"

"Yes."

"How do you know this?"

"We heard them on the big river. They would fire their guns. They may have only been hunting. But it may have also been a signal. To let us know they were coming for us."

"Maybe they were sent from outside. To find you because you were lost. To bring you out."

"No, I don't think so. They are bad men."

"And they are after you."

"We felt them getting closer. The whole time there was something just behind us in the jungle."

"It may have been the jungle itself."

"It's true that we didn't actually see anything."

"But you believe it was these men?"

"Yes."

"And that they are bad."

"That's why we ran away."

We have reached the line of trees at the far end of the garden clearing and the headman takes a single stride into the shade they offer. Props me up against the trunk of the one nearest him and turns to look back at the *shabono*. A flying saucer made of twigs.

"We know about such men," he says. "We are running away as well."

He tells me that their village is one of the last not yet resettled by the government, moved down to the shore of one of the major rivers. There the people are discouraged from building *shabonos* and live instead in pre-fab huts lined up in rows. Along with these, the new village invariably includes a church, a missionary office and a school. There, just as the tour guide on the *Ana Cassia* had said, the Yanomami are taught Portuguese or Spanish or English, and watch television, and have most of their food brought in on river barges once a month. Bleached manioc and meat that comes in tins.

The headman knows this because he is the only one who has seen it for himself. A group of hunters from his village went to a government settlement to trade anaconda skins for new machetes three dry seasons ago but he was the only one of them to return. Something happened to the others there. A spell. Wicked magic that made them want to forget their own names and to learn instead the names of characters on the daytime dramas broadcast out of São Paulo.

For whatever reason the spell didn't work on the headman. But he did stay long enough to learn the *nabah*'s language, and to memorize the maps on the mission wall, with colored pins showing the locations of known *shabonos* and their resettlements. When he left he tried to persuade his tribesmen to come with him, although he knew it would do no good. But he managed to make them promise never to tell anyone the location of their traditional hunting spots, a promise he believed they would keep and, even if they didn't, he doubted they would soon remember how to find these places anyway.

When the headman came back to his village he convinced his people to follow him away from where the government and missionary *nabah* would most likely look for them. So far, this hadn't been too difficult. But now there are others to run from. Small groups of illegal gold miners known as *garimpeiros* fighting for the same land. Mobile teams of half a dozen men who use diesel-powered hydrojets to blast through whatever clay, roots and rocks that stand between them and the meager veins they can find closest to the surface. They work quickly and messily. Then they take what their own backs and a single-engine plane can carry and move on before anybody knows they're there. Anybody, that is, but the remaining Yanomami in the area. And because the *garimpeiros* are desperate thieves who run the risk of being imprisoned for life if they are caught, they aren't above using their rifles on the Indians from time to time. Terrorizing raids meant to push the Yanomami farther in, while they go on with their business, leaving a trail of craters in the shallow soil behind them.

"The fire you came through," he says, closing his eyes as though to protect them from the flames immediately before him. "That was the *garimpeiros* as well."

"We thought it was lightning."

"Lightning doesn't burn forest in the shape of an airstrip."

"That's what we crossed? A runway?"

"A fire that follows straight lines."

"So they're here."

"Not yet. They started the fire and when it cools—and if nobody from outside has noticed it—they will return to clear it flat for their plane. Then they will find us."

"And what will you do?"

"We will move. We'll be gone by the time they come back."

The headman looks at me and must see something worse than before, because he comes forward with his arms out as though to catch my fall.

"No, no, I'll be—" I start, and then begin to move into him just as he guessed I would.

"It's good," he says, guiding my back down against a trunk infested with hirsute spiders. "That is the last of your fever gone."

It may be true. There is no strength in my legs but my head has cleared. The heat shimmering up from the plantain garden as a liquid spray. Through it the sound of the tape player again. The softened strikes of a Rhodes piano. The prog rock of my bell-bottomed youth. Supertramp.

"Party time," I say, looking up at the headman with a smile that I hope conveys an appreciative humor, but he doesn't reply. He appears not to hear me or the music at all.

Soon he begins to speak to himself. Not Portuguese. One word is repeated, its syllables clear enough for me to trace. *Rahakanariwa.* When he says it, he bends back to squint at a moving point directly above him. One point that becomes more than one point, his eyes jerking between them.

"*Rahakanariwa*," he says a final time, lowering his head and looking at me. It is a name. A word he uses for me.

"You think that we're birds?" I ask him.

"I only see you for what you are."

I follow the line of sight he had just held upward. Three dark pricks a half mile up in a sky of cream.

"Vultures."

"You are bad for us even if you don't mean to be," he says, looking up at them again. "There was a *nabah* here not long ago, all on his own. We helped him. And as soon as he was better he left again to find his way out. He said he had been looking for us for many years, but now that we had been found, he only wanted to get away from us. He said the jungle had made him mad. He was a tourist too."

"The guide book."

"He had no book."

"But he had maps, didn't he?"

"He had *nabah* maps, yes. You traveled with him?"

"In a way. We found the guide book that he left behind. It was a comfort to me on the river."

"You find comfort in things," the headman says, shaking his head in an effort at comprehension. "We find comfort in seeing the night end in the morning."

"You said he was bad."

"When he left, he took one of our women with him."

"A wife."

"Not a wife. He took her with his gun. He did not want to die alone, he said. And now they are both dead together."

"They didn't make it to the big river?"

"The *nabah* maps are lies," he says with satisfaction. "But this tourist, he was more sick than bad. And of the bad ones, some are more bad than others. I wonder if that is you. If you're as bad as the worst we have seen."

"We're not gold miners," I offer foolishly. "And our rifle is jammed."

"You have told me this."

"What I mean is, we don't want to cause any harm."

"You don't need guns to cause harm," he says with resolve. "We have seen people like you before. Tourists. Scientists. They have no guns but they kill us as fast as if they did. They bring fevers we have never seen before and that our medicines cannot cure. They start wars between my people and other Yanomami, hungry for trade with the *nabah*. And they take things, too. They take even when they give. Their clothes. A music player. A television we cannot use. We lose ourselves in the gifts they give us."

"We don't have anything to give."

"Only yourselves."

"Only that."

"But that is enough."

The music from the *shabono* reaches us in snatches, cut and shifted in the movement of air over the garden. Once or twice there is also the single clap of hands. A whoop. Roadhouse sounds heard from the parking lot.

"We will feed you and make your friend well," the headman says, looking back toward the sounds with a slack weariness. "And when the *garimpeiros* come—or if the bad men following you come first— then we will decide what to do."

245

"You can't leave us with the men your hunter saw."

"We will decide."

The headman steps into the harsh sunlight and starts back toward the village. There is no offer to help me this time.

After a while—another breeze-chopped song or two—I manage to stand and follow him. Everything a little firmer under me, although no less confused. But for the moment there is no more asking of questions. I have to return to my friends and see how they are, tell them what I know. Be a translator again.

When I step back through the vine-covered entrance the music is louder yet. The galloping rhythm, the Bee Gee–like falsetto.

Good-bye stranger
it's been nice.
Hope you find your
paradise.

On the opposite side, a group of the smaller children have gathered around the headman. Next to them some of the hunters and even one or two of their wives have formed a rough circle. All of them facing its center to watch Wallace.

Wallace dancing a hotfoot jig, one hand waving in the air in front of him and his other gripped to his waist, feet flailing under him like a pub drunk. Bates still lying in the hammock he has been in since we arrived, but awake now, grinning, his head lifted on a rolled-up pair of jeans.

"Congratulations, Crossman!" Wallace calls out, and all of them turn to look at me.

"Congratulations for what?"

"It seems you convinced them to make us dinner. Or is that us *for* dinner?"

When he laughs the children laugh along with him, as though they've understood the joke as well as its teller.

· · ·

For most of the next morning we watch the Yanomami getting ready to leave. All of them, even the smallest children, busy tying pots together along stripped vines, sticking plantain bunches and salted meat into canvas sacks, sharpening machetes for the hike and arrowheads for the hunt ahead. At Bates's suggestion I ask the headman if there is anything we can do to help, but he answers with a hollow look that reminds me that we neither know enough nor are strong enough to assist in as simple a task as gathering wood. And we don't really want to help them anyway. What we really want to know is what they're planning to do about us when they go. For the moment, though, I keep my mouth shut about that. Better not to pester our hosts than demand a response we don't want to hear.

Yet when Bates asks what the headman told me I say, without a half second's hesitation, "He's going to take us with him."

I also tell them a couple of things that are true. That the headman estimates our pirates or their *garimpeiros* or whoever it was that his hunter saw down by our canoe could be as little as a day or two away from here if they were any good at following a trail. If it was the gold miners they would probably linger for a time at the airstrip, clearing away stumps and measuring out the runway length. If it was only them, they'd give the Yanomami a little time to disappear. But if it was the bad men that have been following us, they might not wait that long.

"Two days," Bates repeats.

"Maybe less."

"And the Indians?"

"They'll be leaving in the morning. Tonight they're having some kind of ceremony. A dance or sing-along for good luck. He wasn't too clear on the particulars."

"We've got to get out of here," Bates says, sitting up on the edge of his hammock as though he would start out right now. "If it's the Colombians, we're dead if we stay."

"But where are we—"

"I'm not letting them touch me again, Crossman."

"Then we go with the Indians."

"And where are *they* going to go?"

"Another place like this," Wallace answers for me. He has been standing at the edge of shade, watching the Yanomami work with his arms folded across his chest. I had assumed he hadn't been listening to us.

"This place except far away," Bates adds.

"They can't get far enough away from what's coming for them."

"But they'll drop us off somewhere first, right? They're not going to take us even farther into the jungle?"

"Of course not," I tell him, sounding almost certain.

"They'll probably make a side trip near one of the mission resettlements," Bates says. "Show us the way out and then go on to wherever they were planning on going."

"I expect so."

"*Please*, Crossman," Wallace says, turning to us now. "Easy on the bullshit."

"I'm telling you what the headman said."

"Maybe *some* of what he said. But there's no way these people are going to hold our hands and walk us out of here. Who knows how far away the nearest big river is, let alone a government village. And would they take us anywhere near either even if they *could* reach it? That would be surrender. I can't understand a word they say but I can tell that they're never coming out of here, only deeper in. And if they take us with them that's where we're going, too."

He steps away from us into the sun and looks once more across the open center of the *shabono*, his eyes following the Yanomami bustling about in their preparations. From time to time one of them waves his way or the children will stop to imitate his hopping dance from yesterday. Even the headman turns to him every few minutes, as though waiting for a signal to mark the precise moment to start doing something else.

"You've got everything pretty sorted out," I say, unable to hide the peevish stricture in my voice. "Maybe *you* should be the translator for a while."

Wallace faces me now. Not with anger, or even his usual pity. This time it's an undisguised contempt.

"You don't always have to talk to people to understand them, Crossman."

• • •

"Where is he?"

"Out."

"There is no *out*."

"Well, that's where he is."

"He left us?"

"Don't be stupid."

"I looked around and I couldn't—"

"Relax, Crossman. He's with the leader guy. The two of them went out into the garden to have a talk."

I've awakened from another sudden sleep to find Bates here with me. Along with the Indians, although they keep their distance now. It's only when Wallace is around that the children and women seem comfortable enough to come and finger our clothes, tug our hair.

"Those two seem to have become quite chummy," I say, trying to draw the concern out of my voice. "Little walks in the garden. And they can't even talk to one another."

"He'll come back."

"Of course he will. Where could he go?"

"Anywhere, if he'd like to."

"That's what he keeps saying. I think that herbal remedy or whatever they keep giving him is turning his brain soft."

"I don't think anything could do that."

"Said like a true believer."

"Have you been listening to him since he came out of his fever?"

"I do nothing but listen to him."

"He's saying the most remarkable things."

"Oh? Like what?"

"You can't just *repeat* them. You need to understand them first before you can hear what they mean. He's always been like that. He can bring out what you've already been thinking yourself with just a word."

"And what are you thinking, Bates?"

"Not me. *Him*. It's what he sees in us that matters."

"So he's a mind reader now?"

"He lets you see yourself."

Bates is speaking with a frothy enthusiasm, almost slurred, the words unable to keep up with the notions they stand for.

249

"Listen," I say, clearing my throat. "I know they've been feeding us and we're a whole lot stronger than we were. But let's remember that we still have a touch of the fever. We're not thinking—"

"It's all the worlds becoming one world again. A world that takes everything from you so it can offer it back again."

"More of his free-trade mumbo jumbo."

"There's no economics in it for him. Money's just a metaphor for bringing everything together."

"Into him."

"Not many people are able to recognize their desires."

"No? Greed isn't so uncommon."

"It's not about greed."

"He just wants to have it all to himself."

"No! He wants *you* to have it all."

Out in the circle of bright sand a couple of children jump around each other, one holding a miniature bow and arrow and the other clapping his hands, urging the archer to take a shot. After a moment I'm able to see what their target is. An *anole* lizard, leaping about along with the boys but unable to escape. Around its neck a string tied to a stick screwed into the ground. Target practice.

"I see Barry sometimes, you know," I tell him.

"Barry now or Barry then?"

"I'm not sure."

"What's he up to?"

"Reminding me. Isn't that what ghosts always do? That what happened was real, and that we were there."

"We *were* there."

"And Lydia."

"We were there, too."

"She won't let me forget, either."

"You see her?"

"Hear her, mostly."

Bates stretches out long in his hammock, a bony elbow jutting out over the side where he has draped his arm to shield his eyes. He hears his name, too. Hears it now, probably, just as I do. Our own voices only half obscuring it.

"Do you ever think about her, Bates?"

"Of course."

"Do you try to push her away when you do?"

"I would never push her away."

"Does Wallace?"

"He couldn't do that."

"He seemed able to at the time."

Bates uncovers his eyes and points his chin at me. "He would have been the father of her child. We would have been a family," he says.

"We?"

"Me and Wallace and Lydia."

"And baby makes four."

Bates turns over in his hammock to look out at the boys with the bow and arrow. Only the unarmed boy is jumping up and down now, the other poised, aimed at a point slightly in front of his feet. Steady as a stone cherub. You can't see his eyes and what he aims at at the same time, so I move between them, split-framed.

The lizard continues its dance. Rounding the stake it's tied to, leaping up to show its white underbelly to the sun. The boys' eyes.

The bow releases the shot.

When the heat is at its strongest later that afternoon the Yanomami quit their packing and retreat to their hammocks in the shade of the *shabono* awning. Soon after, Wallace and the headman return from their walk, their shoulders slumped from weariness as well as the burden of serious thoughts. They part without speaking but with a nod that suggests grim agreement. Then the headman walks across the circle to his place and Wallace joins us at ours, falling with his back against the wall and stirring up a cluster of gnats that had encrusted a *kareshi* fruit now flattened under him.

"You were gone awhile," I say, and immediately regret the motherly tone of reproach. "Bates and I were considering going out there to rescue you."

"Bates is asleep. How concerned could he be?"

"I just thought it was strange the way the headman took you away like that."

"He did the same thing to you."

"He had a lot to tell me."

"We had quite a discussion of our own."

He slaps a palm against his forehead and drags it down his face. The flies buzzing onto the skin like crows feeding on earth exposed behind the plow.

"So what did he have to say?"

"It was more me telling him. Surely you could appreciate the irony in that, couldn't you, Crossman? The unilingual kid getting more across than the bookworm translator."

"Hysterical."

"Take the gold cities in the jungle, for example," he goes on. "El Dorado. All the stuff about unreachable cities and pyramids and mines the tour guide told us about. You'd have thought the headman would have known about it. That the adventure stories would have found their way to the place where they come from. But it was all news to him. I guess these people never had the benefit of a good guide book."

"You were your usual entertaining self. What else is new?"

"What's new is that he believed it. I pointed into the jungle in the opposite direction from the *garimpeiros*' runway and the fire, right smack into the *middle* of it, and said 'gold' and 'safe' and 'home,' and drew a map of where it was on my forearm. That's all it took."

"Congratulations. You sold the Indians an acre of swampland."

"I believe it, too. I've sold myself on it."

"That's a dubious accomplishment, Wallace, considering that there is no El Dorado."

"Yes, there is. And that's where I think all of us should go."

"*Go?* Go where?"

"The place that nobody can get to."

"If you can't get there, what's the point?"

"Coming to the end of things."

"You're crazy."

"I'm *expanding*."

"Same thing."

"This is where I was supposed to end up, Crossman. You can live a hundred lives in this place, because it's no place at all."

"What's wrong with *finding* yourself? Isn't that what most people are looking for? But not you. You're running the other way."

Although I should have the advantage in this, given the nonsense Wallace is speaking, my voice dries up into a feeble croak, fighting against new facts that are no less true for being recently made up.

"I *demand* what most others only wish for," he says.

"You want to live forever."

"Now you're talking."

"Everybody dies, Wallace."

"That's generally the precedent in such matters."

"Except that you've found an escape clause."

"If it's the self that dies when the time comes—*me*, this Marcus Wallace, born at the Owen Sound General Hospital on November second, 1975, the *me* I have been disciplined to adhere to—then one has to occupy other selves in order to go further."

"What the fuck does that mean?"

"Think of every experience you've ever had," he says, calming his voice in order to run through a calculation all too familiar to him. "It could be wrong or right or beautiful or dreadful. It's only the *thing that happens*. But even in doing it you recognize all the things you could have done in that same instant but didn't. Why didn't I leave instead of stay, destroy instead of create? The moment lived speaks also of the moments denied. And that's where all the disappointment comes from. That's the pathetic, rusted-out human trap. So I've decided that I will be more than myself. The universal translator, acting out all of our choices at once."

"Wonderful. Sounds like your Hypothesys pitch again."

"That was the idea. But Hypothesys is only a simulation. The medium *itself* is a simulation. You can turn on a computer and look at dirty pictures or buy a Russian wife or have your morality determined by an anonymous focus group. Call it a technological revolution if you like, but it's just another glowing box that must now be installed in every household. I admit that figuring out how to sell things to all the people sitting in front of the glowing boxes was interesting at first, but after a while I discovered that the money was virtual, too. That's what I didn't see coming. Being rich and finding there wasn't anything I wanted to buy."

Wallace's head is obscured by orbiting bugs. Wee-wees now joining the pudgier *baretos*, all spinning around him.

"Then we came here," he says. "And for the first time my experience of the world wasn't wrapped in cellophane or stamped with a barcode. It demanded my attention and I gave all of it over. Now I just want to see more."

"There's nothing more to see."

"There's a whole world."

"We have to go *back* to the world now."

"We can't go back. We'd be those people."

"What people?"

"The ones with *tragic stories*," he almost screeches, so that even the flies jerk back from him. "Authors of harrowing memoirs. Celebrated damaged goods. We'd confess, be forgiven. And then? Then nobody cares. They never really did. And we're left as the answers to trivia game questions. Everything will forever be the time *before* and *after* that terrible experience in the jungle, a fact that nobody will let you forget, and you won't be able to anyway. So why go all the way back there just to be a lame survivor, when you could stay here and be something *better* than you were?"

"You're fucked, Wallace."

"Don't you feel different now?"

"I feel like I'm losing my mind."

"But something else too."

"Like what?"

"Like you're not what you were."

"I'm the same. If you could take everything else out—if you could take all *this* out," I say, waving my arm at the sleeping *shabono* around us, "I'm the same."

"But you can't take this out, can you?"

"You can try. Otherwise there's just letting yourself go. And that's madness. Like our believing there's some bogeythingy following us in the jungle."

"You *do* believe it, though. And you also know the days of being able to remember who you were are long gone."

"Tell me how I'm different, then."

"For one thing, you're ten times stronger than you were before you came here," Wallace says, casting his eyes down my front as though appraising my choice of outfit. "And you know why? Because you've been given a very rare gift, Crossman. *You've seen awful things.* Like it is in a war. If you go back now you'll lose the power that comes with that. You'll *need help.* There will be counseling and support groups and pills to make the nightmares go away. So why not stay in the nightmare? We're already used to it."

"I'm not used to it."

"Maybe it's just me, then." He shrugs. "Maybe this place suits me."

Of course it does. It suits him perfectly. At ease with the languages of technology and relentless entertainment, a kid so intrinsically *hooked up*, the horseshoe buried so far up his ass—and here he is expressing a preference for a grass hut at the center of nothing. He has always required room to maneuver. *Larger than life*, as it is said of those with the most conspicuous needs. Wallace wants free trade, but of a cashless sort. A new kind of marketplace where the currency is alternative identities, the give and take of who he is with who he could be. What I hadn't considered is that knowing this about him comes at the price of not knowing who he is at all.

"I did this to us," I say. "I was a part of it. With the pirates. I brought them to us."

"Oh, *yes*," he says, his voice flat, computerized. "I know you did."

Wallace's face doesn't express anything new, but the shroud of flies around him would hide the most subtle changes. For a moment I'm not sure I've heard him correctly. The buzzing of wings now jarring and discordant. An amateur string section screeching their instruments into tune before the performance.

"They didn't just pop out of the trees, Crossman." His voice comes from somewhere behind the insect noise. "The pirates *had* to have known things. Where we would be that night, which boat we were on. And you were the only one they didn't hurt in the hole. Even then I wasn't certain. But out on the river, when we had all that time to make each other up—I looked at you and I *knew*. And as soon as I knew I forgave you."

I believe him. That he looked into me in the river's intensified light and saw the truth, just as I had looked into him and seen all of his wants. That's what frightened me about him. But he had forgiven me and in return I had betrayed him, over and over, lie upon lie. He had forgiven me the moment he recognized who I was, but I never would. I didn't have the strength for it.

"You didn't say anything," I manage through a choke of instant sobs.

"It was for you to say something, not me."

"And now I have."

"Not everything."

Although he wasn't moving before, there is a stillness now in the way he leans against the wall, legs pretzeled in front of him.

"It was never my plan. I only listened," I start, and Wallace closes his eyes. "On the one afternoon in Manaus when you went to the hotel mini-zoo, I bump into the concierge in the lobby. I had been trying on bikini tops at the boutique, looking for something to wear to dinner that night and he recommends one for me. *You look like a real Brazilian girl now*, he says. I buy it without once looking in the mirror to see for myself. And then gently—so gently I don't really notice—he takes me by the elbow and walks me out through the revolving doors, down to the benches outside the tennis courts. It's only after we get there that I realize he must know who I am because he'd been talking to me in Portuguese from the second he said hello. Once we're sitting there, though, he starts asking me questions about what we're doing in Amazonas, which boat we'd be traveling on, how many are in our traveling party, on and on. I don't look at him. He's too ugly for that. I know what he's getting at is too ugly. So instead I keep my eyes fixed on this middle-aged Japanese wife returning serves from her tennis coach. Her chocolatey skin tucked inside her whites, so clean and starched they're like bone, a kind of exoskeleton. This tiny woman bouncing on her toes and smacking back every single shot. Half of me listening to the concierge, while the other half keeps thinking *Even here* to itself. *The world wants its three-times-a-week tennis lessons even in the jungle.*"

Wallace's knees pull back farther into him. It makes me speak faster, working to unravel him with the turn in the story he's waiting for. And yet I don't skip over anything, as though I'd written it all out before this and am now reading it out loud.

I tell him how the concierge moves so close to me on the bench that I can feel his polyester pants itch down the length of my bare thigh, and I wonder at how hot he must be in that stupid colonial uniform they make him wear. But I don't actually ask him. I say very little the whole time he talks to me.

And does he *talk* to me! You'd never guess the big Frankenstein had it in him. Pours out this stream of bits and pieces that don't seem to connect at first, harmless stuff about the relative tipping habits of different nationalities, how he gets to see *all sorts* come through this place, the only decent hotel for two thousand miles. Political leaders, hookers, missionaries, bird watchers—he'd done favors for all of them, and they'd all paid him back. And I'm listening to him, half hypnotized. Watching the Japanese wife lobbing balls back over the net like a metronome.

Then, without any change of tone, without moving closer or farther away, the concierge slips entirely inside my head.

He tells me that he knows me. It's clear he doesn't mean this literally, and that it is also true. What he knows is the anger so well hidden that only others that shared it could see the stain it left on the skin. The concierge has a *gift* for anger.

But anger at what?

He knows that, too.

"I'm not unhappy, you know," I tell him. And he laughs briefly, horribly, leaving my ear wet as though he'd stuck his tongue in it.

"You're getting along," he corrects me. "And getting older, certainly. But you've never really had luck, have you? Not like *they*

257

have. But it's OK. You'll just have to step outside for once. Lose yourself. Make a little luck of your own."

It's a fight not to fall into his words. To not lay my head against the side of his neck and feel the voice box trembling inside of him, an egg about to hatch in his throat. But I manage to stay where I am. The arc of the yellow tennis balls the same every time.

Perhaps I manage to say some things too. I must, because some of what he says are questions. What's a trade mission, exactly? What's a Hypothesys? Do any of us carry weapons? The answers rise out of me like vapors. But when I stop long enough to ask why he wants to know so much—why he *already* seems to know so much—he tells me straight out.

"We're thinking of kidnapping your friends," he says.

I tell him no at first. The smallest *no* and only that.

The concierge may not even hear it. Without a pause he's telling me about these men he knows. *Class acts*, he says in English. They keep their operations so tidy, so efficient, it's only the most technical reading of the law that would count them as wrongdoers at all. The concierge calls them his friends. Professionals. Among their talents are painless, 100 percent guaranteed foreigner nabbing. Tells me that they arrange this sort of thing all the time—the concierge selects an appropriate target from the Tropical's offerings and then the professional friends move in to hustle whatever bunch of Americans or Germans or Brits off their tour bus or chartered plane, whisk them to a comfortable jungle lodge and cell phone their families or their companies for a quick ransom, which, once received, is laundered through worldwide drug interests—kidnapping is a *business* down here.

"Guns," I barely hiss. "They'll have guns."

"Of *course* they will," the concierge hisses back. "But they're just part of the performance. To make things believable."

Nobody gets hurt because nobody ever resists, the concierge assures me. Most people with money who come down here have special insurance policies for events like these, so there's no real loss. Let alone inconvenience. The whole thing takes about forty-eight hours, often less. And because the professionals would be wearing masks, we wouldn't be able to identify them, and would therefore be allowed to move freely about wherever they took us. It would be as good an Amazon holiday as what you could get from any travel agent. As soon as the ransom was cabled, we would be motored back to the designated drop-off point on the Negro, no more than a half day's journey upriver from Manaus. Hey, we'd all be back at the Tropical for cocktail hour!

"There won't be any surprises," he says, and surprises me with a playful slap on my knee. "None that you won't already be in on. You'll be part of the team."

The concierge gives me a serious hug around my shoulders.

Before us the Japanese wife moves to her backhand without a break in her rhythm.

When the concierge asks if I'm interested in making some money, I nod. He never tells me how much he intends to give me and I never ask. Just go along without a second thought, without any thought at all, like I've been expecting an invitation like this from the moment I arrived in Brazil and now it is a simple matter of saying yes.

"Which you did," Wallace says, head buried against his legs so that I can't see his face.

"Automatically," I say.

The memory of the concierge's frame next to mine accentuates how thin Wallace has become, rolled up into a ball spiked with elbows and kneecaps. But his voice is still strong.

"Why didn't he come to any of the rest of us? We might have said an automatic yes, too."

"You were the rich ones. I was the hired help. He knew I had more to gain, and would therefore be more likely to keep a secret."

Wallace raises himself against the *shabono* wall again, slowly opens his eyes. Takes up the space he usually does. Not the size of the concierge but just as threatening in his way. The sinewy promise, tightly wound.

"What did you give him about us that he didn't have before?"

"I told him where the boat would tie up at the end of each day of our tour. All the relevant phone and fax numbers. Everything I knew. On the things I didn't know, he sent me away to find out."

Wallace is silent, but I know what he's asking me.

"For the money," I say. "That's what I told myself at first. I'll do this thing and set up a new life when we get home. But I couldn't even imagine what shape that life could possibly take, so instead I told myself that it might do me good to be on the inside of something for once."

"That's all it took?"

"I said yes to the concierge that afternoon. But it wasn't until that night that I knew I would go through with it."

"The restaurant of meat."

"Even before we got there. When you laughed at me while we waited for our taxis. Laughed at what I was wearing, my body, Lydia's lipstick on my mouth instead of hers. You laughed at the fact that I might dare be a woman. A woman who wanted *you*, no less."

"Jesus, Crossman. I thought you were laughing along with me. You looked so—"

"And then there was your little trick at dinner."

"What trick?"

"You made me guess who you were thinking of."

"And you assumed I was thinking of myself."

"But you wrote *my* name on the napkin."

"It was only a game."

"No, it wasn't. It was a humiliation. You showed me that I didn't exist, even to myself. That's not a fucking *game*."

"So you guessed wrong."

"As you knew I would. That was the fun part, wasn't it? I'm staring at my own name like it belongs to someone else. So who am I if that's not me? Thirty-eight years old and I don't have a clue. And the second I realize it, it splits me in half," I say, scratching a line down the center of my face with a fingernail. "I'm looking at my name and it's telling me that I've been dead my whole life. We played that game and I knew I had to do it to make my name *mean* something."

"Collaborating with guerrillas is a rather extreme remedy."

"There's no easy cure for hate. Or love."

"And you hated me?"

"You had everything. So comfortable in the *now*, while I couldn't even bear to look at it. You reminded me of how out of place I was."

The flies exhaust themselves all at once, settling over Wallace's skin like black lace. Stay there even when he speaks.

"Tell me," he says. "Was making your name mean something worth it when you saw what they did to us at their camp?"

"I asked them to stop, but they told me it was part of their plan. I said that wasn't the plan I'd heard about. That's when they told me the purpose of their operation had changed."

"Changed how?"

"They didn't just want a ransom anymore. Now they wanted to know about the perfect bomb."

"Bates's girlfriend," Wallace says with something like warmth, as though recalling a dear friend.

"The concierge recommended that bar to you, didn't he? Told you about the girls."

"The monster."

"You saw him there?"

"Bates did. A man stepping out of a Volkswagen to watch us from across the street. Bates called him the monster. I assumed it was nothing more than the *cachaça* having its way with him."

"No, that was him."

"Why didn't you tell them we didn't know anything about perfect bombs?"

"They didn't want to accept that. And after a while I started to get the feeling they didn't really care whether we were weapons experts or used-car salesmen. They were just having a laugh seeing how far they could push us before we fell apart."

"But we didn't, did we?"

"You got us out before we could."

"They saw a white kid wearing basketball shoes worth more than their entire lives and they figured all he wanted was to cry his way home." Wallace shakes his head. "But you know something, Crossman? When they handed me that gun I didn't think—I put it to my head and fired. The bullet would determine whether it would be there

261

or not. And even if it was, I know it wouldn't have been the end of me. Some version would keep going."

"Like Lydia's baby."

"That was one, yes. But there are always others."

He means me. Lifts a bony hand and lets it fall across his eyes. An announcement that I am part of him again. Wallace languidly splayed against the straw wall, the flies thickening around his head, but with a thin smile that tells me more than if he had put the same thought into English.

The leaving celebration starts after the Yanomami bring out their pipes. This is what I assume them to be, anyway, although they look like nothing more than hollow reeds, about three feet end to end. Only the men appear authorized to hold them. The presence of the pipes alone causes ambiguous shouts of eagerness and worry from the women. For the first time, the children keep their distance.

"This town is about to get very strange," Wallace says from his hammock.

"You mean it wasn't strange before?"

"Compared to what it's going to be like in a couple hours from now? No."

"How would you know?"

"Because those things are how they administer the medicine the headman has been giving me. *Yakawana*, they call it. A speedball, muscle relaxant and acid trip all wrapped up in one. They only used to let the shamans take it to have their visions and communications with the gods. But now that all the shamans have moved to government villages to watch *The Price Is Right*, everyone gets to have visions and communications with the gods."

"What's it like?"

"In turns terrifying and euphoric, I've found. It also has a tricky way of being terrifying and euphoric at the *same time*. I tell you, Crossman, I'm not at all sure I want to see the whole *shabono* whacked on the stuff."

Bates woke up at the sound of Wallace's voice. His nose flaring and sealing shut, as though in preparation for his own dose.

"And you've been on it since we got here?" he asks.

"It has therapeutic properties as well," Wallace says. "And my hits were minuscule. I have a feeling that their intentions for this evening are of an altogether larger scale."

The headman waves at us. Wallace waves back.

"I see you're having a warm-up party!" he shouts.

The headman shakes his head and points directly at each of us.

"Well, well," Wallace says, rubbing his hands together. "We have been summoned."

We make our way over to the men, who have now placed the pipes in a pile next to a low fire. Crouched down, their bare backs shining up at us, murmuring and busy with the work at their feet. The headman speaks to me in Portuguese and I translate for the others, yet he never faces me. Only Wallace. All of his words directed at a person who cannot understand what he says. And yet Wallace nods as though he does, often before I have a chance to tell him in English. Laughing before I interpret a joke, shaking his head at the mention of possible danger.

The headman is telling us the story of how *yakawana* is made. His tone buoyed by pride as well as an awestruck wonder. The way one speaks of something that is technically understood, but without knowledge of anything close to its full implications.

Everything begins by a search for *yakawana* trees. Once found, the bark is ripped off in strips, but only partially, so that the trees may recover and be harvested again later. Only the men are permitted to do this. When they return after a *yakawana* quest there is the same excitement as after a successful hunt. Unless they have gone especially long without food, the drug is regarded as more important than meat.

Women are allowed to handle the material only in its initial stages of processing. They are the ones who dry the bark in the sun, laying it out on the *shabono* roof until it is as brittle and thin as parchment. After they take it down it is torn apart and ground into a powder. The ash from the burned bark of another tree is added, along with a few drops of water.

263

This is what we're watching now. The men kneading the mealy liquid over a blanket of palm leaves until it thickens, sudden as cream after beating it with a whisk. Except this stuff is gummy and green. One of the men turns to pass me a wad and I stretch it out between my index fingers until it thins into an elastic band. Let one end go and it recoils back into its original shape.

The men rub bits of it between their palms until they are as hard as ball bearings. Each of these is placed on a gas can lid that has been heated over a flame. The balls jump once or twice before disintegrating into tiny piles of fine powder. This is the end product. Not much more than what a cigarette produces if allowed to burn down to the filter. Yet the men make approving coos as they watch each of the balls fall apart. Smack their lips while the remains are lifted off the lid and onto tinfoil wrapped around the ends of cooking spoons.

"The *yakawana* lets you see," the headman tells us, still without turning from Wallace.

"Do we *have* to take it?"

The cowardly squeak behind the question offends even me. But when the headman turns to address me his expression is soft, returned to its setting of mild amusement.

"It brings visitors into the *shabono*," he says. "Even you."

This is to be a celebration. A ritual request to the gods for good fortune on their next journey deeper into the forest. But it's also an initiation for us. One that Wallace has already passed. He's been one of them ever since he snorted the stuff on what appeared to be his deathbed two days earlier. And now he's an insider all over again.

As the *yakawana* ash cools the hunters take up their pipes. Around us the children tighten their circle, as do the women just behind them, one or two allowing shrieks of anxious anticipation. The men form two rough lines, each running out from a meeting point next to the fire. The headman at the front of the one and Wallace at the other.

All at once the men start whooping. The sort of sound one hears at fraternity drinking parties, boys urging other boys on a dare. Except the hunters' call mimics the trumpeting of a gallinule, one that we heard mocking us through all our days on the river.

Whoop-ree! Whoop-ree!

It brings the headman and Wallace to their knees at the same time.

Wallace knows what he's doing. Takes a thick pinch of the green ash and jams it in his end of the pipe. Puts his mouth around it with cheeks puffed out as the headman screws the other end into his nose. Blows until you can see his ribs shivering through his skin.

Within the first second, every point of entry to the headman's skull becomes a tap turned on full. Dripping eyes, spitting lips. It would be disgusting if the violence of it weren't so interesting. And kind of laughable, too. The headman stands up but tottering on his heels, arms propellering, Chaplinesque. Every few seconds he punches his own face.

Eventually all his moving parts freeze at the same instant and he falls straight back onto the ground. It seems at first that he's dead. But the Yanomami men only smile and gather round him, lift him up at the shoulders. The headman coughs. Blows a pint of mucus out his nose.

When his eyes find their irises again the headman scrambles over to the pipe to perform his part of the service for Wallace, already there waiting for him. Then Bates. Soon the *shabono* circle fills up with stumblers, arms extended like the blind searching for a wall to tell them where they are. All of them oozing green.

The headman shows me his teeth now. Stuffing his end of the pipe with another wad.

My turn.

The women around us cluck with new excitement. Apparently an exception is to be made: the *nabah* woman has been invited to have her brains pureed along with the men.

I lower myself to my knees as the others had done and take the end of the pipe in both my hands, balancing it along the end of my fingertips like a flute. But instead of putting the mouthpiece to my lips I stick it an inch up my right nostril.

The headman takes in an impossibly long breath, his mouth still fixed into its toothy display. When he's finished it clamps shut around his end of the pipe. Starts to blow. Slow at first, building to a vigorous blast at the end. All of it funneled directly into the core of my head.

There is a pause of a sort. Long enough to ask, completely but already too late: What the fuck is *this?*

It's a pair of bricks shoved up whole into my sinuses, grinding hard against the bone. A boxer's fist knuckling what's left of my brain straight out my ass. And there it is: mashed into a black syrup, leaking out the bottom of my shorts into a meager puddle around my heels.

But for all this, I feel pretty good.

And soon even better than that. Emerald snot pouring off my upper lip, but otherwise happy as a clam. Aware that I've been made sick by some jungle hallucinogen that likely hacks ten years off your life and stunts the growth of the next four generations of the user's progeny, but none of it seems to matter much. A poison ripping its way through whatever it chooses but doing the favor of killing the pain along the way.

Not to mention the special effects. Colors and sound and movement all fractured into stuttered chunks. Everything presented at once and then held there so that it may be considered, admired, dismissed. And then another scene arrives. The only thing that joins them together is the soundtrack. The wobbly ghost voices of wine glasses rubbed along their rims.

It takes awhile to understand that I'm spinning.

Not just another chemical impression, either, but busily half-stepping round and round. Just as Wallace did yesterday. Arms out straight from their shoulders, cutting through air, turning so fast that the *shabono* wall becomes smooth, impenetrable. The jungle unseen and beyond reach somewhere on the other side. It's the child's game of turning the details into a blur. And at the end, just as it was as a child, I end up toppling blind to the ground.

"Crossman!"

Wallace's face rotating slowly over me, until it slugs to a stop.

The lowering sun flashes through the trees tall enough to peak over the wall. Beams onto him like the light from a projector's lens. Images playing out across the needling of his first wrinkles: a lit match exploding to life, blue lips meeting his own in a kiss.

His skin is a movie screen.

"It's a world, Crossman," he says, his eyes full, as though urging it to be greater than it is. "A world. A *world*."

Dancing.

So close to the fire that I can see the hair on my arms curling into black pinheads. The skin doesn't burn, though. Not that I would notice. I'm *dancing*. We all are. Circling the flames with hands and feet trying to escape from the rest of ourselves, feeding the fire with motion so that it rises above the height of the *shabono* wall and sends up sparks that hang there, flicked on and off like stars.

There is no ceremony. No ooga-booga ritual worthy of anthropological study, nothing *primitive* or *tribal* or *Indian*. Just dancing. The ghettoblaster cranked, the startled cries of minds being blown—*waah!*—coming from those recently injected by the pipe and now lurching over to join the crowd of us other circling nose droolers.

My body moving but only according to its own spastic inclinations, colors and light left as smears in the air. Nothing holding still long enough to be identified let alone understood.

I am *fucked*, as Bates might say in his precise use of the term. Perhaps even *royally fucked*—a category reserved only for the doomed or insane. Cranked on some ash that has pinched all sense out of my brain stem, leaping around a straw village unnamed on any map.

And yet all of it is somehow familiar. The orange flames fingering over tans, portable rock-and-roll, the adolescent laughter that seems always to be an indirect reference to sex. There's as much bush party to this as bushmen.

Someone has caught one of my fleeing hands. I'm being led away from the fire. Tripping into the abrupt shadow, the cool that tickles.

"We wanted you to be here for this, Elizabeth," Wallace says from somewhere close.

"I *am* here."

At first I think they want me to see something. But Wallace and Bates do nothing but lie next to each other on a blanket laid out on the ground, raised partway upon arms unfurled at their sides. I notice as well that they are naked. White bands across their middles marked by two islands of pubic hair, the nodding heads of their cocks. That their free hands stroke each other there. Slow, avid, punctuated by wet clicks.

I fall forward and slide up between them. Their bodies already indiscernible, shared. The multiplied parts coordinated by a single set of commands.

Dreamer
You know you are a dreamer

Wallace touches me. Both of them do but it's his hands that I follow. Pressed against the front of my neck and then sliding down. Wiping away an invisible coating over my skin. I feel this but keep my eyes on his smile. Not mocking this time, but an invitation. His smile bringing me harder into the touch of his hand until I'm leaning full against it. Drawing it inside.

When he pulls his hand away I collapse into him, and he eases back, until the two of us lie side by side on the ground.

He kisses me.

What is this moment aside from the jump from the possible to the unstoppable? Lips, of course. The decision to open eyes or leave them closed that is never actually made because in the end they'll do as they please. A tight bow around the small intestine gently pulled free.

A kiss that lets me leave who I am.

And with this departure comes the fullness of desire. Wallace half-rolled over me now and I'm guiding him down, tongue out, catching whatever drops fall off him.

I think he says something when he's close. A whispered name. A promise. But it's only his lips opening to take a bite of air before he closes them again and pushes inside.

Dreamer
You know you are a dreamer
Well can you put your hands in your head?
Oh no!

What, exactly, is delivered when he enters me? Ideas, mostly. Plural, unrelated, kaleidoscopic. Too nimble to capture. You couldn't put a name to a single one. Strung together in a kind of sequence, though, so that the impression they leave is one of existence, of *every* existence, yielding to this scramble of shared thought, this beautiful anxiety. I am occupied by a population of ideas, each claiming *This is it*.

I'd forgotten how fucking could do this. The assurances it made, the resistance that is only the most eager acceptance. The gasps of surprise and pursuit, the absurd novelty of exposing yourself to yourself.

Wallace is already there. And Bates cradled in my hand, burgeoning, both of us finding our ways to my mouth. There is no hunger anymore, or the galling insistence on keeping the record straight. I am merely full of them and can finally see what I thought was not permitted me.

This is it.

Floating above everything that is particular, the already done, the small and fixed and disgraced parts that come with being anyone at all. I am *new*. And when I ask—not with words but with a tremor of physical pleading—they give it to me. Let me see what can only be revealed in the inarticulable, the untold, in what, in previous times, might be called the mysterious.

They let me see the future.

It is still night. Though it could be the same night, or any before, or after. I take a shuddering intake of air as though I hadn't done so for some time. There's an ancient taste to it. Chalky and vegetative, suggestive of both beginnings and ends.

The Indians are leaving. This is what I see when I open my eyes and find myself propped up against the *shabono* wall. A long line of them moving out through the opening in an odd hush, as though they and all the stringed and bagged things they carry are weightless, imagined.

Bates is here with me—I can feel the weight of his head, asleep in my lap. But everyone else is on their way. The men in front, then the women carrying the babies across their chests and cloth bundles on their heads, the children lashed with sacks of food. Followed by Wallace and the headman a few feet behind. Both of them bent under the load of their packs, barefoot, Wallace now wearing the same waist string and lolling penis sheath as all the men. Only his height and the spectral glow of his skin distinguish him from the Yanomami, so that he brings up the rear as a freak version of the others, a giant albino.

He doesn't turn around to see if we're awake. He doesn't show his face. The two of them move with the same impossible quiet as the others. Step through the vines and are gone.

Before I can stand straight I release a spume of vomit so broad that at first I'm certain it's the parasite finally taking its leave. Yet there is no pain, so that as I empty myself I let my eyes drift upward to study the stars. They send back a blinking circuit board of activity. Binary messages—yes/no, here/there—bouncing between themselves and the earth.

When I'm emptied dry I take a couple of stumbles after them but the effort threatens to pop my eyes out from their sockets. The first stage of *yakawana* hangover. An instant pressure that feels like it's enlarging the cavity inside my skull to make way for something new.

It doesn't stop me from finding my way out to the plantain garden. Half the line of Yanomami have already marched into the trees, but Wallace and the headman remain at the rear. A hundred feet from where I stand with my hands cupped around my mouth, ready to call after them.

But nothing comes out. What's happening can't be stopped anyway. I could scream and they wouldn't hear. It would be like trying to alter the course of events in a film by shouting at the screen.

Wallace ends in the ellipsis of his silent steps into the trees. I watch him go with his words filling my expanding head, bits of jokes and sales pitch and argument, all of it in the voice I believed I would never forget.

But as I watch his body disappear from sight his words disappear with him. The forest stealing his voice as well as the memory of it, so that when he is enveloped by the night's green it's as though he had never lived outside of it at all.

10

I'M back on the river. Alone in the canoe this time, drifting near the shore but a glance behind shows that I'm in one of the fat sections where the current slows to almost nothing. The jungle leans close enough that the smallest breeze can be heard in its leaves. Everything as I have seen it a thousand times before, and yet only in its general character—the light, the pointillistic forest, the pekoe water—and not in the details. This bend not exactly like any other. This silence more silent.

On my knees, watching the shoreline and waiting for the worst thing I can think of to appear.

You've seen awful things.

"Elizabeth," a voice calls, but not from the spot where I've been looking. A little to the right, maybe. Then thirty feet to the left. "Over *here!*"

I look both ways again but when there is something to see it's in the place I was staring at to begin with.

"They only let me go long enough to do this one thing, Elizabeth. So just stay still, all right? They're quite strict with their *shed-yool.*"

"Lydia," I say.

Her skin white as the underside of a mud fish, ribbed blue with veins. Steps closer onto the quicksand shore to show that she's naked. Rope burns around ankles and neck and wrists.

"You didn't come back," she says. "I thought old girls like us stuck together. And do you know what they did to me after you left? Can you *guess?*"

I may try to reply but nothing finds its way out.

"Didn't you hear me call your name?"

As though appearing only now, lines of cuts seep down the length of her body. These from a knife blade. But fingernail scratches, too. Musical staffs across her chest, her inner thighs.

"Well, I want to make *sure* you hear it this time, Elizabeth."

She pulls Bates's rifle from behind her. Wags it like a pissing cock grown out of the broad V of her pubic hair. Then she brings it up, buttressing it with her other hand. Points it at my head.

"It's jammed," I say.

"It is?"

I follow her now lowered eyes to find bubbles breaking through the water's surface directly in front of me.

"Maybe we can get a second opinion on that," she says with a laugh of false politeness.

The canoe ducks abruptly toward the shore from a weight pulling on the side. Without moving I glance down to see Barry holding on to the edge. Instead of white his skin is black leather. He spews a comical spout of water out from pursed lips.

"Didn't you hear her, Crossman?" he says. "I know *I* did."

"I *didn't* hear."

"You really are a terrible liar, aren't you?" he says, swallowing the river in gulps until he sinks back under. His torn face still visible, blinking up at me an inch below the surface.

"Yes, Elizabeth," Lydia calls again, and I look to see that she's walked up to her waist in the water, but with the rifle barrel still pointed at me. "You really *are* terrible!"

She pauses, tilts her head back as though she's heard someone calling.

"Lydia. *Please!*"

Returns her eye to the site. Pulls the trigger.

At first there is only a sound like a quick kiss. Then the fire ripping through my throat. A shroud of blood falling over Barry's grinning, upturned face.

And another.

Lydia wrapped in smoke, firing into me so that I'm cut apart from myself, piece by piece. An arm splashing into the river. An ear slapping down against the hull. Blasting away until the bullets sing straight through and I am nothing at all—

—shots from outside the straw wall. Distant cracks maybe a half mile into the forest and, farther yet, the low kettle-drum of thunder.

I pull myself up to find Bates already standing over me. Holding the rifle before him just as Lydia had held it.

"It's them," he says.

"They're early."

"I'd say they're right on time."

The *shabono* is empty. In the open center, the fire circle still sends up tails of smoke, but everything else is remarkably clean. They've taken not only the things they packed before the ceremony but the bits of kindling and handmade toys and feather ornaments that were strewn about the ground as well. The only thing they've left behind is the television set, staring at us with its one gray eye.

"I saw them go," I say, unable to look directly at Bates and see what may be there on his face. It's not embarrassment over what we allowed to happen only a few hours earlier. It's worry over having the reality of where I am confirmed. "Last night," I tell the crisscross of tiny beetles beneath my hammock. "Or early this morning."

"I know."

"Wallace went with them."

"I know."

"Maybe you know everything."

"The important things," he says, brings the rifle up and holds it across his waist. "But there aren't many of those now, are there?"

A shock of lightning so bright it finds every gap through the straw wall. For a strobe flash the jungle is made visible on the other side, a ring of dark figures standing together arm in arm. Then the first drops pelt against the earth, kicking up splashes of sand. Turns the ground into a leopard skin rug.

"Welcome to the rainy season," Bates says.

More gunshots now. A steady tolling of a dozen or so, but as far-off sounding as the ones that woke me up.

"What are they doing?" I ask, placing a hand against my ear as though the noise of their guns is being made directly next to it. "If they're still looking for us, they're not being very discreet."

"They don't need to be. They know where we are."

"What are they waiting for?"

"To sound their warning."

"I think we've been adequately forewarned, wouldn't you say?"

"Not for us. For the Indians. Whoever it is wants to scare them off first so that there will just be us left."

"And how do you know that?"

"The headman told Wallace that's what they'd do. What *nabah* who want the place all to themselves have done before."

"The headman couldn't have told him that."

"Why not?"

"Wallace can't speak Portuguese."

"Wallace is an excellent communicator."

"So the people firing their guns—they *counted* on the Yanomami leaving us behind?"

"They want *us*, Crossman. Not a bunch of Indians."

"Well, that's what they've got."

"Two-thirds, anyway."

Bates leans the rifle up against the nearest pole and digs a hand into his pocket. Pulls out the Palmcorder. It's casing and black-pupilled lens still polished and unscratched. It makes me think of money. The sort of gadget I could never afford back home and therefore dismissed as a discouraging sign of the times, a useless novelty, as I had done with all the laptops, cell phones and wireless organizers I had been unfairly denied.

He glares at the camera for a moment, tossing it an inch or two into the air as though gauging its significance by how it much it weighs. Then he bends down and gives it to me.

"I think you should keep this," he says.

"I don't know how to use it."

"You don't have to. Just hang on to it."

I slip it into the front pocket of my shorts and it scuttles away.

"There are things of importance recorded on that thing," Bates says, jabbing a finger at me. "But I don't need it anymore. I can see every-thing on my own now. The whole world clear even with my eyes closed."

And he does close his eyes. His lips folded up into his mouth as though savoring an overwhelming flavor.

"You know, you can take this back with you as easily as I can," I tell him.

"I've got the gun."

"It's jammed."

Only now does Bates open his eyes again. Wherever he's gone has made him appear older. Or perhaps he's had something removed from him, the goofiness that overextended his smiles, the nervous jittering of his knee, the shyness that would lower his eyes if directly met.

"Why did he go?" I ask, and I can see in the way he lets his fists open and close that Bates has followed my thoughts.

"Because he had to. And I stayed because I had to."

"Couldn't it just as easily have been you wandering off into the jungle?"

"Wallace can't go back. And you can't go back on your own."

"You're staying for me?"

"We can't just let you die here alone."

"Why would Wallace care about that now?"

"About you?"

"About anyone but himself?"

"He's *always* cared," he says, almost pleading. "It's only that he can't stay with us anymore. And we can't go with him."

"You could."

"Maybe. But definitely not you. Wallace wants you to have the life you think you've decided to live. There's no way that can happen here."

"And you're doing as you're told."

"It wasn't an order. It's the only way things can work."

"You want to hear an alternative theory?"

He shrugs again. Places a hand on the butt of the rifle.

"Wallace left because he knew that if he went back he'd be charged," I let out in a rush. I hear myself and realize that I'm saying anything now that might keep Bates here with me.

"What are you talking about?"

"C'mon, Bates," I say, now a desperate split in my voice. "He threw Barry over the side. He killed a man. Out here that may be a shrewd improvement of our chances of survival. It may be an *experience*. But back home it's something else."

Bates startles me with an adult laugh. Assured, almost tender, allowing itself the time to wind down to its end.

"Wrong again," he says finally.

"You think so?"

"He didn't kill Barry."

"Look, don't worry," I say, watching his hand on the rifle, the fingers spidering down. "I'm not going to tell anyone."

"You don't understand. Though that's not a surprise," he says, shaking his head. "Wallace didn't kill him, Crossman. I did."

Bates swings the rifle up with one hand and grabs it around the stock with the other, smooth and conclusive as an honor guardsman. A sneer returns to his lips, although he may not be aware of it. Or that he's waved the end of the gun around so that it's aimed between my legs.

"Holy Christ, Bates."

"Funny." Bates laughs his old man's laugh once more. "That's just what Barry would have said."

"I'm glad you find it amusing."

"It's only what's done."

"He was our friend."

"And we were sinking."

"Does that cancel out who he was?"

"It doesn't matter who he was. If the canoe went down, we would drown. That, or make it to shore and starve. Either way, we had to stay afloat."

"And you figured Barry was a lot of dead weight to hang on to."

"Weight that was a couple days from dead, yes. He was also costing us more than his share of food, half of which he couldn't keep down for more than ten minutes. But why am I telling you this? You were there too, weren't you?"

"I didn't kill anybody."

"Of course not. You're not capable of anything but judgment."

"I'm only trying to hang on to right and wrong here."

"So am I," he says, his voice rising in a way I've never heard from him. "And I was *right* when I woke Barry and told him he had to help me and he put his arms over my shoulders all on his own. When I lifted him up onto the side, and when I took the shoelaces out of his trainers because I thought we might be able to use them later on. When I grabbed him by the wrists and eased him into the current. I was *right* when I watched him scratch his way along the outside of the canoe, jerking to get his head up for air but he wasn't strong enough. When I didn't even think about helping him, and he went slack like a fish you've had on the line so long it's got nothing left. I was *right* the whole time."

Now Bates realizes where he's had the rifle pointed, but leaves it where it is. Jiggles it slightly, as though testing to see if it will crack in the middle.

"Are you saying he knew what you were going to do to him?"

"Barry wanted us to live. And he made a sacrifice for that," Bates sighs. "Is that right? Is that wrong? I'll leave that to you. You can muddle it over for the rest of your life, if that makes you feel further away from the doing of it."

"I didn't do anything."

"You can tell yourself that, too."

"You sound like Wallace. What he said when he wouldn't let me go back for Lydia."

"See? You're lying again."

"So tell me the truth."

"Wallace didn't stop you from killing yourself for Lydia's sake. If it happens to be convenient for your conscience that he made an argument otherwise, fine. But don't pretend that made any difference."

Behind him, the rain has hardened into metal rods, sticking through the *shabono*'s roof and piercing the ground. It's still not enough to unsettle the air, although the first drops reach us through the straw cover to soak Bates's skin dark. It makes him look feverish again. Enraged.

"It's only you alone," I almost have to shout. "Is that it? Whether it's me being a cowardly bitch or you forgiving yourself. There's no way to decide one way or another. It's just *you*."

"That's what it's always been, Crossman. Aristotle, the Torah, the

Ten Commandments, Hypothesys.com—they're people cooking up some outside authority to tell them what to do. But there's still only what you can live with. And I can live with what I did. You, on the other hand, seem to be having trouble with what you didn't."

Bates pulls the gun back and rests it over the hooks of his jutting hip bones. Turns around to study the rain as though he'd only just noticed it. Paces with his legs horseshoed in a wide cowboy stance, each step requiring the lift of a bum cheek. Then I remember that this is only the way he walks now, has to, after the pirates did what they did to his balls.

"You're getting used to being a hero, aren't you?"

"I'm not a hero," he says when he's in front of me. Bends down to stroke his fisted knuckles across my cheek. "I just decided to stop being frightened."

There's another round of gunshots from the jungle. Closer together this time. Maybe closer to the *shabono* now too, though each shot seems to come from a different direction, the sound splintered by the rain.

"More warnings," I say. "Maybe we should take the hint."

Bates slides his palm under my chin, cupping it tenderly as though my head is a small bird.

"Bates?"

He rises to look out at the rain again, takes its measurement. The shots overlapping each other so that they make their own fierce echo.

"Hey, man. I *really* think we should go now."

He begins to pace again. Except this time when he reaches the point where he would pivot and come back the other way he keeps going. Out into the open center, the rain pulling his T-shirt halfway down to his knees. Just a skinny kid. The rifle thick as each of his legs.

"Where are you going?"

He doesn't stop. Hip-rolls his way to the entrance, divides the vines with the end of the gun and is gone.

"*Bates!*"

The shots have stopped. Without our voices to close us in, the *shabono* is now perfectly bald. The rain pounding it away, the

Yanomami's dancing footprints already smeared into a muddy soup. And when I cross to leave I look back to see that mine have been instantly obscured as well.

I scan for Bates across the plantain garden and find him maybe fifty feet in, hunched down with his back to me and the gun planted upright next to him like a staff, so that at first I see him as a misplaced lawn ornament, a gnomish shepherd. Not hiding, just squatting in an overgrown field as he would have done to relieve himself back in his tree-planting days.

There's nobody else that I can see. Although with the rain and darkened sky there could be a topless chorus line standing just inside the wall of trees and I wouldn't be able to detect them. I was expecting to have had something happen already, so that now it's unclear what I should do next. If they've been waiting for a human target to appear I'm as good a one as they're going to get. A graphite outline against the yellow *shabono* wall.

There are thoughts about falling flat and crawling over to Bates, or waving my arms in surrender, or simply running away. Instead I walk forward, stepping over the thorny weeds and plantain bunches with deliberate choices of where to put my foot next. There's no bravado in what's happening now. I'm simply not able to do anything else.

Bates doesn't turn when I drop to my knees beside him. He's busy making a hat. Tying what must be Barry's old shoelace around the stem and poking it through the tip of a giant palm leaf lying across his thighs. Lifts it onto his head and pulls it forward as far as it will go so that it might shield his eyes from the rain. The lace scooped under his chin.

When he's finished he still doesn't acknowledge that I'm here. Trains his eyes along the horizon of jungle, one blink to my six.

"Maybe we should wait over there in the trees," I say finally, and hear again the broken terror in my voice.

"There's no point."

"Why not?"

"If it's the gold miners, we want them to see us. And if it's the pirates—if it's *them*, it won't make any difference if we hide."

He offers me a glance that says *But* you *can if you want*. It's scornful, but in a noncommittal way. He expects so little of me there isn't any room left to disappoint him.

What surprises me isn't the look itself but how hurt I am by it. Even now, soaking wet in a slashed and burned acre of Brazilian jungle, awaiting men with guns. Even now when nothing is supposed to matter, I want to impress him. He looks at me and sees only the stark map of things I thought I'd got halfway to hiding.

"We're just going to wait for them here?"

"They're done with their warnings," he mumbles, returning his gaze across the field. "They might think when they step out of there that everybody will be gone. But I won't be."

"And then what?"

The rain hard enough to block words spoken at normal volume, so I try again.

"And *then* what are we going to do? Bates?"

But he's turned to stone. And I stay next to him, shaking in the bits of sky coming down cool and hard as pebbles.

There is no morning or afternoon, the storm a limestone ceiling over the jungle and beyond it. It makes the waiting worse than if we were sitting out in a raging sun. At least then there would be a notion of the day having an end—the heat increasing, holding, dying away. Now there is only our trying to find a human shape in the trees.

Another shot reaches us much later on.

Only one, but closer than any of the others from before. No more than a few feet inside the perimeter of jungle. The mist rising up from the ground mistaken for the puff of smoke drifting up from the barrel.

After that there is only the rain again.

The sound of the latest shot didn't move Bates from his place, so that I wonder whether I even heard it, whether it might have been only a snap of thunder immediately above us. But I can't convince myself of anything but the obvious.

They are here now. And what we heard was a signal from one telling the others that we are here, too.

Yet nobody shows themselves. The earth turning to slippery clay around us, the dug-out troughs where the plantain has been planted now creeks racing into each other. The day will be drowned before it will end.

"I saw you that last night on the *Ana Cassia*," I whisper to him. "When Wallace was kissing Maria. I saw you watching them."

Bates says nothing, but perhaps stiffens slightly more than he already has inside the plaster cast of his clothes.

"I wished it was me, if that's what you're asking," he says after a time. "And what were *you* thinking, Crossman?"

The same thing.

I want to say this, but it's blocked by something hard in my chest, an India rubber ball of longing I hadn't known was there until now.

I wished he was kissing me, too.

"I was just watching," I say.

"You're good at that, aren't you?"

"I guess I'm a better watcher than a watched."

"Most are," he says, nodding. "The watchers were our prime market."

I consider telling him what I had already told Wallace the day before. My deal with the concierge. My awful thing. But something in his expression tells me he already knows. *I forgave you*, Wallace had said. "I" meaning both of them, as it always had. And they'd brought me along with them anyway. They had done for my sake what they thought they would never do for anyone. Separated themselves. The Siamese twins pulled apart so that one half could live a dozen lives at once, and the other to see my way home.

Bates freezes his eyes on a point at the forest's edge the same moment I do. There is nothing there but another pocket of darkness, one among a thousand others, side by side. But we both choose the same one to stare at.

We know they're here before we actually see them. Everything as it was before but intensified. The rain a maddening buzz, radio static turned up full. A feeling like when the house lights begin to dim in a theater, yet so slowly that at first you're not sure if they are or not.

It's why when the men finally step out of the forest I believe that I have created them. That I've been expecting to see them for so long that my waiting has acted as a summoning, conjuring them from the shadows. They even have the vague, floating quality of phantoms.

Advancing without seeming to move their legs or touch the ground. The only thing that commits them to reality are their guns. Heavy looking and distinct even from this distance. I can make out the different wood grains of the butts. The sites rising as sharks' fins at the ends.

They walk forward without particular caution. Beside me Bates levels the rifle with the horizon and pulls it left and right across the line of men, as though personally identifying each one.

"It's them," he tells himself.

But something's wrong. Or different from what it should be. A half dozen men in matching green shirts and baggy nylon pants, the kind that dry out immediately in the sun. The pirates didn't wear clothes like this. Definitely not these matching outfits, with what could be a coat of arms stitched over their hearts.

"Wait, Bates," I whisper to him, but does he hear? He raises the rifle to his shoulder, snugs his cheek against the butt to line up with the man directly ahead of him.

"Bates?"

"He's here."

"Where?"

"There," he says. Points without moving any part of himself. "The tall one."

I squint at where he's looking but the men seem to be of more or less the same height. Then I realize who he has in mind.

"No, Bates."

"I've got him."

"It's not who you're thinking of."

"The fucking undertaker."

"No, it's—"

"I've *got* him."

They come a little closer and the rain carries a selection of their sounds all the way to us.

Boots crunching through the cut weeds.

The metallic clack of safeties being flicked off.

Cartridges falling into place.

And their words. Along with the recognition that they aren't speaking among themselves but to us.

Drop your weapons.

It's over now.

We know who you are.

All of these statements and commands arriving at the same time. What's more is I can hear them in a language I can understand. It's because the figures coming up through the plantain garden are speaking Portuguese. And the pirates could only speak Spanish.

Bates stands. Scans the rifle once more along the line of approaching men until his site finds the one at the end.

"It's not him, Bates."

"Oh yes it is," he whispers, but only to himself. "It's *always* been him."

Bates holds still. Gathers himself up in a single breath and becomes nothing but what is about to happen.

Não! one of them calls across the garden. *Não! Pare!*

Without meaning to do anything like it I'm standing up a few feet behind Bates, waving my arms over my head as though directing a plane in for a landing. An effort to signal them away but I'm offering them a target instead.

Words, I think, letting my arms fall. *Tell them not to do it.*

But when I try I've forgotten the phrasing of it. For a second or two the verb tenses and the selection of the precise term—*disparar? atirar? balear?*—is too complicated and nothing comes out.

Without turning his head, without moving at all, Bates sees me behind him.

"Get down."

Give it up. I search for this but it slips away. Or *C'mon now, buddy* or *We'll never make it if you do this* or just *No.* Not even that. The first word a child learns, the original denial. There is no language that might be thrown against him.

All of the green men are able to tell him to put the gun down, though. No longer calming but urgent.

"Get down, Crossman," he says again without turning to me, and this time I do.

All at once the men raise their shotguns. Close enough that we can see down each of the barrels. Little mouths prepared to speak.

283

"I'll see you back home, Crossman."

"Bates, *no!* It's not—"

He fires.

Although it is the rifle that sends the shot it seems that it comes from Bates himself, his hips thrusting forward, his spine lashing his head like the end of a whip. He willed the thing to work but his body was still surprised when it did.

The shot takes a second to figure out. Not only where it has come from—Bates's rifle? one of the men's?—but where it has gone. All of us looking at each other across the plantain garden as though the referee's whistle has blown and we're awaiting the call.

The pause gives us room for a thought. Bates fired his gun. But because he wasn't used to firing guns or he never expected the thing to actually work or he was only a boy and was hesitant to aim directly at a real, living man and pull the trigger without Wallace telling him he must, the barrel had reared up and sent the shot high over the heads of its intended targets and into the leaves behind them.

What is also clear is that he will not be permitted to try this again.

"Drop the gun, Bates," I think I say, but I can't be sure because the ringing in my ears smothers my voice.

Across the garden the men pull their elbows in tight. Evenly spaced as fenceposts.

"Just let go of it and they won't shoot," I say, louder this time. But in the middle of speaking there is a new sound to get in the way of its being heard.

A single pop from the farthest green figure on the right, the last one to push out from the trees. A hollow echo following it, distant and playful as a schoolyard laugh.

Bates's body reels back. Flaps and spins, all of it sudden as a crash test dummy. The rifle thrown aside. Bates dancing into impossible shapes, yet still goofy and harmless, a puppet show.

And I'm going to him.

There's the idea that he can't be allowed to fall, that so long as he stands there in front of me no harm will come to either of us. My hands reaching out to prop up against his hips but as I take a half step closer

Bates twists around to look back at me. White fingers splayed out over his chest. Blood spitting from a neat hole beneath them.

I say his name but go no closer. He may try to answer—the lips buckle, a puzzled effort blinks his eyes shut—but there is only a gnashing from somewhere down his throat.

And then the echo of three more shots slapping through his ribs.

Even now he stays up for another moment all on his own. Knees locked straight, as though the bullets have given him strength. And then, all at once, his head is thrown back up to the sky in a gesture of recognition.

"Bates?"

He falls and I scramble to him in the grass. The pain pulls his long face longer. I hold his mouth open so I can look straight down into him, the blood coughing up high enough that I can see it lapping against his molars. Pink stains in the silver fillings.

"Bates, it's me."

"Lydia?"

"It's Crossman."

"Where's Wallace?"

"He's gone."

"Where?"

"Into the trees."

"The snow."

"The trees."

"We're a family now, aren't we, Crossman?"

"We are. And we're going to get out of here."

His right hand jolts up to stroke my lips.

"Crossman?"

"I'm here."

"Barry used to call us the Siamese twins. Remember? But he'd have to say that we're the Siamese triplets now, wouldn't he?"

"That's us."

Bates shivers.

"Just pretend," he says.

"Pretend what?"

"Pretend I'm a girl."

"Is that what Wallace said to you? In the snow? Or is that what you said to him?"

"I saved him," he says, then shakes his head as though to correct himself. "He saved me."

"Just stay with me now, Bates. Hang on," I tell him over and over, picking him up by the shoulders.

There is a release of the muscle below his stomach and with it the blood stops its heartbeat spurts and turns into a steady flow, shining and quick. The last of him rushing into the mud and over my legs even as the men arrive to form a circle around us, rifles still trained on the boy's forehead. They couldn't yet see that they'd got him well enough, to count the holes they'd put in him and how much had already spread out to touch the bunches of plantain lying around us.

I rock him back and forth and click my tongue against the roof of my mouth the way my mother did to get me to sleep as a child. It sounds strange coming from me. A lullabye for this boy dying in an imagined Ontario forest of snow.

The men are close enough to have faces now. For me to see that the insignias on their chests are all the same. Brazilian flags with a ring of embroidered Portuguese words. *Comissão Amazonas Parque.*

Amazonas Park Commission.

"Where are your other friends?" one of them asks me.

"One was left behind. One died on the river."

"And the third?"

I can hear the worry in his voice. They're thinking that somebody might be hiding in the bush with another gun pointed at them.

"He's gone."

"Gone?"

"He left with the Indians. The Yanomami. Into the jungle."

"Which way did they go?"

"I don't know. There would be no way to say it even if I did."

"This is an ecological preserve. A park," he says and pauses, as though this alone explains everything. And then, almost with embarrassment, "We've been looking for you."

"To take us home."

286

"Every effort was made."

"Is the concierge with you?"

"Who?"

"The tall one. The undertaker."

"We have no undertakers."

"He must be here," I tell them. "He's been following us, too."

The men shuffle slightly. Looking down at Bates along with me. Watching how his eyes sparkle. Not as eyes do when they reflect sunshine or candlelight, but from within. It is as though all along he'd failed to appreciate their proper use, peering into the wrong end of a telescope so that everything appears farther away. Only now could he see things in focus. Not the outside things but into his own neglected parts, the stark realization of *who he is*. And now that he has seen it, it's too much even to be surprised.

And then the light goes out.

So abrupt you think it can't have happened this way. Now his eyes are no more than bits of chalk in his head, his lips fallen into a childish frown. An accidental expression of disappointment, as though he'd ripped through the wrapping to find not quite the toy he wanted for Christmas. Over the course of these few seconds I watch the boy's face give way to a man's. He was wise, then a petulant infant, and then he is dead. Or this is the way it appears in my mind that is already shaping these things into memory. While Bates dies in a torn bundle pulled across my chest I'm building a version of him that can be carried out of here and through what might pass for a normal life. Translating even now. Piecing together what I have a chance of understanding while editing out what I can never know. The gaps of nothing. The simple horror.

"He is gone now," one of the men says from above us, and when I look up at him I can see that he is telling himself more than me. It hadn't yet struck them that each would spend part of their lives wondering which one had found his target.

"He is gone now," one of them says again, with a little more force this time. They want me to pull away from Bates so that they can start the business of sticking him into an empty supply bag. But I don't let go. My mother's lullabye sound in my mouth.

In one of these seconds he goes from a loose weight to nothing at all.

There are no angels or tunnels of light for him. Yet there is a woman. One that changes from woman to woman. Features shifting so that she is never fixed. A woman without any single identity because she is always in the process of becoming someone else.

First it is his mother. The natural perfumes he assumed he'd been too young to remember, the reassuring essence of adult cocktail party—smoke and gin and Chanel No. 5.

Now it is Lydia, her face more distinct than is possible, all the unforgiving blotches and renegade hairs. Her green eyes softened with wrinkles.

And now it is *his* Lydia. The one to whom he had described the perfect bomb in a language she didn't understand. His not because he had paid her to be but because he had given her a name.

So there is an angel after all. Or angels. But what does it matter? He's just so grateful that he can let all the work of being a man go, now, after coming to believe he would never be allowed to be himself, just a boy, ever again. Along with the desire to say something. Maybe a word about *love* or *forever* or *nothing*. But the woman that is his mother and both of his Lydias rolled into one is shushing the notion right out of him, out of the whole darkening world, so all that's left is a boy stepping into a woman's arms.

Mine.

AFTER

AFTER I returned home—within weeks, not months—the technology market took a spectacular dive. Actually it wasn't so spectacular really, at least not in the way that sunsets or breakaway goals or over-sized moons caught between rooftop chimneys can be spectacular. "Spectacular dive" was just how most anchorpeople and newspaper headlines referred to it, so I did my best to see it that way too, as a phys-ical thing instead of an economic abstraction, as something real, and not just a declining number with a decimal point stuck in it. I even started to imagine how a market could be alive. To envision it as "nervous," or "buoyant," or simply not in the mood at all, refusing to get out of bed as it "remained flat today."

Soon after the spectacular dive, as though directed by a conductor waving a stick at them from his elevated podium, the press changed their tune from revolutionary trumpeting to I-told-you-so's. For a time, there were some questions raised about Western society having had its moral core rotted out by greed. I saw the word *democracy* a lot. But they seem to have shut up about all that now. It's a rather difficult tone to sustain, I imagine.

When they brought Bates's body back to Canada there was some-thing of an unofficial state funeral for him. His father and Memory, his mother and the Halifax orthopedic surgeon flew in from their respec-tive coasts, along with the headmaster at the school in the woods and the same prefects who had tried to kill them and who, now in their besuited late twenties, were showing the first signs of balding and desk-job stomachs. Barry's wife and daughter came up from Georgia, both blond, unsuspecting, pearl necklaced, as dignified as Barry was gentlemanly. The same Minister of Foreign Affairs we had last seen screeching like a spider monkey on the deck of the *Presidente Figueiredo* was there too. Even the prime minister placed a gloved hand on the casket and said a word about the particular tragedy endured by "Canada and the world" for having lost "not just a remarkable young life, but a vision of a new future."

I met the prime minister there for a second time, although he seemed not to remember me from our first introductions at the consulate reception in São Paulo. I told him again that he had my vote. And again, it was a lie.

After that, because Bates was so determinedly dead, they all decided to go looking for Wallace. There was a series of newspaper stringers in Brazil and Colombia that traveled as far as the now abandoned Yanomami village we stumbled upon. An overnight fan club unaccountably working out of Tuckerton, New Jersey, which sent me complementary copies of the first two editions of their newsletter, *The Wandering Wallace*. Even Ed Bradley was buttoned into a safari suit and sent along with an entire *60 Minutes* crew to look for him.

In the end, though, each could do no more than produce a different theory.

He'd gone mad.

He'd been mistaken for a white god by a native tribe whom he now led in conducting gruesome rituals on animals and children.

He'd discovered the lost city of El Dorado and lived inside its ancient vaults of gold, impossibly rich but unable to ever return to the civilized world.

He was alive.

He was dead.

Naturally, I played a role in these reports. Somebody had to sit under the studio lights and distribute the grave details and the tears. A publicist was required. I became what even the journalists themselves referred to, admiringly, as *semi-famous*. There were radio "phoners" with morning dj's, afternoon TV talk shows hosted by women who held their chins in their hands and turned to the camera to say, "Next up, how to get those *really* tough stains out of your carpets," a network Special Presentation that took me back to Manaus and a riverboat ride a few miles up the river to get some shots of me gazing thoughtfully into the jungle. I was pretty good at it, and found a certain shameful pleasure in the attention, although less than I might have expected. What finished it for me was wanting to please them all too much. As a result it became little more than a performance that, after a time, failed to convince even me.

But it all stopped before I ever got around to putting an end to things myself. The media, along with all the others. The letters from university sociologists, anthropologists, psychiatrists, teachers of Women's Studies and Cultural Studies and Bible Studies, all requesting my answers to questionnaires or the delivery of a guest lecture or, once, the sticking of electrodes to my temples and genitals in order to monitor my reaction to repeated images of bestial, anal and aquatic sex. The e-mails from apparently unemployed and imbalanced strangers. The lunches—with film producers, agents, publishers, docu-novelists, method actors, presidents of sports wear and nutritional supplement companies, negligence lawyers, government public relations officials—the *lunches*. It all dried up at the same time. At the exact same *moment*, as though the one thing these various people had in common was a faculty for detecting the most grim human novelty currently available, and now, like dogs responding to a whistle only they can hear, were off bothering the woman who had her face ripped off in a cougar attack or the guy who spent the first twenty-four years of his life chained to a rack of preserves in a Wisconsin fruit cellar.

They all asked about the tape. They really wanted the tape. They made exorbitant offers to buy the tape.

But over and over again I assured them that no such tape existed. Yes, Bates had carried a Palmcorder with him the whole time. And yes, he sometimes shot the events going on around him. But nobody knew where this tape might have gotten to. Buried in some snake hole by now, or turned into a souvenir hung about the neck of some Yanomami warrior. I told them that I certainly didn't have it, in any case.

This particular lie was permissible, I reasoned, because even though there was such a tape in my possession, it had nothing on it. Or almost nothing.

A few weeks after returning home—a few weeks of useless grief counseling but an interesting carousel of antidepressants—I played it on my VCR. It starts with a shot of Wallace standing next to the concierge at the entrance to the Tropical Hotel. Looking into the camera, though the concierge is too tall for his face to be in the frame.

Just Wallace and the concierge's navy blue suit. And Wallace's voice. This one his *step-right-up!* ringmaster.

"Ladies and gentlemen, welcome to the beginning of our great jungle adventure! What you will see recorded here is the discovery of untold mysteries! Breathtaking natural scenery! The conquest of lands forgotten by time and man alike! History in the *making!*"

Then it ends. I've fast forwarded it right through maybe half a dozen times to make sure. More than once I've even sat through fifty-nine minutes of static until the tape clicks to its finish. There's nothing there. Bates hadn't been using it the entire time.

Why did he want me to bring home a tape he knew had nothing on it? He may have simply forgotten it was blank, of course. Or had the camera stuck on Pause the whole time. It may have been an understandable mistake, given his condition. But I like to think the tape's unfulfilled promise carries a message that Bates was wholly aware of. I insist on seeing it this way, as a matter of fact.

And what I choose to see in the screen's vacant static is who they were. They had dreamed of being heroes and I will do what I can to remember them as such. That's what Bates wanted from me by giving me the tape. Their memories not to be inscribed on a loop of wax but in me, their translator, the bearer of their living histories.

As it turns out I brought back something else from the jungle. I thought it was a parasite at first. One that made me sick in the mornings and slowly grew, so that my belly started pushing out against my clothes. Started to move.

But it wasn't a monster that wanted to consume me. It was a child becoming itself.

From time to time people ask me, or come close to asking, who the father of my daughter is. I tell them it was my decision to have her all on my own, the man in question not being the sort to stick around in basement apartments, in going-nowhere-fast domestic situations of the only kind I could offer. This is fine with me. He was a good man, I assure them, and not just any knock-up rogue. An extraordinary man, really. I believe that I cared for him as much as I'm capable of such things. Although I don't say these words aloud. They seem misplaced, almost crude when applied to him.

Is he ever going to visit? they ask. To see his little girl?

No, I say. He trusts me to get on with things on my own, which I will.

Was it one of the boys from the jungle? only the bravest will directly inquire. Was it the missing one, Wallace? Or the dead one, Bates?

I say neither yes nor no to this, which I confess to enjoying a little. What I tell them is that the girl's father is no longer with us, and that this is satisfactory to all concerned.

As for my daughter, she is beautiful in the way that all mothers think of their babies. More than this, she is beautiful in the *no, really, she is* especially *beautiful* way that all older, first-time mothers see their children, the women who for one reason or another almost missed the chance. And the truth is I'm grateful beyond reckoning. I catch myself in mirrors when I'm carrying her in my arms and I have this goofball smile buttered over my face every time. Nothing can be done about it. The foolish joy of the third-drink drunk, the born again, the unlikely survivor.

Already my baby is teaching me things. How to leave yourself behind and not look back, for one. To see anger as a burden, envy as a sunny day wasted indoors.

I've named her Lydia.

There is little of me to be recognized in her face, but I've been told that this is by design. Babies are meant to look more like their fathers for the first few months so that they won't be rejected. Soon my lines and droops and dimples will emerge, though. Even now when I lie in bed at night listening to her breathe beside me, I can summon her face in the darkness more clearly than my own.

One thing appears to be established for good, however. She has her father's eyes.

It's not that I see him when I look into them, but there is the same hunger he had, an absence in her widened pupils that no amount of lullabies or kisses can fill. It frightens me a little. She is mine. But when I look into her sometimes it is she who takes me in. Along with everything else. All the toys in her crib, the night-light down the hall, the sky of glow-in-the-dark stars stuck to the ceiling. Two widening shadows that desire nothing less than the world.

ACKNOWLEDGMENTS

Leah McLaren, Anne McDermid, Iris Tupholme, Mari Evans, Sarah McGrath, Jon Cooley, the crew and passengers of the *Clipper*, Marko Sijan, Heidi Rittenhouse, Jacob Hoye, Shaun Oakey, Napoleon Chagnon (*Yanomamo, Fifth Edition*: Harcourt Brace, 1997), Peter Fleming (*Brazilian Adventure*: Northwestern University Press, 1999) and to Martin Levin for its recommendation, Patrick Tierney (*Darkness in El Dorado*: W. W. Norton & Company, 2000), Neyda Jáuregui, Débora Senra da Rocha—

Many thanks